Praise

Miss Espy Estrada is a ⬚⬚⬚⬚⬚⬚
She possesses that rare j⬚⬚⬚⬚⬚
fiction. Her romance ma⬚⬚⬚⬚⬚
with the son of a leading citizen in 1892 Maine. **Excellent story!**
    —LYN COTE, author of *La Belle Christiane*

Her Good Name is a story with strong characters and gripping emotions woven through a **fascinating plot.**
    —LENA NELSON DOOLEY, author of *Maggie's Journey, Mary's Blessing,* and *Love Finds You in Golden, New Mexico*

Her Good Name is a GOOD book! Espy and Warren come from two entirely different worlds and only God can bridge the gap between them. Any good author, no matter what the genre, will invite the reader into the characters' world to take the same journey the characters take. And that's exactly what Ruth Axtell does. **I loved this book.**
    —TRACEY BATEMAN, author of *The Widow of Saunders Creek*

Her Good Name delivers a compelling story about class differences in late 19th century Maine and how God's grace can fill the seemingly insurmountable gap. **Axtell's vibrant characters kept me cheering for them until the end.**
    —CHRISTINE JOHNSON, multi-published author of *All Roads Lead Home*

You don't want to miss Ruth Axtell's *Her Good Name*. **Her characters engage you** from the first page and have you rooting for their happy ending.
    —MERRILLEE WHREN, award-winning author of Christian romance

Her Good Name is a perfect blend of history, faith and romance. This heartwarming tale entertains in the best possible way. **I loved it!**
    —VICTORIA BYLIN, author and ACFW Carol Award finalist

HER GOOD NAME

a novel

RUTH AXTELL

MOODY PUBLISHERS
CHICAGO

All Scripture quotations are taken from the King James Version.

Edited by Cheryl Dunlop Molin
Interior design: Ragont Design
Cover design and image: John Hamilton Design
Author photo: Tabitha Griffin

Library of Congress Cataloging-in-Publication Data

Axtell, Ruth.
 Her good name / Ruth Axtell.
  p. cm.
 ISBN 978-0-8024-0627-9
 I. Title.
 PS3601.X84H47 2012
 813'.6—dc23

                                         2012016658

We hope you enjoy this book from River North Fiction by Moody Publishers. Our goal is to provide high-quality, thought-provoking books and products that connect truth to your real needs and challenges. For more information on other books and products written and produced from a biblical perspective, go to www.moodypublishers.com or write to:

River North Fiction
Imprint of Moody Publishers
820 N. LaSalle Boulevard
Chicago, IL 60610

1 3 5 7 9 10 8 6 4 2

Printed in the United States of America

Therefore if any man be in Christ,
he is a new creature: old things are passed away;
behold, all things are become new.
—2 Corinthians 5:17

Thank you Adaja, Lisa, and Patricia
for your insights and encouragement.

1

HOLLISTON, MAINE, JUNE 1892

Why are you in such deep thought, Brenty?"

Espy Estrada stepped from behind the thick trunk of an elm tree, blocking Warren Brentwood's path.

He jerked to a stop. Embarrassed at being startled, then annoyed at being embarrassed, Warren only managed a stiff nod. "Hello, Espy."

"Hello yourself, Warren." She planted one slim hand on her hip, leaned a shoulder forward. Amusement lit the depths of her thickly lashed eyes, her irises an unusual shade like umber, halfway between amber and brown.

The sunshine dappled her smooth skin through the tall elms shading the road. "What's the matter, cat got your tongue?"

Her lips curved upward as if she knew exactly how distracting her smile was and would use the knowledge to her advantage. Such straight white teeth—for someone who'd grown up in the shanty town in the outlying district of Holliston, Warren would expect her to have lost one or two by now. Against her tawny skin, they shone all the more vividly.

"Where did you come from?"

"I was here all along. You sure seemed lost in thought. What were you thinking about?"

He swallowed, resisting the urge to step back a pace. Lately, their paths seemed to cross often. Since he'd returned to Holliston a few weeks ago, every time he ran into her—or she into him—it struck him forcefully what a young woman she'd become from the little barefoot girl in her faded calico dress sitting in the front row of the one-room schoolhouse they'd once attended.

Instead of replying to her question, he asked his own. "What are you doing on Elm Street?" It certainly wasn't anywhere near her part of town.

If his pointed question ruffled her, she didn't show it. Thrusting out her bottom lip slightly, she focused her large, deep-set eyes at him.

"I have an *ap-point-ment* here this afternoon." She enunciated the syllables as if to stress the importance of the event.

"Do you?" He couldn't help the surprise in his tone.

She nodded, a saucy look in her eyes. He noted the soft curve of her cheek. It was golden, showing the Portuguese origin on her father's side, unlike the fashionable peaches and cream women of his acquaintance. It complemented her hair, which was gathered in a loose chignon, tendrils curved like glossy serpents against the slim neck. Her straw bonnet had fallen back, held only by the ribbon pulling against her collarbone.

He noticed her outfits hadn't changed much, although what was inside them definitely had. He quickly averted his gaze, disconcerted by the direction of his thoughts.

With an abrupt nod, he made a move as if to walk past her. "If you'll excuse me, Miss Estrada, I was on my way back to the office."

"I love it when you call me Miss Estrada, all stiff and starchy like. Is that the voice you use all day in your office, sitting behind the great big desk at the mill?"

He stared at her, wondering what she meant by her words. Before he could think of a suitable rejoinder, she matched her steps to his, swinging her bare arms on either side of her. He couldn't help a quick glance up the street, to see who was about.

What an incongruous couple they would make, he in his suit— her description of "starchy" came back to him—and she . . . he let his eyes stray once more over her silhouette, in a dark blue cotton skirt and gingham blouse with elbow-length sleeves. He glanced downward, surprised she wasn't barefoot, the way she'd run around in summer as a girl. But dusty lace-up boots were visible beneath the hem of her petticoat.

"Aren't you curious where I'm going?"

He picked up his pace to make it clear he had no time or inclination to stand about making small talk. Instead of answering with a decisive "no," and ridding himself of her once and for all, he found himself saying, "Where are you going?"

"The Stocktons."

His eyes widened. George Stockton was a professor at the local high school academy.

"That's right." She clasped her hands behind her. From the scrawny, underfed looking girl of eight or so, she had grown into a tall, willowy woman.

A flush crept up his neck.

"Mrs. Stockton might hire me," she continued.

"I see." *Of course, a position as maid.*

"What is that supposed to mean, 'I see'?" She mimicked his tone.

Had he really sounded so pompous? The mimicry after the description of "stiff and starchy" rankled.

"I assumed it meant Mrs. Stockton might wish to hire you to help her around the house."

The dancing light disappeared from her eyes and her mouth pouted. He averted his gaze and forced himself to focus on what she was saying.

"I overheard her talking to Mrs. Ellison the other day at Watt's Clothing. She told Mrs. Ellison that Annie had up and left her and she needed a girl to help clean and do the heavier work." Her smile reappeared. "So, I'm going to quit my job at the cannery and go to work for the Stocktons. Mrs. Stockton said I could dust her husband's library."

The professor, a history teacher, had a well-stocked library. Warren had borrowed many a book throughout his high school years. "That should certainly keep you busy."

"Maybe he'll let me read some of his books."

He raised his eyebrows a fraction. "Do you like to read?" Espy had been a few years behind him in grammar school, so he hadn't paid much attention to her. When he'd gone off to the high school academy, his world had no longer overlapped hers.

"I adore reading! But I don't have much of a chance to get my hands on books. That's one of the reasons I'm interested in working at the Stocktons'."

She had been a bright student in grammar school from the little he recalled. He frowned. "Doesn't the cannery pay better?"

"Yes, but pay isn't everything."

The words, coming from her, gave him pause. "I would think the pay you bring home from the cannery would help your mother to a great degree. Don't you have quite a few brothers and sisters still in school?"

He'd never been able to keep track of all the Estradas. There always seemed to be a new one entering school each fall, the younger ones trailing after the older ones.

"Six are in school, Alvaro and Angela are all finished, and the two youngest are still home.

Warren's mind swirled at the list. "How many are you in all?"

10

She lifted her pert chin. "Eleven."

He tried to think of something to say. "What are the oldest doing these days?"

"Angela's at the cannery. Between us working different shifts, she and Mama and I are able to look after the younger ones. Alvaro's looking for work." Espy glanced sidelong at him. "Maybe he could work at Brentwood sawmills."

He nodded, his interest waning. Most able-bodied young men ended up employed at the mills if they weren't fishermen. "Sure, just tell him to apply."

"I thought maybe you could put in a good word for him, you know, since your dad put you in charge now."

"We'll see." He took out his watch and glanced at it. Father was a stickler for punctuality. "Well, Miss Estrada, I really must be getting along."

"What's your hurry?" She plucked at her bonnet ribbon, drawing his focus to her collarbone. "You always seem to be in such a rush."

His irritation growing, he raised an eyebrow. "Don't you have an appointment? I shouldn't think you'd want to keep Mrs. Stockton waiting."

Espy shrugged. "Mrs. Stockton said to drop by any time this afternoon."

"I, on the other hand, have to be back at the office at one, so if there's nothing in particular you wished to see me about—" he lifted his hat from his head an inch and then set it back down, in the exact gesture he'd seen his father use hundreds of times when he wished to cut short an encounter without appearing rude, and finding the same inflection in his tone as he parroted his father's words "—I shall bid you goodbye—"

Before the words were completely out of his mouth, she smiled. "That's all right; we can walk a few minutes."

"As you wish." The words came out clipped.

As they continued walking, Espy chattered on about the people and goings on of Holliston while he'd been away, so happy to have a few minutes in Warren Brentwood's company.

At the bend in the road before the bridge, Espy stopped and smiled at Warren. "Maybe we'll run into each other again tomorrow."

"Perhaps." With a brief tip of his hat, he left her, his long stride carrying him toward the bridge.

His one-word reply was neither encouraging nor discouraging. She'd have to content herself that he hadn't said no.

She watched Warren a few moments longer, disappearing onto the covered bridge spanning that portion of the river. If anything, Warren Brentwood had grown handsomer than she'd remembered him. She'd always admired him from afar, as a high school star whose athletic achievements matched his scholarly accomplishments, making him the most lauded student in the community.

Of course, she had never gotten as far as high school. Around that time, her dad had been injured, and as the eldest child, Espy had had to go to work at the cannery to help out.

But she'd watched Warren on the ball field and read about him in the *Holliston News*.

Those years away at college had only broadened his already broad shoulders and deepened the hue of his green eyes. It had certainly added . . . she searched her mind for an adequate word and couldn't come up with any. But he seemed more a man than any of the local men his age. Her mother would say, "He's a looker."

Espy knew there was more to Warren Brentwood than good looks. He not only had a good head on his shoulders, but he had a heart. She remembered his kindnesses to younger children in grammar school days. He was a leader; others followed the good example he set. And he was no sissy. He'd beat up any boy who dared tease a girl or bully a younger child.

But each time she had encountered him since his return home, his manner was either excessively reserved or he was rushing off somewhere. *Had the time at a fancy private college and a couple of years traveling to all parts of the globe turned him into a replica of his father?* She certainly hoped not.

Fiddling with her bonnet ribbon, she wondered how Warren remembered her. A skinny, young girl in pigtails? Well, she planned to make sure Warren Brentwood noticed how much she had changed in the intervening years.

She smoothed down the front of her skirt with a nod of satisfaction. She'd come a long way from that girl. A knot of doubt formed in her stomach. Could Warren see the attractive woman behind the faded work clothes? She was prettier than most girls of her acquaintance. She checked her thoughts. *Forgive my vain thoughts, Lord, but I know it's true. I just hope Warren notices.* With neither money nor education, her looks were one of her few assets, and she knew she had to use them to advantage while they lasted.

She started, realizing she was still standing gawking down the empty road. If she didn't go to her appointment, she'd never get the job and then could forget about running into Warren Brentwood again.

With a pat to her hair, she turned her attention to the white mansion standing back from the rising swath of bright green, neatly clipped grass. Not a dandelion leaf in sight, she noted, comparing it to her own front yard.

As she approached the picket fence, Espy straightened her apron at the waist and uttered a last minute prayer. *You know how badly I want it, God.* Taking a deep breath, feeling like Scheherazade preparing to tell her story to the king in the tattered copy of *The Arabian Nights* she'd read in school, she unhitched the latch of the white picket fence.

The gate opened silently. Clicking it shut with trembling fingers, she turned and proceeded up the flagstone path to the front door. Shiny black rectangular shutters were evenly spaced at each of the eight windows of the equally rectangular white clapboard structure. Window boxes spilling over with brightly colored petunias and geraniums were the only nongeometric form, like splashes of paint against a bleached white canvas.

It had once been a sea captain's mansion, built on the bluff overlooking the river. For the last few years it had been occupied by the professor and his wife. Standing before the black door, Espy took a deep breath before grasping the brass knocker. She let it fall with a thud. After a moment, she wondered if she should knock again.

Before she could decide, the door swung open and Mrs. Stockton herself appeared in the shadowy entrance hall. She was a middle-aged woman of medium height and build, with nondescript brown hair pulled back in a careless bun. She smiled at Espy. "There you are. I was expecting you. Come in."

Espy bobbed her head. "Thank you, Mrs. Stockton. I came as soon as I cleared up the dinner dishes at home."

"I understand. Well, come out of that hot sun. It's a scorcher today, isn't it? It's a good thing we live on the river. It never gets too hot inside here with the breeze blowing in through the back porch."

Espy stepped inside, welcoming the coolness. It must have been at least ten degrees lower than the unshaded portions of the street.

She glanced about her, falling in love immediately. There was something so restful and elegant about this old house with its wide, uneven floorboards covered in soft carpets. A bouquet of flowers sat in a shiny copper pitcher in the entry. Not wildflowers like she picked, but a variety of garden flowers.

Espy followed Mrs. Stockton down the hallway bisecting the house, glimpsing a tall case clock with brass pendulum and weights, dark wood cabinets, tables topped by curious ornaments, and gilt-framed paintings on papered walls. She barely had time to note these things before they entered a sunny kitchen at the rear of the house.

"Please, have a seat, Esperanza."

"Espy, please."

"Espy?"

"Everyone calls me that," she said with a smile. "Since I was a girl."

"Very well, Espy it shall be."

Mrs. Stockton's features were mild, her skin pale. She reminded Espy a little of her mother, though clearly this woman wasn't as careworn.

"I am so glad you heard of my need for a girl of all work. This is a large house, too much for me alone. I am not always well, you know. We have a cook and a handyman, but I need a good strong girl to do the daily housework."

Espy smiled, growing more confident. "I'm your girl then."

Mrs. Stockton went on to detail some of her health problems and Espy made sympathetic noises and nodded her head. She'd learned to do that with Mama every time she complained of something. "You just show me what needs doing and you don't have to worry, it'll get done. I've got the energy of two people, my mama always says."

"That is exactly the kind of person I need. Let me take you around and tell you what I would like you to do. You may start today if you will. The downstairs rooms need dusting something awful. I will introduce you to Mr. Stockton. He is home for the summer, you know, with school out. But he spends a good deal of time in his study."

Espy nodded, impressed by a gentleman who would have his own room just to study.

They toured the ground floor rooms of the large house, Espy oohing and aahing at each one, which seemed to please her new employer. Last of all, Mrs. Stockton gave a soft knock on the only closed door.

15

At the masculine voice bidding them enter, she opened it and ushered Espy in. "Dear, I would like you to meet Espy. She is replacing Annie as our new housemaid. I hope you will let her dust in here this afternoon."

Mr. Stockton looked up from a large slant-top desk. Espy recognized him from church and the academy although she'd never attended the school. It was a private high school in East Holliston. Even though Holliston had boasted its own high school since mid-century, the academy had existed since colonial times, and was where the Brentwoods and other lumber barons sent their sons and daughters to board.

Espy was in awe of Mr. Stockton as a scholar. He and his wife had only lived in Holliston a few years but had quickly gained the community's respect. He was considered an authority on history and his wife was admired for her civic work on various committees and charities.

He rose as soon as the two women entered and held out his hand. "Hello, Miss Esperanza, how do you do?"

He was in his forties, Espy would judge, with short cropped brown hair a shade darker than his wife's, and mutton-chop whiskers and moustache enhancing the strong planes of his face.

Grayish-blue eyes smiled down into hers.

She found herself blushing at the intent way he was looking at her. "Oh, please, it's just Espy. Everyone calls me that."

"Well, then, Espy it is. Welcome to our home. I hope you will find the job rewarding."

"I know I will." Her eyes couldn't help roaming over the books lining the walls. "It looks like a real library in here."

He followed her gaze. "Do you like to read?"

"I love to read, when I get a chance, that is—and a book," she ended ruefully. "That's not as often as I'd like."

"Well, we must remedy that, mustn't we?" He turned to Mrs. Stockton.

"Why, certainly, if you say so, John. Although I am sure Espy will be quite busy while she is here."

"Indeed. I don't want to interfere with your arrangements, my dear." He turned his twinkling gaze back on Espy. "But if you are a good worker and satisfy my wife, I do not see the harm of borrowing one of my books now and then, as long as you bring it back as soon as you finish reading it."

Her eyes widened at the offer. No one had ever been so generous with books before. She took a deep breath and looked at the shelves again, as if a treasure trove of gold were staring back at her. "Oh, my, I don't know what to say. I would take care of any book you lent me and bring it back as soon as possible. I'm a fast reader."

"Are you then? We shall see about that."

Mrs. Stockton cleared her throat. "You shall dust in here and keep things tidy. But don't be moving about any of Mr. Stockton's papers on his desk."

Espy looked at its cluttered surface. "No, ma'am. I won't move a thing."

Mr. Stockton chuckled. "You needn't look so frightened. Mrs. Stockton is very protective of my work. Come, have a look. I am currently researching a book I will be writing in the autumn."

Espy followed, curious and fascinated by a man who actually wrote books.

"I am detailing the local sea battle off our coast during the Revolutionary War. Not much has been written thus far. I have to dig into all sorts of old journals and papers filed away at our town office and at the historical society to piece together events."

Espy listened as he showed her old ledgers and leather-bound notebooks with spidery handwriting on their yellowed pages.

"You may dust around, but please put everything back exactly where it was."

"Yes, sir."

Mrs. Stockton came up to the desk and cleared her throat.

"Come along, Espy, I will show you the grounds now."

With a last look at what was sure to become her favorite room in the house, Espy said goodbye to Mr. Stockton and followed her new employer.

• • •

Warren left the head office of Brentwood & Co. at half past six and made his way down Main Street, greeting acquaintances he passed. Since returning home, he still enjoyed the sight of the bustling street that partially followed the river before curving inland toward the fields and meadows of the outlying farmland.

The street boasted a couple of savings banks; a dry goods store; a clothier's; blacksmith; bookmakers and notions shops; a few eateries; two newspaper offices; and a law office. Warren crossed the other major street, which intersected Main Street halfway down, aptly named Center Street, where his father's bank stood, a solid brick building with white columns in front.

The newly built brick post office and customs house stood at the end of the street, facing the courthouse and jail. Two hotels and stables, where the stagecoaches left twice daily for Bangor and Calais, were down that way as well.

The white clapboard church halfway down Center Street with its slim pointed steeple helped define the skyline of the valley town along the curving river.

Lots of people filled the plank sidewalks at this hour, the sun still high in the sky on this early evening. Warren turned southward at the bridge, passing the two sawmills and gristmill that stood on the small island bisecting the river. The sound of the roaring falls beneath his feet always soothed him after a long day poring over ledgers. The rapids at this part of the Holliston River signaled the divide between the hustle and bustle of Main Street and the refreshing shade and quiet elegance of Elm Street, the town's nicest residential neighborhood.

Warren entered the shadowy depths of the covered bridge spanning the other half of the river.

The noise of the thundering water gradually faded as he left Holliston River behind and followed the curve of the road southward. Centuries-old elms and oaks filtered the afternoon rays, creating a dappled pattern on the sidewalk like a giant lace doily.

Warren scanned the wide street, remembering his encounter earlier in the day with Espy Estrada. She wasn't there now, only a few others like himself hurrying home to supper.

His shoulders relaxed, thankful to enjoy solitude for a few moments to ease the transition into his mother's world.

This town had been his family's domain for more than a century since the first Brentwood had arrived on the shores of Holliston Bay in the mid-1700s. Now that he'd seen a good portion of the world, Warren realized how true the adage was that there was no place like home.

About a half mile down the road, he turned off at his own gate. The white Greek Revival, set back from the road, had a deep front porch behind Doric pillars. It had been built by his great-grandfather. Warren fully expected to raise his own children in it one day.

That wouldn't be anytime soon, no matter how much his mother seemed to expect him to marry.

In his years away, he'd only met one young woman who'd stirred his heart. But she'd not reciprocated his feelings, so for the last few years he'd concentrated on seeing the world, stopping at the ports of call where his father's schooners sailed.

A servant had already seen him approach the door. It opened silently as he stepped up to the porch.

"Good evening, Mr. Brentwood."

"Hello, Samuel," he replied to the old family retainer, still unused to being addressed so formally. He remembered Espy's use of

"Brenty" and frowned. Even "Mr. Brentwood" was preferable to that degree of familiarity.

"Your mother is awaiting you on the terrace."

"Thank you." He handed the white-haired man his case. "I'll go right out."

"Very good, sir."

The late afternoon sun was still shining brightly over the back gardens in contrast to the shade of the terrace under a navy blue awning. Warren stepped onto the wide flagstones, hearing the clink of glasses and murmur of voices before he saw the occupants.

"There you are at last, Warren. I was beginning to wonder."

"Hello, Mother." He strode toward her and bent to kiss her cheek. "I had a few things to finish up before I left."

"Your father is home from the bank already." Her cultured tones held a note of reproach. "He'll be down in a moment. Come, say hello to Christina."

Warren walked to the cushioned love-seat swing where a young lady of long acquaintance held out her hand with a smile. "Hello, Warren. We were beginning to despair of your ever arriving. Surely your father doesn't expect you to work late every night?"

He chuckled to hide his irritation at the chiding over the time of his arrival. "My father has nothing to do with it since he's at the bank." Despite his father's having put him in charge of his lumber business, Warren chafed at everyone's perception that his father was still in control. Perhaps because it was still all too true, he was coming to find out.

Warren clasped her hand for an instant before letting it go. As always, his childhood friend presented an attractive picture, looking poised and cool in her light blue frock, her dark blond locks arranged in a stylish mode around her head.

"Christina has been asking me about your stay in Paris. Why don't you tell her while we await your father and sister?"

"Very well, Mother."

Christina scooted over on the seat and Warren was forced to sit down even though he would have preferred a wide, comfortable chair of his own. He eased carefully against the wicker. By now he should be accustomed to summing up his trip abroad. People smiled expectantly but didn't really want to hear the details of his experiences, he'd come to find.

"Did you see the Arc de Triomphe?" she asked.

"Oh, yes." That was the one thing educated people usually thought of Paris.

"How I would love to see Paris." Christina folded her slim hands beneath her chin and gave a drawn-out sigh. "Papa has promised me a trip to Europe every summer, but, alas, we have not yet found the opportunity to go."

"You would enjoy it." She would fit right into Parisian society. Her profile was finely shaped, from the smooth curve of her chin to the straight, narrow projection of her nose. She turned blue eyes to him with a smile.

"Would I indeed?"

"Yes. Parisians may seem like snobs, but they would embrace you right away. All you need are a few introductions by the right people."

Her eyes lit up. "Could you arrange those for us?" If he didn't know better, he'd say her dark golden lashes batted at him coquettishly. Christina was not a flirt . . . not the way some women were.

"Certainly. I'll speak to your father at the next opportunity. I should see him at the men's business breakfast tomorrow."

She laid a hand on his arm. "There's not such a rush as that. We are not going to take the next ship over. Why, you've only just arrived home. It seems an age since I've seen you. I feel we must become reacquainted." A soft laugh followed her words.

He set an elbow against the love-seat arm, used to the subtle signals of encouragement given by women of his circle. Just as quickly, he dismissed the notion that Christina would behave so.

They'd been friends their whole lives. Whatever her encouragement, Warren felt no desire to respond.

Since Charity, whom he'd met his freshman year at college, no young lady had drawn him. Charity, the daughter of one of the professors, had been sweet, ladylike, and beautiful, and Warren had been smitten from the moment he met her.

His mouth turned downward. Warren had been like a grisaille painting, gray and lackluster, beside the man she'd given her heart to. It had been a humbling experience for him, not used to being bested by another man—and one who was nothing but a working-class fellow. But Charity had had eyes for no one else.

He focused on Christina's remark. "I don't think a few years away have changed any of us all that much."

"I suppose not." She adjusted the frill of lace at her neck, giving him a deprecating smile. "You must forgive my apprehension. I'm just afraid a trip to so many parts unknown will have given you such sophistication you will look down on all of us as hopeless country rubes."

He chuckled, relaxing once more. "Never fear. I'm not such a snob. Besides, I find people pretty much the same as I left them. Those I respected then, I continue to do so now. A trip to another land doesn't change that."

His mother handed him a tall glass. He took the cool lemonade with a grateful smile. "Thank you."

She settled into the cushioned wicker rocker nearby and picked up an ivory fan. "Speaking of those you've known all your life, Mrs. Hawkins said she saw you walking this noon with that girl—what is her name? Emily? No, something foreign-sounding. Maria? Helena?" His mother pursed her lips, a slight crease forming between her eyebrows.

22

2

Warren stared at his mother, remembering once again his encounter with Espy. "You mean Esperanza Estrada?"

"Mrs. Hawkins said she was behaving with an unbecoming familiarity toward you."

Their busybody neighbor must have been spying through her lace curtain. Some things hadn't changed in Holliston. "I knew Espy in grammar school. That was ages ago. I hardly remember her; she was only a child."

"Espy. What a quaint name." Christina's voice intruded at his side.

"What did she want with you?" His mother leveled her gray eyes on him.

"Let me guess," Christina answered for him, "to find her a job in one of your father's firms?"

He turned to her, not responding to her amused tone. "Why should she do that?"

Christina's lips curled up at the corners. "Perhaps to help feed that brood of kids her mother is forever producing?"

"Well, what *did* she want?" His mother's tone became more insistent.

He shrugged to hide his growing annoyance and dismay. Would every encounter of his be subject to scrutiny? He'd grown accustomed to being his own man during his years away, but since he'd returned, he was under his father's watchful eye at the office and his mother's evening cross-examination from the moment he stepped in the door. "She was just welcoming me home."

His mother lifted her chin a fraction. "What was she doing in this neighborhood anyway?"

"She has found work at one of the houses on this street."

"In this neighborhood? What would she want here? Don't her people all work in the cannery down at Hollistonport?"

He turned the glass around in his hand, feeling the sweat beads dampen his fingertips, trying to keep his voice indifferent. "Yes, she mentioned something about that. But I think she wanted a new sort of employment."

Christina chuckled softly. "A new sort of employment? You make her sound like a young man rising up the company ladder. How can someone like her find anything better than the cannery?"

Although he tended to agree with Christina, her condescending tone caused a stab of pity for Espy. He remembered her words about loving books. He shook his head, hardly able to imagine her as a scholar, though she'd been bright in school. He pictured the bold way she held herself.

Feeling a flush grow along his collar, he shifted on the swing, hoping his reaction would go unnoticed. He wished Christina weren't seated quite so close. "I don't know, but she seemed pretty sure of herself."

"Whatever she may be doing here, I'd caution you against being seen in her company."

"Surely you are overreacting, Mother. It was nothing but a casual conversation between two old schoolmates."

Christina laid a hand gently on his sleeve. "I think what your mother is saying is that this is a small community and no matter how innocent an exchange may be between a gentleman and a young woman, it can be easily misconstrued."

He tried to smile at her indulgent tone, although he felt an unaccustomed rebellious streak rise in him at their censure. What would they do if he suddenly started squiring Espy around town? He smiled at the image, realizing how unlikely that would be. "You are both blowing something out of proportion, but in any case I don't believe I shall see her again."

Christina patted his arm before removing her pale hand. "Doubtless you are right. Let us talk of something more interesting. You're attending the concert in the bandstand tomorrow evening?"

Before he could shift his thoughts, his sister stepped onto the terrace. He rose immediately. "There you are, Annalise. Where've you been keeping yourself?"

His sister's cheeks reddened as she advanced to him. Even though he thought his sister the prettiest girl in town, he felt sorry that she was so timid. "I was just finishing something up," she said softly. "I came down as soon as I heard you come in."

"Come help me entertain Christina, who is probably bored to death with my limited conversation."

Warren took his sister by the elbow and propelled her to the place he had vacated by Christina. With a firming of her lips, Christina edged farther away on the seat.

Annalise resisted under his hands. "That's all right. I can sit over there."

"Nonsense, this is fine." He nudged her downward and she ceased her protest.

With a contented sigh, Warren took the wide wicker rocker on his mother's other side and stretched out his legs. Even though he appreciated his mother's attempts to have his friends over each evening, sometimes he yearned to merely come home and enjoy some quiet time.

His glance drifted to the terraced gardens, which descended gradually to the river. For a few moments he could forget the struggles at the office, the faint but certain butting against his father's will.

"Are you going to be as unsociable tomorrow night as you are this evening?"

"Pardon—?" He looked around his mother toward Christina.

His mother's eyebrows were drawn together. "Christina asked you a question, Warren."

"I'm sorry—"

Christina laughed, with an arch look he recognized as one that made the recipient feel she was questioning his mental capacity. "I asked if you planned to attend the concert tomorrow evening."

He hadn't thought that far ahead. "I suppose so." He turned to his mother and then to his sister. "What about it? Is it on the calendar?"

His mother's hands were clasped in her lap, her shoulders straight. "Of course, dear. Your father is on the philharmonic committee. We are expected to be present."

He smiled at Christina with a casual shrug. "You see, the Brentwood family will be there in full force."

"Good, Warren, you are home."

They all turned at the peremptory tone of Warren Brentwood Senior. Warren began to rise but his father waved him back and then strode briskly across the flagstone. "Good evening." He nodded to his wife and then turned with a smile and hand held out to Christina. "How lovely to see you, my dear."

"Thank you, Mr. Brentwood. It is so nice of you to have me over." The words flowed easily in her well-modulated tone.

"Don't mention it. You are always welcome here. You know you don't need a special invitation. How are your mother and father?"

"They are both well, thank you."

"I'll be seeing your father tomorrow morning most likely at the breakfast."

"So I've heard."

His father came toward him and patted him on the shoulder. "Although I admire your energy, Son, I just want you to know you don't have to try to remake the company the first weeks you're home." He chuckled, addressing the others. "Brentwood and Company has flourished nearly a hundred years. I don't expect it will fall apart anytime soon."

Warren listened to everyone's indulgent laughter as he met the steely glint in his father's eyes. Ever since Warren had questioned a few of the procedures down at the mill, his father never failed to bring up the successful way things had always been done at the company. "Of course, Father. No one is implying otherwise."

His father crossed to an empty chair. Warren's fingers slowly unclenched from the rocker's arms as he attempted to brush aside his father's words. It was one thing to come against his father's will whenever his father dropped by Warren's office from his new post as bank president, just to see "how he was getting along." It was another to receive his sly ridicule at home.

• • •

Espy stepped along the dirt road leading toward the northwestern edge of Holliston. Daisies bright as halved hard-boiled eggs grew in thick bunches along the road. The heat rose the farther she walked inland, leaving the river valley behind.

She plucked a daisy and stuck it behind her ear. With a sigh of relief she turned into a small grove of forest separating the rest of Holliston from her small neighborhood. The air around her was filled with the spicy scent of balsam fir and spruce. The ground was spongy beneath her feet from the layers of fallen fir needles. She followed the path for a quarter of a mile before emerging once again into the sunshine.

Laundry lines crisscrossed the backyards of the weathered houses. Abandoned toys and tools littered the front yards. She trudged behind the houses, slapping a twig against the fence posts. Paint chips scattered to the ground. The twig skipped over the gaps left by missing pickets. When she reached her own backyard, she had to step over the fallen fence, which had blown over after the last snowstorm and never been repaired.

She bypassed a rusted bucket tipped on its side and stopped before the wire fence at one side of the yard. "Have any eggs for me today?" she asked the hens picking through the sandy ground. "Let me get you some more feed." She made her way to the faded red barn and dug into a feed sack. Returning to the hen yard, she flung the corn over the wire. The hens went clucking after the scattered corn.

"I'll be back later and expect some eggs," she called over her shoulder as she headed for the back door.

She pulled on the door, which always stuck, then let it bang behind her.

Her sister Angela looked up from the sink. "You finally home?"

Espy nodded as she fanned herself with a newspaper on the table. The kitchen was just as hot as the sunny backyard. The woodstove held a large bubbling cauldron and a teakettle. "Why don't you leave the back door open?"

"Then I'll have every fly in here."

Espy ignored the warning and propped the door open with a chair. "Where's everybody?"

"They're around. Mama's lying down. Has a headache, she says." Angela rolled her eyes and went back to peeling potatoes.

A young boy entered the kitchen. "Espy's home!" he yelled over his shoulder. Some of her younger brothers and sisters trooped in behind him on bare feet.

"Hi there, Gus." She ruffled the dark, straight hair of her ten-year-old brother. "You need another haircut. You're looking pretty, Gina. Who put that ribbon in your hair?" she asked her eight-year old sister, then bent down to four-year-old Alicia, who stood sucking her thumb and holding three-year-old Julia by the hand.

Espy pulled the girl's hand gently away from her mouth. "Didn't I tell you it's not good to suck your thumb? You don't want your teeth growing in all crooked nor have Julia copying you." She hugged the curly haired Alicia to take the sting out of the words then picked up the youngest, whose chubby body was clad only in a thin petticoat. Espy nuzzled her neck. "How's my sweetie pie, Julia?"

"Where you been, Espy?" Gus eyed her satchel.

"In town and around." As she spoke, she dug into it and extracted a newspaper packet. "Here, some sardines for supper," she told Angela. "I'll fry them up in a bit."

"Nothing else?" asked Gus in a forlorn tone.

"Let me see," she said and made a show of inspecting the very bottom of the bag. "Hmm. I don't see anything. Oh, wait, what's this?" With a look of awe, she brought out two peppermint sticks.

Gus and his sisters' wide eyes followed the red and white sticks as she drew them up high out of their reach.

She looked at the expectant faces. "There's only two and we'll have to save some for your older brothers and sisters when they get home. Guess I'll have to break these into pieces, huh?"

They all nodded. Espy hit the candy against the edge of the scarred wooden counter until it cracked. She handed each child a piece.

The sweets went into their mouths right away and the kids turned to leave.

"What do you say?"

Her words halted them and they looked back at her. "Thank you, Eth-py," they said around the candy in their mouths.

"That's better. All right, off with you."

In seconds, the thundering of the floorboards ceased, leaving the kitchen quiet except for the simmering sounds off the stove and the scrape of Angela's knife against a potato.

Espy lifted the lid and stirred the soup with a long enameled spoon, dislodging a ham bone, some celery stalks, carrots, and turnips. She replaced the metal lid at an angle.

Espy set down the spoon. "My, it's hot even with the door open." She bent to unlace her boots and remove her stockings, then went to the sink and took a dipper from the bucket of clean water and used it to wash her hands and face. She rolled her shoulders around. She hadn't done such heavy housework in an age. "I got a job today."

Angela's hands on the potato stilled. "A job?"

Her sister, although dark-haired like Espy, didn't look anything like her. Instead of oval, her face was round and plump.

Espy's smile grew. "Yep." She picked up a potato peel and twirled it around.

Angela's eyes widened. "You never did!"

Espy walked around the kitchen like a queen in a parade. "I did."

"At the Stocktons' like you wanted?"

Espy nodded with satisfaction. "She wanted me to start right away. That's why I'm late today."

Her sister shook her head and turned back to the potato in her hand. "So, you're going to leave your good job at the cannery to clean someone's house."

Espy threw the peel into the bucket at Angela's feet. "I told you, it's not just anyone's house. It's a professor's. He even told me I could borrow his books. Isn't that amazing?"

Her sister shook her head and continued peeling.

Realizing she would get no further with her and that she'd have to savor her triumph alone, she looked around the kitchen. After the neat, spacious kitchen she'd been in an hour ago, the shabbiness of her own family's kitchen hit her more than usual.

Dirty dishes sat on the small wooden table covered in oilcloth. Work boots of various sizes lay like a pile of rubble by the back door. The door had never shut right after Papa had kicked it repeatedly late one summer night when he couldn't get it open, cursing it as if it had been an animate object, his invective growing louder as it refused to budge, not realizing in his drunken state that his hands still clutched the door handle as his boot attacked the flimsy panel at the bottom.

That had been shortly before he'd left the first time.

The walls, once a buttery yellow, showed ugly brown blotches and the ceiling was water- and soot-stained.

With a weary shake of her head, she began to collect the dirty crockery from the table. As she headed outside to the pump, she spied her fifteen-year-old brother, Alvaro, coming into the yard.

"Where've you been?"

Her brother shifted the stalk of timothy from one side of his mouth to the other. His dark brown hair fell into his wary eyes. "Who's asking?"

"You need a haircut."

"Costs money."

"Didn't you look for work today?" After he'd lost his job at the feed store, he'd been unable to find work.

He shrugged. "Why bother? They'll just say no."

She pushed down hard on the pump handle until a jet of water gushed out. "That attitude won't get you anywhere."

"I been everywhere already and just got the door slammed in my face."

Suddenly she stopped in mid-pump. The water slowed to a trickle. "I've got an idea."

Her brother didn't react to her tone of enthusiasm.

She tried another tack. "Guess who I ran into today?"

31

Alvaro shrugged and continued chewing on the long stalk.

She pulled the pump up and down in exasperation. "Aren't you the least bit curious?"

"Should I be?"

"Maybe." When he said nothing, she finally continued. "Young Warren Brentwood."

"What's so special about that?"

She finished filling the bucket with water before straightening. "Maybe he could give you a job."

He pulled the stalk from his mouth and stared at her. "You're kidding."

"Well, why not? He's managing his father's sawmills." She shrugged. "I saw him on my way to the Stocktons' and stopped to say hello. We used to be in grammar school together."

Alvaro's lips stretched unevenly into a smirk. "Bet he didn't even remember you."

She put a hand on her hip, her annoyance growing. *Why did younger brothers have to hit a certain age and become the most unpleasant people on the face of the earth?* "Of course he remembered me."

"What'd' ya do, tell him you had a younger brother who needed work?"

She blushed, remembering how direct she'd been with Warren. "Well, yes. I got to thinking. His family owns two sawmills, a lumberyard, a few schooners. They've got to need an extra hand somewhere."

Alvaro snorted. "As if he would want to hire me."

"Why shouldn't he? You're a hard worker. Just because you had some hard luck this spring doesn't mean nobody can appreciate what a good worker you are."

"So, you think I should go up to him and ask him for a job?"

Espy tapped a finger against her lips. She hadn't really thought it through. But Warren had been friendly enough, a little stiff perhaps, but he'd certainly seemed interested in her new employment. "Why don't we go to his office together tomorrow before I have to be at work?" she said slowly, thinking aloud. "If he sees you with me, he'll be more inclined to give you a second look." She liked the idea the more she thought of it. It would give her a chance to see Warren again, for one thing.

She nodded. "Yes, I think that would be best. But you'd better spruce up a bit. I'll cut your hair and iron a clean shirt for you tonight."

"Don't think it'll do any good," Alvaro mumbled, turning away.

She picked up the bucket, following him to the kitchen, the cold water sloshing onto her feet. "Of course it will. Warren Brentwood always looks like he stepped out of a haberdasher's. It won't hurt you to look neat and clean."

• • •

The next morning, Warren pored over the column of lumber shipments to Boston in the last quarter. He looked up from his desk at the sound of his clerk clearing his throat.

"You have some—er—visitors to see you."

Warren put down his pencil, an eyebrow raised at the bespectacled young man. "Yes? Who?"

"A young woman and man." Before he could speak further, Espy appeared behind the clerk, followed by a young man who resembled her in looks and coloring.

"Hello, Warren," she said breezily, walking by the clerk as if he were nothing more than a file cabinet. Warren immediately rose.

"Good morning, Miss Estrada." She was dressed in the same skirt and blouse—or ones very similar in appearance—as the day before, but her straw bonnet was fully on her head and no dark wisps of hair had as yet escaped to swirl about her neck.

Before he could get distracted, his eyes flickered to the young

33

man. He appeared no more than fifteen or sixteen, well-built though slim, his dark hair slicked back from his forehead. Warren remembered her saying one of her siblings was looking for work. "What brings you here this morning?" he asked politely though he had a good idea he knew exactly what it was.

Espy eyed the chairs in front of his desk.

He gestured toward them, irritation rising in him at her presumption that he would drop everything to see her and her family member. "Won't you have a seat?" He nodded to the clerk who was staring wide-eyed at Espy. "That will be all, Thurgood. I'll call you if I need anything further."

The clerk stepped back. "Yes, sir."

When they were all seated, Warren folded his hands atop his desk. "What can I do for you, Miss Estrada?"

She leaned forward, her expression eager. He couldn't help noticing once again the vivid tint of her lips. "Remember I told you about my brother?" She gestured to the young man. "This is Alvaro. I thought if you had a chance to meet him, you'd see that he'd be perfect for one of your mills."

The young man looked at Warren with sullen eyes. "How do you do, Alvaro?"

The youth ducked his head.

"What experience do you have?"

Espy answered for him. "He can do anything you ask him to. Alvaro is a good worker."

Warren picked up his pencil, studying the young man. The boy's glance slid away. Suddenly, Warren experienced a surge of compassion. He remembered how he had been at that age, shy and unsure of himself one moment, ready to take on anyone and anything the next. "How old are you, Alvaro?"

The boy sniffed and half-shrugged. "Fifteen."

Warren nodded. "Have you worked anywhere before?"

The boy slouched further down in his chair. "Unloaded hay for Taylor's for a while till he fired me."

Espy leaned forward. "Mr. Taylor said Alvaro wasn't pulling his load. It was clear the old man had it in for him from the beginning 'cause—"

"Miss Estrada, I think Alvaro can speak for himself," he said gently. "You had problems with Mr. Taylor?"

The boy shrugged again, his eyes on a point on the floor in front of him. "He said I wasn't takin' orders right, but I did every-thin' he tol' me to, exceptin' when he tol' me to clean out the whole stall just 'cause I was leaning against the door talking to Lester and he thought I was loafin'—"

Warren cleared his throat. "Yes, I understand." He laid his pen-cil down carefully. "I don't know if we have any positions available at the moment. I shall look into it and be sure to get back to you." He looked straight into the boy's eyes. "Why don't you come back here in, say—" Before he could finish his sentence, the door to his office opened and his father stepped in.

"Warren—" His father stopped at the sight of the visitors. He did not smile in any recognition. "Is there a problem here?"

What was his father doing here again?

Warren stood as soon as his father spoke, his irritation at both interruptions mounting. "Not at all. Miss Estrada and her brother, Alvaro, merely stopped in to see about employment possibilities for him."

His father's dark eyebrows drew together. "I'm sorry to waste your time, Mr.—er—" He glanced at Warren as if for corroboration.

"Estrada," Warren supplied, beginning to feel a familiar ten-sion.

"Yes, er, Estrada. There are presently no positions open at Brentwood Mills. I'm sure you'll find something elsewhere. There are always opportunities for able young men willing to work hard—and start at the bottom."

The implications were not lost on Alvaro, Warren could see by the set of his jaw. Espy glanced quickly to Warren but he remained silent, feeling caught between two opposing forces.

Hardly giving them a chance to say a word, his father went to the door and held it open. "I wish you good day, then, Mr. Espinoza—" With a sharp nod, he turned toward Espy, who half-stood from her chair. "Miss." He waited until they were both forced to stand.

Espy looked to him once more, but still Warren remained where he was. He should be glad his father had rid him of his unwanted visitors so quickly. Instead, he felt the familiar band of tension around his chest at his father's high-handed manner.

With a forced smile, he approached Espy and her brother. "I'll let you know if anything opens up here." He held out his hand to Alvaro.

The boy hesitated a second, then accepted his hand. Warren gave the limp hand a firm shake and let it go. "Good day to you and all the best in your search." He nodded to Espy. Something about her steady look perturbed him. "I'll be seeing you, Miss Estrada."

She shrugged and turned away without a smile. "Perhaps . . ." She flounced out the door, her brother in tow.

His father closed the door firmly behind them. "Now, then, I came to tell you that the *Alma Mae* is in port. We can ride down to the dock and inspect the cargo."

"Father, you didn't have to treat the Estradas so roughly. I had the situation well in hand."

His father glanced at him askance. "What—? Oh, those." He dismissed them with his hand, taking the seat so recently vacated by Espy. "I thought I did you a favor."

Warren resumed his own chair, trying to contain his temper. "Weren't you a little hasty?"

His father settled himself across from him. "I'm a good judge of character. It only takes a moment or two to sum a man up."

Warren could only shake his head in frustration.

"You don't believe me? Wait till you've lived as many years as I have. Look at that boy. Slouching, hardly meeting a man's eyes. Trouble on the yard."

"I see." Warren fingered the edge of the ledger he'd been going over. "That leads me to ask how you have summed me up?"

His father studied him frankly, his fingers steepled beneath his chin. "Bright and ambitious. You've received the finest education money can buy. You've a good head for business." He gave a satisfied nod. "Don't you worry. You'll make your mark on the world. I've given you every advantage. Your future is secure."

Instead of making him feel good, the words left Warren strangely uncomfortable, as if he must step into a box already marked out for him. Like a coffin. "I see."

"Forget about those and come along to the wharf."

Warren cleared his throat. "Don't you have things to do at the bank?"

He regretted the hasty question as soon as he'd said it. Thunderous silence thrummed between them. "I need not remind you, Son, that I am still owner of Brentwood and Company. When a boat comes in, I make it my duty to see that everything is in order on that bill of lading."

Warren looked away from those piercing green eyes so close in shade to his own. "Very well. Just give me a moment to clear up my desk."

"I'll meet you outside at the carriage."

After his father left, Warren turned his chair away from the desk and stared out the window toward the lumberyard down by the river. Men worked on the bank, stacking planks of lumber from the freshly cut timber to be loaded onto the schooner once it had unloaded its cargo.

His father's soft words made it clear who was in charge of the company. Warren's position as manager was in name only. He was there for his father to train and mold to carry on the operations exactly as his father would do if he were here in person.

He considered his father's assessment of him.

Bright and ambitious. Good head for business.

Throughout his boyhood Warren had dreamed of being a famous ballplayer. He'd been captain of the baseball team at the academy in his last two years. But he'd dreamed of becoming a professional one. He'd never voiced it aloud to his father, but to his best friends. He'd follow in the footsteps of Joe Start, John Clarkson, and Charlie Ferguson. Like Jim Creighton, he'd bring some innovation to pitching, continuing to elevate it to an art form.

Warren smiled. Boyhood dreams and ambitions knew no bounds.

He'd always known he'd take his father's place. His father had groomed him to assume control of Brentwood & Co. someday. *The finest education money can buy.* But that time had always seemed far in the future.

Now, the time had come to begin his apprenticeship in earnest. It seemed every day, the harder he tried to fit the role carved out for him, the less he seemed to be able to conform to it and to yield to the strong yoke imposed on him by his father.

3

Espy let the scrub brush fall back into the bucket of soapy water and stood up from the pantry floor. She rubbed the small of her back with both hands, letting a sense of satisfaction fill her at the sight of the gleaming floor.

An image of her own dirty and dilapidated house rose before her and she shrugged it away. She'd given up trying to improve things there. No sooner did she scrub a floor than someone tracked muddy boots across it.

After dumping the dirty water and rinsing everything, she turned to see what else Mrs. Stockton had left on her list.

Her employer came into the kitchen at that moment. "You've done a splendid job today," the older woman said, a smile creasing her face. "Everything in the parlor looks so shiny and smells of beeswax."

Espy let out a breath in relief, feeling a weight off her shoulders. Until that moment she hadn't been sure if she'd pleased her new employer. "Thank you, ma'am. I tried to do everything you told me to." She waved at the piece of paper on the table. "I was just going to look at your list now. I finished up the kitchen and pantry floor."

Mrs. Stockton glanced around at the clean floor. "Wonderful. Why don't you sit and have a glass of lemonade for a few minutes and take a little rest? You've been working since you came in this morning."

"Thank you, ma'am. I don't mind if I do. I don't mind working though," she hastened to add. "I like to see things get cleaned up." She blushed, realizing how that sounded. "I mean, not that your house is dirty." Not compared to hers. "Or untidy. Everything already seems shipshape to me."

"With just John and me, things stay tidy. But they do get dusty. We have so many knickknacks from his travels. Of course, I haven't ever been very strong for the heavy work."

"You leave that to me," Espy answered right away as Mrs. Maguire, the cook, brought her a glass of lemonade.

As soon as she'd finished drinking it, she stood.

"Why don't you dust Mr. Stockton's study now?" her employer suggested. "He's generally finished with his work by this time of day. I know you'll find it dusty in there. I don't dare touch his books," she added with a nervous laugh.

"I'll take some rags and the feather duster with me and get right to work."

Espy entered the professor's quiet domain with trepidation and a sense of anticipation. The moment had finally arrived. The reason she had accepted this job to begin with! She breathed in the scent of books—hundreds of their gold-embossed spines stood in row upon row before her eyes. She closed the door softly behind her and gazed in awe at the wonderful room with its thick navy and maroon carpets, glossy dark bookshelves, and shelves of books.

She heard a noise and turned startled eyes to the gentleman seated behind the desk. "I'm sorry, Mr. Stockton, I didn't realize you were still here."

"Miss—?"

"Espy," she supplied quickly. "I'm here to dust."

He rose and came toward her. He was a tall, well-built man and seemed to fill the room. He took her hand in his and seemed to swallow it up. His grip was firm. "Ah, yes. Miss Espy." His grayish-blue eyes twinkled as he said her name, and she felt herself blush, thinking he saw how paltry her wealth of knowledge was.

"Mrs. Stockton—your wife—uh, told me I—I might come in here now and dust a bit. I hope I'm not disturbing you. If I am, just tell me. I can come back when you're all through here." She stopped, realizing how nervous she sounded.

He chuckled softly and let her hand go, waving around him. "Not at all. Do whatever you need to do." His eyes lingered on her a few seconds longer before he stepped back, seeming to give her room to breathe.

"Thank you, sir. I'll be as quiet as a mouse."

His eyes continued to smile at her and finally with a bob of her head she moved past him and approached the first shelf.

"Don't be afraid of them. They're just books."

"What—?" She twisted around to him and then laughed, realizing he was making a joke. "Yes, I know. I just don't want to damage anything."

"Just treat them as your friends and they'll be your friends."

"I can imagine how that can be." She ran her fingers over the spines in front of her, feeling the smooth leather and ridges and indentations under her fingertips.

"Remember what I said. If you see something that catches your fancy, feel free to borrow it."

"I do remember, sir." She smiled, beginning to feel more comfortable with Mr. Stockton. He really was a nice man.

She got to work with a new will, hoping to finish soon and have a few moments to choose something before she headed home.

It took her a good hour to finish dusting all the rows of shelves and tabletops and windowsills. Besides books, the room held intricate curios and vases. She had never seen such unusual objects, from brass figurines to porcelain vases. She handled everything as if she were picking up a newborn, lest she break anything or risk even a dent or scratch.

"I found that at a street vendor's in Bombay."

At the sound of Mr. Stockton's low voice directly behind her, Espy almost dropped the ivory-inlaid box she held. "Bombay?"

"That's in India."

"Oh." India conjured up pictures of elephants and turbaned men.

"I traveled there many years ago when I was a young man. A fascinating country."

She looked at the small wooden box in her hand. "You must have traveled a lot." The only other person she could think of who had traveled anywhere outside the region was Warren. Her face burned, remembering his father's summary dismissal this morning.

And Warren had just stood there, not saying a word.

"You will probably never figure out how to open that box." Mr. Stockton's voice intruded into her thoughts. She scrutinized the box. "It opens?" There seemed to be no hinges on it.

He smiled and held out a hand. "May I?"

She placed the box in his hand and watched as he slid a panel from one side, then with a fingernail gently shoved down a panel on another side. Little by little, the sides of the box were moved, until finally the top slid open to reveal a cavity inside the box. A pleasant aroma permeated the opening when he handed it to her with a smile.

As if guessing her thoughts, he said, "Sandalwood."

"Oh." She took a deep breath.

"Clever people to invent that."

"Yes." The word came out softly as she turned the box around in her hands, examining how it was fashioned.

When she gave it back to him, his hand pressed it toward her. "Keep it."

Her eyes grew round, unable to fathom the notion that someone would give her something so precious.

He seemed to read her mind. "It's a trinket. I have lots more. You can put your special things in it. Don't you young ladies have lots of keepsakes you want hidden from all eyes?"

She blushed at the intent way he was looking at her. "I couldn't take it, sir. I don't even have anything to keep in it—"

"Maybe you will someday." He stepped back from her, leaving the box in her hands. She didn't know what to do with it. It didn't seem right to take something so valuable from a stranger. "Don't worry about it," he said. "It isn't worth much. Come, let me show you some books." He moved to one of the bookshelves and drew out a volume. "Have you read any Emerson?"

She shook her head, following him, the box still in her hands. "Not since grammar school."

When she finally left the Stocktons late that afternoon, she carried three books in her satchel, two novels and one book of poetry. And the inlaid box. She held the satchel close to her side, aware of the treasures it contained. How was she going to keep these things safe from the dirty fingers and curious eyes of her brothers and sisters?

Her breath caught at the sight of Warren, approaching in the distance. Without planning it, her departure had coincided with his return from work. She couldn't help admiring him. He looked so tall and handsome in his suit and hat, his step brisk.

Then she remembered her brother's humiliation in his father's office earlier in the day, and her heart hardened. Instead of making her way toward him as she would have done a day ago, she crossed to the other side of the street and hastened her step. She'd show him she and Alvaro were worth the time of day!

Out of the corner of her eye she watched him. He raised an

arm as if hailing her. She looked deliberately away, but as he drew near, he called out, "Miss Estrada. Hello!"

She straightened her back and stuck her chin in the air and marched on.

"Miss Estrada. Espy—"

A part of her thrilled that he'd addressed her three times. But abruptly his voice stopped and she didn't dare look behind her.

Conscious that her pace had slowed a fraction, she quickened it again, though every fiber longed to stop and see what he wanted.

But no, she would show him she wasn't dirt to be brushed aside.

●　●　●

Warren stared at Espy's retreating figure, ready to call out again in case she hadn't heard him. But no, that was impossible. She had only been across the street. Her name died on his lips. It was clear she was ignoring him.

Was she upset about her brother's not being offered a job at the mill? He shook his head. Did she expect to just march in and have everyone scurry about to accommodate an ill-looking youth? His father was undoubtedly correct in his assessment. The boy would probably show up only when he felt like it.

Warren turned away, surprised at the disappointment he experienced at not being able to talk with Espy for a few moments. He'd felt bad about his father's summary dismissal and had wanted to explain things a bit better. But, clearly, she wanted no explanation from him.

It was better this way. With a glance around the neighborhood, he resumed walking. At least the neighborhood busybodies would have no tales to carry to his mother.

A couple of hours later dusk was descending when Warren and his family left their carriage at the livery stable and walked toward the pavilion on the town green. The band was playing a rousing march and a crowd was already gathered.

After leaving his mother and father near the bandstand, he held out his arm to his sister. They began to stroll about the long rectangular park.

He glanced down at Annalise. "Anyone you'd especially like to greet?"

Her eyes shot to his an instant before focusing straight ahead again. "No. Unless there is for you."

Sorry to have alarmed his timid sister, he covered her hand with his a moment. "I didn't mean anything by my remark. It's just that I've been away and need to reacquaint myself with your circle of friends. Look, there are the Whitney girls. Would you like to say hello to them?"

"If you'd like." Her manner seemed to return to its normal quiet acquiescence and the two walked toward the pair of young ladies.

As they chatted together, the ladies plying him with questions about his travels, Christina approached with her mother. "Good evening, Warren, Annalise."

"Hello, Christina. How are you this evening? Mrs. Farnsworth?"

They continued conversing until the band began playing a waltz. A young gentleman whom Warren vaguely recognized approached one of the sisters and asked her for the dance. Warren watched as other couples began to fill the space in front of the bandstand. As he turned back to the group, he found two expectant pairs of eyes focused on him, Christina's and the remaining Miss Whitney's.

He felt himself flush, knowing they were waiting for him to ask them for the dance. Normally, he wouldn't have minded, but this evening, he felt a perverse desire just to stroll and observe others having a good time. *What if I were not to play the role of Warren Brentwood III, leading man in the quiet drama of Holliston, Maine?*

Instead, he smiled and bowed to his sister. "How about

opening the dancing with your old brother?"

Her eyes lit up. "I should love to."

He led her toward the other couples, feeling as if he'd escaped. He enjoyed dancing with his sister. She was light on her feet, yet he knew he'd probably have to ask his friends to go and ask her to dance afterward and be there to make sure she accepted them. She was too shy by far.

As he danced with Annalise, he couldn't help noticing Espy being twirled around by a brawny young man, in tight-fitting jacket and ill-matched trousers.

Ignoring the sight, he smiled at his sister. "How are you enjoying the summer thus far?"

Despite his efforts to keep up a conversation with Annalise, his gaze followed Espy every time she crossed his field of vision. She seemed to put her whole heart and soul into the dance, throwing back her head and laughing at something her partner said. Her thick mane of dark hair was coming loose and a few locks fell down her neck.

Why am I taking such notice of her? Despite the nagging question, his eye continued to watch her silhouette.

His hold tightened on Annalise as he struggled to master his feelings.

"Is something wrong?"

His smile felt forced as he reassured her.

Finally the music ended. As he escorted Annalise back to their party, he spied a man from the mill. "If you'll excuse me, I want to say hello to someone."

"Well, that's very gracious of you," Christina huffed, "leaving us ladies to fend for ourselves."

"You won't be alone long, I am sure of it," he returned smoothly. "In any case, I shall return at once. Save me a dance," he added to stop any further objections.

Her smile sweetened at once. "You'd best hurry back or you may not find me available when you return."

46

He chuckled automatically at her sally. "I'll heed your warning."

Without waiting for her reply, he turned away and walked across the grass, feeling like a man who has made a narrow escape. The next second he scolded himself for the ungracious thought. Christina was a worthy young lady, a clear favorite of his mother's.

He hailed his friend and the two stood a moment talking of things at the mill as they watched the dancers. The music was a lively polka. Once again, Warren watched as Espy was whirled around, this time by another young man.

"We received an order from Boston for a few dozen cord o' firewood."

"Yes, I saw it." He hardly heard his companion, his gaze fixed on Espy. Her enthusiasm remained undiminished. Just as she used to answer the teacher's questions with pride and enthusiasm back in grammar school, now she danced as if her whole life were concentrated on the movement of her feet in time to the music.

When the song finally ended, she moved off with the young man. They parted and Espy stood with a woman he recognized as one of her sisters.

"We'll probably work a double shift tomorrow to fill the order before the *Alma Mae* sails out."

"Yes, do that."

Surprised when Espy didn't join in the next dance, Warren found himself stepping away from his friend. "If you'll excuse me."

"Sure."

Warren circled the dancers, glad for the deepening twilight. The gaslights around the bandstand had not yet been lit.

Almost without conscious thought, he stood in front of Espy. "May I have this dance?"

Her dark eyes stared into his a few seconds before she looked beyond him. "No, thank you. I'm occupied."

His glance flickered to the other woman, who gave him a hesitant smile. He inclined his head and then turned back to Espy.

47

"Ahem." When she kept her gaze straight before her, he plowed on, not having intended the words. "I wanted to apologize for what happened in the office today."

She folded her arms in front of her and continued looking ahead. "That's quite all right, Mr. Brentwood. Alvaro has decided to seek employment elsewhere, so you needn't concern yourself with him anymore."

Espy turned away from him as another young man approached. "Care to kick up your heels, Espy?"

"I was wondering what was taking you so long, Will."

Without excusing herself from them, she walked off on the man's arm.

Warren stared at her departing back, unsure whether to be angry or amused. He'd asked her to dance because it was the only way he could think of to explain things to her with some modicum of privacy. Well, she could have her lumbering partner who danced like an ox and would probably break her toes if she weren't careful.

"I don't know what's gotten into Espy. She never acts so rudely."

He remembered Espy's sister. "Have no worry. It's nothing." His tone held the perfect note of indifference. With studied nonchalance, he bowed and excused himself and began to saunter away.

Seeing Christina still standing, he smiled. "Would you care for this dance?"

With an inclination of her head, she allowed him to take her hand and lead her out.

He danced each of the next three dances with a different young lady. When he relinquished the last one's hand, he excused himself. Once again, he circled the now dark perimeter of the green.

He leaned against a maple tree and folded his arms against his chest, watching as Espy continued to dance. Did she never get winded? Another waltz began.

Abruptly he straightened and began walking through the crowd, not stopping until he reached the dancing couple. With a forced smile, he patted Espy's partner on the shoulder. The young man turned a startled look his way.

"Excuse me, may I cut in?"

"Uh—sure—Mr. Brentwood. Anytime." He relinquished his hold and before Espy could move away, Warren took her hand in his and wrapped his other arm around her waist.

The last thing he expected was the jolt that hit him when he touched her hand. It took all his concentration to make sure his feet went where they were supposed to. When she didn't protest but began to follow his footsteps in time to the music, Warren relaxed.

Neither spoke for a few moments. A slight sheen of perspiration covered Espy's forehead and the locks of fallen hair against her neck seemed damp at the edges. "You dance well."

Her dark gaze flickered to his. "Thank you."

He cleared his throat. "What I meant to say earlier, if you had heard me out, was that I wanted to apologize for my father's behavior. You and Alvaro took me by surprise, showing up at the office like that. Most people make an appointment before they come to see me."

When she said nothing, her large eyes still watching him solemnly, he continued. "I was telling you the truth when I said I would see if there was anything your brother might be able to do. I didn't expect my father to come in."

"You said nothing to him."

The statement held an accusing note.

His conduct shamed him. But any further apology stuck in his throat. Finally, he said in a low tone. "You'd have to know my father."

He regretted his words as soon as they were out. Perhaps she hadn't heard them over the sound of the brass band.

"He can't be worse than mine."

His gaze shot to hers. Deep understanding and pain etched the dark depths of her eyes.

He didn't know what to say. How could she speak of her father and his in the same breath? A man who'd abandoned his family? When Mr. Estrada was in Holliston, he was drunk half the time and couldn't hold down a job the rest. All he seemed good for was producing more offspring each year, when he wasn't charming people to hire him on until he'd show up drunk. When he wasn't loafing on the job, he was brawling.

But the raw honesty in Espy's eyes held Warren captive. He hadn't credited her with the kind of sensitivity he saw there.

Then she shrugged and the look was gone. "Anyway, it doesn't matter now. Like I said, Alvaro will find something else."

"I can put in a good word for him somewhere."

She shook her head. "That's quite all right. You needn't bother."

A sensation of regret filled him that he had destroyed something.

When the music ended, he found himself reluctant to let her go. Then he remembered all her many dance partners. *What did she feel in their arms?*

As if conjuring him up with his thoughts, the young man he'd cut into rejoined her. "Maybe we can dance the next one," he said, taking her arm and giving Warren a quick look.

Warren bowed. "Thank you, Miss Estrada. Good evening."

"Good night, Mr. Brentwood," she replied softly.

He backed away from them, reluctant to take his eyes from hers.

Only when the music began again and couples moved around him did he leave the area. He felt her gaze on him as he walked away from the dancers.

4

The next day, Warren left the office in town and walked to one of the sawmills. The roar of the rapids competed with the whine of the band saws, creating a deafening thunder that drowned out all other sounds. The river roared over the dam, which had powered the original sawmill his great-grandfather had founded with the first settlers of the town. Stacks and stacks of lumber filled the yard down to the edge of the river.

The men didn't even look up from their work as Warren entered the shed. Sawdust littered the wood floor. After watching the activity for some moments, he headed out the back.

Warren located the foreman across the space and walked around to him.

"What can I do for you, sir?"

Warren rubbed the back of his neck, not quite sure how to word his request. He looked over the yard at the men who were going about their business. "I was wondering if you could—ah— use another pair of hands here."

Hodgdon followed his gaze. "We're about up to capacity, but we can always use an able-bodied man. Have someone in mind?"

Warren hesitated, knowing he was going in direct opposition of his father, something he'd never done before. "Ye-es." He cleared his throat. "He's a young man—a youth, really. Doesn't have any experience, but I thought we could give him a chance—but only if you're all right with it." He was half-hoping the foreman would say no. That would solve his problem.

But it wouldn't. He'd spent last night and this morning thinking about it. If he hoped to get Espy to talk to him again, he needed to make up for his father's rudeness. And prove to her he was his own man.

Why it was so important to him, he didn't know.

"No problem at all. Send him down and I'll have a look at him." The foreman chuckled. "If he's worth his salt, we'll find a place for him. There's always room for a good worker."

• • •

The soles of her feet sore, her shoulder aching from the weight of the books, Espy entered her house. "Hello," she greeted her mother and Angela in the kitchen.

Her mother sat at the kitchen table peeling potatoes, Julia at her feet playing with the fallen peels. "There you are. Can you see where Alicia has gotten to? I told Gina to watch her."

"Sure." Espy set her things down and removed her hat, hanging it on a peg. "Do you need any help with supper?" she asked Angela, who was frying something on the stove.

"Nope. Just find Alicia and put your feet up," she said with a grin.

"Thanks."

"Alicia, Gina, where are you two?" she called out, exiting the house once more. When she located her younger sisters crouched at a brook a little way from the backyard, she joined them. "What are you doing?"

"Looking for fish," answered Alicia.

"Did you see any?"

"No, but I picked these." Gina held out a fist full of buttercups.

Espy sniffed at them. "How pretty. We'll put them in a jar of water when we get home."

Alicia used a stick to poke at the rushing water.

"I brought you a book to read tonight."

Alicia's large gray eyes met hers. She was the only one in the family to have inherited her mother's lighter colored eyes. "Which one?"

"It's the story about a little orphan boy who goes to live with his rich grandfather all the way in England."

"Can you read it to us now?"

"We have to wait till bedtime."

"Please!" Gina cried.

Espy ruffled her sister's hair. "No. Right now, you're catching fish, remember?" As she spoke, she unlaced her boots and rolled down her stockings and stuck her feet into the cold water. "That feels good!"

Her sisters were already barefoot, and they, too, put their feet in the water. "That feels good!" they mimicked. Espy laughed.

"There you are."

Espy craned her neck to find Alvaro sauntering over. "Were you looking for me?"

Instead of answering her, he stood chewing a stalk of timothy grass, its head bobbing up and down. "Guess I owe you one."

"What for?"

"Your beau found me a place on the crew at the mill."

She drew her eyebrows together. "Beau? What are you talking about?"

"You know who I'm talking about. The great and mighty Warren Brentwood the Third." Alvaro made a derisive sound. "Funny how all of a sudden he found a place for me when his dad was pretty sure there wasn't nothin'."

53

Espy stood, planting her hands on her hips. "You mean to tell me you're hired at the sawmill?"

"That's right."

"And Warren got you the job? How do you know it was him?"

"He showed up here this noontime." He barked a laugh. "Can you imagine his high and mighty crossing the tracks to our neighborhood?"

"Warren Brentwood was here. He came to our house?"

Alvaro's lip curled up at one end. "That's what I said. What'sa matter? Worried he saw the hovel you live in?"

That was exactly what worried her, but she wasn't about to admit it to her brother. "Did you see him?"

Espy glanced down at the girls, but they were now picking ferns that grew along the bank. Gina had left her buttercups scattered on the bank. "Tell me exactly what happened."

"Nothing much. He just tol' me to report at the mill tomorrow bright and early if I was still interested in a job."

Espy chewed on her bottom lip, going over all this. Goodness, Warren had come all the way out here just to offer Alvaro a job. "You said this was noontime?"

Alvaro nodded.

It sounded like he'd come during his noon break. She'd never have believed it if it wasn't her own brother telling her. She swallowed. Did her anger have something to do with it? "So, what did you say?"

"What was I supposed to say? I agreed. That's what you wanted, wasn't it?"

Swallowing back her irritation, she added, "I hope you thanked him."

"Don't remember."

"Well, I'm glad you got the job. I hope you do thank him when you have the opportunity."

"Why don't you? Seems to me like you're the one who ought

to thank him." A sly look entered his brown eyes. "Give you a chance to see Mr. High and Mighty."

She glared at him. "What are you talking about?"

"Aren't you like all the gals around here, dying to be seen on Brentwood Junior's arm?"

"I'm sure that's not something that's likely to happen."

"How do you know?" His tone lost its teasing. "You're just as good as any of the girls he squires around."

She spared a slight smile. "Thanks. I don't think he's been home long enough to 'squire' anyone around. Has he?" she added.

"I haven't noticed since I don't give Warren Brentwood any thought." Guffawing, he turned away and headed back toward the house. "But don't let that stop you!"

Shaking her head at having to put up with her brother's adolescent humor, she gave her attention back to Alicia and Gina, though her thoughts were far away.

What did Warren think of me when he saw where I live? How had he even known? As far as she remembered, he'd never even been near her house. When she'd gone to the grammar school, her folks had lived closer to town in a more respectable neighborhood. Her father had had steady work then and they'd lived in a small frame house near the school.

What must he think of me now?

Curling her fingers into her skirt, she cringed inwardly at the thought of seeing him again.

• • •

Warren looked up from his desk every time anyone walked past his office the next morning. It wasn't that he expected to see Espy show up as the other morning, this time to thank him for giving her brother a chance. He pictured her light brown eyes shining, her generous mouth open in a smile.

He gave himself a mental shake, focusing once more on the papers in front of him.

At noon, Warren went to the mill to see if Alvaro had shown up.

He was sitting on a pile of boards, eating a sandwich, alongside some of the other men.

Nodding to the others and motioning them to stay where they were, he greeted Alvaro. "How's your first day?"

He took a swig from his tin cup and wiped his mouth with his forearm. "All right, I guess."

"Good."

The boy said nothing more, and feeling the eyes of the other men on him, Warren gave another nod. "If you need anything, let me know."

The boy blinked. "Uh, sure."

By week's end, Warren had seen neither hide nor hair of Espy. It rankled that she hadn't even bothered to approach him on the street to give him a word of thanks.

His father was another matter. Only two days after he had hired Alvaro, Warren's father stepped into his office.

"Hello, Father, what can I do for you?"

His father only looked at him a moment, his green eyes keen under his eyebrows.

Warren stood from his desk. "What is it?"

"I saw that shiftless-looking young man on the yard."

Warren didn't have to ask whom he meant. His heart beginning to pound, Warren picked up a pencil and twirled it between his fingers. "You mean Alvaro Estrada?"

"Whatever his name is. I told him there was no work for him at Brentwood Mills."

"I wanted to give the boy a chance. Hodgdon tells me he's doing all right."

"You went against my express wish."

Warren swallowed. "I'm sorry."

"Is that all you have to say?"

"I didn't mean to disobey you. But I thought you were hasty in this instance."

His father's mouth hardened, taking on that look Warren remembered from when he was a boy and had done something wrong. "You mean you thought I was wrong?"

"I mean I thought you were hasty in your judgment," he returned evenly, his eyes meeting his father's steadily even though he could feel perspiration break out on his neck. He hated going against his father.

Finally his father sighed and stepped away. "You'll regret it. I'll refrain from saying 'I told you so' when that happens. Let's just hope it won't cost the company."

Instead of replying, Warren changed the subject. "I was reading about the growth of the pulp mills in the state. Have you given any thought to going in that direction?"

"What's that?" His father clearly hadn't expected the change in topic.

Warren motioned to the papers on his desk, feeling a sense of relief that the topic of Alvaro Estrada had passed. "Have a seat, if you have a minute. I want to show you something."

His father, his countenance more relaxed, took the indicated armchair before Warren's desk.

By the time he left, however, Warren's shoulders were slumped and he felt worse than he had when his father confronted him about Alvaro.

He went over his father's words. *Our business is lumber. There are more than enough products without going into pulpwood. We provide lumber for all sorts of buyers. Shakes and shingles and plywood for the housing industry, cut to size for anything from toothpicks to spools . . .*

By Saturday night after a dinner party at Christina's house attended by his family and a few others, Warren told himself to stop thinking about Espy and focus on the girls in his circle.

He was leaving church after the service Sunday morning when he saw her. He stopped short, sending those in back of him in the aisle shoving into him.

"Pardon me . . . so sorry," he turned to say.

When he moved forward again, Espy was leaving the sanctuary. He couldn't go any quicker than a shuffle, the bottleneck at the front of the church caused by everyone stopping to greet one another.

When he finally made it outside to the wide churchyard, he stood with his family, greeting acquaintances as his eyes scanned the crowd.

Espy stood under the shade of an elm tree with her sister and younger siblings. She was wearing the same gown she had on at the bandstand concert, a dark blue skirt and jacket, a yellow parasol in one hand.

A young man who'd danced with her approached her, and the two young women talked with him.

Warren swallowed, annoyed and impatient. He wouldn't go to her, he decided, but would wait to see if she would speak to him at all about her brother's job.

He smiled at a friend of his mother's. "Yes, Mrs. Dalton, it's nice to be home. Yes, I missed our downeast cooking . . ."

• • •

Espy looked across Will's shoulder, watching Warren without seeming to.

She'd been observing him the whole service from her pew at the back, her stomach twisting in knots so badly as the service wore on, she didn't think she'd be able to get up.

She knew she had to speak to Warren, yet she didn't know how she could. Mortified still at the thought that he'd been to her

58

house—how could Warren see her now as anything but dirt? A girl who cleaned for a living and lived in a shanty.

Will shifted from one leg to the other. "So, whad'ya say, Espy, go with me to the grange dance next Saturday?"

She forced her attention to the sandy-haired man. "Thank you, but if I go, I'll go with Angela." She didn't like encouraging any of the young men who seemed forever vying for her attention. Though they were nice enough, none of them interested her in that way. They were all the same, no ambition in life. Any man who wanted to win her had to show something more than just having a good time at week's end.

Her gaze strayed back to Warren, a slight frown marring her forehead. A fashionably dressed young lady stood close to him, making them seem a couple. Golden blond hair was swept up under a medium-brimmed straw hat topped by a furl of ostrich feathers dyed in the same shade of pale blue as her silk dress.

Espy took in the tight sleeves with their full gathers at the shoulder and gored skirt, comparing it to her own navy blue outfit with its bustle and narrow sleeves. The lady twirled a small light blue and yellow patterned parasol over her shoulder, mimicking Espy's own.

Christina Farnsworth. Daughter of Arthur Farnsworth, owner of the granite mine out of town and on the board of the First Bank and Trust of Holliston, whose president was Mr. Brentwood Senior.

Between the two men, they probably owned most of Holliston.

Warren had hardly been home to already have formed an attachment to any young lady. Unless they'd been corresponding all the years he'd been away. *Was there an understanding between them?*

"Hey, you're not paying attention to a word I'm saying."

She blinked, dragging her attention back to Will. "I am so. You just told me you wanted to go to the grange."

"I was talking about the picnic we're going to have this

afternoon at Three-Mile Lake. Are you and Angela coming along?"

"I don't know." She turned to her sister. "Is Alvaro going?"

"He hasn't mentioned it. We'd have to take the young ones. Besides, I haven't packed a lunch."

Espy turned back to Will, sorry to miss an afternoon by the lake but relieved to have a legitimate excuse to turn down his invitation. She didn't want everyone seeing them to think they were a couple. "Sorry, Will, you should have told us sooner." *What would it be like going on a picnic to the lake with Warren and his friends?*

The thought fizzled as soon as it formed. His friends wouldn't accept her. Christina laughed at something Warren said. More people greeted him, a large circle forming. Their laughter and voices drifted over.

"Well, we'd better head home," Angela said. "The children will be hungry soon."

"Yes." Espy sighed. It had been a vain hope to think Warren would be alone. Friends, family, acquaintances ringed him round as if he were a visiting dignitary. Jealousy bit into her stomach at the sight of his carefree smile to all those surrounding him.

Alicia tugged on her hand. "I'm hungry."

Espy smiled down at her. "You're just saying that because you heard Angela."

The child shook her head at her with a smile. Espy looked at Angela. "You go on."

Angela began to walk away, calling to Hortensia to take the hands of the younger ones, while she looked after the others. Their mother as usual had stayed home with Julia, saying she was too tired.

Angela gave Espy a final look over her shoulder. "What d'you need to do?"

Espy looked away. "Just talk to someone." She pretended to scan the area. "Don't see them yet."

"All right, if you're sure. Come along, Josiah, Daniel, Gus," she called out to the older boys who were running around with others their age.

Alicia stamped her foot. "I want to stay with Espy!"

"I thought you said you were hungry," Espy said to her.

"But I want to stay with you."

Espy shook her head in exaggerated perplexity. "Only if you promise to wait patiently."

Angela waved goodbye, looking doubtfully at her before turning homeward , the children marching behind her.

Espy bent down to Alicia. "Let me fix your hair ribbon." Under the guise of retying the ribbon, which was on the point of falling off the girl's braid, she glanced toward the Brentwoods. At least most people had dispersed. Home to their hot Sunday dinners, she thought sourly over her grumbling stomach. The Estradas probably had leftover potatoes and cabbage with a slab of salt pork awaiting them. And Mama was probably just waking up, woken by Julia's hungry cries.

Espy groaned inwardly at the sight of Pastor Curtis approaching Warren. "There you go, dear." She tugged on one of Alicia's braids. "Come along, let's stroll over there. I see Sally Tucker. She's your friend, isn't she?"

"Uh-huh."

As Espy stood talking to the other little girl's mother, she continued eyeing Warren. He seemed to be telling his family to go on. What could the pastor be saying that would take longer than a few minutes? Warren's family seemed to want to stay. Good, he persuaded them to go. Reluctantly, it seemed, by the look on his mother's face. Espy smiled, remembering sending Angela on home.

"Be seeing you," Espy said to Mrs. Tucker and her young daughter.

Now only Warren and Pastor Curtis remained. Knowing it would look strange to be the last one standing around in the churchyard, Espy took a deep breath, grasped Alicia's hand firmly, and walked a little closer to Warren and the pastor. Not close enough to eavesdrop on their conversation but close enough to be seen by them. Maybe they would think she was waiting to talk to the pastor. That would be natural enough.

After his parents and Annalise departed, Warren turned with a smile to the pastor. "What can I do for you, sir?"

The gray-haired man smiled at him. "I didn't mean to hold you up."

"That's all right. I wasn't in any rush." His glance sought Espy. Good, she was still in the churchyard. "But I didn't want to ruin Mother's Sunday dinner." He grinned. "You know how she is about it."

"Dear me, yes. Mrs. Curtis as well. Which is why I should get to the point." His blue eyes looked into Warren's in that alert way they had of making a person wonder how much they saw.

"I've had it on my heart for a while to have the young folks of the church form some type of group."

Warren nodded with interest. "What kind of group?"

"A group that would look outside of themselves and see what service they can offer to the community at large."

"Sounds like a noble purpose. How can I help you?"

"I've been waiting for the right person to head up such a group. When I saw you sitting in church, it came to me." He pointed at him. "You're the man."

Warren took a step back. "Wait a moment there. I'd be glad to participate, but lead it? I don't think I'm the one."

The pastor merely continued to look at him, a slight smile on his mouth, his eyes filled with understanding.

"I'm not a pastor, for one thing."

"You wouldn't have to be. You just need to be a fellow who knows the Scriptures and is willing to do something for others."

Warren swallowed. "I don't consider myself an expert on the Scriptures."

Pastor Curtis chuckled. "You've attended Sunday school since you were a tyke, attended Bible studies under me through high school, and helped teach Sunday school. Oh, I think you're the right man. The question is, are you willing?"

Warren squirmed, knowing it was a moment of examining his priorities—something he'd been able to avoid in the last couple of years of traveling and seeing the world. "What exactly would you want me to do as a leader of such a group?"

"The way I see it, too many young people of our community—especially the young men—aren't coming to church. I don't mean your circle, Warren; you're all churchgoers," he said with an apologetic smile, "but look around you at the community at large." He waved his hand toward the street.

That's when he spotted Espy, holding her younger sister by the hand. He smiled and motioned for her to approach. "Hello there, Espy. Why don't you join us as I explain an idea of mine to Warren?"

With a quick glance at Warren, she returned Pastor Curtis's smile and joined them at once—almost as if waiting for an invitation. Warren wondered if she had been waiting for him. Was she finally going to talk to him about her brother?

"Hello, Pastor; hello, Warren." She nodded quickly in his direction before turning back to the pastor. "What idea is that, sir?"

"I was just telling Warren about something I've had on my heart for a few years—forming a group for the young folks like you and Warren. Maybe you can help me convince Warren here that he's the man to head it up."

Her light brown eyes turned on him. Warren held her gaze, wanting to know how she saw him. Suddenly, he wanted to do something worthy in her eyes.

The pastor continued speaking. "The taverns and dance hall

are full on a Saturday night. But how many of those people show up on a Sunday morning to church?

"We're losing the young people your age, when they leave school and begin to work in the mills or cannery. Life is hard and all they want out of life is to relax a little on a Saturday night and forget about their troubles." The pastor's voice deepened with conviction. "They turn to worldly amusements and forget that real strength comes from God."

He fixed his gaze once more on Warren. "You could teach a Bible class and arrange outings, fun things for these young people in their late teens and into their twenties, who are still single."

He smiled at Espy. "Maybe you could be the first member! Someone for you to recruit." He winked at Warren.

Although he knew the remark was innocent enough, it made him flinch, feeling as if the pastor read his secret thoughts.

"It sounds like a wonderful idea, Pastor," Espy said at once, her eyes alight with eagerness. "I know so many of my friends at the cannery quit going to church. They'd rather sleep in on a Sunday morning. Maybe if they could see what church is really about, you know, not just listening to sermons, but helping people when they're down." She smiled, gesturing with her free hand.

Warren was caught by the enthusiasm she displayed, comparing his own reluctance when the pastor singled him out for the job.

"That's exactly right, Espy. You understand what I mean, an organization that's civic-minded but also fun. It would give young adults an opportunity to be together but in a wholesome way and give them an opportunity to do some good in the community, be an example to others—and be aware of the plight of those less fortunate."

He patted Espy's arm. "You could help Warren recruit members." He chuckled. "Maybe you could be the group's vice president or secretary."

Her color rose. "I don't know about that. But I'd certainly like to help. Maybe we could raise money putting on events and then use that money to help people or send it to missionaries overseas?"

"I think I can safely leave this idea with you, too."

Pastor Curtis touched Warren lightly on the forearm. "I'm serious, don't let this young woman go. She's got a wealth of ideas, and she knows the people I'm referring to. The ones who most desperately need to hear the gospel."

Warren nodded, not knowing what to say.

"Well, I'll be off to my own Sunday dinner. Let me know how I can help. Why don't the two of you toss some ideas back and forth and then come see me next week?"

Without agreeing to anything, Warren could only continue to nod reluctantly.

"Hey, are you going to pitch for our team on the Fourth?" the pastor asked.

The sudden change of topic threw Warren off. "I . . . I don't know."

"I sure hope so. We need to knock the socks off Seal Harbor after our defeat last year!"

Warren blinked at the competitive tone in the pastor's voice. But the older man chuckled, dispelling the notion before bending down and saying goodbye to Espy's younger sister.

Warren stood there, feeling more awkward than he had since he was fourteen and had his first crush.

"Are we going home now, Espy?"

They both started as if the little girl had awoken them from a trance. "Sure, sweetheart." Espy turned back to Warren. "I . . . uh, heard about Alvaro's job . . . I mean, he told me you'd come to see him."

"Did he?" Warren said no more, wanting to see what she would say.

She moistened her lips, and he swallowed, his attention riveted. "Thank you for giving him a chance. He's not a bad boy . . ." Her voice trailed off.

In that instant all annoyance at not seeing her in the intervening week evaporated. He realized what a conceited fool he'd been, waiting for some sign of gratitude on her part. Instead, he understood what it meant to do something *good*.

He grinned. "Well, if he's not, Hodgdon will see it soon enough. He's the foreman at the lower mill, a hard taskmaster but he's fair and he takes care of his crew."

She drew in a deep breath. "That's good. I wouldn't want Alvaro to get hurt. You know how reckless boys can be at that age."

His grin widened. "I do indeed. I did the same job myself many an afternoon after school and during summers, and I survived." He held up his hands. "No missing fingers."

Her eyes widened in alarm before she smiled, realizing he was teasing her. "You worked in the mill?"

"What's the matter, think I'm pulling your leg?" He watched her lashes, long and dark.

"No, but . . . well, I thought you did nothing but play baseball and football after school when you were at the academy."

"I did those, too, but the rest of the time, Father had me at the mills or down on the docks, loading lumber, to learn the business."

She nodded as if digesting this information.

Her little sister tugged on her skirt. "When are we going home?"

Espy smiled down at her, placing a hand on her head. "In a moment, sweetie." She looked at him again. "I guess I'd better get on home."

On the spur of the moment he said, "Do you mind if I walk you home? I mean, that way we can talk about this organization Pastor Curtis wants us to form."

Her face clouded over and he wondered what he'd said wrong, but then she nodded. "Well, maybe partway. I mean, doesn't your family expect you home?" For the first time she seemed unsure of herself.

"They do, but it's all right. I told them I'd be late."

"All right, just to the edge of town." She looked down at her sister. "Come along, Alicia, we're going home now."

As they began walking down the street, hazy with dust, the little girl began to drag her feet. "I'm tired, Espy, can you carry me?"

Espy tugged on her hand. "You're getting too big for that."

Warren again surprised himself. "I have a better idea. How about a piggyback ride?"

Alicia looked around Espy, staring at him round-eyed. Espy smiled at her. "Did you hear that, a piggyback ride? Like Alvaro gives you."

The child nodded. Warren went over to her and crouched down. "All right, climb aboard." Espy helped her sister up on his shoulders, her fingers briefly touching his shoulders as she adjusted her sister's legs. "Hold on to my hat," he instructed the child. "All set?"

"Uh-huh."

He grasped her ankles and stood. "Can you see a lot more?"

Alicia giggled. "I can see everything!"

The two resumed their walk. "So, what do you think of Pastor Curtis's idea?" Espy asked him after a moment.

"It's a good one. I just didn't expect him to ask me to organize it." He chuckled. "He took me off guard. I think that's a specialty of his. Get folks where it's hard to say no."

She joined in his laughter. "He's not as bad as that." She glanced at him under her hat brim, a pretty thing with blue flowers clustered atop it. "Besides, I think he was right. You'd be good at it."

Ignoring the sense of pleasure her remark gave him, he said only, "Think so? I'm certainly not so sure of that."

"You'll be fine. Everyone looks up to you."

The words filled him with apprehension. "I certainly hope not!"

She made a face as if disbelieving his words. "Now you're

joshing me. You know very well you've always been a leader, ever since grammar school. You seem to know the right thing to do and people admire you for that."

He swallowed. "I just try to do right, but I don't do it for people to admire me."

She shrugged. "It doesn't matter the reason. They admire you for it, and it influences them. I think people try to do better when they're around you."

Pondering the words, he said, "I guess that's a good thing, but I don't like to think I'm on some kind of pedestal." He gave a nervous laugh. "It's too easy to fall off."

"You'll never do anything terrible!"

"I certainly hope not."

Alicia tapped on his bowler hat. "You have to turn here to go home!"

"Yes, I know, but thanks for being my conductor."

"What's a conuctor?"

"Conductor," he corrected. "The man on the train who checks people's tickets."

"We're on a train . . . I'm the conuctor!"

"That's right." He tugged on her ankles, saying, "Choo, choo!"

They left the center of town with its commercial buildings and entered a residential neighborhood, its large houses set back from the street. The streets were quiet, most people probably inside eating their Sunday dinner. "How is it going at the Stocktons'?" he asked Espy, wanting to take the focus off himself.

"Wonderful. The work's hard at times but then I get a reward at the end of each day."

"What's that?" he asked, filled with curiosity at the enthusiasm in her tone.

"Mr. Stockton lets me borrow as many books as I can read. I even take home storybooks to read to the younger ones at night. Isn't that right, Alicia?"

"Uh-huh."

So, she had been serious about her love of reading. "What kinds of things do you take?" He didn't think Mr. Stockton kept a stock of pulp novels, he thought to himself, smiling inwardly at his own pun.

"Everything—novels, poetry books, history books." She smiled. "He has a lot of books on American history. Books about plants and animals, too."

"I see. What are you reading now?" The professor must have taken a liking to her and, like any good teacher, having spotted a thirst for knowledge was only too willing to feed it.

"Now I'm reading *Jane Eyre*. I just finished *The Last of the Mohicans*."

He nodded, impressed. His old teacher must be guiding her choices.

"What's nicest is that Mr. Stockton always asks me questions about the books afterwards. He makes me think about the stories." She shook her head. "He also tells me all kinds of things about when the book was written, how that affected how and why the author wrote what he did."

"He was a great history teacher back in my days at the academy. He gave me a love of American history."

They continued talking about Warren's days at the academy. He discovered how Espy had wanted to attend high school but had not been able to continue her schooling due to her father's injury.

They reached the edge of town and Espy stopped. "You don't have to come any farther."

He found himself reluctant to bid her goodbye so soon. "That's all right. Besides, I have a conductor I have to deliver to the station." He pulled on Alicia's ankle with a wink at Espy.

Espy only smiled wanly and resumed walking.

They returned to the topic of the church organization, tossing ideas back and forth. By the time they reached Espy's house,

Warren wished she lived even farther away so they could continue their talk.

He lifted Alicia down to the ground. "There you go. The train has arrived at its station, Estradaville."

The little girl clapped her hands. "Estradaville. I live in Estradaville!"

"Go on in, sweetie. I'm sure Angela has your dinner ready."

Alicia skipped up the walkway.

"Don't forget to wash your hands!" Espy turned to him. "Thank you for walking me home."

He was thinking of something to say when she added, "Will you be at church this afternoon?"

"Uh, no. I mean, Mother usually has company in so we usually don't go to the afternoon service."

She held her hands together in front of her. "I just meant, I thought I might invite some people that I see there. Do you think that's all right?"

"By all means." He rubbed his chin. "You might want to think about a few people who might help us lead this thing first, before we invite the general public," he said with a grin.

She nodded. "That's a good idea. I'll give it some thought and see who would be best. You'll probably think of some people, too."

"Yes, I'll give it some thought as well."

Still nodding, he turned away, then stopped, a thought occurring to him. "Wait, what about our first meeting?"

She moistened her lips. "What day is convenient for you?"

"Let me look on my agenda and . . . and let you know. Where should we have our first meeting?" He glanced at her house, realizing simultaneously how unsuitable it would be and that his look must be giving the fact away. Slowly, he met her gaze again, thinking that his own house would be just as unsuitable as hers, though for the opposite reason.

Her friends wouldn't feel comfortable there, just as his wouldn't here.

She said nothing, her lips puckered. Suddenly her eyes lit up just as an idea hit him. They both said, "The church!" at the same time. Then the two laughed, relief washing through Warren at the first sticky hurdle they'd crossed.

Waving goodbye, he turned away again and headed down the dirt road.

What other hurdles would there be?

But at least it gave him a chance to see Espy.

For the more he was in her company, the more he craved to be in her company again.

5

Late that afternoon as Espy sat in church once more, she couldn't help imagining what Warren was doing. Eating a fancy dinner at a long table covered by a white linen cloth, using silver candelabra such as she'd had to polish in Mrs. Stockton's kitchen, with delicate china dishes before him?

She peered around her, looking for the honey blond hair of Christina Farnsworth, but she didn't see her. *Is she at the Brentwoods'? Sitting beside Warren, knowing just which knife and fork to use?*

With a shake of her head, she turned her attention back to the pulpit. She was here to hear God's Word preached, not to daydream about a man she had no business thinking about.

She should be grateful that she'd be able to see him often now that she was part of the new church group—thanks to Pastor Curtis, the dear man who didn't seem to notice the difference between Espy and Warren and where each came from.

. . .

Bowing his head for a quick grace, Warren was spared a few seconds longer before he had to give an account of where he'd been. As he was chewing his first bite, his mother set down her fork and dabbed her mouth with her napkin. "What did Pastor Curtis keep you so long for?" She glanced the length of the table to his father. "Your father and I were getting concerned."

Warren finished chewing and swallowed. "He had an idea he wanted to talk to me about." After taking a swig of water, he said, "For an organization, a sort of church club for young folks."

"I wonder why he thinks we need another group. There are so many groups to join already," his mother mused, sitting back.

"I believe he feels too many young people are straying away from church once they reach adulthood."

She frowned. "Goodness gracious, where did he get such an idea? The church is full of young people on Sunday morning. Why, Christina never misses a service, nor either of you." She gestured toward him and Annalise.

"Of course not." Christina, who had been invited to dinner, nodded. "All my friends attend services regularly."

He found himself forced to elaborate a little on what he had tried to avoid. "But not all young people attend, if you take Holliston as a whole."

"You mean the riffraff," his father grunted.

"I wouldn't call all those who work for us in the sawmills or on the docks riffraff."

"Of course not, but a good many of them attend church, especially the family men." His father shrugged. "It's the single men who are the most wayward. But what they do in their free time is their own business."

Warren pushed his plate away a fraction, his food half finished, his appetite no longer what it had been when he'd walked in. "What they do does affect us when it involves drinking and carousing in their free time."

73

Christina laughed. "You make it sound like it takes place at our very doors. Any of that goes on away from here. It's disgraceful, of course, but if it's contained to a certain area of town," she said and shrugged. "I think it's just one of those things one can't really control."

"Men need an outlet after a hard week's work," his father put in as if the subject were closed.

"An outlet, yes, but not drunkenness or gambling."

His father glared at him. "I don't think our town is facing the kinds of problems you see in the city. Leave well enough alone, I say."

Warren tamped down his growing frustration. "I believe Pastor Curtis would like these men to *want* to come to church, to show them that there'll be something for them there as well." He was fumbling, unable to defend the pastor's idea, but thinking there was something right in it.

His father gave a "harrumph" before getting up from the table. "Well, I'm going to have a cigar." He nodded to the women and excused himself.

"What did Pastor Curtis want you to do, Warren, with this new group?"

"He wanted me to . . . lead it."

"Lead it?" His mother sounded horrified.

Christina leaned forward. "Do tell us more. Perhaps you can form it the way you want. It could be quite good fun for us, Mrs. Brentwood."

"I suppose it is an honor," she conceded. "But be careful whom you invite, Warren." She shook her head. "You don't know how unruly some of the elements in town can be. You've been away quite some years."

Warren hid a smile. "Mother, do you imagine I have seen nothing unsavory in the different ports I've visited?"

His mother, too, rose. "I shall leave you young people to discuss *the club*."

Warren finished eating his food, as Christina offered him suggestions.

"I think we should invite Emily and Mabel. Also Dexter and James." She turned to Annalise. "And you, of course. Let's see, that's seven of us. We need one more male."

Warren chuckled. "This is not a social club. It doesn't really matter whether everyone gets paired off."

Christina pursed her lips. "I think it would be ever so much more fun if we kept the numbers even. I hope you don't think it will be all work and no play." She smiled. "I don't know how you expect to attract young people if all you want them to do is labor."

Warren fiddled with the handle of his knife. "Pastor Curtis has also invited Espy Estrada to join. I imagine she will invite some of her friends."

Christina's mouth formed an O. Annalise looked at him with a question in her eyes.

Christina was the first to recover. "Espy? Goodness." She gave a brittle laugh. "Pastor Curtis certainly meant what he said about inviting the riffraff. What will he do next? Go to the tavern on Saturday night and issue a general invitation?"

Annalise looked shocked. Warren reined in his irritation. "I'd hardly classify Espy with a bunch of drunks."

"There is her father . . ."

"I don't think we ought to be judging people by other members of their family," he said stiffly, not understanding Christina's hostility.

Christina raised her brows. "My, aren't you quick to rise to her defense!"

"I just don't like to judge people hastily. She seems a decent, hardworking person."

Christina turned to Annalise. "Did you hear that? Miss Estrada has risen in your brother's estimation to quite some heights. You had better keep an eye on him. Who knows whom he'll invite next."

"I don't think . . ." began Annalise with hesitation.

Warren finished for her. "It's all right, Sis. I don't think anyone has to worry about me. I'm used to taking care of myself and have seen a lot more of humanity than anyone around here gives me credit for."

The joy he'd taken in discussing Pastor Curtis's idea with Espy dissipated the longer he sat at the table. By the time he rose, he felt it was going to be one more chore in his list of duties as heir to the Brentwood name.

• • •

Espy walked with Angela and the two friends she'd managed to convince (coerce and cajole were more like it) to attend the church club's first meeting. She glanced at Will and Henry, whom she'd had to promise to have an ice cream with at the local parlor afterwards.

Even Angela hadn't been very cooperative, saying she preferred to stay home after a hard day's work. Thankfully, their mother was at home to look after the children.

They arrived at the church and went to the side door leading down to the basement. Hearing voices, Espy led the way into the main room, which was usually used for church suppers and other community events. She breathed a sigh of relief seeing Warren already seated, but just as quickly frowned at the sight of Christina at his right hand.

With an impatient head shake, she looked at the others, two young men, Warren's sister, and two ladies she only knew by sight.

Warren smiled when he saw her and the tension eased from Espy. "There you are." His glance encompassed her companions as he stood from the table. He nodded to Angela and then turned to the young men. "I don't believe we've met."

Espy ushered them forward. "This is Will Trafton and this is

Henry Freeman. They work at the cannery with Angela."

The men shook hands and murmured "pleased to meet yous."

"I'm glad all of you could attend the first meeting of our new church group." Warren grinned. "We don't even have a name for it yet, but that's one of the things we can discuss today at our organizational meeting."

Will and Henry muttered, "Sure," already looking a little beyond their depth.

Espy motioned to Angela to take a seat and Warren sprang forward to pull it out for her. Espy took the chair beside it for herself.

When Warren was once again seated, he asked Espy, "Do you expect anyone else tonight?"

"No, these are the only people I asked."

He looked around those present. "Well, then, I move we officially begin our meeting."

Christina smiled at him. "I second the motion."

"Yes, now that you've roped us here, let's get this show on the road," Warren's other friend joked with a smile.

"This smart aleck is Dexter Ellis," Warren said with a smile, "and these are Emily, Mabel, and James—and my sister, Annalise."

Dexter, a young gentleman with dark blond hair, smiled at Espy and Angela. "We meet at last. I've seen the two of you in church but have never had the pleasure."

Espy nodded. "Likewise, I'm sure."

James and Emily merely stared at her and then looked away. Warren's sister smiled at them.

"Well, now that introductions are out of the way, let me give you a little background." Warren proceeded to tell them about Pastor Curtis's idea for a young people's group.

Espy glanced around the table, noticing that Warren's friends all sat at one end and her friends at the other. It was probably just coincidence, since the former had arrived first. But she had hoped

77

they could have a close-knit group, working for the good of the community. Would it turn instead into a club made up of two different groups of people, her friends and Warren's?

She clasped her hands on the tabletop. She wouldn't let it.

When Warren finished speaking, Christina smiled. "I think it's a laudable idea. I would suggest we begin by electing officers for this club."

Warren cleared his throat. "Why don't we discuss what we're going to do as an organization first?"

If Warren's gentle disagreement bothered her, she gave no sign. "I thought Pastor Curtis already gave us the vision?"

"But only in very general terms." His glance encompassed them all. "Why don't we hear from all our members? Whatever ideas we toss around, I'll be sure to discuss with Pastor Curtis. What about you, Will, any thoughts of what you'd like to see in a church club?"

Will turned red in the face. "Hadn't thought much about it, I guess," he mumbled, looking down.

"Well, what about you, Henry?"

"Have fun, I guess," he answered with a self-conscious grin.

Will joined him with a snigger.

Dexter clapped his hands. "I heartily second that!"

Warren turned to Angela with what Espy thought was a strained smile. "Angela?"

Angela shook her head and mumbled something unintelligible.

Espy, reining in her impatience with her companions, prepared to say something about what she had thought over since walking home with Warren.

But Christina spoke first. "Why don't you ask this side of the room?"

"Of course. I didn't mean to leave anyone out. Please, anyone who has something to say, please feel free. We're a small group, and this is only a first meeting to figure out what we'd like to do as a group. James, Dexter, Emily . . . any of you have any thoughts?"

"I'm here for a good time," Dexter said, with a wink Espy's way. The others didn't say anything.

Espy got ready to speak her piece, but once again Christina spoke before she had a chance to muster her thoughts. "What about a beautification project?"

At Warren's blank look, she continued. "We could choose a site in town and improve it. I daresay there are dozens of places that could use some beautifying," she added with a short laugh.

"You mean a garden?" Mabel asked. "That's a lovely idea. We could plant flowers."

Christina turned to her. "That is what I was thinking. You know that abandoned lot by the riverfront, between Tupper's Dry Goods and Sawyer's Livery? We could mow the grass and put in a garden bed. Perhaps a park bench."

Warren nodded.

Espy squirmed in her chair, glancing at either side of her toward Angela and the boys. Seeing she'd get no help from any of them, she took a deep breath. "Excuse me." When all eyes on the other side of the table turned to her, she felt the blood rush to her cheeks. "I thought the purpose was to help those in need."

"Yes," began Warren.

Christina looked at her as if only just noticing her. "What better way to help everyone in the town but to do away with an eyesore? That lot has become a place to deposit trash. It's unsightly."

"I've even seen tramps sleep there at night." Emily shuddered.

The other gentleman, James, leaned forward and drawled, "What I say is we raise money to have the organ repaired. It sounds atrocious. My ears can scarcely bear it on Sunday morning."

The group at that end of the table began talking at once. Espy met Warren's glance.

"Hey, what about Espy's idea?" Will shouted loudly enough to be heard. "Why don't you all listen to her, or don't you think her ideas are as good as Miss Christina's?"

"I believe *Miss* Christina has a very good point," James said with a smirk. "If we don't begin taking pride in our town, how can we take pride in anything?"

"By not having anyone go hungry in it."

"Some people don't want to work and then complain when they don't have enough to eat."

The men's voices rose. Henry joined Will and soon Dexter was trying to calm the others but his voice grew as loud as the others. They were standing, pointing their fingers at each other.

"Everyone will have a chance to be heard if you'll just sit down—" Warren's voice was drowned out by the rest.

Espy turned to Angela. "This is ridiculous."

"I knew it would be a waste of time to be here," Angela muttered.

Espy stood and looked around the room, searching for some-thing—anything—to get the men's attention. Spying a hymnal on a nearby sideboard, she marched over to it. She brought it back to the table. On impulse, she stood on her chair and let the heavy book fall to the table with a thump loud enough to make everyone jump.

In the instant of silence, she plunged ahead. "Pastor Curtis wants us to reach out into the community and show the other young people that church isn't a building—but it's people like us who are willing to show the love of Christ to our neighbors."

As gracefully as she could, she lowered herself from the chair but remained standing. "There are plenty of people who work hard in this town, but still can't get by." She stared James down, daring him to contradict her.

"I know a woman on Chestnut Street who just lost her hus-band. She works at the cannery all hours of the day. She's got five mouths to feed. What she makes barely pays the rent and food. How can she provide for her children?"

They were staring at her. She plunged on while she had their attention. "Her oldest son just finished grammar school. He's been wanting to attend high school since he first began school. But his mother needs him to earn money. That woman hasn't come to church because she's too exhausted on Sunday to do much more than sleep. Her children have only come when someone from church has been kind enough to stop by for them—and provide them with some decent clothes their own children have outgrown."

She took another breath. "Those are the kinds of people we need to be helping." She went on to describe two more individuals she knew of firsthand from her own neighborhood. The longer she spoke, the more she forgot who she was addressing and the more impassioned she became. All she could think of was the plight of the people she had grown up around and worked with, and how important the help they'd received from the church had been to them in their time of need.

When she finally paused, Warren took over, giving her a brief smile. "Thank you for sharing this with us." He looked around at the astonished group still staring slack-jawed at Espy. "These are the people Pastor Curtis would like us to reach. What if we organize some things where we can raise some funds to help this boy who wants to go on to high school?"

"If we just give handouts to people, they'll become more shiftless than ever," James said.

"As my mother says, the more you give people, the more they'll take without making an effort for themselves." Christina's words were said dispassionately but her eyes shot daggers at Espy.

"We can put up safeguards to prevent that. Espy and others," Warren gestured toward her friends, "can let us know of real cases of need. A woman who's just been widowed maybe needs some help to tide her over. Now, why don't we spend some time to come up with some ideas of how to raise some money?"

"As long as it involves fun," Dexter drawled.

"Of course it can be fun if we approach it with the right attitude," Espy countered. "We could sell something—perhaps at one of the church bazaars."

"Oh, yes, selling doilies and embroidered tea towels should pay this boy's way through high school," Christina said, making no attempt to mask her sarcasm.

Emily tittered, adding, "I have a doily I just finished. It took me a couple of weeks to complete."

Christina turned to her with an over-bright smile. "Wonderful. In a few months we may have enough to put out at the Christmas bazaar." They dissolved into laughter.

"What about a food sale?" Warren asked, ignoring the ladies' laughter. He leaned forward on an elbow, rubbing his chin thoughtfully. "We could do something now when there are the summer visitors."

Dexter raised an eyebrow. "The Fourth is coming up in a couple of weeks."

Warren smiled. "I like the way you're thinking. What about a meal in town with donations to go to a young man's education and some of these other needs? Could we organize something so quickly?"

"We could do a lobster feast," James said, his tone serious but approving. "I'm sure we could get the lobster donated from some fishermen. My father's grocery can get some corn at wholesale from Portland."

Espy glanced at Christina to see how she received the idea. From a frozen expression, she suddenly blinked as if waking up, and smiled. Her face was transformed into that of a lovely, sweet young lady. "We could ask for donations and state the worthy cause the funds would be used for."

Once again, everyone began to speak at once, but this time not in anger.

Espy sat back down, feeling a sense of satisfaction on one hand, a sense of letdown on the other. It was as if she'd fought hard for something and now it was out of her hands. She had no control over it.

She gave herself a mental scold at such vain thoughts. *Thank You, Lord, for bringing peace to this group.*

She looked to the far end of the table to Warren.

He was responding to something Will had said but as he spoke, his gaze strayed to her as if he sensed her eyes on him.

A corner of his lips lifted in acknowledgment then he gave his full attention once more to Will.

Espy's heart felt full to overflowing with goodwill.

Thank You, Lord, she repeated silently.

6

Warren sat back in his chair, able to relax for the first time since the meeting began. Now, everyone was discussing the lobster cookout for the Fourth of July in an amicable way, and he could feel he'd taken the first step in what Pastor Curtis had asked him to do.

He could not have done it without Espy, he conceded. He had to admit, he hadn't been too happy when Pastor Curtis had invited her right off the bat.

She was speaking in the animated way she had with her companions, as if trying to draw them in. He wondered why she'd brought the two young men, who hadn't added much to the organizational nature of the meeting, except for almost beginning a brawl.

Christina—another person he wouldn't have invited initially, though for other reasons. She had latched herself to him without awaiting an invitation. It had seemed easier to go along, especially with his mother seconding the idea so enthusiastically.

Now, watching Christina with a pencil and paper in hand, he thought perhaps it hadn't been a bad idea. She seemed to be a natural organizer.

She smiled at him and he smiled back automatically. "I believe we have accomplished enough for the first meeting," she said. "Well, if I haven't earned a spot on your slate of officers, I'm not sure what else I must do!"

He shifted in his chair, reminded of the election of officers. "We can probably discuss nomination of officers at the next meeting, or better yet, after we've pulled off this first project, and see which of us still remain committed to it."

The others joined him in chuckling.

Christina looked down at her piece of paper. "Well, then, before we adjourn for the evening, at least we can decide who is in charge of what." She tapped her pencil against the table. "We'll need those to oversee the cooking, setting up, hosting, cleaning up afterward, greeting the public, and taking donations."

"I can help cook the lobsters," Henry volunteered, raising his hand.

"I shall put your name down." She held her pen above the paper, an expectant look in her eyes. "Mr. —?"

"Henry. Henry Freeman."

She wrote it down. "Now, how about Espy—isn't it?" She glanced across at Espy with a question in her eyes. "Espy can accompany you. You have experience at the cannery, so you'll know how to cook those lobsters to perfection." She smiled at Espy.

"Sure, put me down with Henry."

"I'll put myself down to greet people and sell the tickets. Why don't you accompany me, Warren? You know everyone and are good at figures." Before he could refuse, she turned to Annalise. "What about helping wait tables, Annalise? Don't worry, it should be fun. It will all be folks you know and everyone will be served the same thing."

"A-all right." She gave a nervous laugh. "As long as it's nothing where I could fumble people's orders."

Christina patted her hand. "No fear of that. You won't be alone.

What about you, Emily and James, would you be willing to assist Annalise with serving the dishes?"

Emily waved a hand. "It sounds like fun to me. I don't think I'll ever be working as a waitress, so it will be my foray into what it's like to wait tables." The ladies laughed.

After assigning a few more tasks to the remaining members, the group began breaking up. Warren stood and collected his few notes. He wanted to talk to Espy, thank her for having spoken up when things began to get out of hand, but as soon as she stood, her two friends stood as well and put their hats on. He heard snatches of their conversation over Christina's words to him.

"All right, it's time for that ice cream!" he heard Will say.

"Warren, why don't you stop by my house and we can hammer down a few details before the next meeting—"

"What's that?" he asked Christina while straining to catch Espy's reply to Will. It sounded as if the group had plans for the remainder of the evening.

But Dexter approached him from behind. "Good meeting, Brentwood. Can I see you a moment, or do you have to rush home?"

He gave Dexter a brief acknowledgment. "Sure. Let me just say goodbye to everyone." His glance crossed Christina's. At least he'd have an excuse not to walk home with her.

"May I have your attention, everyone?" he said in a loud voice. When they stopped talking, he continued. "Since we have so little time for the event, can we get together in a couple of nights—say Friday—and discuss what else needs to be done? Everyone can report on what they've been able to accomplish."

After getting everyone's assent, he stood, watching Will pick up Espy's shawl and hand it to her. She thanked him, smiling up at him before walking toward Warren. "It went well, don't you think, after a shaky start?"

He nodded, suddenly feeling tongue-tied.

She adjusted the shawl on her shoulders. "Well, I'd best be on my way."

"I—perhaps we can get together to discuss—" *Think, Warren, think, what needs to be discussed*—"the . . . the lobster—the menu, I mean."

She nodded right away. "Yes, that would be good." She glanced to the side, and he remembered Christina, standing just behind him, probably catching every word despite the noise of everyone else's conversation. "I'll be at the Stocktons', you know, at the usual times."

He let out a breath of relief. "I'll look for you tomorrow."

"Well, good night, then." She nodded in Christina's direction. "Good night, Miss Farnsworth. Good night, Mr. Ellis."

Warren heard no answering reply from Christina, but it could have been drowned out by Dexter's voice. His friend bowed over Espy's hand. "Good night, Espy—may I call you that?"

Espy smiled. "Of course, everyone does."

"It's a cute nickname. What's it short for?"

"Esperanza."

"Esperanza," Dexter repeated with a completely Spanish pronunciation. "*Hope.* What a beautiful notion."

Espy's cheeks filled with color. "Thank you. Hope is something I have a lot of, so I guess the name fits."

Dexter nodded, his eyes seeming to caress her features.

Dexter finally let Espy's hand go. "Good evening, Esperanza."

Espy laughed. "Good evening, Dexter. Nobody has called me that since attendance was taken at school."

Their laughter echoing in the church basement, the group left. Only Christina, Annalise, and Dexter remained.

Christina eyed Dexter. "Warren promised to walk me home."

"Oh." Dexter's gaze shifted from him to Christina and back.

Warren hastened to correct her. "Dexter just asked me to discuss a few details. I can stop by later, if you don't mind," he suggested to her.

Christina firmed her lips and then her features eased. "I suppose that will have to do. Come along, Annalise. I shall see you later, Warren. Don't keep him long, Dexter." With a wave, the ladies left.

Warren collected his things and turned to his friend. "What's up?"

"Nothing too important."

Wondering whether to be annoyed at his friend, he motioned forward. "Shall we?"

As they exited the church and walked toward the street, Dexter shook his head. "Wasn't she grand?"

Warren wondered what Christina had done to capture his friend's attention. "What do you mean?"

Dexter laughed in unbelief. "What do I mean? Didn't you hear her? *Grand*, that's the only word for it."

Warren stopped in mid-stride. "Whatever are you talking about?"

"Esperanza."

Of course.

"A spitfire! A dynamo. If you don't watch out she'll be leading you by the nose—and you already have Christina," Dexter added with a chuckle.

"I don't 'have' Christina—nor she me," he growled.

"Could have fooled me. She has her nails dug in deep; it's a wonder you don't feel it." Dexter sighed. "I guess it's better if it's painless."

"I don't know what you're talking about. Christina and I have been friends since childhood, but it doesn't mean we're courting."

Dexter raised an eyebrow at him. "Do your parents know this?"

Warren rubbed the back of his neck. "I haven't discussed Christina with them. Mother's throwing every eligible young lady my way, it's true, since I've been home. I suppose they hope Christina's in the front running because the two families have been friends for ages, and of course, Father and Mr. Farnsworth run the bank."

"It would make things nice and tidy."

"I have no intention of settling down anytime soon."To change the subject and prevent Dexter from probing any further into his personal affairs, he asked, "So, what did you want to speak to me about?"

"Espy, of course."

They had almost reached the bridge. Warren glanced sharply at his friend. "Espy?"

Dexter eyed him as if he were a child. "Yes, slow top. Espy. What did you think I wanted to speak to you about? Not our fund-raising event for the poor and needy." He laughed. "Though she did have me almost weepy for a moment there as she described their plight."

Warren had to rein in his annoyance, knowing his friend's non-chalant attitude toward everything. "So, what do you want to ask me about Espy?"

"Are you interested in her?"

Warren shoved his hands in his pockets, schooling his features. "Why should you think that?"

"I saw you dancing with her at the band concert. And then I see you both organizing a church committee. If I didn't know bet-ter, I'd say you had an interest in this young lady."

Warren pretended to look in a shop window. Dexter had no-ticed the dance? How many others?

"The only reason we're on this church committee together is that Pastor Curtis happened to see her standing in the churchyard and you know how friendly he is. He waved her right over and roped her into helping me." Warren gave a laugh, which sounded false even to his ears. "There you have it."

"And holding her in your arms in a waltz? Was that also a duty?"

Warren refused to meet his friend's eyes. He could picture their

89

amused skepticism. "I needed to talk to her about something and it was the only way to have some privacy."

"A private conversation so soon? You, my friend, are lost."

Warren picked up his pace. "It was just about her brother. She was trying to get him a job at the mill."

"When they start asking favors, you know it's only a matter of time before they'll be asking for something for themselves. I hear the strains of the wedding march." He began to hum it.

A garbled sound of incredulity and irritation issued from Warren's throat. "Where did you get from a mere acquaintance to a wedding?" Warren shook his head in disgust. "You're worse than my parents."

Dexter chuckled. "My folks have been trying unsuccessfully since I finished college. I think they've resigned themselves that I'll be the bachelor uncle."

Glad the focus was off him for the moment, Warren glanced at his friend. "I hardly think you're hopeless at the ripe old age of twenty-four."

"Am I that old already?"

"You're the same age I am." Warren sighed. "Time to put aside childish things as the Good Book says and become responsible adults."

"How tedious."

"It means shouldering one's responsibility and not being a burden to one's family." As he spoke, he felt the weight that had settled over him since returning home. "I suppose that does include marrying and having a family at some point before becoming a stodgy bachelor like old Mr. Wentworth."

Dexter chuckled at the reference to the town's reclusive citizen who shook his cane at children. "What makes you think I'll be stodgy? Maybe you, my friend, with your Brentwood family code drilled into you from birth."

"Seriously, Dexter," Warren tried to get beyond his friend's banter, "don't you envision someday finding that woman to spend the rest of your life with?"

Dexter plucked a thin twig from a passing hedge and flung it aside. "I think that's the stuff of poems and ballads. I see the older folks around us—my folks, your folks—and they seem stuck with each other more than boon companions."

Warren thought about his own parents. "I don't know. My mother seems to dote on my father, and he respects her."

Dexter gave an exaggerated sigh. "'Dotes,' 'respects'? All very well for them, but what about passion, real companionship, *wanting* to spend time with that one individual not just for a few months or a year or two, but for a lifetime? No, my friend, I can't imagine finding such a woman."

Warren didn't bother arguing with his friend. He'd thought he'd found it but his feelings hadn't been reciprocated. He certainly couldn't imagine it with Christina. With her, it would mean settling down and becoming just like his parents. Having the same circle of friends, enjoying the same social concerns, keeping up appearances in the community. He'd probably find his greatest outlet in his work, just like his father did.

A vision of Espy rose in his mind. What would life be like with someone like her? Someone with such zest for life? Someone whose ideals reached far beyond the world she'd been born into?

He was being ridiculous. She was not in his social circle. She had a dozen young men of her own set trailing after her. Doubtless in a year or two she'd snag one of them and then begin having a brood of kids the way her mother had . . . if she didn't start before marriage.

He hid a shudder. He could never give his heart to a woman so ill-suited to his world, no matter how attractive.

• • •

Espy entered the Stocktons' house by the kitchen door in the back, whistling as she did so.

"Good morning, Mrs. Maguire," she said to the cook, who was leafing through a cookbook at the kitchen table. "How are you this fine morning?"

The stout, middle-aged woman looked up without smiling. "Bracing for a scorcher. My ankles feel swollen already and my bunions are aching and it's only nine o'clock."

Espy chuckled, having learned to ignore the woman's complaints. "I've heard it'll rain this evening, maybe some thundershowers, so that'll cool things off."

"That'll get my rheumatism going."

Espy hung up her satchel and put on the apron left for her. She approached the kitchen sink and tackled the breakfast dishes, humming a tune under her breath.

"Don't know what you always find to be singing about," Mrs. Maguire muttered, lifting her girth from the straight-backed chair with effort.

"Life," she answered promptly.

With a "harrumph," Mrs. Maguire entered the pantry.

After getting her list of chores from Mrs. Stockton, Espy tackled them with a will, glad to be busy so the time would pass quickly. She wasn't sure when Warren would look for her, when he went home for lunch or when he went home in the evening.

Just to be on the safe side, she wandered outside during her lunch break, but she saw no one. She couldn't linger since she had a lot to do before she could go home for the day.

Mrs. Stockton put her to washing windows, so it was nice to be both inside and out during the hot summer day.

By day's end, she was exhausted but she looked at the gleaming first floor windows with satisfaction.

Mrs. Stockton entered the front parlor where Espy stood. "They look lovely, my dear. Tomorrow, if it's nice weather, you can wash the curtains. We'll leave the second floor windows for another day."

Espy lifted her apron to wipe at a spot on the window facing the front yard. "The room looks so light and bright without the curtains."

Mrs. Stockton gazed around her at the chintz upholstery. "Yes, it does. Unfortunately, without the curtains, everything will soon fade."

They both laughed. "Yes, I guess you're right about that. Well, we'll soon have them back up again."

"You've done a wonderful job, Espy. Why don't you call it a day?"

"Thank you, ma'am. If you don't mind, I'll stop off at Mr. Stockton's library before I leave. I have a couple of books to return."

"And I'm sure you'll be taking a few more home," her employer answered with a smile.

"I guess you know me by now."

Mrs. Stockton shook her head. "My, I've rarely seen anyone read as fast as you do. Well, go ahead."

"Thank you, ma'am." Espy picked up the last of her rags and headed to the kitchen.

When she knocked on the library door, her books in her arm, Mr. Stockton's voice bade her enter.

She poked her head in the door and glanced toward his desk. "Hello, sir. I just wanted to return these before I left for the day, and perhaps borrow a couple more."

Mr. Stockton stood from his desk and approached her. "Thank you, Espy. You are a bibliophile's delight. Returning books promptly and in perfect shape." He took the books from her with a smile and turned them over in his hand as he spoke.

"What did you think of *Jane Eyre*?"

"It was wonderful."

"Come, sit a while and tell me what you liked most about it."

"All right." Her heartbeat quickening with the mixture of anticipation and nerves that she used to get when called to the front of the classroom to recite a piece, she ventured into the room and took the chair he indicated.

Mr. Stockton settled back in his desk chair and steepled his fingertips. "Did you find yourself identifying at all with Jane?"

She tilted her head to the side, not expecting that sort of question. "I . . . suppose so . . . a little. I mean, I wasn't an orphan or had a terrible aunt and cousins I was forced to live with, but I did feel as if I knew Jane. I could feel what she was going through."

"Did you find yourself outraged by the things that were happening to her and championing her as she grew into womanhood?"

"Yes, yes," she began, her enthusiasm gathering as she followed his leading. "When things finally began to improve for her at Lowood School, I could understand what she must have felt. To be able to become a teacher like Miss Temple, the one she so looked up to. And to become a lady when everyone had so put her down as a child."

Mr. Stockton asked her a few more questions and she found herself thinking more closely over what she had read and admiring him for already knowing the answers.

"And what of Mr. Rochester, how did you find him as the hero of the piece?"

"I didn't like him at first. He seemed to be teasing her all the time and . . . and trying to . . ." she motioned with her hand, searching for the right expression, "trick her," she settled on finally, although dissatisfied with the word. She wished she had more words at her command, the way Mr. Stockton did. "And the way Mr. Rochester carried on with that odious Miss Ingram."

Espy pressed her lips together in distaste. "But that was nothing to the fact that he was already married." She shuddered. "To discover that on her wedding day. It must have been terrible for her."

"Did you hate Mr. Rochester so much then?"

She blinked at his mild tone. Of course, he had read the book countless times, so he was used to the story. Espy chewed her lip, giving Mr. Rochester's behavior more thought. "At first I did. Well, not so much hate," she amended, "as feel horrified, the way Jane must have felt." She swallowed, remembering the scenes in the book. "After he explained things—and after seeing his crazy wife, I felt badly for him—as badly as Jane must have felt." She shook her head. "Poor man, to be shackled by a madwoman, and to be tricked into marrying her in the first place."

"He is what is known in literature as the Gothic hero."

"What does that mean?"

"As you may remember from your schooldays, 'Gothic' refers to a type of architecture in the late medieval period. Think of the great cathedrals built in Europe at that time. But earlier in this century, a type of literature arose that usually takes place in an old mansion or a ruin of a cathedral or monastery of this type of medieval architecture. The setting is gloomy, and there is usually a hint of a ghost." He smiled.

Espy smiled back, thinking of Mrs. Poole and the strange goings-on in Mr. Rochester's house.

"The hero falls under suspicion in these types of novels as odd things are said about him. The heroine, usually a helpless young woman, begins to fall under the hero's allure, but she is torn between her doubts of his character and her growing attraction to him."

As if listening to a story unfolding, Espy leaned forward. "But Jane stands up to Mr. Rochester when she finds out the truth about him."

Mr. Stockton looked at her as if in approval. "Very good. She is unique as a heroine in fiction because from a seemingly meek young girl, she demonstrates a strong backbone and doesn't go against her moral principles. There are signs of that strength in her even early on when she is a girl. Do you see them?"

Espy pondered some more. "When she refused to buckle under the headmaster's accusations at Lowood School?"

Mr. Stockton looked even more pleased. "Yes."

From discussing *Jane Eyre*, they went to *The Last of the Mohicans*. By the time Espy rose to leave, she felt she had to shake her head to get all the information to settle. "I can't believe an author puts so much into a story."

"The best ones are certainly gifted even when they're not aware of the process. It remains for us the academics—and readers like yourself—to delve deeper and discover the hidden truths beneath what appears a simple romance or adventure story."

She nodded, considering this fact. Then she remembered Warren. "I'd better be off."

She looked at the case clock in the entry hall before leaving and gasped at how late it was.

She rushed down the walkway and onto the sidewalk. There was no sign of Warren. She wasn't sure where he had meant to meet her. He had left things vague. She hurried down the street in the direction of his house. No one appeared in the front.

How she longed to go up to his front door and ring the bell. From her conversation, Christina seemed to be accustomed to dropping in at the Brentwoods'. Shoulders slumped, she turned away from the façade that seemed to taunt her with the fact that the likes of the Estradas would never darken its doors.

After a moment of dawdling, she continued on her way home, her steps slow. By the time she reached the covered bridge into the main part of town, the euphoria over books had dwindled, leaving only disappointment at not seeing Warren.

But the talk of books had so enthralled her that for a short time, she'd forgotten everything else.

Adjusting the strap of her satchel, weighed down with the new books she'd taken from the shelves, she turned off Main Street with no more hope of crossing Warren's path that day.

7

Warren hurried down Elm Street, his eyes scanning the distance for any signs of Espy. He'd made sure to leave the office in time to catch Espy when she left work. He knew she left at five, a bit early for him to be leaving the office, but he wasn't the manager for nothing. And he usually stayed longer than the other employees.

Funny, no matter how much his father liked to talk about the enterprises being Warren's one day, Warren always thought of them in terms of his father's.

Perhaps it was because Brentwood & Co. seemed to be his father's very lifeblood.

He certainly didn't take the carefree attitude of his friend Dexter. But neither did he seem to have his father's drive when it came to work. It worried Warren. He wanted to succeed and make his father proud of him. More than that, he didn't take lightly the fact that many people depended for their livelihood on Brentwood & Co. It would be not only irresponsible, but downright criminal, for Warren not to give his best to making the mills and docks operate at their best capacity and efficiency.

Shaking aside these troubling thoughts, he picked up his pace, deciding to walk all the way to the Stocktons' even though it was beyond his house. He hadn't specified to Espy where he'd meet her. Too many people had surrounded them at the meeting the night before.

He'd surprise her and be waiting for her outside the Stocktons' gate when she left for the day.

But when he got there, there was no sign of her. He looked at his watch then decided to continue farther down. He didn't want to linger outside; it would raise questions of the neighbors. With a shake of disgust, he remembered Mrs. Hawkins. But he kept looking back over his shoulder. At the end of the road where it turned, following the curve of the river, widening into Holliston Bay and the sea beyond, he stood under the shade of a maple tree. He would not arouse too much suspicion there, a solitary spot at the outskirts of Holliston.

He waited a quarter of an hour, then another. Tired of waiting any longer, he finally made his way back, slowing his pace to give Espy more time to appear.

She must have left earlier today—or she forgot. Shoving down his sense of disappointment at not seeing her, and his frustration at not being able to go up to the door and knock, he shoved his hands deeper into his pockets and walked past the Stocktons' residence and continued on to his own, glancing back every few paces to make sure she wasn't emerging from the house.

So much for Espy's high-flown rhetoric the night before—all those grand ideas but no follow-through. *Grand.* The word reminded him of Dexter and his interest in Espy.

Well, he can have her—with pleasure!

Warren pushed open his white picket gate, bracing himself to face his family, who'd wonder why he was home a bit early this evening.

He groaned inwardly, remembering he had to shepherd Christina and Annalise to a friend's birthday party.

98

. . .

"So, how was your day at the Stocktons'?" her mother asked, turning back from the pot she was stirring.

"Good." Espy rolled her shoulders. "I spent most of it washing windows. Tomorrow will be washing curtains if the weather holds up."

"I guess that's a sight better'n standing cutting herring all day or stuffing cans."

"I'll say."

"Have they paid you yet?"

"Mrs. Stockton said at the end of the week."

"Hope so. Rent's due soon."

"I know, Mama." Espy sighed. She doubted she'd have anything left from her first paycheck after seeing to the family's needs.

She heaved the kettle off the stove and poured the boiling water into the dishpan.

After shaving some soap into the steaming water and mixing in some cold, she began piling the dirty dishes into it. "We'll do all right between your earnings and Angela's and mine. Alvaro should be getting a check soon, too. I haven't had a chance to ask him how it's going. Have you?"

"So far so good. He's complained they're working him too hard, but he hasn't quit yet, so that's a good sign."

Espy would have to talk to her brother. *Didn't he realize how fortunate he was to have secured that job?* She swished the dishrag into the sudsy water and began on the first dish, old food encrusted on its surface.

"Heard you've been seen with that Brentwood fellow."

She stared at her mother's profile, her hands stilling on the hot dish. "Where'n the world did you hear that?"

Her mother glanced sidelong at her. "People will start to talk. That'll ruin your reputation in a blink."

Espy let out her frustration scrubbing the stubborn food remnants off the plate. "I haven't done anything wrong. I've just talked with Warren about a church activity."

"Doesn't matter what the truth is. It's folks' talk that counts."

Espy gave a sharp laugh. "I can't think what folks would talk about. I've hardly seen him. But Pastor Curtis asked him to get together a young people's group, and then he asked me. I'm just helping to organize it—but so is Angela, you can ask her, and some of Warren's friends."

"Ellie Anderson told me she saw you waltzing with him on the green."

Espy dipped the dish in the rinse water. "Well, he asked me." She shook her head, a smile forming on her lips. "I refused him at first, but then he cut in later. What was I supposed to do? I danced with a lot of fellows that evening. It's not as if he was the only one."

Her mother didn't say anything right away. Finally, she sighed. "It sounds like he's after you, not the other way around."

Espy said nothing, preferring not to reveal her own feelings in the matter of Warren Brentwood.

"Be careful, Espy."

"You make it sound like I'm in some kind of danger." She attempted a skeptical tone, though inside a shiver passed through her.

"All I'm saying is not to get too chummy. Types like him may take an interest in someone as pretty as you, but they'll never marry the likes of us."

Espy laughed in disbelief. "Who said anything about marriage? He's just someone I knew back in school who's recently returned to town. Besides that, he's a nice person, about as upright as I know. He'd never just lead a girl on. Warren's not like that."

"He may be the nicest boy in town, but you be careful. That's all I'm saying. You don't want to end up like me." Her lips firmed. "Your father promised me a lot of things when I was young and pretty like you."

Espy looked at her mother's pale, drawn features, her light brown hair drawn into a careless bun. Had she ever been as pretty as Espy? She often said so. Would Espy end up like her?

The next morning, Espy walked to town on her way to the Stocktons', her mind going back to her mother's words. Her mother's views were clouded by her own failures. Still, Espy respected her opinions and knew her mother only meant them for her good. She didn't want Espy to end up where she was—or worse.

Espy had no intention of ending up there. She had plans, and no man was going to trip her up, not even Warren Brentwood.

Yet in the deepest hours of the night, she could dream. Dream of Warren falling in love with her and *wanting* to marry her.

But in the clarity of day, she was realistic enough to put such dreams aside.

Fog shrouded the town and river when she approached it, but the sun was already shining through the mist as a fuzzy yellow ball, so she knew it would be another hot day after the previous night's thundershowers.

She was crossing the bridge over the roaring water of the river gorge when she spied Warren entering it from the other side. She wondered whether she should stop and wait for him or walk to meet him.

He saw her at about the same time she saw him and seemed to be making his way toward her so she paused, fingering the drawstring ribbon on her blouse, trying to determine if anything was out of place in her appearance.

"Good morning," he said, stopping before her.

She smiled brightly, even though he wasn't smiling. "Good morning. You're about early."

"Yes, since I left the office a bit early yesterday afternoon, I thought I'd go in earlier today."

"Oh. You left early?"

"Yes, I wanted to see you when you left the Stocktons'." He was regarding her steadily.

"Oh . . . yes." Her cheeks grew warm and she felt as if she were at fault. "I—I'm sorry about that. I left a bit later than usual and when I looked for you, I didn't see you anywhere."

"Yes, well, there's nothing to do about it now." His tone was clipped. He looked past her. "I have to get going." Then he looked straight at her again. "Don't forget tonight's meeting with the group. Unless you've changed your mind about being a part of it."

She bristled. "Of course I haven't changed my mind. I'm sorry I wasn't in time yesterday." She looked at her feet. "The truth is I was on the point of leaving when I returned some books to Mr. Stockton and he kept me a bit, asking me about the books I'd finished." She shook her head, still looking down at the planks. "I was so caught up in what I'd read. I never knew there could be so much to literature. He made me really dig into the story and think about it—about things I never would have seen on my own."

"That's what a teacher is for." His tone gentled.

She nodded, daring to look at him again. "I'm sorry. I just lost track of the time. It won't happen again."

"Don't worry about it. I could as easily have been held up at the office." He pulled out his pocket watch and glanced at it before looking at her again. "How about this evening? If you think you could arrive at the church a little earlier, we could go over the things I wanted to discuss with you before the others arrive—that is, if you don't think you'll get caught up in another literary discussion," he added, a twinkle visible in his green eyes.

She found her mouth curving upward, unable to resist the humor in them or the warmth in his tone. "No, I've only just begun the first pages of one of the new books I received. I'll be at the church a half hour earlier, is that all right?" She'd just make it home and grab something to eat. Hopefully, her mother and Angela would be able to handle supper on their own.

Warren's lips returned her smile. "Good. I'll see you this evening then." With a tip of his hat, he left her.

She glanced after his broad back and decisive step, then with a renewed vigor, resumed her walk to work.

• • •

Warren arrived at the church basement promptly a half hour before the meeting was scheduled to start and was surprised to see Espy already there.

He had schooled himself to expect her to forget again—or at least be late.

At the sound of his footsteps, she turned and smiled. "Hello there."

He smiled back, feeling a sense of relief—and something more that he didn't care to analyze—at the sight of her. "Hello. How are you?"

Her smile widened. "Fine. Tired but fine otherwise."

He drew his eyebrows together in concern. "Do the Stocktons have you working so hard?"

"Not at all. Mrs. Stockton keeps me busy, but I'm strong." She shrugged. "I think she saved all her spring cleaning till I came."

"Be careful. You don't want to overdo." Even though she looked robust enough, he didn't think she should be doing heavy work.

"Don't worry."

Swallowing, feeling suddenly embarrassed as if he had been discussing something too personal with her, he gestured to the table and chairs. "Shall we get started? The others will be here soon. At least I hope so." He grinned, pulling out a chair for her. "I never know about Dexter. If he's having fun, he'll continue, but the moment it starts seeming too much like work, I don't know . . ."

"We'll just have to make sure he enjoys the work," she quipped, taking the seat.

103

He sat catty-corner to her, glancing more closely at her expression, remembering Dexter's question regarding her. Did she mean to see to Dexter's entertainment, or was it merely an innocent remark?

But she wasn't looking at him, but at a piece of paper and pencil she had extracted from her satchel. As she spread the paper out before her, she clasped her hands atop it and met his gaze. "So, what did you want to discuss?"

He withdrew a sheaf of papers from the breast pocket of his jacket and a fountain pen, taking his time to respond. He didn't have a clear idea what he wanted to say, but he felt instinctively that Espy was the right person to attempt to express it to.

When a minute had passed, she asked in a low voice. "What is it? Is anything wrong?"

He finally looked at her then. "No-o. Nothing's wrong—yet."

Her eyes grew round. "Yet?"

He made a motion of dismissal with his hand. "I didn't mean that to sound the way it did." He smiled. "Nothing dire. I just mean—" He took a deep breath, making another attempt to put his vague concerns into words. "I mean, I want this group to be what Pastor Curtis envisioned. I don't want it to be just another church group. You know, just *doing* things, making ourselves feel good about what we're doing."

Espy nodded slowly, a look of understanding in her eyes. "I see what you mean. Maybe we jumped too quickly onto this idea of a Fourth of July dinner without thinking enough about what we want to accomplish. The purpose, from what I understood from Pastor Curtis, is to get young people in the community interested in . . . in God's work." Her words stumbled on the last part, as if she, too, felt self-conscious uttering them.

He smiled in relief. "Exactly." A load was removed from his shoulders. "I wanted to discuss with you how to keep this club 'spiritual' enough." Again, he uttered the word sheepishly. He didn't consider himself a "spiritual" person by any means, but he did respect Pastor Curtis and did share his burden to reach out to that part of the community, especially its young people, who didn't feel welcome in church.

Espy fingered the edges of her paper. He noticed how slim and fine-looking her hands were despite all the housecleaning she did. Her nails were neatly rounded, the edges very white. "I think one way is to make our aim clear." Her eyes looked earnestly into his. "Whatever money we make, if we send a couple of the members— maybe those who may not understand our real purpose as well— to present it to the family in need, perhaps that would help bring home to them how important it is to help those in need."

He nodded, digesting her words.

Her gaze drifted down to her paper and he noticed how long and dark her eyelashes were. "Another thing is to think of activities where both our groups of friends could enjoy themselves."

He knew exactly what she meant. "That's going to be the biggest challenge, as I see it. You saw what happened Wednesday night. How can those people we invite to join us feel comfortable if we don't feel comfortable among ourselves?"

"Perhaps we could begin by studying the Bible together."

He considered. He didn't want the group to be just a Bible study. The church already had such groups, and he doubted he could invite many young men from the sawmill to study the Bible. "Yes, that could be a beginning . . ."

As if reading his thoughts, she hastened to add, "I don't mean just a Bible study, but maybe we could start our meetings, or whatever activity we plan, with a short Bible study." She tilted her head at him. "Have you ever led a Bible study?"

He was ashamed to admit he hadn't. "No. I've attended my fair share though," he said with a grin. "But I taught Sunday school a bit back in high school."

"I love studying the Bible."

He looked at her curiously. She was not someone he'd have pegged as a student of the Bible.

"Maybe it's the way Pastor Curtis teaches it, but I find the more I study it, the more there is to be discovered. And suddenly, there's something that just gets me right here—" She patted her chest with her clenched hand, bringing his attention to the thin cotton covering her front. "I feel what the pastor calls 'conviction'— as if God is talking right to me about something in my own life, even though the words were written thousands of years ago!"

The amazement in her tone jerked his attention from her bodice to her words.

He hadn't felt that kind of conviction since he'd been a young lad sitting in church. Guilt would sweep down on him like a cold spring shower. He could look back and smile at them now—small iniquities like taking a dessert from the tray Cook had left cooling by the kitchen window ledge—knowing his mother had strictly forbidden him to have anything "to spoil his dinner"—or telling the teacher his homework had blown into the river on his way to school . . .

"What's so funny?"

He started at Espy's sharp question. "I'm sorry. I wasn't smiling at your words, just at the times I was convicted when I was a boy, things that seem so trivial now."

"I can't imagine you ever being convicted when you were young. Your behavior always seemed so perfect."

He looked at her in amazement.

"I was always the one who felt I had so many shortcomings in school—I hadn't mended my dresses; my homework looked all smudged by the time I brought it in . . ."

"But you didn't lie about having lost your homework on the way to school," he countered.

Her eyes widened again. "You never did!"

He nodded, almost in pride.

She burst out laughing and he found himself joining her.

"This is a cozy tête-à-tête."

They both jumped at the sound of Dexter's voice across the room. He was leaning against the doorjamb. Warren wondered, *How long has he been standing there watching us?*

Warren cleared his throat, shuffling the papers in front of him. "You're early—or is it already time for the meeting?" He pulled out his watch to avoid meeting Dexter's amused gaze as he sauntered across the room. There was still a quarter of an hour before the others were to arrive. What in the world was his friend doing here so early? Dexter never arrived early.

To hide his irritation at his friend's interruption, he gestured to a seat. "Pull up a chair."

Dexter complied. "What's so funny?"

"Nothin'—"

"We were remembering our childhood sins," Espy said at the same time.

With a lift of his eyebrow at Warren, Dexter then turned his attention to Espy. "Childhood sins? I'm all ears. What dastardly crimes were you involved in while you were still hanging on to your mother's apron strings?"

Espy laughed. "I'll never tell."

Warren's irritation grew at how naturally Espy treated Dexter. Her laugh was no different than when she'd laughed at what he'd said. "Ahem. Maybe we should get ready for our meeting. Let's jot down an agenda."

Dexter waved aside his words. "Time enough for business in a few minutes. Isn't the purpose of this group to have fun as well? Or did you just promise me that to rope me in?" He winked at Warren but returned his gaze to Espy. "Now, let's have the scoop."

Her color high, Espy straightened in her chair. "Oh, the usual childish things." She leaned forward conspiratorially. "But can you believe Warren actually committed a few in his boyhood years?"

"No!" His mouth fell open, and he stared at Warren. "Not

107

our Warren Brentwood the Third. Tsk tsk."

Espy smiled, her gaze also on Warren. "Do you think his parents know?"

"I'll warrant they still suffer under the delusion that their son is perfect."

Espy burst into laughter once again. Warren's neck grew hot and he had to restrain himself from saying something unpleasant. He swallowed, at a loss for an easy rejoinder. "Far from that," he said dryly.

As if sensing his discomfort, Espy turned back to Dexter. "What about you—have you repented of all your past deeds?"

Warren's emotions warred between awareness of Espy's sensitivity to renewed irritation that her interest was now focused on Dexter.

He continued watching her profile, hardly listening to Dexter's riposte. The two laughed easily, dispelling the notion that he and Espy had shared anything special in the moments before Dexter appeared.

He'd never competed with his friend for a girl. Their tastes were different, for one thing.

It showed how easily Espy interacted with the opposite sex, whether of her own social sphere or his. It seemed to matter little to her. She had an ability to shine before men.

He tried one more time to cut their chatter short. "The other thing I wanted to discuss—" he glanced at Dexter before focusing on Espy again—"was the invitation list, some of the folks we could continue inviting. Have you given any more thought to friends of yours who might contribute to this group?"

Espy nodded, resuming a serious demeanor at once. "Yes, I have been thinking about it. It goes along with what we were speaking about earlier. I know a few young women at the cannery who have stopped coming to church for one reason or another, but who miss the fellowship."

"That's good. Maybe you can talk to them about the Fourth of July dinner. They may want to pitch in and help."

"Yes, I'll be visiting them this week."

Dexter drummed his fingers on the tabletop. "How about Ben and Ralph?" he asked about some of their mutual acquaintances.

Warren rubbed his chin. "I don't know . . . they strike me as a couple of partygoers. Do you think they'll be interested?"

Dexter shrugged. "Isn't that the type of person you want to attract?" His amused gaze strayed to Espy. "Save them from their evil ways?"

Before he could say anything, Espy answered, "Sure, invite them. Who knows, maybe they'll be convicted." She turned to Warren, a glint in her eye, telling him she remembered their earlier conversation.

He acknowledged the look with a brief nod. "All right. You can ask them, Dex. We'll put them to work during the Fourth."

"If I'd known you were all meeting earlier, we would have been here." Christina's heels clicked across the floor as she crossed the room, followed by Annalise, Emily, and Mabel. Christina had promised to stop by and collect Annalise when Warren told her he'd be coming from town. He had not elaborated as to the reason, allowing her to assume he'd be coming from work.

Now he stood, feeling as guilty as a schoolboy caught red-handed, and as quickly annoyed that he should feel that way. "Hello, girls, nice to see you. We haven't started the meeting yet." He pulled out the chairs as he spoke. "Have a seat and we can begin."

Christina was the first to take a seat, on Warren's other side at the head of the table, as she had during the first meeting, and began pulling off her gloves, fingertip by fingertip. "You could have fooled us. It certainly sounded as if you were taking care of business."

"Afraid you'd be left out of club business?" Dexter drawled, leaning his head against a fist as if he were too tired already to sit up straight.

Ignoring them both, Warren smiled at his sister. "Glad you could make it, Sis."

She smiled at him. "Mother said she missed you at dinner but hopes you'll have a productive meeting."

"Thank you."

The other members drifted in and took their seats.

After helping the ladies to their seats, Warren stood once again at the head of the table and smiled at everyone, his gaze coming to rest on Espy. "I see everyone made it to a second meeting, so I guess that means I didn't scare you all away after the first."

8

Espy watched and listened in admiration as Warren opened the meeting. He was a true leader—modest yet with the kind of inner strength people sensed right away and that caused them to want to follow him.

After he had summed up the last meeting and asked them to each report on what they had done since then, he sat back and listened to each one and jotted down notes.

"My father says he'll see to the lobsters. He's talking to the fishermen now," Emily said.

Espy remained silent as each of Warren's friends offered a donation on behalf of their parents. *What would it be like to have a parent who could pull out a checkbook and write a check for a good cause like this?* All she could do was donate her time and energy to the event.

"Why don't we elect our officers," Christina suggested, "so we can have a secretary take notes for you, Warren?"

Everyone murmured their assent.

"I think it goes without saying that Warren should be president," she said.

Warren looked around the group, a question in his eyes. "If anyone else feels led to hold this position, please go ahead. Pastor Curtis merely suggested the idea of this group to me. I feel no compunction to run it if there is anyone else interested."

Dexter grinned. "None of us want such responsibility, I'm sure. Any takers?"

The others shook their heads. "Very well," Warren said, "I'll put down my name and we'll still put it to a vote."

"I nominate Espy as vice president," Dexter said immediately, smiling at her.

She smiled back, feeling surprised but pleased at his nomination.

"Hear, hear!" put in Will and Henry. She blushed at her friends' championing.

"Very well." Warren wrote her name, giving no clue to his feelings. "Anyone else?" he asked, looking around.

Christine looked straight at her. "You understand that the position of second-in-command means you are ready to assume the leadership if for some reason our president cannot?"

Espy swallowed and nodded.

"Since one of the primary aims of this group is to raise funds for worthy causes, as you so eloquently put forth for us in our last meeting," Christina continued, "one of the responsibilities of the office of vice president should be making others in the community aware of our mission. This person should be well-connected, as our president is.

"The vice president is the president's right arm, so to speak." Christina slowly looked at each person around the table. "This will entail maintaining good relations with business leaders and the more prominent members of our town—to keep them abreast of our activities, so when the time comes when we may need donations, as now with our dinner, they don't feel as if you only come around to ask for money."

Christina smiled at Espy. "Do you feel you'd be able to adequately carry out these duties?"

An uncomfortable silence fell as Espy felt everyone's eyes on her. "I . . . don't know . . ."

"Perhaps you would be better able to assume this office," James put in, addressing Christina.

Espy nodded immediately, relieved despite her disappointment at not being Warren's right hand. When Pastor Curtis had described the club, she'd never envisioned it as something that involved asking for money from the town's wealthier citizens. But she realized perhaps it had to be if they hoped to do some good.

"What about Espy as secretary?" Angela spoke up, to Espy's surprise.

"That's an excellent idea," Christina answered before her gaze turned to Annalise. "Only I had thought Annalise with her beautiful penmanship might want to do that?"

Warren's sister began to shake her head, her concerned eyes on Espy.

"That's a good idea. My writing is so sloppy, I wouldn't be able to read my notes myself," Espy said with a hearty laugh she hoped didn't sound forced.

His pen hovering over the paper, Warren eyed her with a question. Espy smiled. Warren turned to his sister. "Well, Annalise, would you like me to put your name down as secretary?"

She gave a half-shrug and nervous laugh. "If you think I should."

"I think you'd make a very good secretary. You remember details very well and you're always scribbling away at home."

Espy was touched at how his tone gentled with his sister. "I'm sure you'll do a wonderful job," she said.

Annalise smiled back at her, as if in gratitude and relief. "Very well."

"That leaves treasurer," Warren told them, looking around the room. "Any takers?"

"Since James works with numbers at his father's store, he would be a natural," Christina offered.

A brief look of irritation seemed to cross Warren's features, as if he shared Espy's annoyance that Christina had in effect nominated all the positions for the group.

Warren quirked an eyebrow at James. "Well?"

The young man shrugged. "Put me down."

"Anyone else?" Warren's gaze roamed slowly over the members present one last time.

"Very well, let's put it to a vote. When I call the name, all those in favor say 'aye,' and then all those opposed say 'nay.' Got it?" Warren said.

When they all murmured their assent, Warren proceeded with the elections. In a few moments, the group had its officers and Espy found herself in the rank and file. She tried to console herself with the fact that doing what Pastor Curtis had wanted them to do was not about holding office or being in the lead, but to quietly go about helping others to Christ.

"Second order of business is to come up with a name for us," Warren informed them with a smile. "Any ideas?"

The elections forgotten, they bandied about names for a while, Dexter and Will keeping them in stitches with absurd ones.

Espy was content to merely listen, cowed by what had taken place during the elections. Finally, when it seemed the others had run out of steam, she ventured, "What about the Holliston Lights?" As their attention turned to her, she felt the need to explain, "We want to be a light to our community."

Dexter nodded. "It can be a play on words with Northern Lights, since we can see them at times in this part of the country."

The others began to murmur their assent. Espy noticed that Christina remained silent.

Warren turned to the others. "Let's put it to a vote. All in favor of 'The Holliston Lights,' say 'aye.'"

It seemed everyone assented.

"All opposed, say 'nay.'"

Silence greeted them.

"Holliston Lights it is." Warren grinned. "If I had a gavel, I'd do like an auctioneer and bang it."

After their laughter died down, he became more serious. "All right, now it's time to get down to business. We only have a week left. Let's get everyone mobilized for our first big event."

The rest of the meeting was spent in making sure everyone knew what they had to do between then and Independence Day.

Espy left with her sister afterward, satisfied that they were moving ahead, her momentary disappointment forgotten. It didn't matter what title she held; what mattered was what she would be doing.

She waved goodbye to the others, sorry not to be able to speak with Warren alone. Christina stood by his side closer than a river leech on an ankle.

. . .

On the Fourth, Espy was up at dawn even though she and Angela had worked past midnight baking biscuits for shortcake.

But the sky was already light at five thirty in the morning. She jumped out of the bed she shared with Angela, ignoring her sister's groan.

By the time she and Angela marched out the door, Espy already felt damp with perspiration. Since she would be cooking all day, she had dressed in her lightest frock, a slightly faded calico in a light blue check. It wasn't fancy, but she feared ruining anything newer with lobster broth and clam juice.

Barricades had been set up along Main Street where the parade would be passing. Red, white, and blue bunting, banners, and festoons lined the storefronts and lampposts. The sidewalks were filling

115

up with people guaranteeing themselves a good location.

Once Alvaro deposited the cart of biscuits in the basement church, he took off. "Don't forget to look after Gus!" she called to his back, but he only shouted back, "Josiah and Daniel can do so!"

With a sigh, Espy turned to her work. From the open basement doors, they could hear the band music, which signaled the start of the parade.

Dexter appeared in the large kitchen. "Come along, ladies, let's catch a glimpse of the parade when it passes near the corner of Center and Main Street."

Espy looked around him doubtfully. "I don't know. There's so much still to do before noon."

"There'll be time, come along."

"The rolls have to rise anyway," Emily said, taking off her apron.

"That's the spirit. We can watch the parade and hear the anthem and be back in plenty of time to finish."

"Where's Warren?" Emily asked. Espy was grateful that the other girl had asked. Espy pretended to arrange some shortcake biscuits on a platter as she listened to Dexter's reply.

"He's on one of the floats. The Brentwoods always do one. He sent me down here to make sure everything is running smoothly and to apologize for not having a chance to come himself."

Emily covered a tray of rolls with a dishtowel. "You can let him know everything is shipshape. I know his father wanted him by his side today at all the ceremonies."

"Do you concur, Miss Espy?" Dexter moved to her side. "May I tell him you have everything under control in the kitchen?" He took a hulled strawberry out of the large bowl and popped it into his mouth.

Reacting as she would to one of her young brothers, she swatted at his hand. "You leave those strawberries alone or we won't have enough for the shortcakes we'll be serving for dessert."

He merely smiled as he chewed. "Mm-mm. Sweet and juicy." His blue eyes regarded her.

With a firming of her lips, she turned away and continued tidying up the area. *If he thinks I'm an easy catch, he has another think coming.*

Instead, he moved away from her. "Come along or you'll miss the parade."

"Is Christina on a float?" Angela asked. "We haven't seen her all morning."

Dexter grinned. "She is. She told me she'd be by in time to usher people over to our banquet area. Warren said he'd make an announcement after the ceremonies, as well, to draw people over."

Emily took off her apron and folded it up. "Well, all right, I suppose we can take a little time off to catch the parade."

Despite her height, Espy had to stand on her tiptoes and crane her neck to glimpse the parade. They could hear the band playing a rousing march a block down.

A couple of young men carried the American flag and the State of Maine flag. Then the brass band marched by, the men's cheeks red and puffed out as they blew their trumpets and trombones.

Several floats pulled by draft horses went by, each depicting something typical of the area, from a white schoolhouse with a schoolteacher standing in front and children seated cross-legged waving to the crowds, to a mock sawmill with two men in red flannel shirts holding the ends of a two-man saw across a thick log.

Espy sucked in her breath, recognizing Warren as one of the loggers. His hair was hidden by a thick woolen cap. He wore corduroy pants, suspenders, and thick work boots.

Everyone clapped and laughed with the passing of the floats.

"He's going to have to do a quick change into a suit before the ceremony," Dexter said close to her ear as if reading her mind.

"How will he manage that?" she couldn't help asking, continuing to watch Warren until his float passed.

117

"He'll pop into a friend's place, one of the houses on the green, where he's left a suit."

She pictured one of the large white houses with their colonnaded fronts and pretty flower gardens facing the green. Of course, he would have friends there.

When the parade ended and the crowd moved along to the town green for the raising of the flag, Espy and the other women made their way back to the basement kitchen.

A few minutes later, Will and Henry shouted down the stairs, "We've got the corn here—ten bushels straight from New Jersey via Zuckerman's Grocery."

"Start shucking it," Espy shouted back. "I'll send whoever is free to help you."

Soon, James arrived with a wagon. "I've brought the lobsters, right off the wharf, and the bushels of clams, dug at yesterday afternoon's low tide."

Espy forgot about Warren as they lit the fires and set up the big cauldrons of water outside in the yard behind the picnic tables.

"Everything looks quite festive, doesn't it?" she said to her sister as she surveyed the tables. Annalise and Emily had contributed dozens of small bouquets of red carnations and white daisies, which now sat in vases at each picnic table. Blue ribbons were draped like garlands across the ends of the tables.

One of the stores in town had offered yards of blue muslin, which they'd spent the last week cutting up and stitching into napkins.

"It's lovely," agreed Angela, almost reluctantly. "I hope it's worth it."

Espy frowned at her sister. "Don't you think so?"

She raised her eyebrows skeptically. "I hope so. Part of me sure would like to spend the Fourth watching the races and the games."

Espy nodded. They never missed the games on the Fourth. Except for Sundays, it was one of the few holidays of the year, when all the stores and factories closed for the day, giving their workers the day off. "I wonder if Alvaro will win the foot race."

"Twenty dollars would sure come in handy, if he doesn't spend it on drink."

Espy glanced sharply at her sister. "Alvaro's not like Papa."

Angela shrugged. "He's got a new set of friends since he began at the sawmill—older men who could lead him astray."

"We should bring him along to this group."

Angela snorted. "Come on, there's more to be done."

They had heard the band strike up "Hail, Columbia!" off in the distance and knew the ceremonies on the green had started. "If we get everything ready, we may be able to catch part of it," said Espy, stoking the fire.

"Nothing but a bunch of speeches," Angela muttered, heading toward the basement. "At least it's cooler down in the kitchen, even with the ovens going."

Leaving Henry watching the fires, with the promise to relieve him soon, a group of them set off toward the long rectangular park flanked by the brick courthouse on one end and a congregational church on the other. On the other sides were some of the oldest homes in the town.

Just as they arrived, the flag began to rise; everyone fell silent and looked solemnly toward the flagpole. Warren stood on the platform alongside his father and other important men of the town. Pastor Curtis was there with two other ministers from local churches, the principal of the high school and the headmaster of the private academy, and a few of the lumber barons. With the exception of Warren, all were graying or white-haired men.

When the music died down, Reverend Curtis stepped up to the front of the makeshift platform and bowed his head. Everyone followed him in a prayer.

Then the band struck up "America the Beautiful."

After more patriotic songs, it was Warren's turn. The chairman of the Fourth of July festivities, Christina's father, introduced him as a new leader in the town—one of the young gentlemen "to keep an eye on" in the coming years.

Espy felt a rush of inexplicable pride.

"He's gone away to further his education, he's traveled and seen more of the world than most of us except for our sea captains, and yet, he's come back home. He's a true son of Holliston. Please give him a hand of applause as he steps up to read the Declaration of Independence to remind us what we are celebrating this day."

Espy clapped her hands until they hurt. As the applause died down, Warren stepped to the lectern and placed his hands on either side. He reminded Espy of a statesman or a minister.

He greeted them briefly and then turned his eyes to the document in front of him. "When in the course of human events . . ."

As the first words sounded forth in a strong, steady voice, the final murmurs and rustlings of the crowd died. For the next several minutes, there was silence among the sea of faces surrounding all four sides of the green.

Espy's eyes misted at the sight of the flag flying at one end and the Revolutionary War memorial on the other.

When it was finished and the resounding applause had ended, Warren reminded the crowd about the lobster banquet and spoke briefly but eloquently about the new church group's aims.

He hurried off the platform, but before he could make it down, the older men delayed him with handshakes and pats on the back. How proud his father must be of him, thought Espy, observing the dignified man standing beside Warren, only a fraction shorter, with brown hair edged with gray at the sideburns.

Would Warren look just like him in a few decades? Would his eyes acquire that hard look in their green depths? Espy tried to move forward but found it impossible in the crowd. Instead, she watched Christina climb the platform and stand in front of Warren, addressing him with a warm smile. His father's face softened as he said something to her.

Something sharp twisted in Espy. Why was she standing there when there was so much to be done? With a shake of her head, she followed her sister and the others back to the church.

The next hour was so busy she had no more time to think. Espy turned from the large iron cauldron filled with water and almost bumped into Warren.

"Oh—you're back." All she could do was stare at the sight of him. He had come—and he looked so handsome in his dark blue suit and red print silk tie.

He smiled—right into her eyes.

The spurt of joy filling her evaporated at the sight of Christina and Annalise at his side. "I'm sorry I haven't been able to help out. How is everything going?" His gaze turned from her to scan the churchyard. "Everything looks beautiful."

"Yes, it does, doesn't it?"

Annalise echoed the sentiment as Christina's eyes narrowed on each table setting, as if searching for things out of place.

Espy smoothed the front of her apron, conscious of her old garment before their fancy clothes. "We heard your reading. It was . . . quite moving."

His face flushed, his smile sheepish. "They roped me into reading it."

"It was flawlessly delivered," Christina said, slipping her hand into the crook of his arm.

Was that a faint look of annoyance crossing his face? Espy couldn't be sure.

Before she could decide, Dexter slapped him on the back. "Well done, old man. I couldn't have delivered it better myself."

Warren's face cleared and he smiled at his friend. Espy took a step back as others gathered around him. As they offered their congratulations, she could tell he felt embarrassed by the way he shook his head and turned the compliments away from himself.

"I just wanted to tell you that I'm sorry I couldn't be here earlier to help out. And to tell you that all of you are the real troupers here—the unsung heroes. Everything looks grand."

Dexter saluted. "Thanks, boss."

Warren's green eyes came to rest on her again, and a feeling of pride surged through her. "It's almost time to begin. Why don't we bow our heads and ask for a blessing over this event?"

At their encouraging words of assent, he began, closing his eyes. "Dear Lord . . ."

Espy watched him a second longer, liking the look of his long dark lashes against his skin and the almost vulnerable quality about him with his eyes closed, before she, too, inclined her head and closed her eyes, joining with the rest.

"Amen," they all echoed him as they reopened their eyes. Warren smiled and rubbed his hands together. "Well, Christina and I had better get to our stations. I'm sure we'll have lots of hungry people to feed over the next few hours."

Espy took her place at one of the large iron cauldrons, which now bubbled with water. Henry dumped in the live lobsters, Espy stepping back to shield herself from the scalding drops.

"On to the next world!" With each splash, Henry made an irreverent comment. Espy used a long wooden pole to stir the pot, making sure the lobsters stayed submerged.

Soon, her hair and blouse were sticking to her. Every few minutes she had to wipe her brow with her forearm to keep the beads of sweat from trickling into her eyes.

A line of people wove down the length of the sidewalk and orders came fast and furious. James stepped up with a tray of plates. "We need four lobsters."

"Coming right up." Using a large pair of tongs, Espy lifted out the ones that were ready, let the water drain off a few seconds, and loaded them onto the plates along with an ear of corn. "There you go."

"Thanks!" He marched back to the tables. Espy took a few seconds' respite, watching him. He seemed to be enjoying his stint as waiter. Annalise assisted him, serving the strawberry shortcakes and making sure each table had an adequate supply of melted butter, a basketful of rolls, and pitchers of lemonade. Meanwhile, Will was busy clearing away dirty plates as soon as people had finished eating and vacated their places.

Emily and another young woman who'd volunteered to help came behind him, sweeping off the tablecloths and setting out new place settings.

The line continued for more than an hour. Warren and Christina were kept busy taking money and handing out tickets, but they didn't seem to mind. Each time Espy had a chance to glance their way, they were smiling and chatting with all who came by.

Espy wondered how much money it would bring in. They hadn't charged too much, preferring to attract a lot of people—especially working people who might not normally enjoy a restaurant meal. She should feel elated by their apparent success.

Instead, she felt hot and bothered, and couldn't help glancing at Christina again. Despite the ninety-degree heat, she looked as cool as the dollop of whipped cream that topped every strawberry shortcake.

She and Warren sat under a large red, white, and blue striped umbrella. Instead of dressing in Independence Day colors, she wore a pale pink suit of an iridescent silk weave. A neat little narrow-brimmed hat in matching pink straw covered her blond, upswept locks.

Espy turned away, tucking in the strands falling from her own knot. She'd been right to wear this old gingham. It was drenched with lobster stock and clung to her like fish scales. Too bad the wet material didn't cool her down. The steam coming off the cauldrons of lobster, clams, and corn enveloped the whole area.

A good thing Warren was too busy to look her way.

None of them had had time to eat any of the delicious food being served, but Espy didn't even feel hungry with all the heat. She wondered how her mother was faring with the younger ones. Both Christina's family and Warren's came to the lobster feast, as well as those of the other club members.

Espy felt a pang of envy. Her mother was probably buying something off one of the food stands set up along Main Street, or going home to feed the children before coming back in the afternoon for the games.

Just as she was hauling out more ears of corn from the pot, she caught sight of Warren standing from his place to hail someone. Holding the cob in a pair of tongs, she stared, seeing her mother turn back and approach the table warily, Julia in her arms, Alicia and Gina holding her skirts, the boys trailing behind. Warren smiled. Her mother looked puzzled by what he was saying.

Then she broke into a smile. The next moment, Warren was escorting her mother and the younger children past the picnic tables toward her.

Espy quickly set the corn onto a platter and pulled up her apron to wipe off her face. "Hello, Mama, what are you doing here?"

"She and the children have come to eat," Warren answered for her with a wink.

Gus skipped over, peering into the steaming lobster cauldron. Espy grabbed him by the arm. "Watch you don't get burned."

"Can I have that one?"

Warren looked to where he was pointing. "The biggest one?"

Gus nodded vigorously. "Yep!"

"All right. I'll give you fifty cents if you manage to eat it all." He turned to Espy. "You heard the young man. The largest lobster in the pot."

Before Espy could respond, Warren spoke to her mother again. "If you'd like to get out of the heat a while, there are some tables down in the basement where it's much cooler."

Her mother used a handkerchief to wipe her neck. "That would be lovely. Thank you, sir."

As he escorted them toward the basement doors, he glanced back at Espy and said, "I'll send the boys up to get their plates."

"Th . . . thanks," she managed, too bemused to think of anything else.

Part of her was grateful that he had singled her mother out, the other was ashamed that he'd offered her charity. All the other parents had paid their way. Even Henry's and Will's. And why had he taken her mother downstairs, out of sight? Was it because she hadn't paid, or truly because it was cooler down there?

"We need some more clams," James said, holding out a serving bowl.

Espy turned her attention back to the food. Was she just an object of pity in Warren Brentwood's eyes—or a valuable member of the club?

9

Warren got up from the stool and stretched. "I guess that about does it." The line of people wanting to eat had finally ended, although about half the picnic tables were still occupied by diners.

Christina surveyed the area. "I think we can call this first venture of the Holliston Lights a resounding success." She held out her hand. "Congratulations."

He shook it, returning her smile. "Thank you for all your hard work."

She squeezed his hand, her eyelids fluttering downward. "It was my pleasure."

"Well . . . ," he continued, feeling awkward all of a sudden. He let her hand go when she gave no signs of ending the handshake. "I don't know about you, but I'm famished. I wonder if there's any lobster left."

"Don't worry about what's left. Mother and Father wanted me to ask you to join them at the house for our buffet luncheon. I think there's time before the afternoon games."

He rubbed his chin, wondering how to turn her down. All he wanted at the moment was to sit down at one of the picnic tables with the club members who had worked so hard. He looked at the cash box. "I have to count this and put it in a safe place. That will take me a bit. Then I need to oversee the cleanup here before the games. Please give your parents my thanks and . . . regrets. Perhaps another time."

He watched her smile turn stiff. Before she could say anything, he looked around the churchyard. "If you'll excuse me, I must find James. As treasurer he can help me count the proceeds."

Spotting Pastor Curtis coming toward him from the street, he smiled in relief. Picking up the cash box, he addressed Christina, "Go join your parents."

With a curt nod, Christina turned away from him. An instant later, she turned back. "I shall see you at the ball game later, won't I?"

"Yes, of course."

He walked between the picnic tables to the back where Espy and Henry were emptying out the cooking pots. "You both did a masterful job keeping everyone fed in record order." He eyed the platter heaped with leftover lobsters, another with corn. "I'm glad to see some left for us. I don't know about you, but I could eat a couple of those."

Espy set the pot down and wiped her face with the back of her hand. Her skin glowed, her dark hair clinging to her nape in swirls. Warren swallowed. He lowered his gaze. Her bodice was open at the neck, the thin, faded material outlining her shape like a second skin. Her sleeves were rolled up, revealing slim, shapely arms.

He cleared his throat. "Why don't you all sit down and have some dinner now?"

"Don't mind if we do," Henry answered promptly. "As soon as we wash out these pots and set them to dry."

Espy nodded. "We'll bring these platters down to the basement for the others. I'm sure it's cooler down there." She paused, then moistening her lips, she didn't quite meet his gaze. "Thank you for inviting my mother and the children. You didn't have to do that."

"Hey, for the chef who slaved all morning to see everyone well-fed? It was the least we could do." He smiled.

She gave a tentative smile, as if it were difficult for her, and he frowned, wondering why. "Is something wrong?"

"No, nothing at all." She shook her head vigorously and before he could question her more, she bent over the pot.

With an effort he averted his gaze. "I'm going to get James to help count the proceeds. Then I'll join you all down in the basement. Save me some food," he added with a chuckle.

Will walked by him with a pile of dirty platters. "You'd better not be too long, or I can't guarantee anything."

With a wave, Warren walked away.

When he returned to the churchyard, Annalise was shaking out a last tablecloth. "We're just about to sit down to our own feast. Did you get everything squared away?"

"Yes, all counted and under lock and key." He took the bundle from her. "Come on. I hope there's still some lobster."

"There's plenty, I think."

"I'm looking forward to some of that strawberry shortcake," said James as they walked down the stairs to the basement.

"This feels good, much cooler," Warren said with a sigh, looking around to see who still remained. Espy and Angela were at the sink washing and drying dishes.

Some of the others were already seated at a long table. Warren walked over to Espy and her sister. "Come on, leave those for now, and eat, unless you already did."

To his relief they had not, so he ushered them to the long table, where he pulled out chairs from them.

"Well, Mr. President, did we break even?" Dexter eyed him, a large dish towel wrapped around his neck like a bib.

"I'll tell you after I get something in my stomach. I hope you left us some lobster."

"I was tempted to gorge on some more, but I took pity." Dexter waved to the platters along the length of the table. "Seriously, there's plenty left. We only just sat down ourselves."

Warren took off his jacket and sat down, looking in satisfaction at the plate of lobster, corn, rolls, and steamed clams Espy set before him. He took a whiff, giving her a grateful smile. "Smells delicious. Anyone say grace?"

"We did, but you'll have to say your own," Emily said with a smile.

He bowed his head and said a blessing for him and the others who'd just sat down. Rolling up his sleeves and tying a wide, checked napkin around his neck, he prepared himself to get to work.

"Don't get so full you won't be able to pitch at the ball game this afternoon," Will warned.

James looked up from his corn. "What time will it start?"

Warren wiped his mouth and took the dessert plate Annalise offered him. "Three o'clock on the ball field."

"Maybe I should eat your piece of shortcake." Dexter reached over. "I wouldn't want to see you get indigestion."

Warren chuckled. "No one's taking my shortcake. I didn't sit out there for two hours getting my hands dirty with all that money to be cheated out of my dessert. My, but it looks good. Who baked it?"

"Angela and Espy did," Will answered around his ear of corn.

"Can't wait to bite into it. But first, I have to polish off this lobster."

"Just so you still beat that team from Seal Harbor! No indigestion, you hear?"

The men continued to jibe him, saying they had money on his team. "Hey, I haven't played ball since my college days. That's been two years now, so don't expect much."

When he'd satisfied his hunger, Warren pushed back his plate. Taking a swig of lemonade, he cleared his palate and then took his knife to tap the side of the glass. When he had everyone's attention, he allowed his gaze to fall briefly on each member.

"I just wanted to thank everyone for giving up a good part of the holiday. We raised—" he paused, stretching out the moment of suspense—"two hundred dollars."

Amidst the exclamations and looks of surprise, he settled back in his chair, feeling satisfied. His glance met Espy's, who still looked astounded by his announcement. He raised an eyebrow, as if to say, "Don't believe me?" and then said aloud, "Our treasurer James will confirm the figure."

James wiped his mouth and set down his wide napkin. "I counted every bill and coin myself. I must add that the sum includes a few generous donations by some of our town's citizens."

When everyone had quieted down, Warren said, "We can decide at our next meeting how we'll distribute it."

The men groaned. "Why don't we discuss it now? We've had enough meetings for a while."

"Very well. We'll skip next week's meeting. Everyone deserves a well-earned rest. All in favor, say 'aye.'"

A loud chorus arose. With a smile, he added, "All opposed, say 'nay.'"

Silence met him. Grinning, he reached for his plate of shortcake. "Good, that's settled then. Now, for dispensing the money raised."

Espy rose from the table. "Anyone want some coffee? We put some on the stove earlier."

"Coffee and shortcake. Sounds just the ticket."

As she poured it out, they discussed the money.

Finally, they decided to give fifty apiece to the families in need, including the mother of the boy wanting to go to high school, and hold the final portion in reserve for other projects or emergencies.

"And you, as president, can make the first presentation," James said. "The rest of us can take turns."

A short while later, they started getting up. Warren began clearing the table.

"Hey, you're the president; you don't have to clean up."

"Of course I do. Why don't the rest of you go? I'll wash up since I came so late."

Espy and Angela insisted on staying with him, Angela saying with a sniff, "I don't trust a man to wash dishes."

He was secretly pleased that finally he could have some quiet time with Espy—even if her sister was along. He preferred that, since he didn't want anyone to misconstrue their being together.

"Are you sure you have time for this?" Espy frowned at him. "You have a ball game to go to."

He smiled. "This will aid my digestion. Are you and Angela going to watch the game?" He held his breath, suddenly feeling as if he were asking a very important question.

"Of course. Since I missed my brother's race, I certainly don't want to miss the afternoon's activities," she said in an offhand manner, her focus on her hands plunged into the dishpan in front of her.

"I'm sorry about that," he said immediately.

Espy shot him a smile. "Mother told me he won, so he must be crowing somewhere." She shook her head. "He really wanted to win those twenty dollars."

Warren whistled, taking up a plate to dry. "That's a lot of money for a fifteen-year-old."

Angela clucked her tongue from where she was wiping down the long table. "If I know him, it'll burn a hole in his pocket. Hope Ma makes him put it in the bank."

Espy rinsed another plate and set it on the drain board. "I'll talk to him. Maybe I can make him see it's better to wait and see what he really needs." After washing and rinsing another dish, she asked him, "How is he doing at the mill?"

"Fine as far as I know. I haven't heard any complaints from Hodgdon."

A look of relief crossed her features. "Good. You would let me know if there were any?"

"Sure." He wiped at the dish he was drying, weighing his next words. "If you'd like, I could talk to him about his winnings."

She pursed her lips, scrubbing at a serving fork. After a few seconds, she nodded. "I'd appreciate that very much. I'm just not sure how he'd take it, coming from you." The last words were uttered slowly, her dark-fringed eyes somber.

He swallowed, his throat feeling like sheep's wool. "I . . . understand. I'll see how he reacts to me. Don't worry."

She nodded, a smile going from her eyes to her lips. Realizing he was staring, he yanked his gaze back to the plate he was rubbing.

Finally, the last dish was dried and put away. Warren looked around the tidy basement kitchen. "I think that does it." He glanced at Angela, crooking his lips upward at one corner. "What do you say, does it pass muster?"

She didn't return his smile but followed his gaze across the room. "Good. It doesn't look as if we'd been here at all today."

Warren waved his hand toward the exit. "Shall we make our way to the ball field, then?"

• • •

As twilight deepened, Warren stood in the shadows of the elms, once again on the green, listening to the band play from the gazebo. He stifled a yawn. He'd been up since before dawn, running around from almost the moment he'd opened his eyes—the parade, the ceremony on the green, greeting people and collecting their money, congratulating all his fellow workers, then the hours on the ball field. Finally, a few hours at home, but family from near and far had dropped in for the annual get-together his mother organized.

He'd been a prime focus for his aunts, uncles, and cousins, since this was his first Fourth of July home after the two years he'd been traveling abroad. More questions and looks of admiration. More polite replies without really saying what he meant.

Now his mother and father sat with Annalise in one of the front rows of folding chairs that had been placed for the more important guests. He had excused himself on a flimsy excuse of speaking to someone but in reality because he was feeling restless.

He was not prone to restlessness. Was it merely because he'd returned home after living away so long? Would he gradually settle down to the quiet rhythm of life in Holliston after six months or a year?

His gaze rested fondly on his sister. She shunned any kind of role that drew her to others' attention.

His lips curved in sympathy. Poor dear, her life, like his, was destined for center stage in Holliston. Even now, their mother was grooming her to take on more and more of her charitable and community functions.

At least he didn't mind most of those "duties." It was only that lately he'd felt oddly dissatisfied with everything, but he had no real reason why.

He should feel elated. He'd been able to play his favorite sport and help his team to a win. There was an age-old rivalry between the two towns. It had felt good to achieve that victory.

His smile died. He was a man now, learning to step into the footsteps his father had planted for him, eventually manage the empire his father had spent a lifetime building.

His thoughts broke off. His gaze fell on Espy. She was making her way under the large trees toward the concert area. His mood soured. She was escorted on either side, Will on one, a fellow he didn't know on the other, and Henry bringing up the rear.

How many fellows did she need?

They were smiling and talking, their moods evidently high, which only brought his lower.

As if sensing his glowering look, her eyes met his. For a second she looked startled. Then with a short nod of acknowledgment, she turned away, to catch something Will was saying.

Warren turned his back on her and marched back to where his parents were seated. He forced himself to listen to the concert, denying himself the desire to look around.

Later, as people made their slow way toward the waterfront to watch the fireworks, he saw no signs of Espy . . . and her fellows.

He took Annalise's arm and shepherded her in that direction, making a path for his parents behind him.

"I must say it's been an excellent Fourth," his father said. "Perfect weather, a good turnout." He slapped Warren on the back. "A spectacular win for our team, thanks to you, Warren."

"I think I had little to do with it."

"Nonsense," his mother said. "You had everything to do with it. Hitting three home runs in the last innings. My, my. There's such a thing as being overly modest."

"Your mother's right. Our team has lost the last two years. I don't call that coincidence."

His mother reached over and patted his hand. "But we're much more proud of your place alongside your father on the podium during the ceremony this morning. You looked very distinguished, my dear. Your elocution was perfect, the words so moving."

Knowing his mother expected an answer, he said, "Thank you, Mother," although the compliment only made him feel uncomfortable.

Full darkness fell and the entire town lined the riverfront. Pinpricks of light on the water signaled the boats where some men were preparing to set off the fireworks.

As they gazed upward, the sky was illuminated with explosions of color and light. Annalise jumped with each bang, covering her ears. Warren put an arm lightly around her shoulders.

At least he hadn't had to escort Christina this evening. He'd seen her with her family and there had been enough of a crowd between them to preclude either of them reaching the other.

He tried to regain the spirit of the day as the shower of red, white, and blue sparks fell from the sky, but a damper had settled on his soul, and he didn't know how to dispel it, since he didn't understand its root cause.

10

When the fireworks display was over, Warren's father turned to his mother. "I've asked Samuel to have the carriage waiting for us by Main and Center."

"Wonderful. I'm quite done in. Come along, Annalise." Her eyes lifted to Warren. "You've had a long day, I'm sure."

"Yes," he said absently, his gaze drifting over the dispersing crowds. "I think I'll walk home, if you don't mind."

His mother blinked. "Walk? I should think you'd want to be off your feet by now."

He smiled though his heart wasn't in it. "The fresh air and solitude will be even better."

"If you say so." Looking a bit miffed, she took her husband's proffered arm. "Don't be too late. We don't want Samuel to stay up waiting for you."

"Please tell him to go to bed. I can see myself in and lock the front door. I won't be long." It was an effort to maintain a light tone. Before letting his irritation come to the surface, he bent and gave Annalise a quick kiss on the cheek. "'Night, Sis. Hope you had a nice day."

She nodded without saying anything. For a moment, he wondered what was going on in her head. He hadn't had time for a really good chat with her in more than a week. Just one more thing pulling on him. With a sigh, he straightened.

Even before they were a few feet away, Warren was already turning to eye the crowd.

"Good night, Warren." Friends and acquaintances waved to him as they passed by. He felt like a rock impeding the current. Moving aside, he strolled along the riverbank, his eyes restless, seeking, searching . . .

He stopped, disgust filling him. Espy stood, smiling and laughing with the same fellows. As Will and Henry finally lifted their hands in farewell and walked away from her, the other took her arm and seemed to want to lead her away.

She removed her arm with a smile and stood still, shaking her head. He attempted to take her arm again. He was a hulk of a young man.

Without thinking Warren moved forward. "Good evening."

Espy turned to him, smiling in recognition. "Hi, Warren. Weren't the fireworks beautiful?"

"Yes, indeed." With a nod to the other man, he continued addressing Espy. "Were you here the entire time?"

"Oh, yes." She motioned with her chin. "Right over there. We had a perfect view, didn't we, Jim?" Was it his imagination, or did her voice seem nervous?

"Reckon so." His voice was deep, the words pulled out as if unwilling. "Ready to go, then?"

Espy's glance went from him to Warren.

Warren took another step closer. "Excuse me, Espy, but I wanted to ask you something about . . . the luncheon this noon."

She nodded quickly. "Sure. I'm sorry, Jim, I shan't be going home right away."

137

"I'll see her home," Warren put in before the other man could say anything.

His brain seemed to be processing Espy's words and then his eyebrows drew together, and he glared at Warren. "It's gettin' kind o' late, Espy."

She swallowed. "I know, but the fireworks just ended. They know that at home."

Warren held out his arm to her. "Shall we?"

She tucked her hand in it. "Yes. Good night, Jim. See you around."

He merely grunted.

Wanting to avoid any unpleasantness, Warren crossed the street away from the river. "Where's your brother?"

She craned her neck around. "I saw him earlier."

His irritation returned. He asked in a clipped tone, "How about Angela?"

"She took the younger ones home ages ago. She and Mother decided not to come back for the concert or fireworks. They were quite tired." She chuckled softly. "Angela's exact words were 'same old fireworks every year.'"

Instead of laughing, he said, "You shouldn't have stayed in town by yourself."

"Oh, I was all right. Will and Henry were with me."

He smiled grimly. "I doubt if my parents would consider three young men appropriate escort for Annalise at night."

She stopped in the middle of the street. "What's that supposed to mean? I've known Will and Henry all my life. They're like brothers."

"Except they're not. They're men like any others. And they left you with Jim."

He took her arm to continue walking.

She pulled against his hold. "You needn't bother seeing me home. I know my way."

138

He only tightened his hold.

"Hey, watch it. I'm not a rag doll."

He realized he was behaving no better than Jim.

"I don't know what you're so bent out of shape for. I can take care of myself."

He made an effort to bring his anger under control, slowing his steps and loosening his hold. "I beg your pardon. You seemed to be having difficulty turning Jim down and I thought I'd offer my assistance. Forgive me for intruding."

She waved a hand in dismissal. "Jim's just a bit overprotective."

He wouldn't call it overprotective. More like possessive, but he clamped his mouth down on any further comments.

They walked without speaking for several blocks.

"Thank you for offering to take me home," she finally said quietly. "It was kind of you. I was trying to find a way to shake free of Jim."

"It's what I'd do for any unescorted young lady at this hour of the night," he said gruffly.

They left the town behind and walked past the fields.

"It was a lovely evening. Didn't you think the fireworks were splendid?"

Distracted by her proximity, he only replied, "Mm."

She stopped in mid-stride and gazed upward. "What a night. The sky is so clear, not a peep of fog to spoil the display. Look at those stars. There must be a million."

He followed her gaze. The sky was indeed filled with an innumerable number of twinkling lights. The gauzy veil of the Milky Way draped across the midst of it. "Millions," he corrected in a low tone.

"How far away do you suppose they are?"

"Light-years." His anger evaporating like the night mist, he pondered the vast celestial wonder.

A soft chuckle erupted from her throat. "Ah, yes, Mr. College Man, you probably studied that."

He frowned at her dreamy tone of voice, a new suspicion seeping into his mind. "Have you been drinking?"

A second later, her eyes glared into his and her finger jabbed him in the chest. "Drinking? Me, drinking? Do you honestly think I'd touch the stuff after seeing what it's done to my dad?"

Contrition filled him. "I beg your pardon. That was a thoughtless question."

She turned and they continued walking in silence.

His thoughts a jumbled kaleidoscope pattern, he stumbled on like a blind man clinging to a guide's arm. Their footsteps the only sound on this dark, silent night, he finally managed, "It's just that you seemed so . . . exuberant. More than most girls—young ladies —I know."

She sighed. "*Exuberant*. What a lovely word. Is that one you learned in college?"

His tension eased a fraction. "I suppose it is."

"What does it mean?"

"Let's see . . . full of life, on top of the world, filled with joy spilling out of you."

He could feel her gaze on him. "Is that how you see me?" Wonder filled her tone.

"Hmm," he replied, trying to keep his tone noncommittal.

"How nice." She sighed again, but he kept his eyes forward.

"Exuberant," she repeated, as if committing it to memory.

They continued walking some minutes, Warren straining to see the path as they left the last farmhouse behind.

As he stepped forward, her hand came up to his arm again and she tugged him toward her. "This way."

He peered in the direction she was leading him. A dark mass of trees seemed to block everything. "Where are we going?"

"It's the shortcut."

As they entered the forest, he said, "It's kind of dark."

"There's a path. I know the way, don't worry."

He focused on the path, hoping no tree roots would trip him. The last thing he needed was to go sprawling. Thankfully, she kept her light hold on him.

He cleared his throat. "Were you going to let Jim take you this way?"

"Jim?" she asked in a surprised tone.

"Yes," he said shortly.

"First of all, I wasn't letting him take me anywhere."

"But if I hadn't come along," he insisted, "do you really think you could have dissuaded him?"

"*Dissuade.* That's another of your college words."

"Really, Espy, you need to take better care whom you allow around you."

She stopped dead again, this time seriously endangering him with tripping. His free arm flew out, but he was able to right himself in time.

"Take better care? I've been taking care of myself in this town since I was about four, and I think I've done a pretty good job."

"That's not what I meant. But appearances are deceiving. People see you with so many young men trailing after you, they think, well . . . they think—"

"What do they think?" He didn't have to see her face to tell her eyes must be narrowed.

But he refused to be cowed. "That you're no better than you ought to be—" he finally blurted out, the dark air between them as stiff as a wall.

"No better than—?" The next second she threw her head back and emitted a rich stream of laughter, dispelling the tension between them.

He stepped back, unsure of himself. The last thing he'd expected was laughter. He could imagine Christina's or even Annalise's outrage if he'd made that remark to one of them or to any female of his acquaintance.

When her laughter had subsided, she said quietly, "What do you think, Mr. Warren Brentwood, the Third? Did you offer to walk me home to protect me or because you thought you could have something, too?"

His body was rigid with anger. "How dare you?"

Suddenly, she stepped away from him on the narrow path. "Well, maybe if you can catch me, you'll find out for yourself if I'm 'no better than I ought to be'!" With more laughter, she was gone.

He heard the crackle of twigs and the light patter of feet as he reached out.

"Espy!" He stood on the pitch dark path, unable to see his arms in front of him. He inched forward, expecting to fall at any moment.

• • •

Espy didn't heed him, her feet like wings on the path she knew so well.

The anger added to the heady feeling she'd experienced since the fireworks, when Warren had offered to escort her home—the man she'd yearned for since girlhood coming to her like a suitor and offering her his arm as if she was as good as Christina or his sister or any of those young ladies from his circle.

But his outrage at how he thought she was behaving had brought all those dreams to an abrupt halt. She wasn't going to let him catch her. Let him fumble in the dark and find his way out of the woods by himself.

She looked over her shoulder, hearing Warren calling her name.

"This is not funny! You could break an ankle."

At the concern in his voice, her anger waned and her footsteps slowed. She stopped before a slight bend in the forest path and gripped a tree trunk, her breath coming in gasps.

At the snap of twigs, her anger disappeared completely and worry for him grew. She wouldn't want *him* to break an ankle. She turned back toward the sounds.

The next second she bumped hard against him. "Oh—" The breath came out of her in one whoosh. "I wouldn't have left you alone in the woods," she began, breathing in the scent of his jacket—it smelled faintly of masculine cologne and a hint of tobacco. "I—"

Before she could get another sound out, he grabbed her, his fingers digging into the soft flesh of her upper arms. He dragged her body flush against the immoveable wall of his. His lips consumed hers, gently probing hers apart.

She'd never let a man or boy touch her so, but with Warren it was different. She trusted him completely. Like a spark catching fire, her own passion rose to meet his.

He plunged his hands into her hair. Her hairpins loosened, and her knot tumbled. His fingers combed through it. He breathed deeply, his fingers entwined in her hair, burrowing his nose in the side of her neck.

"Espy," he whispered against her as his touch gentled.

Her fingers stroked his jaw and earlobes and temples, reaching up to his short hair.

He drew her face toward his, once again seeking her lips with his.

She remembered all her mother's warnings. . . . No, Warren would do nothing wrong to her. He was a gentleman.

"I'm sorry—" His lips separated from hers and he leaned his forehead against the top of her head.

"It's all right," she sought to comfort him with her words, her hands smoothing his broad shoulders.

"We shouldn't—" His words slurred as Espy reached up again and pressed her lips against his once more, silencing him. She didn't want him to stop, didn't want the dream to be over.

He drew back again, this time taking her two hands in his and removing her from himself. He took a step away from her.

The cool night air brushed her face and she shivered.

"Come, I'd better take you home. It's late."

"What's wrong, Warren? Why are you acting so cold all of a sudden?" What had she done wrong that he'd pushed her away as if he didn't want her?

He took her lightly by the elbow—as if she were contagious. What happened to turn him so quickly from a man kissing her like she was the only woman for him to one who acted angry with her? Were all her mother's warnings about men true even for Warren?

Did he think she was the kind of woman he'd warned her about? The ugly fear grew in her mind.

"I'm sorry, I shouldn't have taken such liberties with you." His tone sounded formal, so unlike the hoarse whispers of her name against her cheek. "It was unpardonable of me. I have no excuse but the . . . the night."

Hardly aware of where she was going, she tripped over a root in her path. His hold immediately tightened. "Are you all right?"

She yanked her arm from his, crossing her arms in front of her. The night felt cold now, cold and dank as the fog finally moved in. "I'm fine."

"Espy—"

She waited, her heartbeat drowning out his voice.

"Espy," he repeated. When she said nothing, he finally continued. "Please forgive—forget—what happened here tonight. I didn't mean to treat you like that. I—" He seemed to be struggling with words. "I don't know what got into me. I don't treat women like that."

With each word, a fist punched a hole in her hope, leaving it like a torn canvas of a sail, fluttering in the aftermath of a storm. Any dreams she'd secretly harbored that Warren cared for her were destroyed with each stilted, gentlemanly word.

She picked up her pace. All she wanted was to run from him.

"Espy, slow down. I can hardly see where we're going."

"You don't have to see me home," she tossed over her shoulder. "I can manage from here. You . . . you should be able to make your way back with no trouble."

Before her voice broke, she began to run, not stopping or looking back this time.

"Espy!" But as if realizing the futility of it, his voice stilled and she heard him no more.

11

For the word of God is quick, and powerful, and sharper than any two-edged sword, piercing even to the dividing asunder of soul and spirit, and of the joints and marrow, and is a discerner of the thoughts and intents of the heart."

Warren surveyed the crowded pews before him. There sat his father and mother in the front row, Annalise beside their mother. Old Mrs. Hawkins was in the middle of the church, Mr. and Mrs. Grandy with their family wedged between other familiar faces on the opposite side of the church.

Where was Espy? His glance darted about seeking her, but he didn't see her anywhere.

He cleared his throat, realizing they were all waiting for him to speak.

He glanced down at the pulpit, but there were no notes. Only a Bible lay open flat on the lace cloth from where he'd read the Scripture.

His heart began to pump, drowning out the sounds of the congregation. Perspiration beaded up around the edges of his forehead.

Someone coughed, a child whimpered.

What was he supposed to say? He didn't remember the thread of the sermon. He fumbled in his pocket for a handkerchief to wipe his brow and realized he was wearing a Geneva gown.

Warren awoke with a sense of panic of being in the wrong time and place. Light filtered through his window blinds.

His brow felt damp with sweat. He sank back on his pillow, overwhelming relief flooding him at the realization that it had only been a dream. His heart rate gradually eased.

Of course, he should have realized it, as he analyzed some of the incongruities. The church was never so crowded except on Christmas and Easter. Mr. Grandy and his family didn't attend his church, but the Baptist one four blocks up Court Street.

He sat up, adjusting his pillows behind his back, finally able to smile. *Me a minister. That was a good joke.*

The Scripture was an interesting one, though, a powerful one. He wondered if it had some significance for him personally through the dream.

The next second all thoughts of the dream vanished as he remembered the previous night. He stared before him at the striped wallpaper of his room.

What had he done? His mouth went dry as memory tumbled into place.

Espy, running through the dark woods, his frustration toward her, her teasing tone.

He relived the fiery red light bursting in his mind during the kiss, like the fireworks earlier in the evening.

He hadn't been able to see her, and yet perhaps that had made her presence all the more palpable, more enticing . . .

His heartbeat stepped up again, remembering the whole evening. What had possessed him to kiss her like that? Never in his sane mind would he have taken such an unpardonable liberty with a young woman.

The way her body had slammed into his. He'd been so angry

one moment, and the next kissing her like a thirsty man gulping water.

But in the unforgiving light of morning, the folly he'd committed quickly doused any resurging passion. He scrubbed his hand across his face, the roughness of his beard disgusting him.

He was no better than any of the men he'd accused Espy of being free with. *A girl no better than she ought to be.*

She'd taken umbrage at those words, and yet, thinking back now on her words, she'd never denied them.

He ground his teeth in renewed frustration—at himself and her.

She'd provoked him, though that in no way excused his behavior.

He'd traveled enough to consider himself a bit of a man of the world now, even though he was only twenty-four. He'd seen plenty of *that kind* of women, but he'd always shunned them no matter how provocative.

How had Espy gotten under his skin to such an extent that he could throw all convictions to the wind and forget everything he'd been taught and adhered to?

What possessed me? He'd known Espy practically his entire life. He would never kiss a lady he didn't intend to marry—and he certainly couldn't marry a girl like that.

It was more than Espy's obvious shortcomings—her lack of education and breeding—her family situation! In so many ways, she didn't fit into his world.

But his distaste went deeper. She'd given her favors so freely. Did she kiss all the young men who hung around her like cod on a string? Would she have allowed Jim to kiss her like that if he'd escorted her home?

His blood thrummed just remembering her unchecked response to him. She'd never tried to fight him off, but had kissed him back with a freedom and abandon that would have shocked him in any young lady he considered worthy of his attention.

His face grew hot and he struggled to push the memories away.

Throwing back the covers and standing, as if the action would help him escape his recollections, he shook his head. He deeply regretted his loss of control where Espy Estrada was concerned. He still didn't understand it. How could a young woman he'd known since she'd run around like a wild little weed, and who showed no decorum, have so enticed him?

Thank God he'd stopped when he had. How easily he could have taken her. He shook his head to dispel the horror of what could have happened. He bowed his head, thanking the Lord for giving him the strength to put Espy from him before it was too late.

He walked to the window and drew up the blind, eyeing the gardens below and river beyond. An early morning fog still lay on the water, but the sun shone brightly through it like a blurry yellow image.

He drew in a breath, knowing a difficult task awaited him. But the sooner he faced it the better. He had to apologize—again. Last night they'd both been too overwrought. Now, in the light of day, he knew he had to go, hat in hand, perhaps with a small gift of some sort—nothing that would give her the wrong impression, perhaps something for her family—and ask Espy for forgiveness and hope they could remain friends and fellow workers.

He liked her. She'd proven herself an able and valuable partner in the church club. He didn't want to see that destroyed for some folly.

He'd just have to shoulder all the blame himself, tell her he'd been a brute and never meant to cross that line in any manner.

* * *

His family had already breakfasted when Warren entered the dining room. Samuel brought him the silver coffeepot. "Coffee, sir?"

He smiled. "Thanks."

The gurgling sound of the dark liquid was the only sound in the room.

"Where is everyone?"

Samuel lifted the pot and moved the cream and sugar toward him. "Miss Annalise is on the terrace writing. Your mother is in the kitchen consulting with Cook. Your father—"

At that moment his father stepped into the dining room. "Ah, Warren, you're finally up."

Warren swallowed a spurt of annoyance at the implied criticism. "Yes, I'm up."

His father nodded to Samuel. "If you'll excuse us."

"Of course, sir." He directed his attention to Warren. "Would you like some eggs and toast, sir?"

"Toast is fine, thank you." He had no appetite. He felt out of sorts, and attributed it to having woken late.

His father came to sit diagonally from him. "Yesterday went well, I have to say."

Warren poured a spot of cream into his coffee and stirred. "Yes, sir, I think it did. We raised two hundred dollars on the lobster feast." He shook his head. "I still can't get over it."

"Oh, yes." His father seemed distracted. "I was thinking more in terms of the day as a whole. Glorious weather, the whole town must have turned out. You made a fine showing on the podium with the rest of us old men." He chuckled.

Warren set his cup back down in its saucer after taking the first sip, feeling uncomfortable with the praise. What would the prominent citizens of Holliston think of him if they'd seen him in the forest last night?

The cup rattled in its saucer. He let it go, hoping his father didn't notice the tremor in his hand.

"You did me proud, Son. You are the kind of young man this town needs."

Warren kept his gaze fixed on his place setting.

"The years away have only added the polish and maturity you needed. The other gentlemen, all colleagues of mine whom I've known for years, expressed their admiration to me yesterday."

Warren wished he could crawl back into the earth like a worm.

Samuel returned with his breakfast plate. "Here you go, sir. Hot off the skillet."

Warren inhaled. "Thank you—and thank Cook. It smells delicious. Please send her my apologies. I didn't mean to oversleep."

His father chuckled as Samuel withdrew with a murmured, "Yes, sir."

"You were entitled to sleep in after all you did yesterday. That game was a great one. You haven't lost your skill."

Able to smile with enthusiasm at this topic, Warren bowed his head and said a quick word of thanks for his food. "As always it was a team effort, but it felt good to be standing on the pitcher's mound once again."

His father talked a little of the game as Warren ate his food. When he'd taken his last bite and reached for his coffee cup, his father folded his hands on the linen tablecloth. "How do you find Christina now that you've had a chance to squire her around a bit?"

Warren almost coughed on the coffee he'd just swallowed. "S-s-squire?"

His father smiled paternally. "Well, you know, you've been seeing her more than any of the other young ladies in your circle."

Warren set his cup down carefully and reached for his napkin, patting it against his mouth as he sought how to respond. His skin prickled with apprehension. It was one thing for his mother to be matchmaking, but for his father to insinuate something was altogether alarming.

"I don't believe I've seen Christina any more than any of my other acquaintances—of the female variety," he ended with an attempt at humor.

His father didn't crack a smile. "She's been to dinner a number of times, you've been to her house, she sat with our family during the band concert . . ." His father continued ticking off the instances when Christina had been the only female acquaintance of his age, with the exception of his sister, in their party.

Warren lifted his hands palm out as if fending something off. "Whoa, Father. Most of those occasions have been because you or Mother invited her . . . or she's been kind enough to escort Annalise somewhere when I haven't been able to. I think you're being a bit premature to start linking our names together as if I'm courting her."

His father rubbed his gold signet ring with his index finger, a sure sign that he was mulling something over before speaking. After a moment, he quirked an eyebrow. "So, you're telling me it's we who've brought Christina into your sphere and not any inclination of your own?"

Warren shrugged and adopted a light tone. "I'm sure I would have been in her company in any case, since she is among my circle of friends." He met his father's intent look straight on. "But I personally don't feel any special attraction to her."

If his father felt any disappointment, he didn't show it. "A pity. She's a nice girl, beautiful, properly brought up. The two of you have known each other your whole lives."

Warren chuckled. "Now you sound like Mother."

Again, his father didn't respond to the attempt at humor. "As I said, she would make you the ideal wife." He tugged at an earlobe. "Frankly, I'm not sure what you're waiting for. You're twenty-four. In a few months, you'll be twenty-five. I was married and settled down by your age.

"Your mother has been a good wife. She made a home for me. She's raised the two of you into fine young adults. Don't wait too long to choose the right wife."

Warren fidgeted in his chair. His father rarely asked him about his private life, and he'd gotten used to keeping it private since being away. "Father, it's not exactly something one controls." He motioned with a hand, finding it hard to articulate his thoughts. "Meeting that special person . . ."

"Bah! I don't mean to disparage the whole notion of falling in love. I love your mother. But if you select the woman with the right upbringing, the affection will deepen into love over time, especially when you have children together."

Warren said nothing, hoping his father was finished with the topic.

"The *wrong* choice can fill you with regret for the rest of your life."

Warren's gaze narrowed on his father's, wondering what he was getting at. "I don't think you have to worry about that since I'm not singling out any young lady at present."

"Your mother seems to think you've singled out that Estrada girl."

The previous night flashed through his mind. He cast about for a suitably offhand remark. "Well, we did work closely for the lobster banquet."

"It's my understanding that Christina is involved there as well, which is another reason it seemed natural to suppose you and Christina were spending time together."

"You know how people love to gossip." Did anyone see them walking away from the fireworks together? Someone from the mill? He should have expected that.

His father gave him a measured look before standing. "Well, I must leave you and get to the bank. Just consider what I've said. It doesn't pay to be careless of your companions in a town this size. You've been away where you have enjoyed the freedom of anonymity and I didn't ask you to give me an account of your adventures." His father chuckled. "We're all entitled to sow our wild oats, as long as we understand when it's time to settle down."

153

His father patted him on the shoulder. "You'll be heading to the office later, I trust."

"Yes . . . yes, I'll be going right over as soon as I finish here."

"No hurry."

But of course there was. His father expected him to put in a full day's work. Which he fully intended to do.

No matter how distracted his mind felt at the moment.

. . .

Espy dragged herself out of bed early the next morning, only because Alicia and Gina were bouncing on her bed and chattering about the day before.

Espy groaned and turned to the wall, pulling the covers over her head.

"You getting up or planning on laying abed till noon?" Angela poked her shoulder through the thin blanket.

"What time is it?" came Espy's muffled reply.

"Half-past eight."

Half-past eight? She had to be at work at eight. Like a whirlwind, she whipped off the covers and sprang out of bed. "Why didn't you wake me?" As she spoke, she hurried to the washstand, glad that for once there was still clean water in the pitcher.

"Are you joking? With all the noise and you sleeping like the dead? I figured the Stocktons had given you an extra day off."

Drying her face and slipping into her drawers, Espy didn't bother to scold her sister any more. Angela had enough on her plate with getting the younger ones up, especially if Espy hadn't been awake to help.

It was her own fault for going to bed so late—and for letting herself be upset at Warren's behavior.

Her face burned at the recollection of the liberties she'd allowed him to take. The first *and last* time she'd be so gullible. She pulled off her nightgown and pulled on her camisole.

"Espy, will you tie my hair ribbon for me?" Alicia held out a blue ribbon.

"Oh, honey, I'm sorry, but I'm late for work this morning." She glanced at Angela. "Do you have time? I'm sorry I overslept."

Without a word, Angela finished buttoning up the back of Gina's pinafore and went over to Alicia. Her lips compressed, she began to braid the girl's hair. "Here, give me the ribbon." She tied it on the end, her movements efficient from long practice. "Good thing I don't have a shift at the cannery till this afternoon."

Espy brushed out her thick mane, ignoring the pain as she yanked through the tangles. If Warren hadn't pulled it out of its knot or if she'd braided it before falling into bed last night, she wouldn't have this problem now.

Giving herself a quick glance in the small rectangle of a mirror, she smoothed down the front of her gingham. The previous day's garments lay in a pile on the floor. If she'd gotten up in time, she'd have had them washed out and hung out to dry on the line before work.

"I'm off," she told Angela. "Thanks for doing my chores."

Catching only a "humph" from her sister, Espy dashed down the hall, hiking up her skirts and taking the stairs two at a time. She didn't stop for breakfast but ran down the lane, only stopping to walk when she approached Holliston.

She smiled at all those who greeted her but she didn't stop to engage in conversation. Her eyes glanced toward the Brentwood office, but didn't see Warren.

Jerking her head forward, she focused on getting to the end of Main Street and the covered bridge. As she approached it, her heart reverberated against her ribcage, the sound drowned out by the roar of the rushing waters under the bridge.

No sign of Warren. Likely he was long at his work. She needn't worry she'd bump into him.

What am I going to do when I do see him? What about the church club? She swallowed, feeling slightly dizzy. A result of running in the heat on an empty stomach, she told herself.

As the road curved down Elm Street, her heart sank. Of all the people to be out, it had to be Warren, striding down the road toward her as if he'd just left home.

With the sight of his tall frame and broad shoulders in a tan suit, her fingers clutched the worn material of her own gown.

Why this morning, Lord? Oh, please, help me be strong and act as if last night didn't matter at all, she prayed.

He had seen her. She could tell by the slight veering of his footsteps in her direction.

She straightened her posture and slowed her steps a fraction, trying to appear poised and calm. Schooling her features to reveal nothing, she nevertheless feared he'd hear the thudding in her chest.

He stopped a few feet away from her, eyeing her beneath the brim of his high bowler. Her hair spilled down her back and her face was shiny with perspiration.

"Good morning, Espy."

She stopped, her fingers pulling the edges of her shawl together. "Good morning, Warren." She met his serious look with one equally serious.

"How—" He began again. "How are you this morning?"

She nodded. "Very well, thank you. And you?" He certainly didn't look as if he'd tossed and turned half the night as she had.

"I'm fine, thank you." A small smile barely curved his lips. *Oh, dear.* She felt a wave of faintness wash over her at the memory of what they'd done last night, the pain lancing her afresh.

"A little tired after yesterday's festivities," he said. "But I imagine you feel the same."

She lifted her chin. "I'm fine. Right as rain." She wouldn't give him the satisfaction of knowing how little she'd slept.

156

"Yes, well—" He pulled out his silver watch and glanced at it. "I'd better get to the office. I imagine you're going to work, too."

"That's right. I mustn't be late." As she made to take a step, he put a hand out as if to detain her. She stopped immediately, hope springing up in her heart.

"Listen, Espy." He swallowed visibly. "About last night—I didn't mean—that is, I shouldn't have—" He took a deep breath, looking into her eyes. "What I'm trying to say is I behaved in a very ungentlemanly manner and I beg your forgiveness. C-could—do you think you can forget my abominable behavior and g-go on as before?"

A slight breeze ruffled the hair on the nape of her neck, causing her to shiver. His pushing her away had been final. Mustering all her strength, she shrugged. "Sure. I've already forgotten it."

He drew away as if her careless tone had taken him aback. Before he could say anything, she swished past him.

"Espy—" she heard behind her, but she kept going.

When she arrived at the Stocktons', she was out of breath, her dress damp with perspiration. Her fingers fumbled with the latch of the gate and she jiggled it in mounting frustration. *Open, you stupid thing!* Finally, it opened and she banged it shut behind her.

She hurried to the back entrance, hoping not to see Mrs. Stockton until she was more composed.

Mrs. Maguire was drying a dish and turned at Espy's entrance. "There you are, dear. I was wondering if you'd make it in today after yesterday's festivities. My, I must say that lobster feast was fit for a king." She chuckled, setting down the dish and picking up another. "As usual I ate too much."

Espy hung up her shawl and satchel and smoothed down her hair, using that as an excuse to settle herself. "I'm sorry I'm late. I have no excuse except that I overslept a bit." She turned to the sink area. "I don't know why my sister didn't wake me up. Anything I can do here to help you before I see Mrs. Stockton?"

157

"I've got everything under control, thank you, dear. Why don't you run along to Mrs. Stockton? She was in once asking for you."

"I'd better go find her." Worried Mrs. Stockton would be displeased, Espy hurried off.

But Mrs. Stockton was in a good mood, and after talking about the Fourth of July events for a few minutes, she gave her a list of chores to do.

Espy put aside her disappointment over Warren and tackled the list with vigor. There was nothing like physical labor to help dispel low spirits, she'd found. When she'd had to leave school, she'd plunged into the work at the cannery with a will, determined to be a faster sardine slicer than anyone.

And, now, this housework would get her over her foolish yearnings for Warren Brentwood. *He isn't worthy of my affections, that is for sure*, she decided, squeezing out her sponge and using it to scrub the baseboard in the dining room.

When she finished her list of chores, she asked Mrs. Stockton for more, saying that she wanted to make up for having been late in the morning.

"Goodness, Espy, you needn't worry. I understand how busy you were yesterday. Why, you didn't even get to enjoy your holiday."

"That's all right. I was happy to be able to be part of the new church group. Do you know we raised quite a bit of money, and it'll feel good to be able to get it to the needy."

That stopped her short. How was this money going to get to them? When she'd stormed off, leaving Warren with his apology, she hadn't thought about the club. She had no desire to ever see him again, much less work with him.

She took the dust rag and bottle of oil to the study, chewing on her lip as she puzzled what to do about the Holliston Lights.

They certainly didn't need her. There were enough people to help Warren. All she'd done yesterday was stand over a steaming lobster kettle. Let Christina get the glory. She'd bask in it.

Pushing aside these thoughts, Espy knocked softly on the study door. Mrs. Stockton had said her husband didn't mind if she started early on his room, before he'd finished his work—that he'd asked for her.

A sense of satisfaction filled her. At least someone appreciated her talents.

"Come in."

She opened the door and smiled toward Mr. Stockton. "I don't want to disturb you if you're still working, but Mrs. Stockton said it was all right to start on the shelves."

He rose and smiled. "You're never a disturbance, more a welcome change." His gray-blue eyes twinkled into hers.

She found herself blushing, not used to having someone compliment her and treat her as if she truly were someone special.

He motioned toward the couch. "Come, leave your dust rag a moment and sit and tell me about your latest book."

She glanced at the wall of books she needed to dust. "I don't know . . . I should work first . . ."

He patted the place beside him. "Don't worry, if the dust stays another day, I'll not say a word."

She didn't need any more persuading, vowing to work twice as fast as soon as she could. But she needed something to get her mind off Warren.

Talking about books certainly worked. She could trade her own life for another's, where interesting things happened and hardships ended in something good and noble in a character's life.

They discussed the books she was reading, and before she knew it, an hour had gone by. "Oh, my," she said, jumping up, when the clock in the library sounded. "I really must get on with the dusting."

He didn't stop her but remained looking up at her with a smile.

Smoothing down her apron, wondering how he could see beyond her apron to a young woman with a mind, when Warren only saw someone beneath him, Espy finally turned away and fumbled for her dust rag and bottle of lemon oil.

She'd started removing books from the lowest shelf of one section when Mr. Stockton spoke. She jumped when she heard his voice right behind her. He stood, looking down at her pensively. "You're a remarkable young woman, Espy."

"Th-thank you, Mr. Stockton."

"You should consider furthering your education."

She swallowed. There was nothing she'd rather do. She laid her hands on her knees. "I don't know . . . I have my younger brother and sisters still in school." She gave a rueful laugh. "Some not even started yet."

"It's a terrible shame for you not to resume your studies."

He continued looking at her until she grew uncomfortable. Picking up the rag, she began dusting the first book, a thick leather tome.

"I'll tell you what, I'll tutor you."

Her gaze flew up. "Tutor me?"

"Yes." He nodded, continuing to look at her. "Don't be alarmed, it wouldn't involve too much more than we've been doing now, with the exception that I'll assign you some work to do at home."

"I could do that, I guess."

"We'll broaden the subjects, so you're not just reading literature. Some mathematics, history, the sciences, how about that?"

She swallowed, looking up at him. "Would you really do that for me? I may not understand everything . . . it's been a while since I've been in school."

He chuckled. "Don't worry about that. Remember, I'm a teacher; I know how to impart knowledge to students, as long as they're willing to learn."

"I'm willing," she promised fervently. "Thank you, Mr. Stockton, for taking such trouble with me."

"So, we're agreed?"

She nodded.

He held out his hand.

She began to stand, but he took hers in his before she had a chance to. His clasp was warm and firm, his eyes looking into hers. Did he treat all this students this way, as if they were the only ones worthy of his attention?

Finally, he let her hand go and stepped back from her. She clasped her hands together, still feeling the warmth of his palm against hers.

"When you finish your work today, perhaps you can stay a few minutes and we'll have our first lesson. I'll give you a few assignments to complete. Don't worry—" he held up his hand—"I know you're busy with lots of tasks, so I won't overburden you."

He returned to his desk then and she focused on the books to dust, but her mind found it hard to concentrate. To be able to be educated. It was a dream she'd given up.

She could hold her own with the Christinas of this world.

And men like Warren wouldn't look down on her.

Maybe she'd be so busy, she wouldn't have time for his club. Let him see how well he'd manage without her. Let Christina endear herself to the poor in the community.

Hah! That would be the day!

12

W arren called the meeting to order. He'd waited fifteen minutes extra for Espy and her sister to show up at the church basement, but finally he could delay it no longer. The others were becoming restive, Dexter joking about all the places he could be, and Christina reminding him of the sociable at the Smiths' later.

"Very well, I'm calling our meeting to order. I'll open in prayer and then we can begin." He bowed his head and said a short prayer.

He hadn't seen Espy since that brief encounter on the road when she left him in a snit. He didn't blame her, but he'd hoped she'd cooled off by now, more than a week later. Funny, in a town the size of Holliston, he'd expected to run into her, but it was as if she'd disappeared off the face of the earth.

He'd had to tell Alvaro about the meeting date and ask him to relay the information to both Espy and Angela. The boy had sullenly agreed.

Perhaps Alvaro hadn't told them. Warren couldn't believe Espy wouldn't show up otherwise. She cared too much about the purpose of their group to let personal feelings come into it.

Or did she?

Pushing aside the thoughts, he opened his Bible to the Scripture passage he'd chosen to open the meeting with. Even that had been Espy's idea.

Following their short devotional, he began their regular meeting. "Now, then, this is where we stand . . ."

When he opened the meeting for discussion, they began to talk about distributing the proceeds from the lobster dinner.

"Hey, where's Espy, anyway?" Will asked. "Didn't she know we were meeting tonight?"

"I told her brother Alvaro to inform her and Angela."

Henry made a sound in his throat. "That was about as useful as telling her father."

Will laughed. "As far as I'm concerned it's no use meeting till Espy's here."

"Nonsense." Christina leaned forward, her hands clasped atop the table, her gaze surveying all those present. "We have a quorum present. We merely need to decide where we are going to focus our efforts next."

"But what about the money we raised for those families in need?" Mabel asked.

"Warren will deliver the sums we agreed to. As vice president, I can accompany him," Christina answered promptly.

Will glared at her. "Why should you go with him?"

Before things could escalate, Warren cleared his throat. "Perhaps as vice president, it would be better for you to take the second donation. And someone else can take the third. Even better, we'll go in pairs." His gaze roamed over the gathering and paused at his sister. "Annalise, why don't we go together?"

She smiled at him, and he felt a sense of relief at one issue solved. "Good, then."

By the end of the meeting, the hostility from Espy's friends had only increased with every remark of Christina's. Christina didn't seem to notice anything. She carried on, asking the opinion of her friends.

Warren felt as if he were fighting against the tide, trying to keep the unity of the group.

This was all Espy's fault. If she was trying to get back at him by sabotaging the club, then she was certainly succeeding. He stood, smiling and bidding everyone good evening as if nothing was wrong, but inside his annoyance with Espy grew.

"That's a shame Espy and her sister couldn't make it," Dexter said, when the others had left. Christina lingered with Annalise, but the two stood by the entrance to the basement, waiting for him to take them home.

"Yes."

Dexter eyed him, a speculative look in his gaze. "I find it hard to believe she didn't ask you for the next meeting date."

Warren shrugged, gathering his papers.

"You didn't say anything to her?"

Warren looked at his friend sharply. "What do you mean?"

Dexter looked at his fingernails. "Oh, I don't know. Women are funny creatures. Think she got fed up with slaving over that lobster kettle at the dinner and decided to throw in the towel?"

"No. She seemed very happy with the sum raised."

"That's true." Dexter shook his head. "Who is to fathom the mind of woman, eh?"

"I think you're making too much of it. She only missed one meeting and it's most likely her brother forgot to tell her."

"You saw how disjointed everything was without her, didn't you?" He grinned, lowering his voice with a quick look toward the door. "You wouldn't want Christina taking over, would you?"

Saying nothing, Warren turned to go. But he shared Dexter's disquiet more than his friend realized.

Feeling like the lowest scoundrel, and resenting the way Espy made him feel, he approached his sister and Christina with a smile pasted on his face. "Ready to go?"

. . .

The next afternoon, accomplishing little sitting at his desk, he walked to the mill. On the yard men were carrying logs into the mill and piling up the sawn lumber that came out of it to load onto the next schooner.

He frowned, watching Hodgdon approach Alvaro and speak to him. The foreman was serious and Alvaro seemed as sullen as always. Finally, the boy spun on his heel and walked off.

Another result of his friendship with Espy—a surly employee. His father had been right. With a frustrated sigh he headed toward the foreman.

"Anything the matter?" he asked Hodgdon.

The foreman looked uncomfortable. Warren glanced toward Alvaro, who was back to stacking lumber.

"This is the third morning Alvaro has been late to work," the foreman finally answered. "And not by a little."

Feeling responsible for making the foreman hire the boy, Warren said, "Let me talk to him."

After greeting Alvaro, he asked, "What seems to be the trouble that you can't get here on time?"

Alvaro glanced over at the foreman. "He complaining?"

"Well, he has a right to."

The boy shrugged. "I just overslept."

"You know it's not fair to the others to have someone come in long after they've begun working."

Alvaro pushed his cap up. "Yeah, I know. I'll make it on time tomorrow."

Warren had a good mind to sack the boy then and there but he paused. He thought of why he had started the Holliston Lights.

Wasn't it to reach just such youth as this boy?

Repressing a sigh, he gave a nod. "Very well. On your way home today, stop in at my office."

• • •

Espy managed to dodge Warren for more than a week. It meant staying away from church in the morning, which she missed, and having to explain things at home. She'd gotten by with saying she didn't feel well the first Sunday.

Alvaro had told her about the club meeting when he'd come home from work. "By the way, Mr. Brentwood—Warren to you— asked me to tell you they're meeting tonight for that church club."

Espy had been out in the backyard with the dishpan of dirty water to throw over the vegetable garden. Everything was bone dry. The rows of peas looked scraggly and the cucumber leaves were yellowing. And something seemed to be eating at the leaves of the cabbage plants. She'd have to get after Hortensia and the boys who were supposed to weed and water it.

She turned to her brother, wiping her forehead with the back of her arm. "When did he tell you that?"

"'Fore I left work."

"What else did he say?"

"Nothin'." His dark eyes took on a sly look. "What'dya expect him to say?"

"None of your business." Her own eyes narrowed on him. "How's the job?"

"None o' *your* business."

Too tired to argue with him at the moment, she walked past him. When she entered the kitchen, she replaced the dishpan in the sink. "Alvaro said there's a church club meeting tonight," she said to Angela, picking up a towel to dry the dishes.

"We don't have much time."

Espy didn't reply to her sister. She was waging a battle inside about whether or not to go. She didn't want to shirk her responsibilities, but neither did she have any heart to attend. Not when her heart was broken and empty. But she didn't want to keep her sister from the club.

"Aren't you going to get ready?" Angela asked when she'd put away the last of the food and seen no movement on Espy's part to leave the kitchen.

"Uh . . . no." Espy continued scrubbing at a spot on the edge of the soapstone sink with her rag. "You go ahead," she added.

Angela's footsteps sounded across the kitchen floorboards. Espy saw the tips of her shoes peering from the hem of her dark skirt. "You mean you're not going?"

Espy let out a breath, her eyes coming up slowly to meet her sister's. "That's what I mean."

Her sister's arms were folded uncompromisingly across her front. "Why not?"

"I'm kind of tired."

"And you didn't feel well on Sunday. That's not like you." The two stared at each other. "All right, out with it."

Espy looked down. "I would just rather not tonight. That's all."

"It's that Warren, isn't it?"

Her eyes flew back up. "Am I wearing some kind of sign across my forehead with Warren Brentwood's name stamped across it? Good gracious, he's not the only person I think about!"

"But he gets under your skin, doesn't he?"

Angela probably knew her better than anybody in the world. Espy said nothing, as they continued looking at each other.

"Well, I'm not going either then."

"No, Angela, you mustn't stay home on my account."

"What do I need some church club to go to? I have enough to do around here. I'm tired, too."

"But—"

167

Angela turned away from her. "I'm putting the children to bed. Don't worry, Warren has enough of his friends now so they won't even notice we're not there." She gave a harsh laugh. "Christina'll be happy. She can have him all to herself now."

The thought gave Espy no comfort at all.

• • •

Warren had forgotten he'd asked Alvaro to stop by his office until the boy showed up. Warren stopped himself from looking at his watch. The last thing he wanted was to talk to some ungrateful youth with a bad attitude. Instead, he smiled. "Come in, Alvaro, and have a seat."

The boy shuffled toward the desk and sat in the chair opposite Warren. Warren sat back in his own seat, thinking about how to approach this meeting. "How are things going?"

"What do you mean?"

"Oh, I don't know, life in general."

"Fine, I guess."

Warren hit on a topic. "Hey, I've been meaning to congratulate you on winning that footrace."

A glimmer of animation flickered in his eyes. "Thanks."

"I'm sorry I wasn't able to watch it."

"That's all right."

"You must have been pretty fast to beat everyone else. And twenty bucks in prize money." He whistled. "That's a small fortune."

Alvaro smiled. "Yeah."

"Any plans for all that money?"

His face shut down again, suspicion darkening his eyes. "A guy always has plans."

"Sure. When I was your age," *oh, no, now I sound like my father,* "I had a lot of plans. I worked at the mill then, too, but didn't get

168

paid very much." He grinned. "My father kept me on a short leash. He didn't think young men had any cause for much money."

Alvaro shifted his lanky frame in the chair. "So, what kinda things did you want money for?"

"Hmm, let's see. It's been a while. A new baseball bat, a new uniform for the team. Enough to take out a girl I was sweet on for an ice cream after school, things like that."

Alvaro nodded. "You played good on the Fourth."

Maybe that was some common ground. "You like to play ball?"

The boy shrugged. "When I get a chance."

"Would you like to toss a ball around a bit some afternoon?"

"Maybe."

"Good. How about Sunday? You can bring some of your friends, too, if you want. We can have a small game."

His eyes lit up again then quickly smoldered. "You're not bringing any of your friends are you?"

"Uh, I hadn't thought about it. Not if you'd rather I didn't."

"They're a bunch of swells."

"Not all of them. But it'll just be your friends for now, all right? We can meet on the ball field, say around two o'clock."

When Alvaro had gone, Warren stood and looked out the window toward the river. The dream of preaching from the pulpit came back to him. Other dreams, he'd forget by the end of the day.

What does it mean, Lord? he asked for the countless time. *Does it mean You want me to be more involved with the things You care about? Things like befriending this young man who's had few good examples of manhood in his life?*

Warren had been a churchgoer and a believer for years. It was just that so many other things had come before church—his studies first and foremost. Coming in anything less than head of his class was unacceptable to his father. Then athletics, his first love when he was younger; then college, where he'd grown to enjoy his studies for himself, without needing his father's approval. There, he'd been exposed to so many new ideas that church was only something he ran to on Sunday morning, sliding into the back pew as the choir was already singing the first hymn.

And then it had been seeing the world, and now business, which was first in his life.

None of these endeavors had filled him.

He'd thought the love of a woman would do it. But after his first tentative experience with love, he'd decided storybook romance was not for him. He was cut from his father's cloth. You married someone of your own society in order to "settle down," which consisted in setting up a household and begetting children and presenting a united front in your community endeavors.

Why then did he go against his parents' wishes where Christina was concerned? Perhaps because he saw his own parents' union. He wouldn't call it unhappy, but neither would he call it happy. They merely coexisted, each one involved in his or her own sphere. The main things they discussed together were Annalise and himself.

Perhaps he'd understand the bond children brought to a union once he'd had children of his own. He remembered the emotions colliding in him the night he'd kissed Espy.

He turned away from the window in an effort to block out the images and sensations of that encounter. Espy Estrada was *not* his kindred spirit. The farthest thing from it.

13

On Sunday morning, Espy was happy for the delays that meant that, as usual, they left at the last minute for church. When they finally entered the high-ceilinged sanctuary with its dark oak beams, they had only the last pew available to them.

She didn't see Warren until the congregation sat down after singing the first hymn.

There he was, his head a fraction higher than his father's, on the front right pew where his family habitually sat. She'd been staring at his back for years, since she was about eight. When he left for college, it took her a while to adjust to not seeing him anymore.

But her own life got busy and she grew used to life without Warren in town. She had lots of friends, people who liked her for who she was. She didn't need the likes of Warren Brentwood. The problem was none of her friends understood her desire to do more with her life.

She focused on the preacher's words, shutting Warren out of her thoughts.

When the service ended, she stood. "Come on, let's get out before the aisle fills up."

"What's the rush?" her fourteen-year-old sister, Hortensia, asked.

"No rush," she threw over her shoulder, taking Alicia by the hand. "If you don't see me in the yard, it means I've started home."

Before Hortensia could question this, she squeezed past a portly matron.

"Excuse me, Mrs. Preston."

She made it out the front door just as Pastor Curtis stepped up to greet parishioners.

He smiled. "Where's the fire?"

"Oh—there's no fire." She slowed her steps.

"Glad to hear it. I haven't seen you in a few days. How are things? How's the club?"

She flushed, her fingers clutching her Bible and handbag in one hand, Alicia tugging on the other. "Fine."

He nodded, peering at her as if to determine more than her answer said. "I shan't detain you any longer." He smiled at Alicia before waving goodbye to them both.

Just before leaving the churchyard, she glanced back and caught sight of Warren, only because he stood taller than most around him. As usual he was surrounded by family and friends.

"Come on, Alicia."

• • •

By the second club meeting when Espy and Angela didn't show up, neither did Henry or Will. As Warren discussed the agenda, he looked around the table, realizing it was only his friends and acquaintances who made up the group.

By the end of the meeting, which had consisted mainly of Christina, Emily, and James discussing their next projects, Warren realized it had become what Espy had warned against—another do-gooder group with no real connection with the community it sought to reach.

A few evenings before, he'd finally gone with Annalise to deliver the money raised over the Fourth to one of the families.

It hadn't gone well. They knocked on the door and introduced themselves and explained their purpose.

The young woman at the door, a baby on her hip, two youngsters clinging to her apron, glared at them in suspicion. By the end of Warren's hesitant explanation, she began shoving the door in his face. "Keep your charity!" The door banged shut.

He and Annalise exchanged looks. "What should we do?" she asked.

He gazed at the door with its peeling paint. "I don't know." What he wanted to do was march to Espy's and ask for her help.

But he'd be confounded if he'd go there. She'd probably slam the door in his face, too.

He'd spent every waking moment in bed at night asking God's forgiveness, but he didn't know what else he could do to Espy to make up for it. Seeing her would be worse.

And yet, a part of him wanted to. Wanted to confront her . . . talk to her. But he knew it would serve no purpose but add fuel to the fire.

He put his hat back on his head and turned away from the door. "Come on. We'll have to figure something else out."

Annalise walked alongside him on the weed-choked path back toward town. Yellow and orange hawkweed grew almost knee-deep; oxeye daisy offered a bright white and yellow contrast to the grass growing along the dilapidated fences.

"Perhaps we shall have to ask Espy to explain things to her," Annalise offered.

He swatted at a horsefly buzzing around his face. "Perhaps."

"Would you like me to ask her?"

He blinked sidelong at his sister, who normally was too

withdrawn to make such an offer. He was tempted and then thought better of it. She couldn't go there alone. "I don't want you walking there by yourself."

"Why don't you go with me? Or, if you're too busy, perhaps Dexter or James can go with me."

He slapped unsuccessfully at the buzzing fly. "I'll take you," he said shortly. He could wait at the end of the lane.

"Why don't we go now? She's probably home from work and it will only take a moment. We should be home in time for supper."

"Very well. It's not too far from here." He took his sister's elbow and steered her down a side path instead of the wider dirt road that led back to town.

The street was filled with playing children, men old and young sat on their stoops smoking pipes, and dogs sniffed around the edges of yards. Thinking better of leaving his sister alone, he nodded at the passing men and guided Annalise toward the last house. At the gate, he let go of his sister's arm. "Go on up. I'll walk down the block and back."

Her brows drew together in puzzlement. But she said nothing, too tactful probably to ask him why he didn't go to Espy himself. He watched her walk up the grassy path. He'd forgotten to warn her to watch the broken step. But she was making her way cautiously.

Seeing the twitch of a curtain behind a window, he did an about-face and walked back down the road.

"Your beau is outside."

Espy looked at Alvaro from the couch, where she sat stitching a patch on Gus's trousers. "Who?" she asked absently, wondering whom her brother would construe as her beau these days.

"Mr. High and Mighty Brentwood."

Her head snapped up, and she smothered an exclamation at the needle prick to her forefinger. Bringing it up to her lips, she mumbled, "What are you talking about? Don't be ridiculous."

Before he could respond, they both heard a knock on the door. The two stared at each other, Espy feeling as if she'd been cornered in a cove by the incoming tide.

Why was it Warren always saw her at her worst? This afternoon she was wearing a soiled apron over her oldest work skirt. She'd been scrubbing the kitchen floor at the Stocktons' and only come home a half hour ago. Gus had shown her the rip in his trousers from the school ground. He needed the pants tomorrow morning.

"Aren't you going to answer?" Alvaro continued, leaning against the edge of the window.

"Why don't you? Maybe he's come to see you about something at the mill." Though she doubted he'd walk all the way here to talk to Alvaro about work, even if he had done so to hire him. That seemed an age ago.

Alvaro's face closed up. "I've done nothing wrong." But without another word, he straightened and walked into the entry hall. A moment later, after the sound of low voices, he returned. "It's for you. It's his sister."

Annalise? Hastily, she set aside her sewing and stood, smoothing down her apron over her skirt. Her hand went to her hair. *Oh, what's the use?*

She marched to the door and stopped in amazement. Annalise stood there, her gloved hands clasping her handbag in front of her. She wore a pretty bonnet wreathed in a sprig of tiny daisies and a white gown with a green pattern and green sash. "Hello, Espy."

Espy approached the doorway. "Hello." Her gaze slid beyond Annalise but she saw no sign of Warren. "Are you by yourself?"

"Yes, I mean no." Her pale cheeks filled with pink. "Warren brought me, but he . . . had to walk down the street. He'll be by in a minute."

"I see." Even with his sister along, he didn't want to see her.

"We came—that is, I came to . . . to ask you—"

175

Seeing Annalise's difficulty in talking to her, Espy's heart softened. "Won't you come in?"

"No, thank you. I can't stay long. Mother expects me home soon."

Clearly, coming to her doorstep was as far as Annalise would permit herself to go. "What can I do for you then?"

Annalise moistened her lips. "Well, you see, Warren and I have just been to see Mrs. Robinson to take her the money collected from the lobster banquet."

Espy raised her eyebrow. "It's about time the money was delivered."

"She wouldn't take it."

"Did you try to give it to her directly?"

"Yes."

"Hmm."

"That's what we'd discussed."

Espy looked away, feeling torn. Poor Marie needed it badly, and here Espy had only been concerned with her own problems. "If you'll give the money to me, I'll see she gets it. Maybe I can explain things better to her."

Annalise's eyes filled with relief. "Would you? That's what I was hoping you'd say. I asked Warren to bring me here to ask you."

"Did you?" So, it had been Annalise's idea to come here and not Warren's. And now, Warren couldn't even bear to see her long enough to hand her the money. "Sure you trust me to deliver the money?"

Annalise's dark blond eyebrows drew together over her pretty green eyes. "What do you mean?"

"How do you know I wouldn't keep the money myself?"

Annalise's eyes grew round. "Of course you wouldn't do such a thing!"

The hard cord around Espy's heart began to loosen. "No, I wouldn't. As long as I can work for a living, I'm not going to take something that I haven't earned. Especially not when another person's so needy."

Annalise opened her handbag and reached into it. Extending her hand, she gave Espy an envelope. "Here, the sum we agreed on."

Espy took it. "I'll see she gets it tonight."

"How do you think you can persuade her? She told us she didn't want charity."

"I'll explain that it's not meant to insult them, but be a helping hand for her children until she gets back on her feet. I'll tell her someday she can do the same for someone else. Maybe even one of us," she said with a short laugh.

But instead of being offended, Annalise nodded. "I never thought of it that way, but what a perfect way to persuade her."

"And if that doesn't work, I'll tell her to accept it for the children's sake. They don't deserve to go hungry because of their mother's pride."

"You're so wise."

Flustered by the compliment, Espy took a step back. "Just common sense."

"Well, I'd better be going." She half-glanced behind her shoulder. "Warren will be returning for me." She took a breath. "I hope you can come back to the club. We really miss you."

At a loss, Espy remained silent.

"Warren said you were too busy, but I hope you can find the time. It's not the same without you . . . or your sister or Henry or Will."

Espy frowned. "Aren't they coming? I mean, besides Angela."

Annalise shook her head. "Not since they saw you weren't coming."

Espy's lips flattened with disgust. *I must talk some sense into those good-for-nothings. Can't they do anything without me?*

"I'll see what I can do."

Joy suffused Annalise's face. "Thank you. I know they'll listen to you. Do please come yourself."

Espy merely nodded once. "Maybe."

Annalise took a step back. "Good day then. And—thank you."

Espy closed the door softly when Annalise turned away and walked back down the path.

No sign of Warren. Espy walked to the other front room, hoping to escape Alvaro's notice, and stood near the window, well out of sight.

There he was, walking slowly up the lane to meet his sister. As soon as she reached him, he spoke a few words to her. Satisfied, he offered his arm, and the two turned away.

But not before he'd glanced back at her house.

* * *

Espy considered Annalise's request throughout the following days, debating back and forth about whether to go to the next meeting or not. She needed to tell them about her visit to Marie. Thankfully, it had gone well, just as Espy had expected. But first she would give Will and Henry a piece of her mind.

In the meantime, she kept her thoughts off Warren and his almost-visit to her house by spending much of her time at the Stocktons'. At the end of her workday, she immersed herself in the talk of books and ideas. She completed her assignments for Mr. Stockton by kerosene lamp in the kitchen after everyone else had gone to bed. He corrected everything promptly and discussed them with her the following afternoon. A whole new world was opening up to her. She called it her "secret world," hugging the books to her as she walked home.

By midweek, she still hadn't decided what to do about the church club meeting, though it was becoming clear to her if she wanted her friends to go back, she'd have to go with them.

It stuck in her craw but she also realized she was behaving badly by not showing up. This was about the Lord's work, not her petty life. But she couldn't bear to be in Warren's company and know he didn't care about her—and see the victory in Christina's eyes.

The day dawned gray and cool. She glanced up at the skies, hoping the rain would hold off until she arrived at work but thankful for rain since it meant she wouldn't have to water the vegetable patch when she got home.

She spent the day polishing silver and then pewter and copper for Mrs. Stockton. "Goodness, I didn't think one could have so many metal things," she said to Mrs. Maguire when she was finally able to set down the last candlestick. Her fingernails looked awful, full of the gray paste she'd used for polishing.

The cook chuckled. "And to think, in a few weeks, you'll probably have it all to do again. But for the moment everything looks shiny."

Espy rose from the kitchen table. "Let me put everything back and scrub my hands." She held them out.

Mrs. Maguire clucked her tongue. "Perhaps some lemon peel will help. I'll see if we have any when you come back."

"Thank you."

Afterward, she had to run to town for a list of groceries Mrs. Maguire gave her. "Mrs. Stockton wants me to prepare some of the broad beans from the garden and I've run out of butter and bacon."

On her trip back the rain began to come down hard. Espy threw her shawl over her head as she picked up her pace. By the time she passed the mill, her shawl did little to protect her from the cold, wet drops drumming down on her, and she ducked her head against the assault. She glanced at the mill but no one was outside.

She had a short respite in the covered bridge. Once on Elm Street, she kept to the cover of the large trees but the puddles soaked her legs and hem of her skirt. She fumbled with the gate with one hand, the other carrying her bundle, then ran to the back toward the kitchen entrance.

She pulled open the door, thankful for the small portico above her. She threw the shawl off her head, letting it fall to her shoulders as she stepped inside.

"Goodness, I didn't think it would come down like that—" She stopped short at the sight of Mr. Stockton standing close to the kitchen door. "Oh, I thought you were Mrs. Maguire." She laughed at her mistake. It seemed strange to see the professor in the kitchen.

He smiled, holding the door open for her. "No, I'm not her. I believe she went to consult with my wife. Something to do with some recipe."

"Oh." Espy brushed the sodden locks off her forehead.

"Here, allow me." He took the bundle from her hands.

"Thank you."

As she draped her wet shawl across two coat hooks to dry, she wished she had some dry garments to change into. It would be uncomfortable to go about the rest of her chores in damp clothes. She turned to find Mr. Stockton right behind her.

She put up a hand involuntarily. "I'm sorry, I didn't expect you there." She smiled self-consciously.

He returned the smile, holding up a pair of kitchen towels. "I just meant to bring you these. Why don't you let down your hair and allow it to dry properly. You wouldn't want to catch a chill."

"No." She fumbled with the hairpins, feeling nervous all of a sudden. He was taller than she by half a head. Before she could decide whether or not to move, he draped one of the towels around her damp shoulders. "Th-thank you."

Instead of stepping back, he began to help her with the hairpins.

"You don't have to do that—" she began.

"I know I don't." His voice was a soft burr with an oddly soothing quality as if he were speaking to a child. "It's my pleasure."

Her wet hair fell heavily over her shoulders.

She could hardly breathe, he was standing so close, his broad shoulders blocking out everything, his arms raised toward her head. "There, that should do it," he said finally.

Instead of stepping back, he took the remaining towel to her head.

She immediately raised a hand to begin drying her hair, but he took her by the wrist and gently but firmly lowered her hand. "That's all right, I can do this more competently than you." He chuckled, a low rumble in his throat. From where she was standing, she could see the contours of his shaven jaw and smell the spicy scent of his cologne mingled with the sweet scent of his pipe tobacco.

Her thoughts went to the night Warren had kissed her and involuntarily she compared the scent of the two men. Warren's cologne was more—Espy hunted for a word to describe the difference—more like the outdoors.

Mr. Stockton's gentle, rhythmic rubbing of her scalp, combined with her memory of Warren holding her in his arms, began to mesmerize her. Her head felt weightless.

As if reading her thoughts, he guided her head back, the towel going from the front of her scalp farther down.

From a distance, she heard female voices. Mrs. Stockton and the cook.

Goodness, what am I doing, standing in the kitchen, allowing Mr. Stockton to dry my hair? She shook her head, stepping away from him. At the same time, he let her go.

Instead of looking as concerned as she felt, a slight smile played along his lips. He handed her the towel and turned just as the two women entered the kitchen. "Ah, there you are, Mrs. Maguire. I was just coming to ask if you could brew me a pot of your good Earl Grey."

"Certainly, sir. The water in the kettle should be hot."

"I found Espy coming in from the rain. Perhaps a hot cup of tea would do her good as well."

"Oh, Espy, you're soaking wet." The two women clucked over her, offering to get her some dry garments and pulling her to a chair near the stove.

By the time she was able to look around, Mr. Stockton had left the kitchen.

Her thoughts were in a turmoil. Why did Mr. Stockton behave so strangely?

If it had been any other man of her acquaintance, she would have been suspicious. But he had done nothing unseemly. Mr. Stockton had only been concerned over her welfare, not wanting her to take a chill.

He'd even had the thoughtfulness to have Mrs. Maguire prepare her a cup of tea, which now sat in front of her on the table.

Mrs. Stockton soon returned to the kitchen. "Here you go, my dear, an old skirt and blouse of mine you can wear for now."

"Thank you, ma'am. I'll wash them and bring them back to you tomorrow," she hastened to say, taking the garments.

Her employer waved aside the concern. "Don't worry, I only wear those for heavy cleaning. Now, as soon as you've finished your tea and changed, I'll show you what I'd like you to do."

"Yes, ma'am." She hurried to put on the clothes, telling herself she'd just imagined everything with Mr. Stockton. That went to show what happened when she spent too much time mooning over some fellow who didn't give her a thought.

Mr. Stockton was a thoughtful, upright, married man.

Espy needed to concentrate on her cleaning and shut down her overactive imagination. It came from reading too many books.

When she was ready to leave for the day, she hesitated about going to the library, as she usually did before she left.

Using the excuse that it was raining too hard to take home any books, she decided to leave without seeing him. By tomorrow, she'd have forgotten this incident in the kitchen.

But as she walked past his library door, it opened and he stood there.

"Ready for your lesson?" he asked.

"Oh—I thought with the rain . . . I'd better be on my way." She tried to smile.

"Of course, if you'd rather," he said, his countenance perfectly serious. "But if you leave your assignment, I can go over it for tomorrow."

His tone was businesslike.

She swallowed, suddenly worried. She fumbled in her satchel for her papers. "Let me find it." Feeling guilty for having let her imagination run away with her, she brought out the crumpled sheets of paper. "Here, sir."

He took them without a word. Before he closed the door, he said, "I shall expect you tomorrow afternoon then. Keep dry." A slight smile hovered over his lips before the door shut him from her view.

14

Warren arrived quite a bit before the next club meeting. He'd left the office early and wanted to spend some quiet time alone at the church to think and pray about this next meeting.

Thankful for Annalise's intervention with Espy, he nevertheless did not want to depend on his sister to resolve his problems for him. He needed to face what was happening to Holliston Lights and decide where to go from here, if Espy truly did not want to be a part of it anymore.

He entered the church sanctuary and stopped short at the sight of Pastor Curtis. He'd hoped to find the church empty at this hour.

Not betraying his disappointment, he smiled and walked toward his longtime minister and family friend. "Good afternoon, Pastor. Hope I'm not disturbing you."

"Goodness, no. Come in, dear boy. I was hoping to see you sometime soon."

The two shook hands. "Here for the club meeting?"

Warren nodded. "I'm a bit early, but I thought I'd spend a little time here." He indicated the pews, his mouth turning upward on one side to hide his embarrassment.

"Very wise of you. As leader of anything, it's good to seek the best counsel available."

Warren hesitated, torn between consulting the pastor who'd known him all his life and remaining silent. He longed for an older, wiser man's perspective, he realized.

Pastor Curtis touched him lightly on the elbow. "Anything amiss?"

Warren rubbed a hand across his mouth. "I'm not sure." *No, that was not quite true.* "As a matter of fact, there is. It may be nothing important; I could be blowing things out of proportion."

"Let's sit a moment, and tell me about it. I'll tell you whether it's a tempest in a teapot or something that bears looking into—and praying about."

The two settled in the front pew. Warren nodded, feeling a sense of relief to be able to talk to his old mentor. He took a moment to marshal his thoughts. "I'm afraid the Holliston Lights are becoming what we—that is, Espy," he was thankful her name came out sounding natural on his lips, "and I didn't want it to become."

Pastor Curtis raised a graying eyebrow.

"Another club made up of the privileged of our community to feel good about themselves." Having voiced his fear, he let out a breath. "I looked around the meeting last week, and all I saw were the faces of my friends, those of my 'set,' whom my parents have always approved of."

Pastor Curtis's bottom lip thrust outward considering Warren's words. A few seconds later a crease formed between his eyebrows. "Wait a minute, what about Espy and Angela and their friends? Fine young people, but not . . . the kind your dear parents would exactly invite over for Sunday dinner." He ended with a smile that was filled with sad understanding.

Warren looked down at his hands, kneading his palms together. "That's just it. They're no longer coming."

"Not coming?"

"No." The single syllable was hardly audible.

"None of them?"

Warren shook his head.

"What happened?" Knowing his pastor from his early boyhood, Warren knew it was an invitation to confess all.

He wiped his brow. "It's my fault. I—offended Espy and she hasn't come since. When they saw Espy didn't come, the others lost interest."

"I'm sorry. Have you tried to apologize?"

"Of course, first thing."

"I take it that didn't do any good?"

Warren shifted on the pew. "I'm afraid it's a bit more complicated than a mere apology would settle."

"Would it help if I spoke to her?"

Warren's glance shot to the pastor. "Uh—no, sir. That is, this is between her and me."

Pastor Curtis nodded, not pressing the issue, for which Warren was thankful.

"You know, Warren, the devil will try to destroy what you've started here with the young people of Holliston. I asked you to do something the Lord put on my heart, and you were willing and obedient.

"The devil wants to discourage you. He does not want the young people of this community serving God. The question is whether you will give up or not."

He'd tried. He'd failed. No one would hold it against him. He certainly had enough other responsibilities in his life to make it impractical to head a church group.

But he thought about the afternoons he'd taken Alvaro to the ball field. There had been little outward progress so far, except that the boy had not arrived late to the mill since then. The sullen look in his eye was appearing less and less often when he addressed Warren.

186

Warren looked Pastor Curtis in the eye. "I don't wish to."

Pastor Curtis nodded. "Good. That's the first battle won."

Warren gave a self-deprecating laugh. "You want to hear something funny?"

"I can always use a little humor to lighten my day."

"You'll get a kick out of this one then." Warren leaned forward, resting his hands on his knees. "I woke up to the strangest dream one morning. I only remember it because it was so distinct."

The pastor cocked his eyebrows, waiting.

"I was standing up there," he said and motioned to the pulpit, "addressing the congregation." He laughed though it sounded forced. "The place was packed out. It must have been Christmas or Easter." He tried to continue in a light vein though his heart was pounding in anticipation of the pastor's reaction. The two would have a good chuckle and Pastor Curtis would make some joke about taking his job if he cared—or dared—to.

But the pastor was listening to him, an intent look in his eyes.

Warren rubbed his knees. "I was staring at everyone, and that's what I mean by it being so distinct. I remember individual faces from our congregation. Didn't see you, though," he added with another nervous chuckle. "I was even wearing your robe."

A sweat had broken out on his forehead. He didn't want to reach into his breast coat pocket for his handkerchief. "Another thing I remember is the verse I had just uttered to everyone. Hebrews 4:12, 'The word of God is quick and powerful . . .'" He cleared his throat. "That's when I woke up."

He eased back against the pew. "Funny, huh?"

Instead of smiling back, Pastor Curtis said, "Maybe the Lord is trying to tell you something."

Warren waited, his breath suspended.

"Perhaps He's calling you into the ministry."

The sound between a laugh and snort issued from Warren's lips before he had a chance to hold it back. "I beg your pardon, sir, but I hardly think the Lord would call someone like me."

"No?"

He couldn't help himself this time but had to dig for his handkerchief. After wiping his brow, he smiled self-consciously. "Warm in here, isn't it?"

Continuing with his train of thought, he focused on the handkerchief in his hands, refolding it. "I've never had any inclination for the . . . uh, church. I mean, I've always attended, you know that, but as for joining the clergy, it's never entered my mind. I dreamed of playing professional baseball at one time. But that was years ago when I was still a boy in school."

Warren shook his head. "Preaching is about as far in the outfield as that dream was."

"Preaching is not something we choose. The Lord calls us."

An ominous feeling grew in Warren's chest. "I don't think the Lord would just speak to me like that. I mean, I've been groomed since birth to take over my father's business."

Pastor Curtis shrugged. "I was expected to take over my father's shoe store."

Warren stared at the pastor. "Shoe store?"

"That's right. My father owned a successful shoe store in Bangor, right on Union Street. I was the oldest. Worked there after school since I was twelve."

"What happened?"

"The Lord called me to the church. I attended Bangor Theological Seminary."

Warren looked away, flummoxed, hardly knowing how to reconcile this new information with what he knew of Pastor Curtis. "W-wasn't your father upset when you didn't do as he wished?"

"I would say surprised more than upset. When he saw that I was committed to this course, he accepted it."

"What happened to the business?"

"My younger brother took it over." Pastor Curtis smiled. "He has proved very able, much better suited than I."

Warren's shoulders slumped. "You had a brother. I'm the only male in my family. My father expects it of me."

Pastor Curtis studied him under his brows. "Let me ask you something. What would happen if you didn't take over your father's business?"

Warren considered it. "I don't know. He's always expected it. I've always assumed I would. That's why I went to college, and traveled over the world. I just can't imagine anything else."

"Is it what you want?"

This question stumped him as much as the first. Was it what he wanted? He shifted on the pew, fixing his gaze on the polished wooden floorboards, and let his mind wander beyond the usual borders of his day.

If he could do anything . . . if he had a blank slate, a free hand in his destiny, what would he choose to do with his life?

He pictured Alvaro hitting a ball he'd pitched him. He remembered his work on the Fourth, his days at the office, his frustration and sense of futility at being cooped up with numbers and shipments when he was more interested in the lives of the men on the yard, and, finally, the continual butting heads with his father's way of doing things.

He turned to Pastor Curtis. "I don't know." The moment the words were uttered, Warren felt a weight drop from his shoulders, a weight he didn't realize he'd been carrying. He smiled. "What do I do now?"

"You pray. I'll pray as well, for the Lord to reveal His perfect will to you."

Once again, the doubts and fears filled him. "Maybe you shouldn't." At the pastor's questioning look, he tried to smile but it came out lopsided. "I'm not sure if I want to know the answer."

"We all fear the truth at times. But don't worry, the Lord would never have you do something that's inherently against your nature.

It might go against all you've known until now; it might cause friction and even alienation from those you hold dear, but He will not make you do something against your very nature.

"If there is a call on your life, He will equip and empower you to carry it out, *and* He'll give you the desire for it." Pastor Curtis paused. "And if you go into the ministry, perhaps He'll provide someone else to run your father's business empire."

Warren expelled a breath, still not feeling sure he wanted to pursue this. "Very well. Can you pray for me right now?"

"Of course, son." Laying a hand on his shoulder, the pastor bowed his head and began to pray.

* * *

Espy steeled herself to confront her sister's questions. "I'm going to the meeting tonight."

Angela rested her hand on the outdoor pump where she'd been filling a bucket of water. "When did you decide this?"

Espy shrugged, leaning forward to pluck a buttercup that grew in the damp ground around the well. "I realized I was being childish to give up on this important work just because I was feeling put out with the Christinas of the world. You should have seen Marie Robinson's face when I explained things to her and got her to accept the money."

She met her sister's level gaze. "If we can help people like that, then it's worth putting our time into this club."

Angela lifted the pump handle and began to pump. "I hope you don't change your mind again next week."

"I won't."

Angela merely looked at her before turning back to her task.

A few days ago, Espy had spoken to Will and Henry and badgered them into coming, so she knew she wouldn't be alone.

When Espy walked out of the house after the supper dishes

were done, Angela joined her without a word.

Espy felt better than she had in a long time. She glanced down herself, confident of her appearance. She'd taken special care this evening. She wore a white blouse with a tiny pattern of lavender and blue flowers and a dark blue serge skirt. The blouse was still relatively new. She'd tied a blue ribbon at the collar. Her hair was swept up in a neat coil under a straw bonnet with a wreath of small flowers at the base of its crown.

She felt clean and hoped the walk to town with the sun still high on the horizon wouldn't wilt her appearance. Angela looked pretty, too, in her pink calico dress and bonnet with pink ribbon.

By the time they arrived at the church, the clock on its steeple showed her they were five minutes late. She quickened her pace. "Come on."

She heard voices coming up the basement stairs, telling her others were already there. Moistening her lips, she picked up the hem of her skirt and made her way down.

The voices gradually stilled, the members all standing around looking their way.

"Good evening," she said. Finally, she dared meet Warren's gaze.

He was staring at her as if he had never seen her before. The moment her eyes met his, he snapped to attention. "Good evening." He looked quickly away from her to Angela. "Come on in and have a seat. We were just getting ready to call the meeting to order."

Turning away from them, he motioned for the others to take their places around the table. Dexter grinned, giving her a small salute. Christina and Mabel ignored her and took their seats. Annalise and Emily smiled. There was no sign of any of Espy's acquaintances who had helped out at the Fourth.

Her shoulders slumped. It was going to be a long evening. She and Angela took chairs at the far end of the table.

Will and Henry came clomping down the stairs a few minutes after Warren had prayed to open the meeting while James was reading the Scripture for the evening. Espy smiled widely, relief filling her, and motioned to the empty chairs near her.

"Are we late?" Will asked in a loud voice.

Christina looked pointedly at her silver watch.

"A little," Warren said. "Have a seat and we'll continue. Glad you could make it." His gaze traveled over Espy as he spoke and she felt the irony of his words.

Does he think Will and Henry only come because of me? Fuming, she looked down at the knuckles of her clasped hands, refusing to acknowledge the truth of the fact.

• • •

When the meeting was adjourned, Will got up and stretched, yawning audibly. "Wanna go out for an ice cream, ladies?"

Espy and Angela looked at each other. "I don't know . . . we have an early morning tomorrow."

"As we all do. If there hadn't been so much jawing, we could've been out of here by now. Come on, let's walk outside and not waste the entire evening."

Espy looked toward Warren, but he was talking with Christina and James. To her surprise, however, Annalise approached her. "I'm so glad you two could come tonight." Her cheeks filling with color, she hastily added Will and Henry in her glance before looking away quickly.

Espy returned her smile with a warm one of her own. "Thank you." On impulse she said, "Would you like to come and have an ice cream with us?" She tossed her head at Will. "Will's treat."

Ignoring the surprise on Will's freckled face, she hastened to add, "You can tell your brother that we'll see you home." There, it should be clear that he wasn't included in the invitation.

"I . . . don't know." She looked torn but then with a slight

192

squaring of her shoulders, she nodded. "Very well, thank you. Please excuse me a moment."

"Sure. We'll be right here."

"Now, why'd you have to go invite her?" Will bent down to whisper.

Espy swatted him away. "Be still. It'll be fun. She's a nice girl."

"When she ever brings herself to say more than two words."

Espy ignored him, more interested in watching Annalise approach Warren. With a motion and apologetic smile to Christina who was still talking to him, he bent his head toward his sister, attentive immediately to her. His smile faded as he listened to her, and his glance went to Espy's group.

Espy lifted her chin a fraction and then deliberately looked away. "So, Henry, what have you been up to these days?"

As Henry reddened and stuttered out an answer, Espy fixed a smile on her face, keeping her profile to Warren.

A moment later, Annalise returned. "Very well, I'm ready whenever you are."

"What are we waiting for then? Let's skedaddle," Will said.

Espy took Annalise's arm in hers and hooked her other through Will's, refusing to look toward Warren though her mind imagined him escorting Christina home under the elm trees.

* * *

Warren couldn't help being concerned as he watched his sister depart the church with Espy. He didn't really know Will and Henry. His common sense told him not much could happen with three ladies in tow. Annalise had a good head on her shoulders and Angela would brook no nonsense. It was only to the ice-cream parlor on Main Street. But he couldn't help thinking of Espy's abandon the night of the fireworks.

"Are you listening, Warren?"

193

"Yes, of course." He forced a smile at Christina even though he had no idea what she'd been saying.

"So, will I expect you tomorrow evening?"

"Let me make sure with Mother and Father that there's nothing else going on. Mother usually has something planned."

"I told you, I already spoke to them. They said you and Annalise are free to come to my house. Brian is playing piano. You know he's just come from the conservatory in Boston."

"Yes, I remember." An evening in a warm parlor, sitting on straight-backed chairs, listening to long piano pieces.

He imagined going with the group to the ice-cream parlor. Laughter and spontaneity. But Espy had hardly looked at him the whole evening and went off laughing and flirting—he frowned at the inappropriate behavior—with her friends. He should be grateful that she had left him alone since the evening of the Fourth.

That evening. That confounded, disgraceful, ignominious evening. He couldn't reproach himself enough for his lack of control.

"Warren, are you ready to go?"

He started again at Christina's insistent tone. "Yes. Yes," he repeated more firmly. "Let's go."

He listened to Christina's conversation as they walked through town, offering monosyllabic replies at the appropriate intervals, smiling at passersby.

His mind was occupied by what was going on at the ice-cream parlor, telling himself his concern was for his sister.

When they passed in front of it, Warren's steps slowed. Espy and her group were seated around a small round table at one end of the shop. A couple of other young men had joined them, people he recognized from around town. It seemed that wherever Espy was, young men were sure to follow.

His mood soured as he witnessed each smiling and laughing face. Even his sister appeared more animated than usual.

The words from "Mary Had a Little Lamb" danced around in his head as he watched Espy's vivacious personality at work. Clearly, she was over whatever she'd felt for him. If any other woman had responded to his kiss the way Espy had that night, Warren would've been convinced she was madly in love with him.

Even Christina. Even Espy's sister. No young woman of his acquaintance would take such an act lightly.

No one but Espy. There she sat flirting with every Tom, Dick, and Harry.

When they finally arrived at Christina's front door, it opened as if someone had been on the lookout for them.

"Look who's here," Christina's father said with a chuckle, extending his hand, "our favorite gentleman caller." He turned to his wife, who stood slightly behind him. "Isn't that so, dear?"

"My, yes. Hello there, Warren. Did you two have a nice evening?"

Warren shook hands, replying to Christina's mother's question as Mr. Farnsworth's words echoed in his ears.

As he continued alone to his own house, he sobered. If he wasn't careful, her parents would soon expect a declaration from him. He'd only been back a few months and already he felt as if both sets of parents assumed he and Christina would marry.

How had it come about? Just because Christina was over at his house for dinner, or he had been invited to some function at her parents', suddenly they were paired together.

They hadn't been close during his years away. There had been no correspondence or special feelings on either side. Yet he felt as if Christina had taken possession of him from the moment she'd seen him the day after his return.

The way she'd fixed her gaze on him before her parents appeared at the door, he felt as if all he'd had to do was lean down and kiss her. He could swear he'd felt the pull of her desire.

There was no answering pull, no overpowering force. He'd felt only relief that her parents had opened the door. Until Mr.

Farnsworth's remark, *our favorite gentleman caller.*

Warren rubbed a hand across his chin. Why didn't he want Christina? It would make life so much easier. He opened his gate and latched it shut behind him, his thoughts intent on the conundrum of his life. Instead of walking to the door, he skirted around the side of the house and took the garden path down to the small dock on the river.

A half-moon illumined the flat expanse of water. The family's pleasure skiff lay moored, the water lapping softly against its sides.

Why did the thought of marrying Christina only make him feel like a man being shackled? Almost all of his friends were married or pursuing a particular young lady, with their thoughts on settling down.

Warren's thoughts turned to the young lady who had turned down his offer of marriage. For the first time, he felt no sadness or regret. He felt . . . nothing at all but a pleasant—and somewhat embarrassing—recollection of an earlier time.

He turned the notion over in his mind, too amazed at the novelty of it.

As he gazed across the river to the dim view of white farmhouses and dark silhouette of forest, Espy's laughing face appeared.

But what he felt for Espy was nothing like what he'd felt for Charity. Those feelings had been sacred; he'd held her in such high regard and respect.

He swallowed. What he felt for Espy . . . that wasn't love. The Bible called it by an ugly name. Lust.

The single syllable reverberated in his mind, continuing to taint the kiss he'd shared with her.

No matter what she might permit other young men, she didn't deserve his disrespect. He had no right to take from a woman what he wasn't willing to offer his name and protection for.

He should just ask Christina for her hand and make everyone happy, he concluded. Just do what his father wished at work. In twenty years, he'd be where his father was . . . perhaps. With two children, a lovely home, a socially prominent wife.

The picture gave him no joy. He dropped his chin. *Dear God, show me what to do.*

15

Espy knocked softly on Mr. Stockton's library door. Half of her always hoped he wouldn't answer. Since that afternoon when it had rained, she felt self-conscious in his presence even though he'd been nothing but kind and respectful to her in the intervening time. She'd almost been able to dismiss the memory from her mind during those times she spent with him discussing books and history.

"Come in."

Espy started and pushed open the door.

"Ah, Espy, ready for your lesson?"

"Yes, sir." She held up her book.

"Have a seat."

She closed the door softly behind her and advanced toward his desk. His chair creaked as he sat back in it, raising his arms and lacing his fingers behind his head. "So, Espy, how is life treating you?"

"Excuse me, sir?"

His gray-blue eyes crinkled at the corners as he regarded her. "What do you do when you're not working here?"

Reassured by the simple meaning of his question, she took her seat and smoothed her skirt as she thought of what to say. "Oh—well—I've been doing the reading assignments."

He seemed to be waiting for her to add something, so she cast about in her mind for which of her many activities would interest a man of his stature. "I help take care of my younger brothers and sisters."

"You come from a big family, don't you, Espy?"

He seemed to enjoy saying her name, pronouncing each syllable distinctly. She nodded.

"You're a good daughter."

"Well, my sister Angela does a lot as well. Hortensia, the next oldest, is taking on more, too." She took a deep breath. "I've also been busy with the new young people's group at church, the Holliston Lights."

"That's the group Warren Brentwood heads up, isn't it?"

She blinked. "Yes."

"A fine young man. I remember him at the academy." A reminiscent look entered Mr. Stockton's eyes as he gazed beyond her. "Always ready with the answer when called upon, and it wasn't just rote memory. He was thoughtful with his replies, as if he'd taken the time to look beyond the surface answer. Those are the kinds of students that make a teacher's day." His eyes focused on her once again. "You're one of those students—a teacher's dream."

Her cheeks flushed again. "Th-thank you, sir."

"I knew Warren would go places." He chuckled. "Of course, it doesn't hurt that his father is so prominent in the community. But plenty of successful men produce children who are not driven to succeed. Wastrels, sons who only want to spend their fathers' money, but not Warren." He nodded. "A hard worker, a chip off the old block like his father. Though I don't see that streak of ruthlessness in him that I see in his father."

Espy frowned at this remark.

"Did I shock you with my words? Don't worry, it's nothing

that's not generally known. Mr. Brentwood Senior would probably be the first to agree with my assessment of his character."

"I haven't ever met him personally."

Mr. Stockton regarded her until she felt herself blush once more under his scrutiny. "No, I daresay you haven't. His loss, my dear."

The moment drew out until Espy had to clasp her hands tightly to keep from touching her face or hair to make sure nothing was out of place.

As if sensing her embarrassment, Mr. Stockton looked away. "Literature is full of such ruthless individuals who appear on the surface as leaders of their community. Machiavelli was one of the first to write about them, though of course he was describing a prince, not a businessman. But in the end it comes to the same thing: power."

Espy found it hard to follow him and pretended to listen intently.

As if realizing he was going beyond her, he smiled. "Enough of that for today. We shall eventually read some excerpts from *The Prince,* but for today, let me go over the paper you wrote me last." He moved her scribbled sheets forward on his desk. She could see he had marked it up quite a bit with his fountain pen. "Now then, your impressions of Daisy among the Italians. You defend her actions."

He leaned toward her, the paper between them.

"Yes, sir. I think she was just being herself." She took the essay from him and sought for something she'd written and read it aloud to him.

As the two continued discussing her opinion of Henry James's work, Espy grew more comfortable. She enjoyed their lessons, only feeling out of her depth when he went into other areas. She sensed more behind his words but wasn't sophisticated enough to discern what.

He sat back in his chair, sending it creaking again. "I think that's enough literature for today."

Espy looked at the clock above his desk. "Goodness, I didn't realize it was so late." An hour and a half had passed.

"No one ever does when in the throes of a good discussion." He shuffled the papers on his desk into a neat pile, his voice becoming businesslike. "Now, I want you to write me another list of words that you've never heard before and use the lexicon to look them up and learn their meaning. Use each in a sentence."

"Yes, sir." She felt encouraged by the way her vocabulary was growing.

Mr. Stockton stood. "Come, my dear, let us look at the bookshelves for some further reading material."

She picked up her satchel and followed him, trying to ignore his use of "my dear." *It is just the way he talks to everyone*, she told herself, trying to remember if she'd heard him say it to anyone else.

She hurried to his side, where he was running his fingers over the spines of the books. He drew out a slim volume and flipped through a few pages. The crisp sound of the paper reverberated in the still room. "Shall I compare thee to a summer's day?" He smiled into her eyes. "Thou art more lovely and more temperate."

Taken aback at the words at first, she then smiled, realizing they were poetry. "Who wrote that?"

"The Bard. Shakespeare," he added. "Take this home and read some of his sonnets. Then write me your thoughts on what he says of beauty."

She reached for the book. To read Shakespeare! It was the first time Mr. Stockton had given her something of the great poet to read. She felt as if she was advancing.

The moment she touched the smooth, marbled cover of the book, his hand covered hers.

A chill went down her arm. His hand felt warm. She raised her eyes to him, wondering what he meant.

His gray-blue eyes were fixed on hers. "Espy." The single word was a breath on his lips. Before she could react, his hand slid up her arm, wrapping around her upper arm and drawing her toward him.

"Mr. Stockton—" She tried to push away but he held her fast. The next second his lips were on hers.

Dear God, don't let this be happening. Her throat closed at the faint scent of tobacco on his breath.

The click of the door came to her as if from far away. "What on earth!"

At the sound of his wife's shocked exclamation, Mr. Stockton's hand dropped from Espy's arm. He stepped back from her and turned to his wife. "Nothing, my dear, nothing at all. I was just lending Espy a book."

Mrs. Stockton was obscured from Espy's view by Mr. Stockton's back, but Espy heard the sound of her footsteps approaching. The next instant the lady stood in front of Espy. Espy wished she could throw her apron over her head from the shame she felt. *What must the poor woman think!*

Mrs. Stockton pointed to the door. "Get out of my house."

When Espy hesitated, she raised her voice. "Now!"

Espy's glance went to Mr. Stockton, seeking help. But the professor said nothing. A look of sympathy or sadness flickered in his eyes, and he gave a small shake of his head.

Espy turned back to his wife. "Mrs. Stockton—I'm sorry—I did n—"

The woman turned to her husband. "Get her out of here."

"Of course, my dear." Mr. Stockton held his hand out to Espy. "Come, Espy, my wife is understandably upset. It's best if you left now." Unlike a moment before when his eyes were looking so raptly into hers, now he seemed to be looking somewhere lower. He didn't touch her but motioned with an arm toward the door.

Espy scurried toward the exit, wanting only to escape the house.

Mr. Stockton's soft footfalls sounded behind her. Not wanting to go all the way to the kitchen, she headed straight for the front door, which she rarely used.

"Allow me." Mr. Stockton's hand closed over the doorknob and she backed away before her own touched his. But he merely held it open for her.

Before she was able to step across the threshold, he spoke. "I'm sorry, my dear. Mrs. Stockton is a bit quick to react. I shall explain everything. You'll see. It will be all right."

His soothing tones only deepened her shame and revulsion. Why hadn't he immediately explained things to his wife? She stepped over the threshold but looked at him over her shoulder. "You can tell Mrs. Stockton I'm not coming back."

Before he could say anything, she hurried down the steps, breaking into a run before she reached the gate.

She fumbled with it. Finally, she was out in the street. She didn't dare look back.

It was only when she reached the sound of the rushing waters at the rapids that she was able to think more clearly.

Winded, Espy slowed, daring a look over her shoulder. But she was long past the Stocktons' house. Her gaze went to Warren's house.

Her cheeks turned crimson. She drew a hand up to her mouth and scrubbed at it.

Dear Lord, she cried, *how could Mr. Stockton do such a thing? Why?*

Of course, she knew there were a lot of bad men in the world. But not the professor.

She emerged from the covered bridge, the noise of the mills increasing, the sound of the saws competing with the rushing waters beneath. Averting her gaze from those of any passersby, she hurried along.

She glanced at the mill.

Her face heated once more, comparing Warren's kiss to the professor's. Her fingers went to her lips, remembering how Warren's fervor hadn't scared her or repulsed her, but made her understand the madness that caused women to run away with unsuitable men, the way her mother had done with her father.

Madness, and yet a madness that felt so right in the heat of the moment, compared to . . . the other. When a man kissed an unwilling woman, it was disgusting, revolting, and more—

It felt like a violation of something sacred.

A whiff of tobacco smoke from a loitering man puffing on a pipe brought the scent of the professor to Espy afresh. The feel of his soggy lips, the coarse feeling of the surrounding skin against hers.

Her gorge rose.

Clutching her throat, she picked up her pace, wanting to break into a run. Her satchel bumped her hip, reminding her of her lessons with the professor.

Pushing down any regrets, she tightened her hold on the strap of the satchel, glad she had left nothing behind at the professor's. She never wanted to step foot in that house again.

Thankfully she didn't have any of Mr. Stockton's books, since she'd returned the last ones she'd taken. The slim volume of Shakespeare's sonnets had fallen when the professor let her go. She remembered the thud of the book on the floor beside her.

Now she hoped she never read Shakespeare. It would forever remind her of this horrible moment.

She breathed a sigh of relief when she finally left town and was on the dirt track leading to her neighborhood.

Only then did she realize she was out of a job.

With both Alvaro and Angela working now, they no longer depended on Espy's income the way they used to, but neither could Espy just sit around home.

She'd have to return to the cannery.

• • •

Warren stepped into his father's office at the back of the bank building. His father had been one of the driving forces behind the establishment of the first bank in Holliston. It was scarcely a decade old, but already had weathered more than one panic that had finished other banks in the state.

His father smiled and waved him over. "Hello, Son, come in."

Warren took the leather upholstered chair in front of his father's massive oak desk. "Hello, Father." He set down the portfolio of papers he'd brought with him. The bank was only a few blocks from the mill, yet it seemed another world from its noise and activity.

Here, everyone spoke in hushed tones, and everything smelled of leather and polished wood as if the accumulation and lending of money were holy.

Warren cleared his throat, knowing how much his father hated wasted time. "I brought the information on the sulfite pulping and the groundwood grinders for making pulpwood. I've studied some of the information on the two types of processes that some of the mills in other parts of the state have started to use in the last several years."

A look of displeasure marred his father's features. "I told you I'm not interested."

"But I thought if you saw the tonnage some of these other mills south of us are producing, you'd see the way we could profit with what is scrap wood to begin with."

His father dismissed his words with a wave of his hand. "I made it clear to you I didn't want you to pursue this. We're a lumber mill. That has been and continues to be our business."

"But the lumber business is going west. We have the best wood —fir and spruce—to produce cheap paper. If we change now, we stand to expand in the coming years instead of contract."

Before his father could voice another objection, Warren pushed

205

the papers forward. "I just want you to look over the information. I thought I'd bring it here to the bank where you can consult with others involved in finance—"

"Consult with others? Are you daft? Let the competition have an inkling of what's going through your mind?" He shook his head. "Not in a million years. They'll think we're losing money."

Warren reined in his irritation, leaning forward and opening up the portfolio to extract the relevant documents. "Building a pulp mill will require some investment of capital and we may need to borrow from the bank.

"I've shown our earnings over the last five years and compared it to what I've been able to amass on the volume of pulp down the coast."

His father stood, his face tinged with the ruddy color from when he was close to losing his temper. Warren, too, rose to his feet, refusing to be cowed. His gaze didn't waver from his father's.

"I told you, Son, I am not interested. Now, I consider this discussion over. I have work to do and so do you."

Without a word Warren closed the portfolio. Hesitating only a few seconds, he debated whether to leave it on his father's desk, but he decided to take it with him. With his father in his present state of mind, he could destroy the entire thing. It had taken Warren too many hours to assemble the information.

Swallowing his own annoyance and frustration, he nodded briefly. "Good day, Father."

The rest of the afternoon only further discouraged him. Two men were out sick, a conveyor belt broke down, and a new part had to be ordered from Bangor since the smith was not able to repair it. Alvaro arrived late for the second time that week, Hodgdon told him, and would have been fired if Warren hadn't intervened—again.

By the time Warren arrived home, he was tired, hot, and out of sorts.

"Good afternoon, Mr. Brentwood. Your mother says to join them on the terrace when you have freshened up."

"Thank you, Samuel. Is Father home yet?"

"Yes, sir. He is already on the terrace."

Warren climbed the stairs slowly to his room, not yet ready to face his father again. His father never discussed business with his mother and sister present, but after dinner, he'd probably want to know about the mill.

Pastor Curtis's counsel came back to him. *What do I want? What does God want of me? Shall I abandon all my father has prepared me for? Is it just frustration because Father isn't ready to change his ways? Give him time,* Warren told himself.

Or, were they more, these feelings of frustration and purpose-lessness?

With an impatient shake of his head, he turned away from the glass. It was easier to push these kinds of thoughts aside, bury them for now, and immerse himself in all the activities of his life.

Beginning with going downstairs and being friendly and so-ciable to his mother and sister. His heart sank, remembering their dinner engagement at the Farnsworths'.

He went out to the terrace, a smile on his lips. "Hello there." He bent down and gave his mother a light kiss on the cheek.

"At last," she replied with a smile. "You didn't forget dinner at Christina's, did you? I wouldn't want us to be late."

"No, I did not forget." *With everyone reminding me, it would have been nigh impossible,* he added to himself.

His father lowered his paper and nodded.

"Come, have a seat," his mother said. "You have time for a drink if you'd like. Your father has already ordered the carriage."

"I'll just have a lemonade," he told Samuel with a smile and then sat down next to Annalise on the swing. "Did you have a nice time the other night?" He hadn't had a chance to ask his sister about her evening at the ice-cream parlor.

Her face brightened. "It was lovely. They're all so nice."

He pictured Espy laughing with her friends. "We walked by and saw you. You all seemed to be having a good time."

Her smile deepened. "That Will is so funny. He kept us in stitches."

Their mother frowned. "Who's this?"

Warren answered for his sister. "When the church meeting adjourned, some of the members invited Annalise to the ice-cream parlor."

Their mother's mouth relaxed in a smile. "How nice. Who was with you, dear, James and Dexter?"

A short silence followed. But Annalise spoke before Warren could think how to word an answer. "I was with Espy and her sister and their friends Harry and Will. They're all very pleasant," she added quickly.

Her mother's smile disappeared into a straight-lipped look. "Are they?" Her gaze fell on Warren. "I'm surprised you left your sister alone in such company."

"Mother, they are all members of our church group. I see no reason to be overly concerned if they decided to stop at the ice-cream parlor on their way home." He glanced at Annalise.

An uneasy silence descended. Warren was going to add something more in his sister's defense when his mother said, "I don't want you near *that* girl anymore."

As they stared at their mother, her lips turned downward. "I heard a most disturbing story about her today."

Warren's gut clenched, ready to discount whatever his mother said.

"Who's that?" his father asked from behind his newspaper.

"That half-Portuguese girl, the one Mrs. Stockton hired as a maid-of-all-work. You remember my telling you."

His father merely grunted, his interest having waned as soon as his mother had mentioned a female name.

"I saw Mrs. Tyson today, who told me the most shocking thing."

Warren's fingers tensed around his glass. What had Espy done now?

"Mrs. Tyson heard it directly from Mrs. Stockton herself, so this is not idle gossip. The professor's wife was in tears."

She lowered her voice with a quick glance at Annalise. "It seems she caught Espy making advances to her husband."

"That's ridiculous!"

They all looked at Warren. Embarrassed at his sudden outburst, he lifted his chin. "I don't believe it."

"I don't think Mrs. Stockton would say something of this nature it if it weren't true. Goodness, Warren, it's a shameful thing to have to tell anyone."

"There must have been some misunderstanding." He couldn't imagine how anyone could make such an accusation. Mr. Stockton, his old history teacher, was a man of impeccable reputation. What could Espy have done to have Mrs. Stockton draw such an erroneous conclusion?

His mother sniffed. "Mrs. Stockton caught the girl in her husband's arms!"

The blood seemed to slow in his veins and his mother's voice receded to some faraway point as Warren continued staring at her, the drumming in his ears drowning out everything else.

There had to be some mistake. He relaxed his hold on his glass and forced himself to sit back. Espy was a vivacious person and every time she spoke of Mr. Stockton it was with the utmost admiration and respect. Perhaps there was a bit of hero worship. Mrs. Stockton must have misinterpreted what she saw.

"What did Mrs. Stockton do?" Warren's father snapped out.

"Dismissed her, of course." Warren's mother flicked at something on her skirt, the movement giving substance to her words.

"How awful," whispered Annalise. "There must be some mistake. She seems so nice."

"Annalise, dear, you little understand such women. They appear nice but are vipers."

"So, she's out of a job," Warren said, thinking about the implications for Espy.

"You can't expect Mrs. Stockton to condone such behavior. The reason she spoke to Mrs. Tyson, she said, was to make certain no one else hires her. She was adamant on that point."

Warren set down his glass and stood. "I still think there must be some mistake."

"You seem to be quite certain of what took place." His father's eyes pierced his.

"I've known Espy since she was in grammar school."

"But you haven't known her since she grew up."

"No, but—"

"I've seen the girl." His father addressed Warren's mother now. "I wouldn't put it past that type."

"What 'type' is that, Father?"

"No need to use that tone with me, my boy. You've traveled. You've been in enough ports to know there are two kinds of women. Your mother and sister—and Christina—are one type. This *Espy* as you call her is another. I'm not saying she committed a crime, but maybe she flirted with the man. A man is only human."

A vision of embracing Espy rose in his mind, but it was overlaid by Mr. Stockton replacing him. Warren had to face away from his family. "I hardly think she'd flirt with her employer's husband, not when she's there to clean the house."

"Well, I'm thinking she's not the kind of woman you want to be found in company with too often. Perhaps you should ask her to step down from that church committee."

Warren sensed his father waiting for his reply. "I will do nothing until I've spoken to her."

"Just make sure you aren't seen to give her too much of your

210

attention." His father thumped the arm of the wicker rocker. "Stick with Christina and you'll be all right. You don't want to set tongues wagging."

"Your father's right. I haven't wanted to say anything, but I have been concerned with the time you've spent with that woman. People have seen the two of you together."

Warren felt the prickles of fear rise along his arms. No one could have seen the two of them that night. It had been pitch black in the woods.

His father rose from the chair. "There's no harm done yet." He thumped Warren's back, coming to stand by him. "We're just warning you to distance yourself from a bad apple. Evil companions corrupt. Now, we'd better be getting along to the Farnsworths'. At least you have no worries spending time in Christina's company."

Warren said nothing, his mind fixed on his father's words. *There's no harm done yet.*

Wasn't there?

If something had occurred between Mr. Stockton and Espy, had Warren's behavior been any better?

16

Espy had no trouble securing her old job back at the cannery. She'd told her mother and Angela that Mrs. Stockton hadn't been pleased with her work.

"She doesn't deserve your work!" Angela said immediately. "You're better off in the cannery!" Her mother shook out her apron. "Good riddance to her."

Afterward Angela asked her what had happened. They were both sitting on the bed they shared, each one in her nightgown, a shawl around their shoulders. The younger ones were finally asleep.

Swearing her to secrecy, Espy told her the full story in a low tone.

Angela's hand flew to her mouth. "Not Mr. Stockton! I can't believe it."

Espy nodded, clasping her knees with her hands. "I couldn't either. That's why I didn't move. I was too shocked. Then Mrs. Stockton came in, so of course it looked like I was kissing him. But I wasn't, I swear it." She beseeched her sister with her eyes.

"I believe you." She shuddered. "I can't imagine anyone kissing him. He's such an old man. And a married one."

"He's not so old but certainly too old for us. And goodness, he's married, as you say, and he's my teacher. I would never do such a thing."

After they'd gone to bed, Espy lay staring at the steeply pitched roof. Back to the cannery. She dreaded the notion. Would she ever live down the shame? What would she do if she ran into Mr. or Mrs. Stockton on the street? How could she hold her head up, even knowing she wasn't at fault, when Mrs. Stockton had every right to be angry?

She hoped Mr. Stockton had told his wife the truth. Would Mrs. Stockton come beg her pardon? Of course, she could never offer her her job back, but just to know Mrs. Stockton didn't judge her, that would mean so much.

Espy tossed and turned, reliving that awful moment and wondering what was to come. *Dear Lord,* she prayed, *show Mrs. Stockton the truth. Please don't let her judge me so harshly. Please help me.*

As the hours passed at the cannery, her spirits fell. By the end of her shift, her legs felt shaky from standing all day. Nothing but days at the cannery to look forward to from now on, she thought, dragging her feet as she and Angela made their way home.

Would she ever catch a glimpse of Warren? What was he doing? Did he ever think of that night in the woods?

Would she see him at the Holliston Lights meeting or on Sunday? Would they all know she'd been fired from her job? And the reason why? She shuddered, wishing sometimes that she could just run away and hide.

• • •

Espy had to endure some joshing from her old companions on the cannery line. "You finally realized that factory work was preferable to cleaning." But after the first few days, it seemed as if she'd never been away.

She hadn't been able to avoid Elm Street, but since she and her

213

sister walked it in the predawn hours and then in mid-afternoon, when the streets were quiet, she'd been able to avoid the Stocktons. She had not caught a glimpse of Warren either, a fact that left her in a quandary.

Part of her longed to see him, the other was terrified.

By Sunday, she was anxious to see him in church even if only at a distance. As usual, she squeezed into the back pew.

The hymns and message were a solace, making her feel that God saw her secret pain and would comfort her and make things right someday. But that someday loomed far in the distance. For now, there was only drudgery and work.

It wasn't until after church as they waited for people to make their way from the church that she sensed anything wrong. Henry and Will joined them. But no one else from the Holliston Lights greeted her. They walked right past her as if she were invisible.

But they nodded to Angela, Harry, and Will although they walked right by without lingering.

She craned her neck, searching for Warren. As she did so, Mrs. Hawkins walked near her. The glare in her eyes caused Espy to stagger back. "Wicked girl!" she hissed so that only Espy and Angela could hear the words before she walked past her.

Espy felt faint. Angela grasped her hand.

Espy looked at her sister. "What did she mean by that?"

Angela shook her head.

"Could she know?" she whispered.

"I don't see how." Her sister looked at all the people around her. "I haven't seen Mrs. Stockton—oh, there she is." Her sister's voice dropped. "Oh, dear, should we leave?"

Espy followed her sister's gaze, her heart thumping with dread. Across the churchyard stood Mrs. Stockton and her husband. As if sensing her look, he looked toward her. Espy quickly averted her gaze.

"I'm not going to run away," she said barely audibly. But it took all her courage to remain where she was.

How she wished Warren would come up to her now and smile and stand as a buffer between her and the professor.

Instead, a couple whom Espy recognized as a prominent family from Elm Street walked by her. The woman gave her one look and turned away with a sniff.

She knew! She had to.

Espy's eyes flashed back to Mrs. Stockton. She must have told someone, and the news had spread. Espy's gaze traveled around the churchyard. How many others knew?

It doesn't seem as if Mr. Stockton managed to convince his wife of the truth. Or, had he told her at all?

She sneaked another peek toward him. He was smiling and chatting with a couple from church, as if he didn't have a care in the world.

The bile rose in her throat, bitterness filling her.

Then suddenly she saw Warren. The next second, her heartbeat thumped in her chest. She hadn't seen him since the club meeting —*before* all the ugliness with the Stocktons. If Warren should know. The thought horrified her.

Instead, she straightened her shoulders, fixing a smile on her face, and waited. Of course he would say "good morning" to her.

He leaned his head toward Christina, listening to what she was saying. Then his gaze roamed over the people congregating in the churchyard. Smiling, nodding, his attention didn't stay on any individual for too long.

Was he looking for her?

She took in a deep breath, in an effort to steady her pulse. "Angela," she whispered out of the side of her mouth, "see him?"

"Who?"

"Him."

"Who?" Her sister's voice became more insistent.

"Warren."

"Oh. So?"

"Do you think he's coming to say hello?"

Her sister considered. "I don't know. Looks like a lot of people want to say hello to him, but that's nothing unusual."

"Should we go up to him?"

"You mean 'them.'"

"Yes, of course." Besides Christina, Annalise was at his side, his parents not far off.

"I don't know. It seems kind of forward. If a gentleman wants to say hello to a lady, then he will."

Espy bit her lip. Her sister was right.

"Espy, how long are we going to have to stay?" Gus tugged on her arm.

She smiled down at him. "We're going right now." With a sigh, she turned to Angela. "Come on, we best—"

Feeling someone near her, she looked up and drew in her breath.

Warren was standing in front of her. Color flooded her cheeks.

"Good morning, Espy, Angela." With a quick nod at her sister, his intent regard came once more to her.

The first thing she realized was his lack of a smile. Her own joy diminished immediately. "Hello, Warren." Christina was no longer hanging on his arm, but Annalise was still beside him. "Hello, Annalise."

Annalise smiled at her, although Espy sensed something—a wariness or caution—in her gaze. "Hello, Espy. You're looking very pretty." Then her pale cheeks suffused with color as if she'd said the wrong thing and she looked downward.

Espy gazed down at herself. "Oh—thank you." She had dressed with care that morning, although surely Annalise had seen the dress before, since it was one of only two Sunday outfits.

"I'd like to talk to you."

216

Warren's tone was low but penetrating. There was something imperious in it. She tilted her chin up. "Is that so?"

His nod was clipped. "Yes. Are you free this afternoon?"

Had he heard something? Dread filled her. Deciding she needed to talk to him as well, she said, "Yes."

"I'll stop by around three." Without giving her time to agree or object, he gave another curt nod to each of them. "Good day then."

He propelled his sister away. Annalise turned back with an apologetic smile. "Nice to see you, Espy."

"Nice to see you, too," she said automatically, her mind grappling with Warren's words. She strove to remember each one, his look and tone in the brief time he'd stood in front of her.

"Well."

Espy glanced at her sister to see what she would offer.

Her sister's brown eyes stared into hers. "Wonder what bee's gotten into his bonnet."

Espy hadn't imagined the high-handedness in Warren's tone.

"It sounded like whatever it is he wants to talk to you about can't wait."

"Do you think—?" Espy let the question hang between them, too afraid of voicing what she most feared.

Angela lifted her brows in a sign of uncertainty. "You won't know till this afternoon."

●   ●   ●

Warren left the house at a quarter to three, telling his parents he was going for a walk. As he turned onto Elm Street, he let out a breath. Making conversation and pretending everything was all right when all he wanted to do was run to Espy's house and demand to hear what had happened had been a strain.

As he took long strides down the sun-dappled dusty road, he pictured her this morning in church. She'd seemed unchanged—

217

her dark hair swept up in a pretty arrangement. How could she stand there when everyone in church was gossiping about her behavior?

He'd wanted to shake her and demand some answers, but he could only greet her, knowing his parents were watching the exchange.

At three o'clock, he arrived on Espy's lane. As usual, barefoot children played on it, their shouts filling the hot air.

"Hey, Mr. Brentwood!" one boy yelled and waved at him. He recognized him as Espy's younger brother.

He returned the wave. "Hello, Gus." Two older brothers joined the boy.

Alicia skipped to his side.

Suddenly he wished he had something to offer them, but he hadn't thought to bring anything, his thoughts too focused on his purpose.

As he brought his glance toward Espy's house, he drew in his breath as if gearing for battle. At that moment the front door opened and she emerged, a parasol in one hand. She gave him a brief look before shutting the door behind her and making her way down the rickety wooden steps.

She didn't meet his gaze as she walked down the path and onto the street, where she opened the yellow parasol.

"Hello," he said as he approached her.

Her umber eyes looked into his. She moistened her lips and he felt his stomach contract.

"Hello, Warren."

He indicated the lane with his hand. "Shall we?"

With a brief nod, she walked beside him.

A second later, her brothers and sister ringed them. "Where you going, Espy? Can we come with you?"

She stopped. "No, all of you stay here and continue playing. Josiah, take care of Alicia. I'll be right back."

"Aw, why can't we come, too? Are you going to eat something?"

"No," Warren answered. He didn't plan on going into town—not where they could be seen. "I'll bring you something though." Hoping he'd be able to keep his promise, not knowing if he'd be back, he smiled in reassurance.

Finally, the children turned back and left the two alone.

"Where are we going?"

"Uh—I thought we'd just walk a little ways . . . somewhere where we can talk . . . without being disturbed, that is." Memory of the dark forest rose to his mind.

But she led him past that footpath and continued down the dirt track until they came to a shady area near the forest.

The warm scent of balsam and spruce permeated the air.

She looked at him expectantly, her parasol a shock of color amidst the green backdrop. "What did you want to see me about?"

Realizing there was no pleasant way to bring up the topic uppermost in his mind, he cleared his throat. "Do you know what Mrs. Stockton is saying about you?"

Comprehension immediately filled her eyes, and his heart sank. So, there was some truth to the story.

When she said nothing, he continued. "It's a rather ugly accusation."

"She fired me over it, so I know."

"Espy, what did—why did you—" Not knowing how to say what he wanted, he reached out a hand, making a futile gesture.

She stepped back.

Did she think he was going to take advantage of her again? He took a step back himself, to make it clear there would be no repeat of that night.

"Why did I *what*?" Her tone was steady, her gaze never leaving his.

Irritation rose in his chest. She was making him feel as if he was the one accused of something when he was only there to get to the bottom of things. He raked a hand through his hair, looking at a red squirrel scamper up the white bark of a straight, slim paper birch. "Why did you do something to make Mrs. Stockton accuse you in such a way?"

When she didn't answer right away, he was finally forced to look at her. "Well?"

Once again, she moistened her lips. He clenched his hands and shoved them in his pockets, focusing instead on the image of her kissing Mr. Stockton.

She batted her inky lashes at him. "Maybe I couldn't help myself. But you'll believe whatever you want. There is no point in trying to convince you otherwise."

He wanted to take his hands out of his pockets and grip her shoulders and shake her. How could she behave like that? His jaw hurt from the pressure he exerted to keep himself in control.

Finally, trusting himself to talk, he said through lips that barely moved, "You would destroy a good man and someone's marriage for the sake of—of some flirtation!" His breathing sounded harsh through his nostrils.

She just lifted her chin. "I have nothing to defend."

Still unable to believe she could be so wanton, so unrepentant, he could no longer bear to look at her. Spinning on his heel, he left, wanting only to be away from her.

● ● ●

The forest was peaceful, only the scolding of a squirrel above her on a tree breaking the stillness. Espy had always loved the forest, thinking of it as her private place of refuge whenever there was chaos at home.

Now, its stillness offered her no solace as the shards of her heart fell. She hunched over in pain until she was kneeling on the path, unmindful of getting her best skirt dirty. Her forehead fell among the sharp, dry little needles, the balsam resin filling her nostrils.

Why did you do something. . . . You would destroy a good man and someone's marriage for the sake of—of some flirtation.

Warren's words played over and over in her mind, the hard look in his eyes accusing her before he'd even spoken a word.

Even this morning after church, he'd been cold and aloof, just wanting to see her alone so he could accuse her. Asking her what she'd *done*, the way a parent does to a child when getting ready to take the switch to him.

He'd never even considered that she might have done nothing, that it was all Mr. Stockton, that he was the one to accuse.

Her breath came rapidly, too rapidly, until she wasn't getting enough air into her lungs. She sat up, panic filling her. She was going to suffocate.

Please, God, help me, help me!

Her hands against her chest, she finally was able to draw in a draft of air. She fell back.

Then the tears came. They began slowly, filling her eyes until they rolled down her cheek. She lay on the ground, drawing her knees up to her chest, unable to stop the sobs that came up from somewhere deep inside her. Her body shook with grief. Worse than the pain she'd felt when Mrs. Stockton had accused her and ordered her to leave her house, worse than enduring the condemning looks of the churchgoers, Warren's censure was like a shaft piercing her core, ripping her heart asunder, irreparably damaging it.

• • •

If she thought things couldn't get any worse, she had underestimated Mrs. Stockton's fury.

She debated most of the week whether or not to attend the next meeting of the church club. But this time she decided she was not going to run and hide like a scared rabbit as she had the last time. No, she would stare down those like Christina who would likely look at her as if she were some flotsam washing against the dock pilings on the tide.

By Wednesday night, even Will and Henry had heard rumors. Their information was scant, but as soon as they joined her on Center Street, Will demanded, "What's this about being fired from the Stocktons' for some 'inappropriate conduct'?" He parroted the words as if he'd heard them verbatim from someone.

"Where'd you hear I was fired?"

"I was at Tupper's Dry Goods and I heard one o' those biddies from Elm Street talking to Mrs. Tupper. They glared at me as if I was interrupting their talk on purpose instead of putting a stop to their gossip."

When Espy said nothing but kept on walking, he caught up with her. "What's it all about? What happened? Was Mrs. Stockton jealous of you?"

She glanced at Will. At least someone believed in her. "No." She hesitated, finding it hard to say aloud what had really happened. She just wanted to forget about it, bury it somewhere. Even saying it in her thoughts made her feel dirty.

"Well?"

"It was . . . Mr. Stockton."

She could feel Will's eyes on her even though she kept her own gaze fixed on the sidewalk in front of her.

"You mean . . . he tried something?" Amazement filled his words.

Espy jerked her head up and down then tensed, expecting him to express his disbelief the way Warren had.

He whistled. "You're saying that old professor took liberties?"

"He . . . he tried to kiss me." There, she'd said it.

Both men stopped short on the street. Espy and Angela were forced to stop as well. "Please." She tugged on Will's arm. "I don't even want to think about it anymore."

Will's sandy brows drew together. "You want us to beat him up?"

"Goodness no! Come on, before we attract attention here."

Reluctantly, he allowed her to pull him along. "Really, Espy, it'd be easy. We'll just waylay him some evening on his way home from wherever he goes."

"Yeah, Espy, just say the word. Will and me here'll give him a couple of black eyes, maybe some cracked ribs." Henry put up his fists, feigning a punch, and snickered.

"Shut up, Henry. It's not funny. It's plenty serious," Will said sternly.

"Course it is," his friend asserted. "I'm just laughing picturing ol' Stockton limping to work, his eyes lookin' like raccoons, his ribcage bandaged up."

Will chuckled.

"It's no more than he deserves," put in Angela in a no-nonsense tone.

"That's right." Will patted her arm. "Don't you worry about a thing."

Espy stopped, putting her hands on her hips. "Now you listen to me good. I won't have you going and doing something foolish on my account. I'm back at the cannery and am just going to put this behind me. I don't want any more gossip about me." She glared at them, until she got a nod from each one.

"Good, now come along before we're late again." The last thing she needed was to make an entrance again. As it was, she'd have to endure enough of their scornful looks.

But even though she and her group were on time, the others still standing about the table talking with each other, they all stopped and stared when she entered the church basement.

Before she could decide what to do, Will strode forward. "What're you all starin' at?"

No one said anything.

Espy swallowed, her feet stuck to the ground as if held down with brass weights.

Christina folded her hands demurely in front of her. "We were just surprised to see Espy here, that's all."

"Why should that surprise you? She's a member, ain't she?"

"Her conduct has not represented that of a Christian trying to lead others to Christ, Will."

"Espy's just as good a Christian as any of you here—if not better!"

Warren cleared his throat. "Why don't we all take a seat? No one has decided anything nor said anything about Espy's Christian conduct. Perhaps that is something we can discuss as soon as the meeting is called to order."

They were going to sit and judge her as a group? The floor seemed to fall beneath her as a wave of dizziness overcame her. She clutched Will's arm. His hand immediately covered hers. "Steady there, Espy. We won't let them attack you," he whispered.

He glared at Warren. "This ain't no courthouse to sit in judgment of Espy. She's done nothin' wrong." Will's voice rose, his finger puncturing the air in front of him.

"Then she has nothing to fear," Warren answered quietly.

Dexter stepped forward. "Come, come, we're all friends here. Let's behave like civilized human beings." He smiled at Espy, and for a moment, she could believe he was a friend. "No one's accusing you of anything. We'd just like to know what happened."

"I think it's clear what has happened," Christina said. "But if you gentlemen are going to be taken in by a pretty face, then I shall wash my hands of this group. We have a reputation to uphold in the community. We must be above reproach, the Bible says. If a young woman is going to behave in a way that brings reproach to the Lord and to the rest of the church, I can have nothing to do with it."

Espy had heard enough. "Don't worry, I shan't bring division to this group. I am withdrawing." Not waiting for anyone to say anything more for or against her, she slipped her hand from Will's arm and headed for the door.

"So am I." Henry's heavier footsteps sounded behind her.

"And I." Will quickly joined her and took her arm once more in his.

"I never did feel welcome here." Angela followed them out.

When they stood out in the churchyard, suddenly Will looked at them all and laughed. "Will you look at that! We're half the club. Let them be what they wanted all along—a little club for their own kind!"

The others joined in his laughter.

"Let's go have an ice cream—on me."

They shouted their agreement and headed toward Main Street. Espy kept her stride even with Will's but felt no victory.

Even though her friends' ready defense of her had warmed her heart, the others' quick dismissal of her showed her how futile her dream of ever entering their world had been.

Though Warren had made an attempt at fairness, it was half-hearted at best. The others—with the possible exception of Dexter, and he was too lazy to fight for anything—would have quickly voted her out.

17

Warren stood at the door of the church basement, nodding and murmuring good night to the departing members. Finally only Dexter remained.

"What a pity about Espy."

Warren rubbed the back of his neck. After Espy had stormed out, taking her half of the club with her, he'd tried to proceed as if nothing had happened even though his gut roiled with anger both at Espy and Christina.

Espy for having gotten herself in such a fix and Christina for provoking a showdown tonight instead of expressing her concerns privately to Espy. "Yes." He expelled a pent-up breath. "Maybe I can talk to her—or to Christina."

Dexter chuckled. "Good luck."

"It's not funny. Once again our club is in shambles."

His friend glanced down at his fingernails. "Christina would say it's down to its proper size—all undesirable elements removed."

After a second, Warren said something that had been brewing in his mind throughout the meeting. "I may speak to Pastor Curtis, hand in my resignation this week."

Dexter whistled softly. "You feel that strongly about it?"

Warren motioned to the empty table and chairs. "This is not what either the pastor or I envisioned as a young people's club. This is just another social event for the well-to-do to gather and feel good about themselves in the process."

Dexter chuckled. "I admit, I was skeptical and only came when you coerced me, but I kind of liked it." He sighed. "Ah, well, time to find a new amusement for Wednesday evenings."

Trying to keep the irritation from his voice, Warren said, "You could have spoken up, said something to deter Christina."

His friend spread out his hands. "You know me, never exert yourself if you can help it."

"Come on, let's get out of here." Ushering Dexter before him, Warren turned and closed the door behind them. "In any case, if Espy hadn't gotten in trouble with the Stocktons, none of this would have happened."

They crossed the churchyard. "You think not? Don't you think Christina would have pounced on some other peccadillo? You know she's disliked the notion of having Espy and her friends in the group since the beginning."

"I don't know." Warren was tired and didn't want to think about it anymore. "But it would have been hard for her to get anyone's support if it had been a minor charge."

"Probably."

After a moment Dexter turned to him. "Do you really think Espy is guilty of what they're all accusing her of?"

Warren stopped on the street, not expecting his friend's question.

Dexter grinned at him. "If you could see your face." A second later he said seriously. "Hey, I'm sorry."

Warren resumed walking. "She as much as admitted it to me. Do you really think Mr. Stockton, let alone his wife, would say anything so awful if it weren't true?"

"I suppose not, still . . . Espy seems like a nice girl."

"Yeah, nice, but look how the men swarm around her." *Including me.* Hating himself for the worst hypocrisy, he nevertheless continued trying to convince his friend. "Maybe she didn't think she did anything wrong, but look where she comes from. How would she know it's wrong to flirt with someone like the professor? Maybe she tempted him and then he couldn't help himself." *As happened to me.* "It doesn't excuse his behavior, but a man can only take so much."

Dexter chuckled. "And Espy sure is sweet to look upon. I'd hate to think what I'd do if I found myself alone with her on a lonely road some night."

A rush of anger rose so suddenly in Warren, he had to clench his fists to keep from grabbing Dexter by the collar.

How dare he lust after Espy.

The anger dissipated as quickly as it had arisen. Wasn't Dexter expressing exactly what Warren had done? He grunted, thrusting his hands deep in his pockets. "See? If you imagine something like that, think of poor Mr. Stockton, closeted with Espy day after day, giving her lessons."

"Lessons? What kind of lessons?" Dexter wiggled his eyebrows.

"History, literature, things like that," Warren hastened to explain. "She wanted to improve her mind. She had to leave school early, you know, when her father was injured and couldn't work anymore."

"I see. And while the professor was improving her mind, she thought she'd expand his horizons a bit, eh?"

Sickened by the implications, Warren remained silent. Halfway down Main Street, he was able to leave Dexter.

"Let me know what you intend with the group."

Warren nodded. "I will."

At last he was alone. If he'd stayed much longer with Dexter, he would have ended up punching him in the face. No matter how guilty Espy was of bad conduct, he couldn't stand hearing her referred to in any lewd way.

And now? His thoughts returned to the church group. He'd talk with the pastor tomorrow during his lunch hour.

His mind made up, he headed to the bridge and home.

•   •   •

Espy walked to the cannery early in the morning and walked home in the afternoon, her legs tired from standing. With her mother, Angela, and her all working different, though overlapping, shifts, they were able to have someone home at all hours to take care of the younger ones.

She hadn't realized how much the professor's lessons—though not so many in number—had helped her until she came back to the cannery. She longed for more than that world, a world where people only worked to put food on the table.

She entered her house and immediately sensed a change. It was the smell of tobacco in the air.

Her father was home.

She entered the kitchen with a sense of both apprehension and curiosity. Her father sat at the kitchen table, his thin shoulders slumped, a chipped mug of coffee before him.

"Hello, Papa."

He looked up, his eyes bleary, his still-black hair long and shaggy. "Hello there, Daughter. Where've you been?"

She suppressed a retort that she should be asking him that. Instead, she set down her satchel. "At the cannery."

"Still there?" He took a sip of coffee, making a slurping sound.

Espy began emptying her satchel. Two cabbages and a small piece of salt pork. She took them to the sink, and seeing the water bucket full, she poured some water into a basin and washed her hands.

229

When her father asked no more, Espy said, "What brought you home this time?"

"The usual."

Ever since he'd been injured off a fishing boat, he only came back when he'd run out of money and his back pain became insupportable.

He grunted.

She poured fresh water to wash the cabbages and checked the stove. The fire had gone out. With a sigh, she removed one of the lids and poked around the ashes looking for a live coal.

Seeing nothing but gray and white ash, she stooped to the kindling basket and took the remaining sticks, crumpled pieces of newspaper, and any other combustibles from the household.

As she arranged the sticks in the stove, she asked her father, "How've you been?"

"Middlin'." He rubbed the small of his back.

"Where'd you come from?"

"I was up Danforth-way. Had a job digging the road beds for the rail line they're runnin' up there. Till the back got so I couldn't bend over anymore."

She refrained from asking if he'd brought any money with him. It used to be important, but with all of them working now, his share was no longer necessary.

Gus wandered into the kitchen, expressing no surprise at the sight of his father. Instead, he directed his words to Espy. "Is there anything to eat?"

"Not till supper." She motioned with her chin. "Go refill the kindling basket, all right? By the time you get back, I'll have some supper for you."

He looked over the cookstove top. "What're you making? I don't see anything."

"Pork and cabbage."

"Go do as your sister says." His father's sharp words caused

230

Gus to jump. His lips turned downward, he took the basket and headed out of the kitchen.

"Got any liniment for my back?"

Seeing the fire was going, she replaced the lid and set a cast iron skillet atop it. "There's some bay rum in the cupboard."

"If you could rub some in, it might help."

Espy nodded without saying anything. She continued preparing the dish, slicing up the salt pork and putting it into the skillet with a dollop of bacon fat. As it sizzled and filled the air with its smoky scent, she sliced the cabbage.

Her father didn't ask her anything about her life. She had grown accustomed over the years to his lack of interest. Now, she felt relief. He'd hear soon enough.

He got up with a groan and came to pour himself another cup of coffee from the enamel pot.

"That's probably cold."

"Don't matter. It's as bitter as sin, but it's something to ease the parched throat."

"You could drink water."

He made a face, reminding her of Gus's earlier.

While the cabbage was simmering, she fetched the jar of bay rum and ordered her father to lay facedown on the couch. He pulled his shirt out of his trousers and she rubbed some liniment in her palms and then began to massage it into his lower back.

The spicy fragrance filled the room, mingling with the cabbage and bacon smell from the kitchen.

Children's voices drifted in from the open windows and she glanced into the street to see her sisters playing hopscotch with neighbor girls. Espy turned her attention back to her fingers.

Her father began to groan.

"That hurt?"

"No, it feels good."

A man's voice came from outside. "Hello, children, anyone at home?"

She couldn't see who was speaking, but the voice sounded like the pastor's.

"Who's that?" came her father's groggy voice.

"Sounds like Pastor Curtis."

"What's he doing here?"

"I don't know." She heard footsteps on the steps and the next second a firm knock. "Hello! Anyone home?"

With a sigh, Espy stood and went to the front entryway, wondering what the pastor wanted with them. She hoped he wasn't coming to see her. Not with her father here. She opened the door slowly.

"Hello, Espy."

He smiled and Espy's tension eased a fraction. "Hello, Pastor." She didn't open the door the whole way. "What are you doing here?"

"Just stopping by to see how you and your family are."

"We're fine."

"Is your mother at home?"

Espy shook her head. "But my father's just arrived."

"Oh, may I come in to say hello to him? It's been over a year since I last saw him."

She opened the door wider and stepped aside. She was forced to lead him into the parlor, hoping her father had sat up at least. In the parlor, she viewed the sagging upholstery through the pastor's eyes. Her father still lay facedown, one arm falling limply to the floor.

"Mr. Estrada, I didn't expect to see you here." Pastor Curtis bent down near the sofa. "Are you all right, sir?"

Her father opened one dark eye, gazing upward. "Not so good, sir. It's the back. Got me laid up."

"Oh, dear. Is there anything I can do for you?"

"Don't think there's anything anyone can do for me."

"Let me pray for you."

"All right."

Espy repressed her annoyance at the self-pitying tone. He'd make the pastor think he was at death's door.

The pastor laid a hand on her father's back and uttered a short prayer.

At the "amen," he straightened. "There, I hope you feel better in the coming days. Thankfully, you have some good daughters here who'll no doubt see to all your needs."

Her father glanced at Espy, who stood in the doorway with her arms crossed. "Espy's a good girl. So's Angela. But they're out working most o' the day." He sighed. "Guess I'll get along somehow."

With a nod, Pastor Curtis stepped back and sniffed. "My, it smells good in here. Bay rum?"

Espy moved farther into the room. "I was just massaging his back. Please, have a seat—or would you care to sit in the kitchen? I have to check on supper." Better to have him talk to her in the kitchen away from her father's ears if he came to ask her about the Stocktons.

"The kitchen should do fine. Lead the way."

When he was seated at the table, she held up the coffeepot. "Would you like a cup of coffee or some tea?"

"Nothing, thank you."

Relieved, she checked on the cabbage and set it to the side where the heat wasn't so intense. The kitchen was a little too warm with the fire now. She wiped her forehead with the edge of her apron and approached the table, wary of what the pastor wanted to say.

"Sit down, Espy."

The legs of the chair scraped across the floor as she pulled it out. She clasped her hands atop the table and looked at the pastor.

"I've heard some unpleasant reports about you this past week."

Her stomach clenched. So, as she'd imagined, he'd heard, too.

She shouldn't be shocked, but the words still managed to startle her. "Yes, sir."

"Want to tell me what happened?"

She moistened dry lips. "What did you hear?"

"Mrs. Stockton said she found you kissing her husband."

He didn't pale or blush as he said the words; his regard continued steady on her. Of course, he was probably used to hearing worse things about people, although she couldn't imagine anything worse at the moment. "She opened the library door and found us kissing, but *I* wasn't kissing Mr. Stockton, it was the other way around." There, she'd said it. Would he believe her?

He nodded as if digesting her words. "That's a pretty serious accusation to make about an upstanding man of this community. Are you sure you are telling me the truth?"

Her anger rose immediately. He was as bad as the rest. "Yes, sir. I would never lie about that."

He said nothing. As the minutes passed, Espy's ire grew. She was on the point of getting up and telling him she was too busy to waste time when he finally spoke. "I shall have a word with Mr. Stockton, but before I do, I'd like some more information. What were you doing alone in his library?"

She explained about their lessons.

"How long have you been receiving these?"

She calculated. "About as soon as I started working for Mrs. Stockton, which has been the whole summer, almost two months now."

He looked at his hands, which lay on the table. "Did you never think it might not be appropriate to receive these lessons alone with him?"

She swallowed. It had never occurred to her to question Mr. Stockton's invitation. "No-o, sir. He invited me to pick out any books I'd like to read from his library, and somehow from there, he asked me to spend a few minutes after I finished all my work,

234

talking about what I'd read. He was teaching me all kinds of things about the books. I'd never have seen all that in the stories, if he hadn't pointed them out."

"Did Mrs. Stockton know you were spending this time alone with her husband?"

"Of course she knew."

"And she didn't object?"

"Why should she? He was a teacher. And . . . and she could come in any time she wanted." Her voice came out faster as she became more excited in her defense.

"Did she come in often?"

Espy paused. "No-o . . . ," she said slowly, trying to remember how often Mrs. Stockton had entered the library. It had always seemed the room was the professor's sanctuary.

Pastor Curtis sat back in the chair. "I will make no judgment on what happened in Mr. Stockton's library until I have spoken to him. I just want you to consider a few things."

She swallowed, wondering what he was going to say.

"Firstly, Mr. Stockton has given years of service teaching the young men and women at the high school academy. He is beloved by his students. He is happily married to the same woman of his youth. He is a member of the church and various civic groups in town. The fact that he wanted to add to your education speaks for the kind of man he is."

Espy's hopes of being believed by the pastor sank with each sentence.

"I want you to think long and hard before you accuse this man. His reputation will be damaged beyond repair if you accuse him of making advances to you." He held up his hand when she tried to speak.

"I'm not saying you are lying, Espy. Only God, you, and Mr. Stockton know the truth right now. But, consider this: you are an attractive, very personable young woman who sat afternoon after afternoon alone with a still young, virile man. You . . ." For the first time during his visit, the pastor seemed embarrassed. "You are perhaps not aware of the way you dress, of your manner. You . . . are quite outgoing. You are used to perhaps—" he cleared his throat, a bit of color spotting his cheeks, "flirting with men. There is such a thing as tempting a man above what he is able, even if you did not do it intentionally."

She stood, the chair making a loud noise as it crashed to the floor. "Are you saying it was *my* fault Mr. Stockton kissed me?" Too late, she remembered her father in the next room. She lowered her voice, which shook with anger. "I didn't do anything and he suddenly—"

The pastor stood as soon as she did. "I'm not accusing you of anything. I'm simply asking you to think about your behavior, perhaps unconscious, it's true, not just on that afternoon, but during your entire sojourn at the Stocktons'. Think well on it. Men are not as women. They are easily enticed by a young lady's looks, her easy manner. What you may have imagined as an invitation may have appeared to him as offering him your favors."

Her mouth dropped at what he was insinuating. That she, maybe even without understanding it, was actually giving Mr. Stockton an invitation to *kiss* her? The thought filled her with horror.

Until she remembered Warren's sudden kiss. Had she led him through that dark forest path on purpose? She wanted to refute it but was held captive with the thought.

The pastor soon excused himself, telling her he would pray for her, and went to speak a few words to her father before departing.

Espy remained in the kitchen, having no desire to face her father. She stirred the cabbage and then replaced the lid. Taking up the corn broom, she began to sweep the floor, needing to do something to keep herself occupied. But she couldn't forget the pastor's words. They tainted everything about her. *Had she been inviting Mr. Stockton's advances every time she'd sat alone with him in his study?*

236

All she'd wanted to do was learn and advance herself, and he'd seemed so willing to teach her. He'd behaved so respectfully, except for that day . . . and earlier, that rainy afternoon.

Why hadn't she done something then? But what could she have done even if she had known? She swept the dirt into a pile and looked for a piece of newspaper among the kindling. As she took up a section of an old paper, her gaze fell on an advertisement on the page.

Typists Needed
Will train. Apply Monday–Friday, 8:00 a.m. at
offices of Talbot, Smith, and Asquith.
Young women ages 18–30 sought.

A picture of a young woman dressed neatly in a dark skirt and white shirtwaist and tie, her hair upswept, smiled at her. Espy's heart began to beat hard, her fingers clutching the newsprint.

This is who she wanted to be.

Neat, trim, with a respectable job in a big office. She read the bottom of the advertisement for the address. It was in Bangor. The city.

She stared beyond her, no longer seeing the water-stained wallpaper or dingy linoleum but a large, clean office space where no one knew her, where she could start afresh.

She read the advertisement again. They said no experience was necessary. Finally, she tore it out carefully and put it in the pocket of her apron. Tonight she'd count how much money she had saved in her jar under her bed.

18

As the gossip surrounding Espy grew, Warren resolved to eradicate all feelings for her. By God's grace, he would banish her from his thoughts. He had knelt by his bedside the night before and asked forgiveness for his sin. Again.

Still he tortured himself going over and over in his mind how she'd kissed him—and how she must have behaved with Stockton.

Hopefully, with her no longer working at the Stocktons' or coming to the church group, he'd rarely see her. *Out of sight, out of mind,* he told himself firmly, picking up his pace as he headed to the office.

By noon, after immersing himself in his work, he reemerged on the street. Before heading home, he turned down a side street, needing to purchase a few things at the stationer's.

When he exited after a friendly conversation with the proprietor, the parcel in his hand, his spirits had lifted. It was a beautiful August day; he was hungry and looking forward to a good lunch. If his mother didn't bring up Espy's name.

He rounded the corner onto Main Street. And bumped into Espy. "Oh—!" His hands reached out to steady her. Just as quickly, he dropped them to his sides. "Pardon me, Espy."

She backed away, a tentative smile on her lips.

Her dark hair was shiny as watered silk, her dusky skin as smooth as polished beech wood. "That's all right, Warren."

With a start, he backed away from her, conscious of how he was gazing at her, that nothing had changed since that night in the forest. He wanted her as much as he had then—even knowing what she'd done. A Scripture came to his mind. *Flee also youthful lusts.* "Excuse me, but I must run. So long." He stepped around her, nodding and walking away, flinging the last words over his shoulder.

•   •   •

Espy gazed after him, too stunned to move.

His long stride took him to the end of the block in no time. The next second he disappeared across the bridge.

He'd taken off as if he were being pursued by a host of bill collectors. From surprise at seeing her to a hint of something else—pleasure, perhaps—his green eyes had finally filled with fear.

She noticed a few passersby eyeing her curiously as she stood on the sidewalk.

If Warren looked at her like that, what hope did she have in Holliston? As if coming out of a daze, she walked on, her resolve to leave solidified.

•   •   •

Warren hated how he'd behaved toward Espy, but he didn't see what he could have done differently. He couldn't treat her as if nothing had happened, because it had. Nothing would change that.

He could not go back to treating her just like anyone else. Nor could he forget what the Stocktons had accused her of.

When Wednesday came, he went through the motions of the

church club meeting, but his heart wasn't in it. There was only the skeleton membership of Christina, Annalise, Emily, James, and himself. Even Dexter had told him not to look for him.

He looked around the small group. "Let's focus on a project for the autumn, shall we?"

"What about a harvest fair? The Ladies' Guild is planning a sale of goods here in the basement. We could piggyback onto them and plan our own activity that would complement their white elephant sale."

Warren nodded at Christina's suggestion, appearing to digest its merits although it held no appeal. He hadn't followed up on his decision to resign as president, realizing it would be cowardly at this moment in time. Once the group had regained a few more members and was better established, he'd propose new elections and bow out.

By the end of the meeting, he realized how much Espy had added to the meeting. She was not only the reason her friends came, but she had good ideas, enthusiasm, and the ability to bridge the gap between the two groups of young people.

He escorted Christina and Annalise home but had little to say. He hadn't seen Espy since that day on the street, and no matter how many times he'd told himself he was relieved, he continued to scan the streets every time he went out, hoping for a glimpse of her.

"Why are you so quiet tonight?" Christina's voice intruded on his thoughts.

"No reason. Just talked out after the meeting, I guess."

"We accomplished quite a bit, wouldn't you say?"

"What—oh, yes, I suppose so."

Christina had set forth most of the ideas and everyone else had agreed to them.

"You suppose so?" A note of annoyance entered her fine voice. "I'm not sure what you expect, but I thought it was wonderful to move along at such a nice pace." She let out a breath. "There's something to be said for getting rid of the excess fat in a group and leaving a core leadership. One can accomplish so much more."

He glanced at her in the twilight. *Excess fat.* So that was how she was describing it.

"I'm sorry so many have left," he said quietly, looking across Christina to Annalise, who said nothing but looked at him sympathetically.

"They were nothing but an unruly group with contentious behavior," Christina said with a sniff. "I'm surprised you feel that way."

"It doesn't matter." He was too tired to argue.

"I've heard that Espy has left town. Good riddance, I say." Christina swiped at the front of her skirt as if flicking off a fly.

"Left? What do you mean?" With effort Warren continued walking instead of stopping in the middle of the sidewalk and demanding to know what she meant.

Christina shrugged. Annalise's eyes were wide and Warren wondered if his own face mirrored the same shock.

"Just what I said. Left Holliston."

"Who'd you hear this from?" Probably another old gossip.

"My mother." Christina eyed him. "She heard it from Mrs. Tyson, who belongs to the Women's Guild. They were discussing the fact that Espy has not received any sort of reprimand or disciplinary action from Reverend Curtis. My mother wanted to bring it up at the next board meeting.

"That's when Mrs. Tyson told her it no longer mattered."

Warren looked away, his mind working, trying to remember how Espy had acted that day.

"Slow down, we can hardly keep up with you."

He didn't realize he'd quickened his pace. "I'm sorry." He concentrated on keeping a measured step as if he had all the time in the world, when all he wanted to do was turn around and find Pastor Curtis and ask him what he knew.

No, better yet was to find Angela and get the truth from her. He'd do so tomorrow.

With that, he steered the conversation to another topic, anything to show his indifference about Espy to Christina.

∙ ∙ ∙

"Where did she go?" He stood in front of Espy's door, staring at Angela. It was around eight o'clock at night, a time when he hoped she'd be home from the cannery. She had not smiled in greeting nor invited him to come in—not that he would have accepted. But it made him feel at a disadvantage, as if Angela knew more about him than he did about her.

A flush grew along his collar, wondering if Angela knew about their kiss.

The two sisters were close and he imagined sisters so near in age told each other secrets.

"To Bangor," she finally said.

"Why?" The single interrogative popped out of him before he could frame it less directly.

Angela's brown eyes—a deeper shade than Espy's—stared into his, and he knew then that she must know quite a bit.

He shifted on his feet. "I mean, isn't it kind of sudden? She didn't tell any of us of her . . . uh . . . plans."

Angela released a loud breath. "Why should she tell anyone? Not as if any of you cared." She took a step back into the house. "If that's all, I'm busy."

"Yes, I'm sorry, but I was just . . . concerned." He cleared his throat, growing more awkward with each second "Concerned . . . when I heard she left town, so suddenly without telling anyone."

"Well, she's gone. She had some money saved up and didn't want to spend the rest of her life working at the cannery."

He felt each word was directed at him in accusation. "I can understand that. She was very bright and eager to learn." The statement only brought him back to thoughts of Mr. Stockton.

The awkward silence lengthened until Angela touched the doorknob and began drawing the door closed. "If you've gotten what you came for, I need to be getting the children to bed."

He stepped back. "Yes, of course. Thank you." He wanted to ask if there was any way to reach Espy, but the hostility emanating from her sister silenced him.

As he walked back down the dusty path, his mind grappled with the fact that Espy was gone.

He should be relieved. Happy and relieved. Happy that she was able to start over somewhere else, where maybe she had a better future. Relieved that God had answered his pleas for help. He'd removed that temptation from Warren's path.

The way was now clear for Warren to follow in obedience the path his father and mother wanted him to follow, the one he'd worked all his life for, been trained for.

If that included Christina, then so be it.

• • •

Espy was thrust forward as the stagecoach came to a stop at its final destination. "Exchange Station! Exchange!" the driver called down. A second later, the door swung open and the passengers began scrambling for their things, eager to leave its tight confines.

Despite her impatience to be out of the stuffy, smelly coach, she was wedged at the far end and was unable to stand until the other passengers descended.

Finally, she stepped onto the street, feeling rumpled and thirsty from the long, jostling ride. Ignoring the other passengers around her, she eyed her one bag above, waiting as the driver climbed atop and began throwing things down to an awaiting boy.

She retrieved her carpetbag and looked around her. She hadn't really thought out the next step. She glanced at the large clock atop the tower at one end of the train station. Half-past eight.

Everyone seemed to know where they were going.

Someone bumped her from behind. "Excuse me," she said, moving aside quickly as a burly man brushed past her, a trunk atop his back.

She crossed the street, stepping over the streetcar tracks, and approached the train station. Once inside the cavernous building, she looked around for the ticket office, but it was closed.

She hesitated but when a gentleman started eyeing her, she stepped quickly away, pretending to look as if she knew where she were going.

When she went back outside, she glanced back at the stage-coach stop, but the coach had left and none of the passengers remained. She should have asked one of the women aboard for a respectable place to stay. But she had been reluctant to engage anyone in conversation, afraid of being asked what her circumstances were.

The only ones she'd told were her mother and siblings.

"I suppose it's time you made your way in the world," her mother said, brushing aside a wisp of hair from her face in a weary gesture. "Just be careful, and don't give any man what you shouldn't, you hear me?"

"Yes, Mama." There was no danger of that, she could have told her, now that Warren was out of her life. It still scared her how willingly she would have given him whatever he'd asked. And he was ready to believe something so vile of her.

Espy looked around her, but everything appeared to be warehouses and factories. The buildings were tall, five or six stories high. She'd never seen so many tall buildings standing beside each other. Most appeared closed.

She took out the crumpled newspaper ad from her pocket, wondering where the business was located. Finally, she approached an older man wearing a white apron, bringing in boxes of produce from a greengrocers'. "Excuse me, sir. Could you direct me to a street where I might find a . . . a boardinghouse?"

He eyed her with clear disapproval. Finally, he jutted out his chin. "Down by the waterfront, four blocks, turn right, you'll find a whole string of them."

She scanned the few people left in the street. A large brick complex with tall smokestacks shadowed the street, making it darker than the hovering dusk. The smell was sulphurous and metallic. She glanced to her right. The warehouses hid the river but she could smell its rank odor and spy the tall masts of ships above the rooftops. Hefting her carpetbag and satchel, she began to walk where he'd indicated.

When she reached the river, she looked right and left. Spotting a mild looking middle-aged man, she put on a confident front. "Excuse me, sir."

He stopped, looking surprised that she had addressed him. "What can I do for you, miss?"

"Could you tell me where I might find a . . . a boardinghouse, a reputable one?"

He looked her up and down, and she wondered how unusual it was for a young lady to be alone in the city, at least in this part of the city. "You might try down the street, the waterfront's full of boardinghouses."

She didn't like the sound of "waterfront," but it was getting late and she didn't dare ask him anything more. Bangor was known for its dangerous waterfront, nicknamed the Devil's Half-Acre. She murmured "Thank you," and hurried on.

Shifting the weight of her bag from one hand to the other, she headed forward, trying not to appear ignorant of where she was headed, all the while praying for direction.

The wide Penobscot loomed before her, partly obscured by the dark masts of the moored vessels. Wharves of different lengths jutted out into the river. A few street lamps began illuminating the street.

She had to walk several long blocks with no sign of any hostelries or boarding houses, only darkened factories or warehouses. She reached a block with a string of taverns. Voices and laughter drifted through the air.

She hesitated at the sight of the people walking or lounging against the buildings. They were mostly men. A glance over her shoulder showed the sky turning pink on the horizon, making the silhouettes of the buildings black in contrast.

"Need any help, miss?" a deep-voiced man asked her.

She clutched the handle of her bag more tightly. "No, thank you."

Another man chuckled as she walked past. "That bag looks too heavy for a young girl like you to tote around. I can carry it for you."

"I'm stronger than I look," she tossed back. Laughter followed her and it took all her willpower not to break into a run.

Finally, she reached a block that appeared more residential, the three- and four-story buildings tightly wedged together.

When she heard footsteps behind her, she didn't turn to look but stepped across the railroad tracks to the other side of the street. There were two sets of rails, and she almost tripped over the second set.

Her heart pounding, and the sweat soaking her skin despite the cool evening air, she didn't slow her pace until she no longer heard the footsteps.

She had to find a place to stay before dark. She gripped the handles of her bag, her shoulders aching, her stomach growling, her mouth parched.

She jumped when a shadowy form sidled up to her. "Lookin' for some company tonight, sweetheart?" The husky voice was almost at her cheek. The smell of beer, so familiar from her father, wafted up her nostrils. "No, I'm not!" She began walking away from him but he followed her.

"Aw, I didn't mean to offend you, young lady. Are you needin' a place to stay? I'll keep you warm."

He kept up this garrulous stream as she lengthened her stride. Soon another man joined him, then another. They appeared to detach themselves from shadows between the taverns.

Praying for deliverance, Espy ran, her eyes searching for an escape. One man grabbed her arm. "I won't hurt you, honey, I just want to see what you have." His low tone had an Irish lilt.

Her heart banged against her chest as she pushed him away. "G-g-get away f-from me," she panted. Most of the other men had stopped following her but two others stood in the background. They were mere youths, she determined, eighteen or nineteen years old.

The man drew her closer. "You don't mean that."

She yanked free. The man pulled her back by the strap of her satchel. She clutched it more closely to her side, but he only pulled harder. The two young men closed in on her.

Panic engulfed her, cutting off her breath. She hitched up her skirts and broke through the two young men. Her side aching, her chest on fire, she didn't dare stop or look behind her until she turned a corner onto another wide street, her carpetbag banging against her leg.

She heard a shout and footsteps behind her and picked up her pace, clutching at her side. She turned another corner and zigzagged up a narrow street then around another corner. Too winded to run anymore, she stopped in a sheltered doorway, bending over to gulp in air.

Her breath slowing, she leaned against the door, praying for succor. Finally, she dared to peer up and down the street. A lone cat crossed the street and darted into an alley. Muffled lights came from behind curtains in the upper stories of the buildings but their entrances stood dark.

She pictured her brothers and sisters at their kitchen table with its checked oilcloth, her mother at one end, she and Angela at the other, ready to get up to the stove to dish out more helpings.

She hoped her father hadn't found any of their money. Summer would soon be over and they needed every penny for fuel, some new overcoats, and boots for the children. They seemed to be growing like weeds now.

Had she done wrong to leave? Was it merely selfish ambition and fear?

But she remembered the looks of condemnation on the faces of those at church and those of the club. How could she ever hope for anything better for her life if people thought the worst of her?

She sagged against the doorway, loosening her clutch on her carpetbag and letting it fall to the stone step at her feet.

Only then did she realize she no longer held her satchel. Her eyes snapped open, panic rising once more. She searched around, knowing it was a vain effort.

19

Espy remembered the young man who'd pulled at her strap. He must have taken her satchel when she ran away.

She wanted to march back to the wharf and find that young man and demand her belonging. But the emotion was quickly replaced by fear.

Dear God, what am I to do? All her money was in that satchel. She'd been so careful of it during the stagecoach trip. Now she was in a strange city, at night.

Despair engulfed her. She slid down until she squatted in the doorway. Covering her face with her hands, she cried out to God.

She didn't know how long she sat there but her feet began to prickle from the lack of circulation. Realizing she could not stay there all night, she stood, wincing at the pain.

No signs of life on this street. She'd just have to walk until she found some place to stay. She had no money. Perhaps she could convince some compassionate landlady or hotel clerk that she'd work for her keep, at least for a few days until she could find work in an office.

She felt for the newspaper ad in her pocket and heard its

reassuring crinkle. At least she still had that hope. And she had her suitcase with clean clothes. She had things she could be thankful for.

Reaching the end of the street she found herself back at the riverfront. But instead of taverns, these buildings seemed to be tenements. She looked up and down, debating. Finally, she turned left, upriver, away from the area she'd run from.

She stopped short at the next block, hearing a male voice. Her heart hammering in her chest, she tried to inch back, but the man's voice stopped her.

"Come on, Bill, you'll have a warm bowl of soup and a clean bed for the night."

Another voice, this one slurred and whiny, replied, "Aw, John, I don't like your wife to see me like this. 'Tain't right."

As her eyes made out the figures in the lamplight, she saw the first man had his back to her; the other sat squatting against a building, its unpainted clapboards gray with age.

She began to back away but the drunken man spied her. "Hey, there, darlin', lookin' for someone?"

The first man turned. He was middle-aged, which immediately put Espy on her guard.

He smiled and took a step toward her. She backed away some more. He stopped. "You needn't fear me. Are you in need, miss?"

She debated whether to hightail it back from where she'd come or bluff her way through, pretending she had a place to go. But he had made no further move and stood there quietly as if in no hurry.

The drunk spoke, "A pretty thing like you shouldn't be wanderin' about by yourself. Just come into town?"

She realized he was eyeing her carpet bag. She addressed the other man. "Yes." She clutched the bag tighter. "I'm visiting family," she lied, "but seem to have lost my way. If you could tell me where I might board for the evening."

"Certainly, miss. My wife and I run a boardinghouse of sorts." Without making a move toward her, he gestured behind him. "It's only a couple of blocks from here. I was trying to persuade my friend Bill here to come and have a bed for the night."

She wrinkled her nose at the drunk. What kind of boardinghouse would take in a drunk—and a respectable young woman? She repeated his words to herself, *boardinghouse of sorts.* "What kind of boardinghouse do you run, sir?"

"One for anyone who finds himself without a bed for the night. It's called House of Hope." He added, "It's a Christian mission for the homeless. We'd be glad to offer you a place to stay until you can find those relatives of yours." The way he said it made her think he saw through her.

Did he think she was a . . . a woman of ill repute? She clutched the bag in front of her with both hands like a shield.

Again, as if guessing her qualms, he offered, "My name is John Talbot."

He appeared a gentleman. But then, so had Mr. Stockton. But she had nowhere to go and it was now dark. "I only need a place to stay for tonight."

He inclined his square chin. "That's fine. Why don't you come along? My wife had a pot of stew simmering when I left."

Her stomach rumbled. Thankfully, no one would have heard it over the sound of the river behind them. *Dear Lord, protect me, please. Don't let him harm me.* "All right, I'll follow you." If he led her down some lonely alley, she'd bolt.

He smiled and then turned to the drunk. "I'll come back later tonight and see if you've changed your mind."

The older man waved him off. "No need, John. I'll be fine. You stay home with that sweet wife of yours."

Espy breathed a silent breath of relief that at least he wasn't lying about having a wife.

With a final nod, Mr. Talbot stepped away from the drunk and began to walk down the street with a glance back to make sure Espy was following him.

"Give her my best regards," Bill called after them.

"I will," Mr. Talbot answered over his shoulder.

"How much farther?" Espy asked after they had walked a few minutes and turned down the next corner away from the river. It was a regular street and not an alley. Some people sat on their porches.

He pointed ahead of him. "See, on the next block, that signboard where the light is?"

She peered where he pointed. "Yes."

"That's it. House of Hope."

They arrived at the two-story clapboard house with the pitched roof, dormer windows, and wide verandah in front, a house similar to the others up and down the street, with the difference that this one appeared neatly painted in light blue with a patch of grass in front instead of dirt. The sign she had seen from down the block hung from two metal rings. *House of Hope, established 1884* was etched on the light blue background, the block letters painted in gold.

House of Hope. The significance hit her. Her name meant hope. Had the Lord truly brought her here?

"Here, let me carry your bag."

She drew it toward herself. "No, thank you, I'm fine."

"Come along then." Mr. Talbot swept his arm forward, indicating she should precede him up the wide steps to the porch.

Everything appeared welcoming. A gas light in a glass-enclosed lamp lit the front doorway. More light shone through the oval glass in the door.

Mr. Talbot reached in front of her and turned the brass knob. As soon as the door opened, Espy saw other people within. A woman was walking down the corridor; a man sat in a chair near a staircase.

"You're back early," the man said, his glance flickering to Espy then away. He spoke English like a foreigner, though Espy couldn't identify his accent, unused to foreigners except her own father.

The woman smiled and paused, her attention also on Espy.

"Yes, I found this young lady—" He turned to her with a smile. "I'm sorry, I didn't catch your name."

"Espy Estrada."

"Miss Estrada, in need of a place to stay for the evening."

The other young woman approached Espy, a smile breaking open on her freckled face. "Hello, Miss Estrada, I'm Mary O'Leary." She held out a hand, speaking with an Irish accent.

"Hello." Espy held out her hand automatically, too dazed to think clearly.

"Would you like to wash up before dinner?" Her glance went to Espy's bag. "Been traveling, have you?"

"Yes."

"Why don't you take her up to your room and then bring her to the kitchen once she's had a chance to freshen up? Go ahead and assign her a bed."

Mr. Talbot smiled at her. "I shall find my wife and tell her we'll have one more for supper."

Espy followed the young woman up two flights of stairs. "You'll like it here. It's not at all like an institution or almshouse, as we had back in County Wicklow."

Institution? Almshouse? "I'm not looking for charity. I'm going to find work here in Bangor."

The girl smiled down at her. "Of course you are, miss. That's what I did, too, when I first arrived. But the Talbots, they offer people a good, Christian place to stay until they can get settled."

Feeling somewhat reassured, Espy continued climbing the stairs, glad to arrive at the top.

"Here, let me take that for you, you look worn out."

This time Espy put up no argument. Relieved of the carpetbag, she felt lighter. Until she remembered her stolen satchel and all her money. Her shoulders slumped.

The girl reached the end of the landing. "Here we are, the girls' room." With a flourish, she swung open the door. Espy peered past her into a long room with polished wooden floors covered with rag rugs. A row of narrow metal beds with an assortment of brightly colored spreads ranged down the length of the room, which Espy judged to be the front of the house. Three curtained dormer windows divided the row of beds. Chests of drawers and washstands took up the wall opposite.

"It looks very nice," Espy said slowly.

"We try to make it homelike. We sew our own bedspreads and knit those throws." As she spoke she lugged Espy's bag to a bed at the far end of the row under the steeply pitched eave. "You're in luck; we have a spare bed right now. The girl who was here just got married and they found a floor to rent."

Espy arrived at the bed with the plain white coverlet and folded steamer blanket at the end.

"There." With a sigh, Miss O'Leary set the bag down on a straight-back chair at the foot of the bed. "There's some clean water left in my pitcher if you'd like to wash your face and hands. I'll take your pitcher down to the kitchen when we go, and you can bring up some hot water later."

Espy began to remove her hat. She hardly heard when Miss O'Leary said, "I'll leave you then. Just come back down the stairs and to the back of the house to the kitchen when you're ready. You can't miss it."

Alone, Espy sat on the bed and then realized how tired she was. All she wanted to do was lie back and sleep. Forget everything until tomorrow morning. She leaned forward, her elbows on her knees.

Dear Lord, thank You for bringing me here. I don't know who these people are, but I thank You for bringing me somewhere safe. As she thought how she could be sleeping crouched somewhere outside in the open, she shuddered, awed by how she'd come upon this kind gentleman.

She had been foolish to come the way she did, too proud to ask for anyone's help. But God had been merciful. When she called on Him, He provided her with help.

With a weary sigh, her muscles aching, she got up from the bed, hearing the springs creak under the sagging mattress, and made her way to the washstand. A glance at herself showed her a pale face, the areas under her eyes shadowed. Her hair was falling onto her shoulders from her run to get away from the men.

Taking the remaining pins out, she finger-combed it. Her brush had been in her satchel, and she was too tired to look through her carpetbag for her comb. She twisted her hair up away from her face, securing the bun with her few pins. It would hold through dinner, she hoped.

After splashing her face with water and soaping a washcloth and scrubbing her skin, she looked less pale, at least. She breathed in the rose scent of the soap.

With a last pat of the towel, she hurried from the room, her stomach reminding her how hungry she was.

She found the kitchen easily enough, cheerful voices coming through the open door. A half-dozen people were seated at a long table, a couple of others serving.

Mr. Talbot motioned her forward. "Come in and have a seat. I'd like you to meet Marion Talbot, my wife."

The woman set down a serving dish and came toward Espy. "Hello, dear, so pleased to make your acquaintance."

Espy found her hand taken in the woman's warm, firm clasp. "Thank you for taking me in."

"It's our pleasure." In a brisker tone, she beckoned to the table. "Come, have something to eat while it's hot. We'll have everyone introduce themselves as you eat. Not everyone is here. Some work different shifts at some of the hotels and factories."

The next moment Espy was tucked into a chair between Miss O'Leary and an older woman. The middle-aged man from the hallway sat across from her and smiled, giving a slight bow of his head.

Mrs. Talbot seated herself at one end of the table and her husband retook his place at the opposite end. He bowed his head. "Dear Lord, we thank You for Your provision. Please bless this food and the hands that prepared it. In Your precious Son Jesus' name, Amen."

Espy folded her hands and closed her eyes before the end of the grace. She took the checked napkin at her place and unfolded it onto her lap. She helped herself to the rich stew from the serving dish that was passed to her. Feathery light rolls and creamy butter accompanied it. Afterward, a bowl of fruit was passed around. Espy took a yellow apple.

Mr. Talbot smiled at her. "One of the early varieties." He moved a small wooden board toward her. It had a block of cheese and sharp knife on it. "Try it with a slice of good cheddar. We've been blessed this year by a farmer who's made a piece of land available to us to farm. And in return for help with his livestock and his orchard, we are repaid with dairy products, eggs, apples, pears, and meat when he butchers a beef or a hog."

"How nice," she murmured, cutting her apple in wedges and nibbling on a corner, not quite sure what to make of his information.

The man in front of her was the first to stand. "Well, if you'll excuse me, I'll hit the hay. Early day tomorrow."

"Sure, Stanislas."

One by one the remaining people got up, taking their dishes to the sink and tucking their chairs in. They rerolled their napkins and put them in cubbyholes set against the wall by the door.

Two of them stayed and began washing the dishes while Mr. and Mrs. Talbot remained at the table. Espy was surprised to see that one of the helpers was a young man. She'd never seen a man doing a woman's work.

"Isn't it good?"

256

"What?" Seeing Mr. Talbot pointing to her apple and piece of cheese with the point of his fruit knife, she nodded. "Yes, delicious." The tangy apple mixed perfectly with the sharp cheese in a combination she'd never tried.

Mr. Talbot pushed away his fruit plate and sat back. Espy had the feeling he was preparing for some serious conversation. She braced herself for his questions, shooting a quick glance to his wife, who smiled reassuringly.

"Why don't you tell us how you came to be by the waterfront tonight in not the most savory neighborhood in Bangor?"

She stared at the bits of seeds and core on her small blue and white china plate.

"You needn't be afraid to tell us," Mrs. Talbot's soft voice came to her. "We're not here to judge you but to help you. We've all needed help at one time or another."

At the gentle words, Espy's vision blurred and her throat swelled up so she couldn't get any words out. They seemed to understand because they said no more. The soft murmur of the two people at the sink came to her with the clink of dishes and the opening and closing of cupboard doors.

Finally, she was able to draw in a deep breath. With her napkin, she dabbed at the corner of her eyes. "Th-thank you."

"Why don't you begin at the beginning?" Mr. Talbot suggested.

"I . . . I was robbed, just before you found me—" she glanced at Mr. Talbot—"otherwise I would be in a rooming house now. I came to Bangor to work as a typist."

"Where's your home?" Mrs. Talbot asked.

"Holliston."

"Have you ever worked as a typist?" her husband asked.

She shook her head. She dug into her pocket and extracted the ad. "But it says here that they'll train me. I've always worked hard, at the local cannery since I was fourteen."

Then as if a floodgate opened, she began to tell her story. Mr.

and Mrs. Talbot nodded and murmured their understanding, asking only a few questions.

She said nothing of her friendship with Warren, though several times his name was on the tip of her tongue, and she wished she could pour out her heart to someone about him. Instead she spoke of what had happened with Mr. Stockton. If they wanted to ask her to leave their house after hearing about it, it was better that they do so now.

But they expressed no shock or censure. Feeling more confident, she continued with how it had been in the weeks after she'd left the Stocktons' house.

She kept her gaze fixed firmly on her place setting, only glancing once or twice at either of them. She ended with, "I couldn't stand it in Holliston anymore, everyone looking at me as if I'd done a wicked thing, when I never did anything at all." She took another breath. "When I saw that advertisement I decided to come to Bangor, somewhere where no one would know me. I had a little bit saved up, enough for a day or two in a boarding house until I got a job, but when I arrived, I didn't realize how big Bangor was . . . that it was going to be so . . . so—"

"Easy to get lost?" Mr. Talbot ended with a smile.

She nodded.

He looked at her. "What happened to you at the Stocktons' is not so unusual."

She gulped. "It isn't?"

"Unfortunately, no."

"But everyone respects Mr. Stockton—he's a member of the church, he teaches school, I mean, he's such a nice, gentlemanly—" her face grew hot, "I mean that's why when I saw you—I was afraid—"

He smiled. "Very understandable. A man doesn't have to appear like poor Bill, the drunk," he replied to her puzzled look, and

258

she remembered the derelict Mr. Talbot had been talking to in the street, "to be dangerous."

"My dear," Mrs. Talbot spoke for the first time since Espy had related her story, "how awful for you, and to leave everything familiar. You must have been desperate to get away."

"I was. I couldn't stand being there anymore. But I did hate leaving Mama and Angela, and my younger brothers and sisters, of course. And I wouldn't have, if I thought they still needed me."

She lifted her eyes to them both, as if by sheer will, she could bring them to see. "I've always worked to make things better at home. It didn't matter if I had to leave school even though I loved going to school. It didn't matter that I had to work in the cannery as long as my brothers and sisters could continue on with school.

"When I got the job cleaning for Mrs. Stockton, I was so glad to be out of the cannery. When Mr. Stockton said I could read any books on his shelf and then offered to teach me things I had missed at school—why, it was like a little bit of heaven!"

Mrs. Talbot covered her hand. Gradually, Espy's fist relaxed under its warm hold. "That's very understandable."

Espy swallowed. "Coming to Bangor meant I could finally make something of myself. Was that so very wrong? I wouldn't have left if—if it hadn't been for Mr. Stockton."

"Of course not." Mrs. Talbot's voice soothed her.

"If you get a good job, which I have no doubt you'll eventually do, you can always send your family some money."

She turned to Mr. Talbot, hope rising in her breast. "I can?"

"Of course."

She frowned. "You said 'eventually.' Don't you think I can get work right away?"

He gave a slight shrug. "There are plenty of factories in Bangor. I'm sure you'll get something quickly."

She swallowed. "A factory job?"

"You want to work as a typist, don't you?" Mrs. Talbot asked.

Relieved that she seemed to understand, Espy nodded. "Yes, ma'am. I was so hoping to get something in an office now. I didn't mind cleaning house for the Stocktons, but I wanted to someday be able to live the way they do, and do some other kind of work than housecleaning or cleaning fish."

Mrs. Talbot patted her hand. "I'm sure you'll be able to get the right training here in Bangor."

Mr. Talbot spoke up. "Tell me something, Espy. May I call you that? We're like a family here, so we call each other by our first names. You may call us John and Marion."

She nodded, waiting for his question.

His hazel eyes looked steadily into hers until she felt he was seeing through any pretense. "Did you pray about coming to Bangor?"

The question threw her aback. "I . . . I prayed for God's protection and for His help," she began.

"Did you pray about whether it was His will for you to leave town and come to make your fortune here in Bangor?"

She began nodding her head but as she thought back, she was no longer sure. She'd been so anxious to leave, she hadn't really thought about anything except how soon she could get away. "I'm not sure if I prayed the way you said," she finally answered slowly. "I asked the Lord to help me, but I guess I just didn't think He'd want me to stay in Holliston either."

He simply nodded. "May I see the advertisement you clipped from the paper?"

She handed it to him. He read it and then passed it to his wife.

Espy fretted but then Mr. Talbot smiled. "I can show you where this is. I'm sure they need typists there, but they're a bit hard on women who work there. Before you go, would you like us to pray about it? What if the Lord has a better job for you in another company?"

She swallowed, her hopes rising before plummeting at his words. To think that as soon as tomorrow she could be training to be a typist. "But . . . what would I do if it's not? How do I support myself? I haven't any money left. I don't expect you to keep me for nothing."

"You can help out with the chores, as everyone who lives here does," replied Mrs. Talbot.

"In the meantime, we can take you to a typing school and enroll you in a course. It doesn't take long, six weeks perhaps. Armed with that skill, as well as shorthand, you can apply for any number of stenographer and typist positions. You can become more familiar with the city, see what companies are out there." Mr. Talbot gestured as if the city lay before her. "And see where the Lord leads you."

"But . . . doesn't a course cost money?"

"Don't worry about that," Mrs. Talbot said. "The Lord has set us in this neighborhood, which you may have noticed is full of newcomers, people from many nations. Primarily Irish as you'll soon see. If you'll help us, you may be surprised how the Lord will begin to work in your life."

Espy twisted her lips. "I don't know, ma'am. I'd feel more comfortable working in a factory. It seems church people are sometimes the first ones to treat you badly."

"Sometimes that happens, sadly," Mr. Talbot said quietly. "But perhaps the Lord sent you here to show you another part of His church."

"It's funny. The pastor of my church had asked me to help—" Espy swallowed, thinking of Warren, "form a young people's club to reach out to those in the community who usually didn't feel welcome in church."

"That's very commendable. What happened?"

Her lips turned downward. "It started well, but they were some of the first to want me out when this . . . happened." She clasped her hands together, kneading her fingers against the back of her hand, not wanting to remember it.

"Why don't we pray and see what the Lord would have you do?"

She nodded at Mr. Talbot's suggestion, and to her surprise he reached across and took one of her hands in his. She almost pulled back but Mrs. Talbot took her other hand. When all three had joined hands, they bowed their heads and closed their eyes. Mr. Talbot's quiet yet firm voice began, "Heavenly Father, we come before You and ask for You to show our sister Espy Your perfect and divine will . . ."

After he'd prayed, Mrs. Talbot prayed. Espy was amazed, never having seen Pastor Curtis's wife pray with her husband as an equal. Then they fell silent, and Espy sensed they were waiting for her to pray.

Feeling a strength in the warm handclasps on either side, she finally moistened her lips and took a deep breath, feeling as if she were stepping off a precipice.

"Dear God, thank You for bringing me here." Each word came out slowly, hesitantly. "Thank You for Mr. and Mrs. Talbot and what they've offered me. Please bless them for all they've given me." She realized she was emulating their prayer, which had begun with a lot of thanksgiving and recognition of what God had already done. It made her realize her prayers were filled with a lot of requests.

"Please keep Mama and Angela, Alvaro, Hortensia, Josiah, Daniel, Gus, Orrie, Gina, Alicia, and Julia safe." Her voice lowered to a whisper. "Please don't let Papa find their money and . . . spend it all on drink. Please bless each one of them."

She moistened her lips again. Was she ready to ask God to show her what He wished her to do—even if He told her to go back home?

"Please—" She sought how to word it, then began again, "Please show me what You want me to do. If . . . if You don't want me to work in that office, please show me. Just don't let me be a

262

burden here to the Talbots. Help me earn my keep and . . . and to learn what You want me to learn.

"Amen." She felt as if she'd relinquished something that had cost her, yet experienced a new lightness in the process.

20

DECEMBER 29, 1892

Warren gazed out the grimy window to the riverfront. The water was gray and frozen, great slabs of broken ice leaning against each other where the rapids were. The yard was quiet now, the bulk of the crew gone upriver into the woods for the winter to fell timber, which would come down the river with the log drive in May and June.

His gaze fell to the open letter in his hands. It was written on a fine, creamy vellum with the words Bangor Theological Seminary embossed in a dark blue script across the top, the street address in a small script at the bottom.

The body of the letter was typed, addressed to the Reverend Jeremiah Curtis. Pastor Curtis had given him the letter yesterday evening before the club meeting. All he'd said was that he had written to an old friend and colleague of his at the seminary and he wanted Warren to read the reply.

After the preliminary opening remarks, Warren got to the heart of the letter.

*Thank you so much for your recent communication concern-
ing your parishioner Warren Brentwood III. If the young man is
half what you say—and I do not doubt your evaluation, as I have
known you these many years—we would welcome him at the
seminary. The body of Christ needs such enterprising, searching
souls. We would be happy to receive him here in early January at
the beginning of the new term.*

It went on with some practical details, ending with the encouraging words that he would personally welcome Warren at the
seminary and help him settle in.

Once again, Warren looked at the outside scenery. His life had
mirrored the gray scene since early August . . . ever since Espy
Estrada left town. He'd finally gotten it from Angela that she was
all right, but her family would give him no further details of her
whereabouts.

No matter how many times his head had told him it was better this way—she could make a fresh start wherever she was, and
he, well, he could put that episode of his life squarely behind him
and continue plodding along the course set for him—his heart
found no joy in the facts.

Plodding. The word described exactly what life felt like. After
the passage of a few weeks when it became evident Espy had not
just lit off on a whim, but was gone for good, Warren had forced
himself to buckle down and focus on more important matters.

Work filled most of his time. He joined his father's business
committees, in an effort to have valid excuses not to attend the social events his mother planned—and avoid being seen as Christina's
escort.

He had not quit Holliston Lights but had given up trying to
lead it. He let Christina have her way at the meetings, supporting
her ideas for raising funds. He'd taken pleasure instead in getting
to know the recipients of those funds.

He'd had to enlist Alvaro's help. The boy refused at first, but Warren took pains to cultivate his friendship and those of the young men he spent time with. Warren coached them in baseball. Little by little, he met their families.

His greatest satisfaction had been when Angela rejoined the church club. Will and Henry followed.

His only pleasure in life these days seemed to be when he was actively doing something to help the needy. He put up with the business end of the club meetings, listening to Christina and pretending to favor her ideas, listening to the businessmen in the community as they proposed improvements for the town, but in the end, he concluded it was all words, words, words with no real change.

The joy came for him when he was filling food baskets or arranging a delivery of split wood or coal to one of the houses along the riverfront or on the outskirts of town where the immigrants and cannery workers tended to congregate.

They had just finished the largest project to date: wrapping dozens of Christmas gifts for not only the town's needy children but also for those in the surrounding hamlets.

His own family celebration seemed a letdown after that evening playing Santa Claus.

Opening presents around their tree, followed by a large meal, and then sitting in the parlor receiving guests for the rest of the afternoon merely left him feeling overfed and drained.

He glanced back down at the letter.

His father would not budge on the pulp mill idea despite the figures Warren had presented to him time and again. Shipments of lumber continued to decline as more and more sawmills opened on the Pacific coast.

By the time his father acknowledged the need to diversify, it would mean getting in late to a new industry.

Warren fingered the edge of the stationery. If he were to pursue theological studies, it was now or never, while he was still relatively young and single. He could not ask a wife to uproot herself and their comfortable way of life for a future of uncertainty and possibly poverty. Not that he had any plans to be married anytime soon.

He refolded the letter and put it back in its envelope and slipped it into his breast pocket. Then he straightened his shoulders, already anticipating his father's reaction when he spoke with him this evening.

But first he would speak with Pastor Curtis and pray with him.

21

BANGOR, APRIL 1893

Espy pushed on the brass handle of the front entrance of Peabody's Clothing Manufactory and exited onto Harlow Street. With a glance at the sky visible between the tall buildings filling both sides of the busy street, she breathed deeply of the spring air.

She had a half hour of freedom. Wasting no time, she set off toward the small restaurant where she usually took her lunch.

Just as she reached the corner, she stopped dead.

She blinked. Could it be? Pedestrians brushed past her, but she couldn't move, her feet stuck to the plank sidewalk as if she'd been nailed there, her eyes fixed on the familiar tall young man eyeing the traffic. As he looked her way, his eyes caught hers and doubled back.

For a second she thought of doing an about-face and fleeing.

Warren crossed the street, his long stride heading straight for her. He looked unchanged, his light brown hair neatly combed away from his face, his green eyes staring into hers.

"Espy, is it you?" he asked, his voice filled with wonder.

Suddenly she felt a shot of pure joy. It was Warren and he seemed glad to see her. She nodded vigorously; a laugh slipped out of her.

"W-what a-are you doing here?" he asked.

Her smile broadened. "I should ask you that question. What are you doing in Bangor?"

He shook his head as if in a daze. "It's a long story. Look, where are you off to this minute? I mean, do you have a few minutes to visit with . . . with an old . . . friend?" He stumbled over the last word.

"Yes, yes, I do." She gestured to the building behind her. "I work over there but I just left for lunch. I have a half hour."

He shook his head as if trying to process everything. "W-would, I mean, could I join you? Better yet, may I *invite* you?" Again, he grinned with a certain amount of chagrin. "I don't have a lot of funds, but I do have enough for lunch."

"I don't expect you to buy me lunch—"

Before she could finish, he took her arm lightly in his and began propelling her forward. "Let's hear no more about that. You don't know how good it is to see a friendly face from home. Come along, is there a place you usually frequent?"

She nodded, allowing him to carry her along.

By the time they crossed the street, her wits were returning and she began to think of what he'd said. "A friendly face from home? What do you mean?"

"I've been living here in Bangor since January."

She gasped. Before she could ask why, he added, "I enrolled at the theological seminary up the hill." Warren grinned sidelong at her. "Pastor Curtis pulled some strings so that I could begin the new term after Christmas."

"Theological seminary?" Wasn't that where men went to study for the ministry?

"Where are we going?"

"What? Oh, just here, there's a small restaurant, not too

269

expensive," she said, feeling bad that he felt he would pay for her. She wondered what he meant by not having many funds.

He smiled at her reference to money, and again, she felt a queer sensation travel through her. How could he still have that effect on her? Hadn't she relegated him to her past—her mortifying past, thanks to the Talbots and the new life they'd made possible for her?

"I'll explain it all to you once we've ordered something to eat. I don't know about you, but I'm starving. Is this the place?"

She nodded at the glass-fronted eatery. He held the door open for her and she entered.

"Hello there, Espy." The stout middle-aged proprietor beamed at her from among the crowded tables.

"Hello, Mrs. Pratt. Do you have an empty table?"

With a curious look at Warren, she addressed Espy. "You know how it is at noon. Every office and shop empties out and it seems like the clerks and typists haven't been fed in a week." She chuckled, wiping her hands with the edge of her apron. "But come along, I always find a table for you."

As she spoke, she led them between the round tables, her words drowned out by the high level of voices.

"There you go." Mrs. Pratt invited them to sit at a table covered with a blue-checked cloth. "Who's your new friend, dear?"

Warren held the chair out for Espy. "Thank you," she murmured, feeling unused to having a gentleman be so attentive to her. She addressed Mrs. Pratt, since clearly she would not leave until Espy had answered her question. "This is a—a friend from back home, Warren Brentwood."

"How lovely to see someone from home. Pleased to make your acquaintance, Mr. Brentwood." She smiled at Warren, her plump hands folded in front of her apron.

"Likewise, Mrs. Pratt." Warren took his seat. "I hear the food is good in this establishment," he said with a twinkle in his eyes toward Espy.

Warmth suffused her cheeks and quickly she took the menu card sandwiched between the sugar bowl and salt and pepper shakers.

Mrs. Pratt rattled off the day's specials. After the two had ordered, Espy asking for only a bowl of hearty oxtail soup, wanting to keep the price low, they turned to each other, a silence falling between them.

She focused on Warren's hands folded atop the table, realizing they were both sitting in the same position. She quickly took up her napkin and unfolded it as an excuse to move her hands beneath the small table.

"So."

At his one word she met his look. The twinkle was still in his eyes. "So," she repeated back to him.

"I heard from Angela that you'd headed to Bangor when you left Holliston." All amusement disappeared from his green eyes.

Where was the man who had judged her as harshly as the rest? She pressed her lips together, determined to keep all bitter thoughts away. John and Marion Talbot had taught her the importance of not harboring any root of bitterness in her heart.

Her own reading of the Scriptures had confirmed this and helped her to begin a new life, free from any encumbrances of the past.

But now the past was staring her in the face. She took a deep breath. "Yes. I came here."

He quirked an eyebrow. "Do you have family here?"

She shook her head.

He swallowed. "Angela refused to give me any more details, though she assured me you were doing fine."

"I am."

His eyes scanned hers. "I suppose it made sense to start over somewhere big enough where no one . . . knew you." He looked away briefly, and she detected a slight flush along his jaw line.

"Yes."

271

He cleared his throat. "That was brave of you to just venture forth so far from home, not knowing anyone. At least I had Pastor Curtis to help me."

"I saw an advertisement in a newspaper about jobs for typists. That's why I came here."

His brows knit together. "Typist? I didn't know you knew how to type."

"I didn't, but it said they would train you."

He nodded slowly as if digesting this information. "I see." He looked past her toward the street. "I forget what a bustling place Bangor is. I suppose they are desperate for employees."

"There is a lot of opportunity here. After I learned to type, it didn't take me long to find a job as a stenographer-typist at a large clothing manufactory. They have a typing pool on the fourth floor. One half is devoted to seamstresses, and the other half is partitioned and holds the typists."

At the growing look of wonder on Warren's face, she lifted her chin, glad he could see how well she was doing. "I got promoted a couple of months ago. I'm Mr. Hill's personal assistant now. He's the vice president."

"Goodness, that's wonderful, Espy. I always knew you were smart."

Espy warmed at the praise. "He said I was a hard worker and that he could see I got along with everyone. Of course, he also said he likes a good looking gal in his front office." She blushed, immediately regretting the words, even though they were true. What made her rattle on that way? It was because she was nervous.

"Be careful, Espy."

He didn't think she was going to let herself be in that kind of situation again, did he? "He's a fat old man with a wife who comes in most every day like a dragon, always inspecting what I'm doing as if she expects me to steal something out of my desk." She shook her head. "As if I'd need one of their pencils."

Warren's brow furrowed. Afraid she'd painted too dire a picture, she added, "Otherwise, it's a very good job. I make twelve dollars a week. Two dollars more than I did when I was in the typing pool." She sat back with a satisfied smile on her face when he whistled softly.

"You'll soon be rolling in the dough."

She chuckled, glad the moment of unease had passed between them.

"Here you go." This time it was Mr. Pratt, who came by with their food, setting down a plate in front of Warren and the bowl of soup before Espy. "Careful, the plates are hot. Enjoy." He looked at Warren as he spoke, and Espy realized he was just as curious as his wife about her companion.

When he left, Espy hesitated a moment. "Would you like to say grace?"

He smiled. "Sure." He bowed his head, folding his hands, and she followed suit.

"Thank You, Lord, for this food and for all Your provision." He paused and Espy wondered if he was finished but just as she was about to say "Amen," he spoke. "Thank You for allowing me to find Espy today. Thank You for keeping her safe all this time." He drew in a breath. "Please bless this food to our bodies' use. In Your precious name, Lord Jesus, Amen."

Espy looked at Warren in surprise. His prayer sounded so much like the kind John Talbot said every evening. Before she could remark on it, Warren dug into his food, and she did the same, realizing how hungry she was. She remembered how little time she had and felt a stab of regret.

When they paused in their eating, he said, "You're making more money than some of the men in the sawmill. I'm impressed."

She smiled. "I'm saving money and still able to send some home. I felt bad leaving Mama and Angela carrying on alone, but they said they were doing fine, especially with Alvaro working."

She leaned toward Warren. "I wanted to thank you for keeping him on. Angela wrote me that he is doing all right at the mill."

"He's a good worker." A slight color tinged his cheekbones. "I think—hope—I was a good influence on him." His green eyes looked earnestly into hers, as if seeking her approval. "We formed a baseball team back in the fall, Alvaro and some of his friends, a few of the mill workers and I."

He gave her an abashed smile, making him look more boyish than she was used to seeing him. He was still handsome enough to take her breath away.

As he bent his head to continue eating, she studied him a moment. There was something different about him. It was hard to pinpoint exactly. Before she could figure it out, he asked, "How are your mother and sisters and brothers? I've been away since January." A slight crease formed between his eyebrows. "I don't get news of them anymore."

"The brood? They're all fine, growing like weeds. And Mama —she's fine. She was sick this winter and Hortensia had to take some time off from school to nurse her, because Angela was working. But she's better now, back at the cannery. Papa's been away all winter."

Before he could ask anything more about her father, she hurried on, "Alvaro is still at the sawmill, which I'm sure you know. And the others are in school, except for Julia and Alicia, of course. The boys don't always like it, but Angela makes sure they go."

His gaze was warm and friendly as she spoke, so different from the last time she'd seen him when he'd run off as if she were contagious. Realizing time was running out and she had not discovered anything about him, she hurried on, "Tell me how you are doing in Bangor. You could have knocked me over when I saw you on the street as if you were going to work like any other gentleman."

His expression sobered, and she felt a sudden disquiet. "What is it, has something happened at home? Is your family well?"

He nodded, dispelling her fears with a slight smile. "They're all fine, at least from Annalise's last letter."

She waited, sensing there was more. "She's the only one who writes me. You see, I left Holliston against my father's wishes."

Warren watched Espy's expression as he spoke the words. He'd dreaded—and looked forward to—this moment. When he'd first left for Bangor, he'd determined not to seek her. He was entering the ministry and must put temptations behind him.

What a shock to find her again. All these months he'd banished her from his thoughts and yet, he realized the moment he saw her face in the crowd, her beauty shining, that she'd lurked in the recesses of his mind.

If anything, she was more beautiful than before. Her umber eyes stared widely into his, their black lashes long and thick, her tawny skin translucent. Her ebony hair was neatly coiled at her nape. She wore a starched shirtwaist with a pink pinstripe and short dark blue Windsor tied around its high neck. Its masculine severity made her look all the more appealing.

Her eyes widened at his words. "Against his wishes—what do you mean? Please tell me before I have to go back to work."

Hearing the urgency in her voice, he pushed his clean plate aside. As briefly as he could, he explained the journey he'd found himself on since he'd arrived in Holliston at the beginning of last summer. He studied her face with each word, wishing he could know her reaction. Did she think he was an absolute fool or just naive or misguided, the way most people back home did? Which he, himself, increasingly felt.

"Here I'd spent all this time traveling abroad only to come back home and feel more restless than I'd ever felt. Except this was different." He tapped his chest. "This was inside, where just going off on a trip wouldn't cure me."

He cleared his throat. "I felt the Lord was leading me to the ministry, no matter how farfetched the notion sounds. Go ahead and laugh. You won't be the only one."

"Oh, no, Warren," she said softly, awe in her golden eyes, "I think it's wonderful."

He stared at her. "You do?"

She nodded. "God is so amazing the way He works in our lives, when we allow Him to. Who would have thought He brought you home and then guided you here to study for the ministry? And Pastor Curtis is behind you."

"Yes, he was my only ally. I don't know if Father resigned his membership. Maybe he's attending the Methodist Church these days," he said in an attempt at humor.

"Annalise would have told you, wouldn't she?"

"Yes, you're right. She's not allowed to write me, but manages to, nonetheless. I never thought she'd have the courage to defy Father, though, of course, he knows nothing."

"I think your sister has more grit in her than anybody imagines."

He smiled. "Do you? I think the two of you could become friends." Then realizing how foolish his words were, he cleared his throat. "Listen, Espy, I'm sorry about how . . . how things transpired in Holliston for you . . . that is, that you had to leave the way you did."

To his surprise, she reached out a hand and patted his arm, then as if regretting the touch, she drew back, color suffusing her cheeks.

Warren continued to feel her touch, however.

"It's all right. That's all behind me now. I think the Lord brought me here to Bangor, too. Not that He wanted all that happened in Holliston, but as John says, 'God meant it for good.'"

Warren frowned. "John?"

She nodded vigorously, the color in her cheeks deepening. "John and Marion Talbot are my closest friends in Bangor. I live with them, in fact. He was the one who rescued me the night I first arrived in Bangor."

Before he could hear more, she glanced at her watch and

gasped. "Goodness, I must get back to the office. Mr. Hill will have my hide!"

He stood and put some money on the table. "Wait, let me walk you back."

Thanking him for the lunch, she began wending her way between the tables. Warren hurried after her, terrified he'd lose her again so soon after finding her.

He managed to reach the door in time to hold it open for her. With a grateful glance, she murmured her thanks before stepping into the street.

He wanted to take her arm but hesitated, remembering her drawing back when she touched him. He'd treated her abominably back in Holliston when she found herself shunned. Whatever she did in the professor's house did not justify Warren's cowardly behavior.

He'd learned a lot in the months since. He wished he could go back and change much of his previous behavior. "How do you like Bangor?" he asked, matching her quick stride, trying to prolong their conversation.

She glanced at him with a smile. "Very much." She made a face. "Not at first. But I met John and Marion. They've helped me enormously. I don't think I'd have lasted if it hadn't been for them. They run . . . a house of sorts for people who don't have any place to go to in Bangor."

"What kind of house?"

"It's a Christian house, a boardinghouse called House of Hope. John—Mr. Talbot—is a pastor." She smiled. "Not like Pastor Curtis. He never wears a collar and you wouldn't know it if you just met him on the street. Everyone calls him John. When you begin talking to him, though, you realize how much of the Bible he knows. He's not so different from Pastor Curtis after all."

Intrigued, he probed further. "Does he have a church?"

"No, but we have lots of Bible studies in the evenings. And we attend a church nearby. He calls House of Hope a mission."

"I see." Before he had a chance to find out more, they arrived at the large brick building taking up the block.

"Well, here we are."

He nodded. "W-would you like to have lunch again tomorrow?" He felt as hesitant as a schoolboy.

Her smile reassured him. "Sure. But I don't expect you to pay for me." Her eyes brightened. "Why don't I pack a lunch and we can have it in the park?" She gestured behind her. "The one in back of the Bangor Hotel?"

He smiled, liking the idea. "Yes." He glanced up at the sky. "Let's hope it's as beautiful as today. Tell me what to bring."

She thought a second. "A blanket to sit on, though they have benches, too."

"Same time as today?"

"Noon is fine."

It seemed neither wanted to be the first to leave. "I'd better go in."

"Allow me." He opened the door for her.

"Thank you."

Someone came up behind her so she was forced to enter the building. With a wave and smile, she disappeared as other people pushed through the doorway. He stood a few seconds longer until he realized he was in the way.

Shoving his hands in his pockets, he made his way down the street, his heart feeling lighter than it had in days . . . weeks.

It had been good to see Espy. A friendly face from home. It made him realize how lonely he'd been since he arrived.

She'd looked as beautiful as ever—but so prim and proper. It was more than her altered physical appearance. Despite her friendly welcome of him, he sensed a new reserve in her. He didn't quite understand it and wanted to see her again to see if it was just his imagination. Did it have something to do with her living with a Christian family? She'd been a churchgoer before, yet, besides her eagerness to help the poor, had not struck him as particularly devout. Except for that time she'd told him how much she loved hearing the Scriptures. It had struck him at the time, but he'd forgotten that memory.

Now, he thought about how she'd initiated saying grace over their simple lunch. He compared it to his own spiritual awakening.

He'd come to Bangor at great personal sacrifice. When he'd finally approached his father, his reaction was worse than Warren had anticipated. The interview had ended in a shouting match, which even now pained him to recall.

The next day, his father had assumed Warren was ready to take back all he'd said. When he'd seen Warren's resolve to leave for Bangor unchanged, his father, with no hint of the previous evening's emotion, had stated his terms: *Fine. Have your way then. Get it out of your system. But don't expect any help from your family. As far as I'm concerned, you are abandoning us, so I want it clear there will be no financial assistance or any communication between us.*

Warren had almost given up then. But something inside him held fast to his resolve. He didn't think it was pride. If he'd thought he could submit to his father's plan for his life, he would have gladly done so, if it meant being back in his father's—and family's—good graces.

Pride, moreover, would not have withstood his mother's entreaties. She'd come to him afterward and pleaded with him, tears in her eyes. Pride would not have been able to see his mother's heart breaking and stand unmoving.

Annalise had knocked on his door later that evening when everyone had retired. She'd been the only one to listen to him and attempt to understand why he seemed to suddenly want to throw everything away for something that appeared a whim.

But after he confessed what he'd been going through in the months he'd been home, she took his hand and squeezed it and wished him Godspeed.

279

She made him promise to write her in care of Dexter.

He also corresponded regularly with Pastor Curtis, though for several weeks now he'd found it hard to write. He had little time, between attending classes at the seminary, doing outdoor chores for the professor where he boarded, and holding down a job as night watchman on the seminary's grounds in order to pay for his studies.

He crossed the bridge over the Kendusteag Stream and headed uphill toward the seminary. He had an hour before his class and planned to spend it in the library studying.

Biblical Hebrew and Greek, Old and New Testament, church history, biblical exegesis, philosophy of religion, and systemic theology. He felt overwhelmed most of the time. Much of it was merely catching up with what the other students had already had the previous semester. He spent many of the night hours between his watchman rounds over his books.

Lately, he kept asking himself if he'd made the right decision.

The work didn't scare him. He knew he could work hard if he was certain of his goal. But instead of growing closer to God, he felt that all the academic theological courses were drawing him further and further away from a personal knowledge of God.

His soul felt as dry as the tomes he pored over.

He wondered if something were wrong with him. This made it difficult to write to Pastor Curtis. The man had done so much to help him. Neither could he talk to the professor where he boarded. The man was austere and distant with him, and Warren felt he was putting his family out by taking a room.

The other students seemed dedicated to their program of study. None of them was working a job outside of his studies, so they had time to get to know each other. For the first time in his life, Warren had no outside support; he must work for whatever he wanted or needed.

And he felt as if his purpose eluded him more than ever before.

22

Espy left her office building promptly at noon, carrying the picnic basket in one hand, her parasol in the other. She gulped a breath of air, trying to calm her nerves as she looked up and down the street.

"Hello there."

She jumped at the low sound of Warren's voice behind her. "Goodness, you startled me."

He stood smiling at her, his green eyes softly lit with humor—and gladness to see her, she hoped. "I'm sorry. I didn't mean to, but I saw you looking around."

"H-how long have you been waiting?"

He gave a slight shrug. "Oh, not more than five minutes."

She nodded, finding herself speechless.

"Shall we go?"

Remembering her short lunch break, she nodded.

He held out his hand. "Allow me." He took the basket from her and she noticed he carried a dark, folded blanket. She opened her parasol and walked along beside him.

She didn't have to direct him; he knew the city as well as she.

In a few minutes, they arrived at the downtown park as large as a city block. The trees were just unfurling their pale green leaves. Tulip beds brought splashes of red and yellow to the center of the park. Warren led them to a sunny spot and examined the grass for dampness.

Satisfied, he set down the basket and spread out the blanket. She took hold of the opposite corners and helped lay it out.

Placing the basket in the middle, he invited her with a smile to sit down. "There."

She sat, arranging her blue serge skirt, and then leaned forward to open the picnic basket. "Chicken salad sandwiches," she said, extracting the items, "hard-boiled eggs, some applesauce."

He helped her unwrap and uncover things and distribute the napkins and cutlery. "Sounds delicious. Better than I'm used to eating."

She glanced at him, wondering where he lived.

They bowed their heads, as if by accord, when everything was spread out, and said a brief blessing.

Espy eyed him over her sandwich.

"Mm-mm," he said, his mouth full, and she smiled, pleased that he was enjoying the food.

"Marion helped me with everything, so I can't take all the credit," she said as soon as she could speak. She poured them both some lemonade and washed down the last of her sandwich before sitting back and taking a look around her.

"That was very nice of her."

"What is it like where you live?" she asked, wanting to get a better picture of his life in Bangor.

But he only shrugged. "Typical boardinghouse, I suppose. One of the professors at the seminary takes in students when they need a place to stay, but he also has some younger sons of his own, and his wife seems to have enough on her hands to be saddled with anyone extra." He took a bite of the hard-boiled egg. "It's very nice here."

She looked around her, realizing he didn't want to pursue the topic. The back of the large hotel bordered one side of the park, smaller buildings two other sides, but southward, beyond the railroad tracks, they could see the wide river and the town of Brewer across it. Several schooners lined the waterfront. "Yes, it seems peaceful in the middle of a city."

His eyes met hers as if understanding more than she could articulate. "Quite a bit different from Holliston, isn't it?"

"Do you miss home?"

He took his time answering, finishing his egg first and then taking a sip of lemonade and finally wiping his mouth with the gingham napkin. He leaned back on his elbows and looked toward the river.

"Yes." He took a deep breath. "More so when I question whether I did right in coming here."

"You'd make a good pastor," she found herself saying unexpectedly.

His eyes widened a fraction as if startled by her words. "Do you really think so?"

"Yes." The conviction in her tone grew stronger. "I could see it last summer when Pastor Curtis asked you to lead the Holliston Lights. And whenever you addressed the group—even on the Fourth of July when you read the Declaration of Independence— you sound so confident, a real leader."

A shadow crossed his gaze, as if her response disappointed him. Her own spirits fell, afraid she hadn't given him what he needed.

"I don't think being able to address a crowd is anything special. I'm afraid I don't have what it takes inside to make . . . to make a good pastor." Again he looked toward the river. "Do I have a shepherd's heart?"

She drew her knees up and planted her elbows on them, leaning her chin in her hands. "I think you do. You were the one who rallied us to work together in the club, you gave Alvaro a chance, and from what you said, you've given him and his friends your friendship." Her voice softened. "You do care about people even if you don't think so."

His lips quirked upward. "Thank you, Espy."

Her eyes widened. "For what?"

"You're the first person since Pastor Curtis who's made me feel I've made the right decision."

Warmth spread through her at his words. Before she could ask him anything more, he said, "What about you? You seem—" he hesitated as if looking for a word, "—happy."

She brushed off the crumbs from her skirt. "I am. Happier than I've ever been—except for missing my family."

He cleared his throat. "About what happened in Holliston—"

A slight flush tinged his cheekbones. She knew instinctively he was uncomfortable bringing up the topic. He still thought she was guilty. "I've put it behind me."

He blinked, pulling his face back a fraction, her words taking him aback, she could see. "I see. Well, tell me about your life here."

He'd recovered quickly. Part of her ached with a longing she had thought long dead. A longing to have him believe in her innocence.

She began to tell him about the warmth and welcome she'd found at House of Hope.

He'd listened to her enthusiasm about her lessons with Mr. Stockton and had encouraged her before, but she'd felt he was humoring her like an older person a younger one just starting out on a journey the other had already taken.

Now, it was as if she were telling Warren something new, something he'd never experienced. He asked her a question, whenever she paused, as if afraid she'd stop.

"I feel as if my knowledge of Christ has grown by leaps and bounds since arriving in Bangor. The Lord really showed me that He'll never leave me or forsake me. I arrived with so little." She spread her hands out with a laugh. "What little I had was stolen from me on arrival, and yet, the Lord sent me straight to John. I've learned so much from him and his wife." It was on the tip of her tongue to compare him to Mr. Stockton and his lessons, but she stopped herself. That episode in her life was finished—a closed book.

"I've also learned so much from the Bible. When we're not on the street ministering or running the soup kitchen, we sit around the kitchen table studying the Scriptures and praying for the souls living around us."

Something flickered in his eyes.

She laughed. "My, look how I've gone on and on. I've hardly heard about your studies at the seminary. I've walked by it before. With its red brick buildings covered in ivy, it looks like a place for learned men. I see such serious students and professors walking across its trimmed lawns."

He only smiled.

She glanced at her watch, sorry to see her half hour was up and she'd hardly heard from him. "I'd better get back to work."

He began to put things away and she followed suit.

"Everything was delicious, Espy. Please thank Mrs. Talbot for me."

"I will." They rose and Warren took up the blanket to shake it. She said with a laugh, "You may thank your landlady for use of the blanket."

He made a face. "It's just a horse blanket from the barn. That's all I was able to use."

"Well, it served us very well."

As he took the basket and blanket and they began walking across the park toward the street, she said on impulse, "Would you like to meet John and Marion for yourself?" Her face colored, wondering if she was being presumptuous. "Since you are studying for the ministry and John is a minister, I thought you might find it useful."

Instead of being offended, his eyes lit up. "I should like that very much."

"Let me tell him and I shall let you know which day." She would ask them if she could bring him to dinner.

"I look forward to it."

At the door to her office building, he handed her the basket. "Thank you, Espy. That was a delicious lunch. But your company was even better."

She felt her cheeks redden. "Thank you."

A clerk brushed by her. "You'd better get in if you don't want Mr. Hill bellowing." With a smile and curious look at Warren, he entered the glass door.

Warren held out his hand. "I won't keep you. Wouldn't want you getting yelled at." He hesitated. "May I stop by tomorrow or is that too soon?"

His hand felt warm around hers. "Tomorrow is fine." She was afraid to ask if he meant they should lunch together again and she didn't want to presume.

"I'll be here, same time then." He let her hand go and pulled open the door for her.

As she turned to reenter the building, he said, "If you'd care to have lunch with me, I'll be honored."

Two office girls came up behind her, forcing her through the door, but she managed to nod. "All right, that'd be nice."

Her last impression was of a look of relief passing his features as she walked slowly toward the elevator.

Did he seem as pleased—and as unsure—as she was of their . . . friendship?

● ● ●

The next day Warren talked a little more to Espy about how wrenching his leave-taking had been from his family. He'd hesitated to open that painful topic, especially since, with each passing day, he began to wonder more whether he'd made the right decision.

But Espy asked him about his family and home, and he found himself talking in a way he hadn't imagined he could do with anyone.

He remembered the cloud she'd left under and realized if anyone could understand homesickness and doubt, it was Espy.

She seemed so different, nothing like the girl in Holliston. This young woman seemed so demure by comparison, and yet, more attractive than ever.

He watched the way her thick dark eyelashes covered her eyes when he paid her a compliment, the rosy tint suffusing her cheeks, with a modesty she hadn't possessed before.

This was nothing like what he'd felt for her in Holliston. This was something deeper, as if he'd finally met someone who understood him. He crumpled his napkin and glanced down at his empty plate. He'd spent money he could ill-afford to take her to the same restaurant she'd taken him to the first day. But he didn't care. He wanted to see her every day if it was possible.

"So, now, I'm not sure," he found himself saying, looking into her sympathetic eyes. "The more I study here, the further I seem to be from the life I feel the Lord was leading me to."

She tapped a slim forefinger against her chin. "I think you should talk to John. I'm sure he'll be able to help you. He seems to be doing what you have a heart to do—reach people."

"I don't want to impose on him."

"Nonsense. They said you'd be welcome to stop by anytime. In fact, they invited you to dinner tonight, if that's not too soon."

He swallowed, feeling a keen sense of anticipation. "Not at all, that is, if you aren't tired of seeing me." He laughed self-consciously.

Warren longed to reach out and take her hand but he held back, the memory of how awfully he'd treated her stopping him. He hadn't broached that subject again, afraid she'd stop him as firmly as she had when he'd first brought up the scandal that had forced her to leave. But he felt their own past history lying between them like a logjam on the river. The longer he waited, the larger it seemed to build up, blocking any further deepening of their new friendship.

He had lain awake the previous night, staring at the dark ceiling, considering the irony of the situation.

For he was no longer in any position to offer any woman anything. He had no money, no prospects except some nebulous dream of preaching the gospel someday—he didn't know where or when. This masters of divinity degree he was pursuing would take another year—if he could manage it.

He had been reluctant to marry when his parents wanted nothing more. Now, he longed for the kind of companionship and partnership that true love with the right woman would bring.

What was it about Espy that gave him the confidence to open up, risking appearing less in her eyes by revealing his weaknesses? She never displayed anything less than understanding and compassion.

As far as her fall from grace with Mr. Stockton, Warren wasn't troubled. Espy was much improved and in good hands in Bangor.

Her old life was behind her, he felt sure.

By the time they parted after lunch, he was counting the hours until he could see her in the evening. At five o'clock sharp, he stood again in front of Peabody's Clothing Manufactory, waiting for Espy to exit. They would take the streetcar to her boardinghouse. He would finally meet the couple who was responsible for the new Espy.

A moment later, young men and women, clerks and typists streamed out the department store entrance. Espy emerged and, spotting him, immediately smiled.

Her smile never failed to warm him. He walked forward to meet her.

"All set?"

"Yes. We can take the streetcar at the corner. It shouldn't take long."

He offered his arm, and a second later he felt her hand upon it.

They chatted about her day at the office and his at his classes while they waited for the streetcar and then as they rode along. The car was crowded with people heading home from work.

They exited a few stops after the main train station. "We can walk from here. It's a few blocks toward the river."

He looked around him, not having come to this part of town before. It was the immigrant neighborhood, mostly Irish but with some Jewish and Eastern Europeans as well. The streets were crammed with row houses side by side with warehouses and factories. The air was thick with the soot from the tall smokestacks belching smoke. The clacking of a train thundered past as they approached the tracks near the river.

"It's just up here," she indicated with her hand.

"The train must keep you awake at night."

"You get used to it. I hardly hear it anymore."

As they approached the river, the clapboard houses were hardly more than shanties. Despite the cool spring evening, several individuals lounged or sat on porches. The smell of tobacco and murmur of voices wafted across the street.

His heart sank, thinking that Espy's lot hadn't improved much from her life in Holliston.

Espy led him up the walkway to a wide roofed porch of a two-story clapboard house, which seemed a little neater and better kept than the others. A gas lamp was lit outside the door. He read the sign, *House of Hope*, in wonder.

She opened the door and invited him in. Fragrant smells greeted his nostrils. A moment later an attractive woman appeared, a smile on her face, a hand outstretched.

"You must be Warren Brentwood. Welcome to House of Hope. I'm Marion Talbot."

He clasped the woman's hand. "Thank you for having me, Mrs. Talbot."

"Any friend of Espy's is a friend of ours. Please, call me Marion. I imagine you both must be hungry. Espy, why don't you show Warren the washroom and then take him into the dining parlor? You can meet the rest of the 'clan,'" she added over her shoulder with a laugh.

When he entered the dining room a few minutes later, a large group was assembled, men and women of various ages. Before he spotted Espy, a trim, middle-aged man with graying hair approached him with a smile. "Warren Brentwood?"

At his nod, the man held out his hand. "John Talbot. Please, call me John. I'm sure my wife has already expressed our welcome, but allow me to do the honors and present you to a few of our 'family' members."

Warren remembered few of the names. What struck him was the welcome in everyone's eyes and words.

"Is everything all right?" Espy whispered when she came to sit beside him at the long table.

He grinned at her. "A little overwhelming but otherwise fine."

"It took me a few days to get everyone straight. And new people come all the time as older residents move on once they get on their feet."

"Mr.—uh—John called them 'family.'"

"They are. We're all part of the family of Christ here."

He pondered this as John tapped his fork against his glass. "Let's ask a blessing for our food."

Everyone bowed his head and Warren followed suit.

After they all said "amen," voices rose once more, dishes were passed back and forth, and cutlery clinked against china. Things quieted as people began to eat, but then conversation began again.

Warren was content to listen to snatches around him. People asked about each other's day. He got the impression that everyone was employed in offices or factories. They ranged in ages from Espy's age to men with grizzled hair and graying muttonchop whiskers.

John asked him a question now and again to include him in whatever conversation was going on at his end of the table.

Warren was grateful to go relatively unnoticed. He was hungry, for one thing, and the food was much tastier than his usual fare.

It was only after everyone had finished and left the table that John sat back and invited Warren to linger a while at the table.

Espy joined the others in clearing the table. When Warren made a gesture to rise, she waved him down. "I'll be back in a bit. Washing up goes quickly with so many helping hands."

When she left, John leaned back and smiled. "Espy told me how you ran into each other. Funny, both of you being in Bangor and not realizing it."

"It sure was good to see her—a friendly face from home."

"Espy was quite surprised that you were attending the seminary. My alma mater," he added with a smile.

Warren looked at him with more interest. "You went there, sir?"

He chuckled. "Quite a few years ago."

Warren wanted to ask him much but he hesitated. He'd only just met the gentleman, but somehow felt an empathy with him. Although the silence lengthened between them, there was an unrushed air about John Talbot.

Warren cleared his throat. "Tell me about House of Hope. How did it begin?"

"The Lord gave me the gift of evangelism—that is, to preach the gospel outside the church. I began many years ago, after leaving the seminary, by traveling from church to church taking the gospel of salvation. But in my travels to lots of towns and cities, I began noticing those outside the church—those living in the tenements, those not speaking English well because they'd recently arrived on our shores. So, I came back to Bangor and began preaching in the streets here in this neighborhood where most of the immigrants end up.

"Gradually, it became a ministry of helps as well. You can't just preach to people who lack the necessities. Being a waterfront neighborhood, we also have a lot of drifters, sailors, merchant marines, loggers, which leads to problems with liquor and vagrancy. So, I began a soup kitchen, which we still run. In time, it grew to include a place for people to stay."

He stretched out his hand toward his wife, who was entering from the kitchen. "Needless to say, I couldn't have done any of this without a good right hand, which the Lord was so kind to provide in this dear lady."

A look of mutual admiration passed between the two, before Marion took a seat opposite Warren.

A few minutes later, Espy came in with a tea tray. As John continued to speak about the ministry, she gave each one a cup of tea. Warren smiled his thanks, glad to have her take the seat beside him once more.

Warren asked a few questions, but mostly, he just listened to both John and Marion speak of their years of living by faith.

"Little by little, as we were faithful with the gift the Lord had given each one of us—me to preach, Marion for hospitality, among others—we began to reap the harvest."

Marion took up the story. "Our neighbors began to see how people who came here, people considered outcasts—drunks who would never amount to anything, young women who came to work in the factories but got into trouble—were able to rebuild their lives. Former drunkards could hold a job, perhaps be trained for something new, young women would find good husbands. Those same neighbors who had been most hostile to us began to want to help. They, too, would hear the gospel message. We were able to start a church in the neighborhood."

"You pastor a church as well?"

John nodded. "I did. Now there's a young man who has taken that over. Someone I discipled."

Warren shook his head. "I wish I could feel so used by God. I feel as if what I came to do here in Bangor has no relation with what you are doing."

"Tell me about your journey to Bangor," John said quietly.

Warren looked into his calm gaze and began to tell him everything that had brought him on his journey.

"I incurred my father's ire, my mother's disappointment. I feel as if I'd let down everyone I ever hoped to please in my community, by leaving everything just when I was supposed to take up the mantle I was trained for. My father spent all these years educating me—just so I could throw it all in his face and walk away?" He stabbed a hand in the air in frustration.

He shook his head, expelling a disgusted breath. "For what? To sit in a classroom listening to learned men pontificate on things that seem to have no bearing to what I felt the Lord wanted me to do?"

Instead of looking shocked, John merely smiled.

"I'm glad you find it humorous. I feel terribly guilty now, and wonder if I shouldn't just head home and tell my father he was right and I made a mistake." Warren smiled humorlessly. "Like the prodigal son, except I wasn't going away to live licentiously. I don't believe I've ever lived so abstemiously or worked so hard."

John leaned forward, folding his hands atop the table. "Tell me what you find the most difficult of your circumstances now."

Warren rubbed his jaw. If he hadn't shocked the pastor up to now, his next words might very well. "The fact that I feel so dry inside."

The pastor's eyes remained steady, the warm humor unchanged.

Warren continued, wondering if the man were hearing him at all. "I sit in class under men with letters after their names who've come from the most renowned theological schools of the country, older men, who've lived their lives as Christian theologians. I should be lapping up their words of wisdom."

He shifted in his chair. "Why do I instead find myself restless, seeing little connection with their high-flown language and my present life? I ask myself, is this what the Lord asked me to give up everything for—and worst of all—disappoint and hurt my family for?

"I pore over theological treatises into the wee hours but find little that has any meaning with my present existence."

"Have you studied the book of Acts?"

John's question was like a curveball Warren had tried to copy when young from one of the New York pitchers.

The pastor leaned forward. "If you haven't read it in a while, I suggest you read it again. Look particularly at the apostles' experience on the Day of Pentecost and how the church grew from there."

He'd read the book before but was intrigued nonetheless by this man's suggestion.

"God's anointing—I think that's what you need. It will transform your walk with the Lord—and your ministry." John smiled. "Best cure for dryness I know of."

The pastor's glance encompassed his wife and Espy. "I suggest we pray for Warren."

Marion smiled and reached out both hands. "Yes, indeed."

They all joined hands, a custom Warren was not used to in prayer.

The prayer left him shaken. The soft words spoke of revelation, of having the "eyes of his understanding enlightened," and other things in that vein, as if he were walking around blind.

When he left that night, he kept thinking of what the pastor had told him. He stayed up reading the book of Acts, scrutinizing it as never before.

23

The weeks that followed were such as Espy had never dreamed possible. With the warmer days, frequently they each brought a lunch and shared it in the park or by the river. Warren came to visit the mission whenever he had a free evening, taking part in the Bible studies or going out with John on his street rounds or helping Espy whenever they held a soup kitchen.

With May came the arrival of the river drives into Bangor, filling the lodgings with loggers who'd spent the winter in the woods and had money in their pockets. Every night seemed to bring new brawls and men left penniless after a night of drinking and card-playing.

Warren went out with John almost every night before going to his night watchman job. Usually Marion and Espy stayed in, since the crowd was a rough one. But they did accompany the men, along with a few others from the house, on Sunday nights. It was on a Sunday night at the end of May that Warren told Espy John had asked him to preach.

"You?" Espy breathed in delight. "Warren, that's wonderful."

He searched her eyes. "Do you think so?"

"Yes," she said with all the certainty she could infuse into her voice. "You'll be magnificent."

He smiled crookedly. "I hope you're right, though I doubt I'll be 'magnificent.' Adequate will suit me fine."

"You'll be more than adequate."

As they walked along the twilight street she asked him, having been curious since the night the pastor had spoken of it, "Did you ever read the book of Acts?"

He took a few minutes to respond. Espy hoped she hadn't probed into something he didn't want to discuss with her. "Yes, that same night."

Nothing in his tone suggested he didn't want to speak of it further. "What did you think?"

"It's strange; it was nothing I had never read before, yet it was as if I was reading it for the first time, as if the Lord did answer John's prayer right away, taking away a sort of spiritual blindness and opening my eyes to truth."

Before she could ask anything more, he turned to her. "Have you read it—I mean in the way John suggested—looking for something for your own spiritual life?"

"Yes. Soon after I arrived here, he and his wife suggested I read and study it. Then we talked about it in the Bible study with some of the others. They each had an amazing experience to relate." She marveled still at everyone's individual testimony. "One evening, John asked me if I truly wanted to put the past behind me." She flushed, forcing herself to bring up her past in Holliston. "He led me in a prayer of repentance and of asking Jesus to come into my heart in a way I never had before. Oh, perhaps when I was a little girl. But now, it meant so much more."

"What happened?"

She remembered that night clearly. "I knelt on the carpet in the parlor and everyone gathered around me and prayed for me, the way it says in the Bible, laying hands on me. John prayed for me, his hands on my head, then Marion prayed, then Jacob, one of the men here at the time."

She swallowed, her voice thickening with emotion even now, almost a year later. "I felt this warmth come all over me, and I felt clean, truly clean for the first time in my life. And joy—such joy filled me as I'd never known. I've been happy before when something nice happened to me, or I got what I wanted, but this was different. The pastor told me afterward it was what joy is all about, and I could understand the difference between it and just happiness."

He swallowed, a look of something like yearning in his eyes. But all he did was nod and look ahead again.

They arrived at the place near the majority of boardinghouses where the loggers and lumbermen were apt to lodge. Espy remembered the night she'd first walked along this street alone and afraid.

Against the streetlights, stacks and stacks of lumber sat on the wharves waiting to be loaded onto the schooners moored along the river.

Espy stood with the others and held hands and prayed for the evening. Then they went in smaller groups, armed with leaflets, telling people they were going to have a Christian service and inviting them to come and listen.

Espy walked with Warren and another fellow. John went with his wife and two other men.

They received some jeers, but most of the men were friendly, saying things like, "I'm too far gone to save, but thanks anyway, Rev." "Sure, I'll be along as soon as I've had a drink," followed by guffaws.

But many expressed gratitude. Espy's heart went out to them, seeing the lonely look in their eyes. Some stopped them with hard luck stories. Warren listened politely and then repeated his invitation to the meeting, promising to pray for their situation after the service.

When it was a woman, one who was there to sell herself to any man who'd take her, Espy was the one who issued the invitation. Warren stayed silent even though the women invariably only looked at him.

Instead of feeling annoyance, the way she would have once, she felt only pity. Was this the way she used to look at Warren, seeing only his good looks and nice suit?

"Sure, love, I'll be along to hear the message, if you're preachin' it, brother," one said to Warren, with a laugh.

Finally, they gathered at a street corner and began to sing a few hymns. Together, their voices carried well into the night air, enough to begin drawing onlookers, those whose money had run out, who were bored, or for whom the familiar tunes reminded them of home and better times.

After a brief prayer, John introduced Warren, a "young man who knows the logging business and would like to address a few words from the Scriptures tonight."

Warren thanked him and opened the small Bible he carried. "Thank you, Brother John." He eyed the straggling crowd. "If you'll turn with me to the book of . . ." He fumbled with the pages and then cleared his throat, "Ephesians."

He began to read, his voice becoming firmer with each verse. Espy prayed silently for him, knowing how unsure he was of himself, even though he projected confidence and strength.

Lord, empower him by Your Holy Spirit. Let him experience Your anointing, that he may rest secure in the knowledge that You have called him to preach.

* * *

When Warren returned to his room late that night, he felt too keyed up to sleep. He sat up in bed, rereading the book of Acts.

But ye shall receive power, after that the Holy Ghost is come upon you: and ye shall be witnesses unto me both in Jerusalem, and in all Judaea, and in Samaria, and unto the uttermost part of the earth.

Further on, he read, *And they were all filled with the Holy Ghost, and began to speak with other tongues, as the Spirit gave them utterance.*

He continued reading until he finished the book, marveling at the transformation of the former disciples once they had received that new power from on high. They truly began "to do the works of Jesus," once they had received the power of the Holy Spirit.

Was that what made John's ministry so effective? *Effective* was not precisely the word, Warren realized, although it was partially so. There was more to it. There was fruitfulness in his ministry—the evidence was in the transformed lives he'd witnessed.

His mind compared the people he'd met with the friends and neighbors he'd grown up with who attended his home church faithfully every Sunday. He'd never seen a transformed life. So different from John and Marion and the people at House of Hope. He'd never experienced anything dynamic at his old church.

Even his paltry effort at bringing more young people into church and bridging the divide between the "haves and have nots," as he termed it to himself, had fallen flat.

His body exhausted but his mind still alert, Warren closed the Bible and laid it aside. Then he drew back his covers and knelt by his bed. Clasping his hands and bowing his head, he prayed, *Dear God, grant me what Your first disciples had. I want the power of Your Holy Spirit upon me. I want it with all my heart. I want to be an effective minister of the gospel, if that is what You wish me to be. I don't want to feel this emptiness, this dryness inside of me.*

When he finished, he waited a moment, hoping for something, not knowing what, picturing those tongues of flames described in the book of Acts at the first outpouring, remembering Espy's testimony of her own experience.

But he felt nothing. With a weary sigh, he rose and got back into bed, pulling the covers up over himself, resting his head on his hands, staring up at the dark ceiling.

He arrived at his boardinghouse late the next afternoon after a full day of lectures, hungry, and thinking of the long night ahead on his watchman rounds. He'd been unable to meet Espy for lunch because he had too much studying to do. Final exams were the following week. But he missed having had that time with her.

He entered the house and breathed a sigh of relief at not seeing his landlady. He checked the front table for any mail.

His heart gave a little lurch at the sight of a hand-addressed envelope. He always devoured Annalise's letters like a man deprived of food and drink presented with a feast. But as he neared the hall table, he recognized the black ink as his father's.

He picked up the long envelope with trembling fingers, ripped open the envelope, and unfolded the sheet.

Dear Son,

He read as he walked up the stairs. Once in his room, Warren sat in a straight-back chair reading his father's letter more slowly.

Dear Son,

Please come home. I've spent the past four and a half months thinking about things, and I'm willing to give you full run of the mills if only you'll come home.

I haven't heard a word from you since you left. Frankly, I had expected to see you back long before now, but I should have known that you were made of sterner stuff.

You were taught by me, after all. That was an attempt at humor, if you hadn't guessed.

I'm willing to do whatever you'd like to meet you halfway if you'll come home. I realize now I shouldn't have taken such an uncompromising approach, that you would not have said you felt called into the ministry unless you truly sensed that pull.

I am feeling my years and realize that I need someone to help carry the weight of the enterprise which your great-grandfather established and which I've had the privilege of continuing to build over the years.

The letter went on in this vein for another paragraph. What astounded Warren the most was his father's conciliatory tone. Never had he experienced a willingness in his father to negotiate. He'd raised him with an iron, if fair, hand, and Warren had been accustomed to obeying, trusting in his father's superior wisdom and experience.

This time it had been different. This time, a superior force had called Warren to something else, and now his father was beginning to concede that.

The other thing that amazed Warren but also filled him with dread was his father's reference to age. Warren stared at the strong writing, unwilling to see his father aging.

Yet, something had changed in his tone.

The letter ended with a plea for Warren to come home for the summer so the two could talk before Warren made any decisions about returning to the seminary.

Dear Lord, what would You have me do? I thought Your will was clear, but how can I refuse my father?

He'd be an unworthy son if he didn't at least agree to his father's wish to talk.

He thought about the man who had said he would follow Jesus but that first he needed to bid his family farewell. *No man, having put his hand to the plough, and looking back, is fit for the kingdom of God.*

Warren had left all for God's kingdom. Why would he now be caught in this dilemma?

He remembered his prayer of the night before. Staring at the papered wall before him, he asked whether this was an answer to prayer or a temptation of Satan. *Dear God, show me what to do. Do You wish me to go home?*

The term was almost finished, and he *had* wondered what to do over the long summer months.

Feeling a resolution form within him, he picked up his pen to answer his father's letter. He would tell him he intended to take his final exams and then come home for a visit only. He'd trust the Lord would show him eventually what to do.

His heart sank, thinking of Espy and of John and Marion and the world that had just opened up to him.

The Lord couldn't want to take him from them so soon.

• • •

Espy sat across from Warren in the park, their half-eaten lunch between them. She found it hard to formulate the words, her throat tightening up at Warren's news. "So, you've decided to go back?"

His green eyes scanned hers. "Only for a visit." He rubbed a hand across his mouth, looking away as if in frustration. "Frankly, I don't know what to do, but I feel I owe it to Father to at least hear him out." His chest rose and fell in a tired sigh. "I don't like being estranged from my family. If nothing else, I want them to accept my being here."

"Of course you do. You can't let that go on."

His gaze returned to hers, a warmth lighting his eyes and a slight smile edging the corners of his lips.

The next second his gaze sobered and he looked down at his hands. "But I hate having to leave. I feel as if I've just—" Whatever he'd begun to say, he seemed to think better of it. "I've just met John and Marion, just become involved in the ministry. For the first time, I feel as if there's a real purpose to my having come here to Bangor."

His rueful smile was directed at her once more. "I know, God probably has more important things on His mind than whether I

302

continue my studies in Bangor or go back home and work in my father's mill."

"Warren, that's not true! Of course He cares." The next words cost her an effort. "And He'll show you clearly. You'll see. Just believe in Him and His goodness."

"He sure has changed your life around. I mean, you're so different in so many ways."

Tears pricked her eyes. "It's no longer I that live," she said softly, "but Christ that lives in me."

He smiled in response to the Scripture, no words being necessary between them.

She would miss him, and she had to face the fact that she might never see him again. She wouldn't think about that now. She would rejoice with him that he would be reconciled with his family. How she'd love to go back and visit with her mother and Angela and all her brothers and sisters.

But she was not ready to go back. Bangor had allowed her to begin a new life. She was not going to return to a place where people only saw her as a temptation.

• • •

A week later, Warren was gone. Espy had seen little of him in the intervening time; since he had to study for his final exams and work his night job, he had little time for anything else.

John, Marion, and Espy had accompanied Warren to the stagecoach. Warren asked if he might write to her.

"Of course," she said right away. Then she hesitated. "But I'll understand if you're busy with so many things."

His eyes regarded hers steadily. "I won't be too busy. W-will you write me back?"

Did he want to hear from her, Espy Estrada, or was it just a polite request to a friend? But the intent way he continued looking at her, waiting for her answer, gave her the hope that perhaps this leave-taking wasn't so easy for him either.

"If you'd like me to," she finally whispered.

"I would."

• • •

Warren arrived back in Holliston after several hours. He unfurled his sore body from the seat when the coach finally pulled into Holliston.

The first person he saw was his father. He gave a nod before looking to the side. Warren saw his mother and Annalise beside her. The women ran to Warren and he clasped them both in his arms.

"At last you're home!" his mother said, looking up at him, a sheen of tears over her eyes. He had trouble swallowing, not accustomed to seeing his mother this emotional. He squeezed her shoulder before turning a smile on Annalise, who didn't seem to mind the tears rolling down her cheeks.

"Hey, I hope it's not a time to cry."

Laughter gurgled from her throat. "Tears of joy, Warren."

"Well, all right then," he said with a smile. Gently he let them both go and turned to his father.

"Hello, Father." Tentatively, he stretched out his hand, but his father took a step forward and embraced him.

Neither said anything. Releasing each other, Warren felt uncomfortable, already sensing a noose tightening about him.

"You look good, Son. How was the journey?"

"Fine."

It felt good to be home—if only his heart wasn't back in Bangor.

"Christina wanted to come, but we put her off, saying we wanted you all to yourself this first day," his mother said, her hand clutching his arm as if afraid to let him go.

"Thank you. I appreciate that." He'd made it clear to Christina when he'd left for Bangor that he had no plans to undertake anything serious with any woman. She had asked him in playful voice whether or not he was going to write or was he going to forget all his friends. So, he'd been forced to say of course not. But he had not initiated any correspondence. When he'd received a Valentine's card from her, he'd sent a short note a week or so later. When she'd responded with a long letter, he'd waited even longer before writing another short note.

He did not relish seeing her again now.

His thoughts turned to Espy, already missing her. He'd missed her since the moment the stage had pulled out of Bangor.

Watching the passing fields and forests and mountains from the stagecoach window, he'd thought about how right she was for him. He imagined a life with her—something similar to John and Marion's.

But now, back in Holliston, hearing his parents' news of town over a dinner served by Samuel, with all the accompanying formality he'd grown unaccustomed to in the intervening months of boardinghouse living, he felt his bond with Espy stretching thinner by the minute.

It wasn't until after a leisurely dinner that his father asked him out to the terrace for an after-dinner cigar. Warren knew the moment of truth had arisen, at least for what concerned his father most.

Warren sat in one of the wicker rockers. The lilacs were out, filling the early evening air with their heady scent.

He shook his head at the cigar his father proffered him.

"No?" His father raised an eyebrow. "Don't tell me you've become a teetotaler as well."

"No." Though he had partaken of a glass of wine with dinner, it had been his first in months. The Talbots served no alcohol in their establishment and neither did anyone smoke on the premises.

He understood it, of course. The individuals who came to them generally suffered under the yoke of so many vices that they didn't want to expose them to the pull of the old life.

After a silence when Warren grew sleepy on the warm June night, his father spoke. "I don't want to bring up anything serious on your first day back, Warren, but I would like to know if you've given my letter any thought. Your reply didn't imply much except that you'd come back for a visit. I hope that means a long visit."

He met his father's eye. "I've thought about your words and have prayed about my future." He gave a rueful laugh. "I'm not sure if I have the answers yet, but I'm keeping an open mind, I hope."

His father nodded. "Well, I'm glad of that." Relief was evident in his voice. "Does that open mind include coming to the office? I confess I could use a hand."

"You haven't found anyone to replace me?" He was surprised.

His father shook his head. "I haven't made a serious attempt, hoping you'd come back. But I will, if at the end of the summer you tell me you're going back to the seminary."

The two held gazes for a moment. His heart sank at the thought of being away from Bangor for the whole summer.

But his father had said he'd find a replacement at the end of the summer. Warren knew his father wouldn't go back on his word. Finally, Warren gave a nod. "That's fair enough."

He'd just committed to working back at the mills over the summer. As the weight settled over him, he realized how little he'd missed that work.

And that meant three months without Espy.

24

Espy held Warren's latest letter in her hand.

Hardly a few days had gone by when she'd received her first letter from Warren. In it he'd told her of his decision to stay the summer. The news hadn't surprised her.

She'd replied right away, encouraging him in his decision, and keeping her tone light and cheerful, even though he might not come back to Bangor in the autumn.

For a few weeks their letters went back and forth with a frequency that made John and Marion and the others at House of Hope smile and raise their eyebrows every time Espy took up a letter from the hallway table where the daily post was laid.

She'd always wait until she was alone in her room—choosing moments when she knew no one else was up there, or going out to the back stoop if the room was occupied. She treasured each word, even though he never said anything romantic, except for the ending. He always wrote that he missed her and hoped he'd see her soon. And then he'd write, "Affectionately, Warren." She had to be content with those few crumbs.

The letters were filled with the goings on in Holliston. He

always told her about Alvaro and Angela, and she could tell he made a point of visiting them or seeing them in town. He also was very open about his work at the mills and his relations with his father. He spoke of Pastor Curtis, and the counsel the man gave him.

He sends his best regards and hopes he'll see you back in Holliston someday.

Holliston. Not a day went by that she didn't think of it—her family and friends. But when she thought of her reputation and the townspeople, and those of Warren's circle—and worst of all, the Stocktons, whom Warren never mentioned to her—she cringed, and knew she couldn't go back.

She continued reading Warren's latest letter.

Guess what? Pastor Curtis has invited me to preach next Sunday. Can you believe it? I said no at first, not feeling qualified. It is one thing to preach in the streets at the waterfront, but quite another to stand in a pulpit of the town's main church. But he said something similar to John, that the only way to learn to preach was to preach. I asked him if he wouldn't get in trouble with his board, or the elders, and he said he'd already discussed it with them and they all heartily supported his choice.

I've had several long talks with Pastor Curtis. He told me he has been wanting to train up a successor for a long time, and believes the Lord has brought me back here for a purpose.

Can you believe that? I don't know, myself. I am still praying about it, and would appreciate your prayers as well on my behalf. I will write to John separately, though please feel free to discuss this with him.

I haven't heard anything from the Lord yet. I feel as if I'm waiting for something . . . some sign from Him. I hope that doesn't sound presumptuous, but ever since reading—and reread-

ing and rereading—the book of Acts, I feel the Lord will speak to me in some way and show me the way.

Was this part of God's plan for his ministry? She brought a fist to her mouth, fighting the urge to cry. She could fight the notion that it was Warren's father, his family who wanted him home, but she couldn't go against God's plan for Warren.

Did she fit in all of this? The answer came swift and sure. Of course she didn't.

With a heavy heart she continued reading. There wasn't much left of the letter.

> *Espy, I'd like to ask you a big favor. I know it would be asking a lot of you, but I'd like you to think about it—and pray about it.*
>
> *Would you come and hear my first sermon at church? I know you've heard me in Bangor, but this would be a little different. I'll be a lot more terrified, for one thing. It's like Jesus said, a prophet is not without honor, save in his own country, and in his own house.*
>
> *I feel that way now. I'll be facing everyone who knows me. They'll see me up there and remember the young boy, his shoes unlaced, or the youth having a few high jinks with his friends. I'll feel like a fraud.*
>
> *So, would you come and be a friendly face in the crowd? I know my family will be there, but remember, they would have preferred me to remain as I was, ready to take the reins from my father. This will be a test of sorts—will I sound like a pastor to their ears?*

Even as Warren's invitation sent a chill through her, her heart couldn't resist the plea in his words.

Allowing the letter to fall in her lap, she looked out across the narrow fenced yard. Could she face going back to Holliston? Not just going home, but walking into that congregation that looked at her with condemnation in their eyes?

And Mr. Stockton, would he be there? She didn't think she could bear to see him again.

I will never leave thee, nor forsake thee. Jesus' words came into her mind, and she felt that He was asking her to do this.

She picked up the letter again, wondering what else Warren said.

> *I know you don't want to come back here, and you are probably not relishing the idea of walking into that church, but let me say, first, that I've talked about you to Pastor Curtis and he heartily seconds my invitation. I've told him how well you are doing. I'd also like to say that you are welcome to stay with my family. I'd like them to get to know you.*
>
> *I'd like to cover the stagecoach fare. Please don't be offended by my offer. I am working back at the mill, so my salary is a bit more than what I had in Bangor and my expenses much fewer.*
>
> *Well, I'd better close. Please, please, think about my invitation. Last but not least, I'd love to see you again. The summer seems so very long until autumn.*
>
> *Affectionately,*
> *Warren*

She read the last paragraphs over a few times. *He wants me to stay with his family.* The notion took her breath away. He said he'd *love*—not just like—to see her again, and made it sound as if he fully intended to return in the fall.

If he could offer so much, how could she turn down his request?

She would not stay with his family, nor accept his offer to pay her fare, but she would brave Holliston and the church congregation, the Stocktons themselves, and be not only a friendly face, but his strongest supporter on that Sunday morning.

* * *

Warren paced in front of the livery stable waiting for the stage, stopping and taking out his watch every few minutes to check the time, his nervousness growing with each passing minute.

He hadn't seen Espy in a month and a half. Fears, no matter how silly they seemed, had mushroomed ever since she had replied to his letter.

He fingered his breast pocket, hearing the familiar sound of paper, where he usually carried her latest correspondence, so he could take it out and reread it whenever he liked.

He was disappointed that she'd refused his invitation to stay at his house, but he realized that she was probably wise. She hadn't seen her own family in so long. He didn't know what his parents would have said to have her in their midst, and he had enough hurdles to leap over this weekend without taking on more. He didn't want them to offend Espy by a word or look.

But he had informed his parents of her coming and had asked his mother to invite Espy to a meal or a tea while she was there.

His mother had taken more than a day before she gave her approval. Finally, she'd said Espy was welcome to tea, and if things worked out well, she could come to dinner after church on Sunday.

"After all, Warren," she'd said gently, "we don't know how she would fit with our . . . acquaintances. You don't want to make her uncomfortable."

His mouth had firmed, not liking the words, but respecting his mother.

"What about Christina?"

"I told you, Mother, there is nothing, nor ever has been, between Christina and me. I made it clear to her when I left. And I appreciate

311

the fact that you haven't invited her here since I've returned."

"Well, I didn't think it fair to her if you will only disappoint her." Her mother looked at her hands on her lap. "She is such a suitable young lady. Are you sure you aren't being willful in this . . . this desire to court a young woman who will be so out of her depth in your circle—and worse, one who left here in disgrace?" Her eyes reflected true hurt and lack of understanding.

"I care for her. Deeply." He didn't say more. His parents would have to see for themselves that Espy wasn't the same Espy. His mother stared at him for a long moment before sighing deeply.

"Very well. We may as well meet her." She didn't sound at all pleased with the notion.

His thoughts were interrupted by the thundering of hooves and rumbling of coach wheels. The crowd began to gather closer, impatience a tangible force in the air as the stage finally drew up in front of the livery. Voices broke out at once.

Warren, watching easily over the heads of most in front of him, held his breath as the door swung open and the first passengers alighted.

The women and children stepped out of the coach to be engulfed in the arms of loved ones. Then men began getting down.

As the crowd dispersed, and the coachman and his assistant began to lower the baggage, Warren dared step forward and peer into the shadowed recesses of the coach.

Espy sat in the far corner.

She looked frightened, and his heart went out to her, realizing how difficult this arrival must be for her. He smiled widely and held out a hand. "There you are. I was beginning to think you'd missed the stage."

She smiled tentatively and began to come forward, gathering her things. He helped her down, breathing in the faint flowery scent of her. He gripped her elbow gently and guided her forward, making small talk.

"How was the journey? Here, let me take your satchel. Let's get your bags."

"I didn't bring much." She pointed to a carpetbag the driver was lowering. Warren took it from him with a "thanks" and a tip.

"I brought the buggy." He motioned down the street. "I can take you to your house."

"You didn't have to do that. I could walk."

"Nonsense." He faced her, gripping her bag in his two hands. "It's good to see you."

Her glance skittered away from his, pink suffusing her cheeks. "It's good to see you, too."

"I missed you."

Her umber eyes fixed on his a second before looking to the side again, as if his words made her uncomfortable. "I missed you, too," she finally said.

His heart swelled, but before he could think what else to say, someone hailed her. "Espy! What are you doin' back?"

Warren's heart sank at the sound of Will's voice. Would he spirit her off to her circle of friends—friends who had stuck fast to her when she'd had her troubles, unlike Warren, who'd distanced himself from her?

She smiled, stepping away from Warren.

"Hello, Will. How've you been?"

Will leaned forward and planted a kiss on her cheek. Warren's knuckles whitened on the bag's leather handles. He strained to keep his expression impassive, knowing he'd have to manage a smile in a moment, if Will's attention would ever be torn away from Espy.

She certainly spoke with more animation than she had with Warren, asking Will about their mutual friends.

Finally, she turned her attention back to him. "I'd better go. Angela's probably expecting me."

Will barely nodded his head at Warren, and Warren reciprocated. "How long you back for?"

313

"Only till Sunday."

Warren's heart sank at the news. That only gave them these two days.

Will's face fell. "So short! Can't you stay longer? What's in Bangor that's so important?"

"My job," she tossed back with a little of her old impertinence.

"Are there any canneries in Bangor?"

Her eyes flashed. "I'm not working at a cannery."

"Well, where then?"

"Why don't you come on over later and I'll tell you all about it?"

All Warren's constructed plans began to crumble before him like an elaborate sandcastle in the face of the incoming tide. He wanted to interrupt, tell Espy about his mother's invitation, but somehow, he thought that would only spur her toward Will.

"Sure. I'll be along shortly. I'll bring some of the old gang." With a brief touch of his hat brim, he took his leave of Warren, before smiling at Espy and touching her arm. "Good seeing you."

She looked at Will's departing back until Warren was forced to clear his throat. "If you'd like to get home."

"Oh—sure, of course." She started as if out of a dream.

All the things he'd wanted to say to her dried on his tongue. Instead, an awkward silence filled the space between them. "Come along, the buggy's right here."

She walked beside him, quiet. He chanced a glance at her and saw that she was looking around her as if she were new to the town. "Anything changed?"

She blinked, giving her head a tiny shake. "No-o. It's just strange to be back. It's been almost a year."

"I know what you mean. Whenever I've been away, it was always strange the first few days of being home."

A bittersweet smile tugged at the corners of her lips. "At least you hadn't left in disgrace."

He could have bitten off his tongue for his tactlessness. He strove to find something to say. They reached the buggy. "Well, this time I was certainly in disgrace with my father."

She paused, her hand on the side of the buggy. "I'm sorry, but at least your father has welcomed you back, hasn't he?"

He helped her up. "Yes. I thank God for that. My homecoming has been better than I could have hoped for," he continued as he climbed in on the other side after unhitching the horse from the post.

As he maneuvered through the busy street, he had to focus on keeping a tight rein on the horse, but as they left the town and took the rutted road in the direction of Espy's neighborhood, he was able to return to the topic.

"I'm very grateful for how my family has welcomed me back, but it's a bit of a two-edged sword."

"Oh—what did you say?" She turned from gazing at the trees and pastures they were passing to look at him.

He repeated the sentence, again feeling like a fool. Of course, she wouldn't be interested in what he was going through. She'd been away almost a year and had no idea what kind of homecoming to expect. He should have been more attuned to her. Although if Will were anyone to go by, Espy would have a warm welcome, he thought grimly.

That should have been Warren's prerogative. The thought brought him up short. But he'd forfeited the right—never having stood up for Espy when he should have.

· · ·

Warren's words snapped Espy from her daze at being back in Holliston. "What do you mean 'two-edged sword'?"

He shrugged. "I'm probably being overly dramatic. It's just that my father has been so understanding that I feel it will be harder and harder for me to tell him that I'm still returning to Bangor at summer's end."

Despite his assertion to the contrary, she felt in her heart that he was not going to return to his studies.

Espy looked away. They were passing the stretch of evergreen forest where Warren had kissed her. Then the road curved and they were passing a meadow. The lupine was in full bloom, creating a sea of blues and purples with an occasional white or pink in the mix.

"You did the right thing coming home." The words cost her, but she knew there was little else he could have done.

"I'm trusting the Lord to make things clear for me."

They turned down Espy's lane.

Everything looked the same. Broken fences, playing children, strewn toys and tools, and a goat tethered in someone's yard, munching the grass.

As the buggy approached her house, children stopped to look. A buggy was a sight in this neighborhood, but then they began recognizing her.

"Espy!" Children waved, some jumping up and down. "Espy, you're back!"

She smiled, though her insides felt as twisted as a sheet in a wringer. "Hi! Yes, I'm back for a visit," she replied here and there, smiling and greeting children by name.

Warren stopped the buggy in front of the gate. She noticed it was repaired and the fence was white-washed. As Warren set the brake and hitched the horse to the fence, she began to collect her things.

Warren came to her side just as she was ready to descend. He held out a hand, and she placed one of hers in it. He gave it a squeeze.

A lump formed in her throat.

As she came down to his level, he bent his head, whispering in her ear. "Don't worry, it's not the lion's den. Besides, I'm here to defend you."

Before she could think how to reply, he took the carpetbag from her and tucked her hand in the crook of his elbow.

He pushed open the gate and escorted her into her yard.

"Goodness, everything looks so neat." The grass was clipped short, the bushes trimmed. Someone had even set a few plants in a patch of garden, though they hadn't blossomed yet.

"I think you'll find Alvaro is responsible for keeping the yard clean."

She glanced up at him, wondering how much was due to Warren's influence.

Espy took a deep breath, hearing Warren's decisive knock on the door as a pounding on her heart. The next second the door was flung open and Angela stood there with a wide smile, the younger children all crowded around her.

In the melee, Espy heard exclamations of her name as she was enveloped in hugs.

When she was finally given some room to breathe, she saw her mother in the background with Alvaro. Smiling shyly, she approached them. Her mother patted her on the arm. "Well, aren't you the young lady? I would hardly have recognized you."

Swallowing disappointment over her mother's lukewarm welcome, she smiled at Alvaro. "Who's this handsome man?" She held out her arms and he came to them, but his arms only held her briefly before he let her go.

"You're lookin' good, Espy. Welcome home."

Espy turned back to Angela and her younger siblings. Angela looked the same, though she wore a clean apron over her gingham gown. Her hair was neatly pinned up. The children, too, all looked scrubbed clean. Espy suspected Angela had done this for her homecoming.

Then she noticed Warren, in the corridor, standing by the door. She hurried to him. "Please, come in."

"I don't want to spoil your homecoming. I'll just leave your bag here and get going."

"Let me walk you out." Would she see him again before Sunday service?

"That's all right." He stood on the steps, his eyes scanning hers. "My mother has invited you over for tea. May I come and collect you, a little before five o'clock?"

Tea *at his parents'*? Fear shuddered through her even in her amazement. But Warren was looking at her with such entreaty in his green eyes, and she realized she would have little opportunity to be with him otherwise. "All right."

The next moment he was gone, and Alicia, Gina, and Orrie were clamoring for her attention again. She turned back into the parlor.

25

Warren's palms were sweaty by the time he approached Espy's door once again to collect her for tea. When he'd left home, his mother was overseeing the final arrangements on the terrace. No matter how much he'd asked her to keep things simple, he could see she'd brought out the best linen and china.

He broke into a smile right away when Espy answered the door. "Hello there." She looked so pretty in a white blouse with a high, frilly collar and a deep maroon skirt. She wore a straw boater on her piled-up curls, a pretty yellow ribbon around the base of its crown.

"Hello." Her heavy dark eyelashes swept downward, and he realized she must be more nervous than he was. This was a test of sorts. He wanted it to succeed.

"Ready?"

"As much as I'll ever be."

• • •

Espy didn't say much on the drive to Warren's house. She didn't see many acquaintances on her way through town, so she had no chance to gauge people's reactions to her return.

As they crossed the bridge and then entered the long covered bridge across the second span, her heartbeat began to accelerate. As they came out once again into the sunshine, the road curved and then they were on Elm Street.

All too soon, he pulled up before his stately house. He maneuvered the buggy down the drive, which led to a barn in the back. A boy came out and Warren jumped down, handing him the reins. "Thanks, Jeb."

And then he was before her with a smile, as if understanding her fear, giving her his firm hand.

Voices drifted through the lilac and rhododendron bushes that edged the house. To her surprise Warren led her over a flagstone path toward the back of the house.

Her steps faltered when she saw the gathering of ladies on the large stone terrace. "I didn't realize it was going to be such a big . . . party."

"Neither did I," he muttered, patting her hand and leading her through the terraced flowerbeds that made Alvaro's attempts at gardening look like a child playing with mud pies. They walked up the shallow flagstone steps.

Conversation slowed and finally came to a complete halt as they reached the terrace. "Hello, everyone. I think you all know Espy Estrada. She's visiting for the weekend. I hope you'll make her welcome."

Warren's voice sounded unnaturally hearty. Espy cringed, wanting to burrow behind his broad back.

But Mrs. Brentwood came up to her, a thin stretching of her lips passing for a smile. "Good afternoon, Miss Estrada, so nice of you to come." She held out her hand, palm down, as if she expected Espy to bend over and kiss it.

Instead, she took the limp hand, and after a brief handshake, the two separated.

Annalise approached, a genuine smile on her lips. "How lovely to see you back, Espy." Her handclasp, though not quite firm, at least was not as limp as her mother's.

"Hi, Annalise. It's nice to see you again, too."

Warren bent toward her. "Let me fetch you some tea and goodies. Watch after her, won't you, Annalise?"

Then her lifeline was gone. Espy pasted a smile on her face and ventured a look around. Her heart sank at the sight of Christina, who made no attempt at a greeting. The women had gone back to chatting in their small groups, their hands holding teacups and saucers. Espy realized she was not dressed for this occasion. The women on the terrace presented a palette of color. Even Mrs. Brentwood wore a stunning striped silk gown of teal blue. Annalise's gown was a soft pink with a wide white lace bodice.

Christina's gown was a bright red with red satin bows all along the back.

Dear Lord, what are You trying to show me here? How little I fit in?

But then the words *a child of the most high God* came to her mind. Espy straightened her spine and nodded to the few ladies whose glances she crossed.

She breathed a sigh of relief when Warren came back with a cup and saucer in one hand, a small plate of tiny cakes and triangular sandwiches in the other. He grinned sheepishly. "I didn't know what you like, so I brought a little of as much as would fit."

She took the cup and saucer from him, thanking him, as he held the plate for her.

Mrs. Hawkins stepped over to her. "I'm surprised to see you back, Esperanza. Thought you'd gone for good. What brought you back?"

The accusation was clear in her unwavering gaze.

"I invited her," said Warren in a soft tone that held a steely undertone to it.

"I wished to see my family," Espy answered honestly.

Mrs. Hawkins sniffed. "I hope you've learned some lessons in the time you've been away."

Espy's cup rattled on its saucer. "I have."

The older lady seemed at a loss at the simple words. "Humph." With an abrupt nod, she backed away.

"What is it like, living in Bangor?"

Espy started at Annalise's soft question. Taking a sip of tea to fortify herself, she began to recount a little of her life in the city, glad to find something to talk about. Warren whispered a quiet, "Excuse me a moment," and was gone, handing her plate to Annalise to hold, before she could beg him not to leave her side.

Annalise asked her enough questions to keep the conversation going. Espy was gratified that the girl seemed genuinely interested. A few other young ladies stopped by and listened.

"I don't think I could ever type like that," Emily said. She held out a hand, eyeing her fingers. "I'd be afraid my fingers would get all knobby like an old person's." She tittered and the others joined her.

They moved away, and an awkward silence fell between Annalise and her. "So, what is new in Holliston?"

Annalise shrugged, her mouth twisting in a self-conscious smile. "Nothing, really."

"H-how is the club?"

A degree of animation lit her eyes. "It's doing well, but that's thanks to Warren." She looked earnestly into Espy's eyes. "He's the one who kept it going. He and Angela," her face colored, "and Alvaro, of course, have made progress in the community. Th-that's why Will and Henry came back."

"Came back to what?" Warren asked over his sister's shoulder.

"I'm just telling Espy about the Holliston Lights."

"Oh, that." He addressed himself to Espy. "It was gratifying to see them come back. They've kept coming since I've been away." He sobered. "Though I hear numbers are falling again."

"Only a little since you left. But with Christina president and James as vice-president, well . . . you know how it is," she ended as if sorry she'd begun.

"I do indeed," he said grimly. "Anyway, I came to tell you my father would like to meet you, Espy."

Espy clutched her cup and saucer. "He does?"

Amusement tinged his voice. "You look like a rabbit ready to bolt."

"I feel like one. Wh-where is he?" She was afraid to look around.

"By my mother."

It was worse and worse.

"Don't worry, he's probably more uncomfortable than you in this crowd of ladies. He just stopped in for a moment to say hello. Here, let me take that plate," he said to Annalise before looking at Espy accusingly. "You haven't touched a thing."

"I'm not really hungry."

He set it down on a nearby table then took her arm to lead her through the throng of women, all of whom examined her as she passed.

But no one's scrutiny was more piercing than Mr. Brentwood's. It occurred to her he was about Mr. Stockton's age. Mortification rose in her, wondering what he thought of her, if he believed everything Mrs. Stockton had accused her of.

He gave her a clipped nod. "Hello, Miss Estrada."

She dipped a brief curtsey. "Pleased to meet you, sir."

"Espy was gracious enough to come for a brief visit to hear me preach tomorrow," Warren said in that false hearty tone that made her feel worse than being completely ignored by the company.

"Is that so?" His relentless gaze continued on her.

She could only nod, her throat refusing to work.

"She's working at Peabody's Clothing Manufactory, so she has to get back right away."

"I see. Seamstress, is it?"

"Stenographer," answered Warren.

Mr. Brentwood's gaze traveled the length of her and she felt exposed, as if she were pretending to something she wasn't. "Lot of young women doing that nowadays, aren't they? Taking the jobs from young men who are the breadwinners."

The implied criticism took her aback. "Excuse me, sir? I didn't realize that."

"No, of course you didn't."

"Th-there are a lot of young women working there—in the typing pool."

"Where'd you get trained at taking shorthand?"

"Mr. Talbot. He's a pastor. I met him and—and his wife when I first arrived." She struggled through the explanation. "He suggested a typing course. They were gracious enough to pay for it."

"Pretty fortunate, weren't you?"

"Yes, sir." She looked down at her cup, feeling as if she had done something wrong.

"Very well. I wish you continued success in your endeavors. Nice to have met you." He turned his attention to Warren. "I'm heading over to Jim Keller's. We're planning a men's breakfast."

Mr. Brentwood continued this discussion with his son for a few minutes. Espy let her attention wander, fingering the handle of her teacup as she allowed herself to study her surroundings for the first time.

The terrace had a lovely view of the river, far enough downstream so the lumberyards were no longer visible. Instead, rolling hills, farms, and fields offered a lovely green vista across the river, the darker green of forest visible beyond them.

The gardens beyond the terrace were filled with all kinds of flowers and bushes. A sailboat was moored at a small dock at the river's edge.

She felt someone's eyes and turned to see Christina looking at her. Then Christina leaned toward her friend and whispered something. The other lady looked at Espy, shaking her head with disapproval.

Soon, Christina had a small coterie gathered around her and speaking in low tones, the ones nearest Espy throwing glances over their shoulders at her.

Warren's father left them and Warren turned his attention back to Espy. "Let me see if I can get you another plate."

"No, please, don't bother. I really couldn't eat anything. Will you show me the gardens, please?"

She had to get away from these people. She didn't belong here. What had she been thinking? How was she going to face them all in the church tomorrow?

Warren took her request to see the gardens with such speed that she guessed he was just as relieved as she to leave the stifling atmosphere of the tea party. He gave her half-empty teacup to a passing maid and tucked her hand in the crook of his arm.

Espy felt an immediate peace walking so closely with him amidst the flowering greenery edged with large stones. Flagstones formed walking paths between the terraced layers.

"How pretty," she said. "It must be nice to sit up there in the summer, smelling the flowers and watching the boats go by."

"It is. We always gather here before dinner when the weather is nice."

They ended down on the dock. "I wish you were here more time," he said. "I'd take you for a sail."

She imagined what that would be like, seeing the houses from the river, sailing by Holliston Port and then out into the bay. She wondered if he had often taken young ladies out for a sail . . . Christina.

Espy disengaged her hand from Warren's arm and walked to the end of the dock. Her feeling of well-being warred with how out of place she felt. This was not her world, and if she'd needed any reminding, this tea party had worked a cure.

"Listen, Espy, I'm sorry if you don't feel comfortable among my mother's friends."

She looked back at Warren, his hands in his trousers pockets, looking so handsome in his tan sack coat and darker camel trousers, a brown patterned silk tie against a pristine white shirt. He must have a maid wash and iron his shirts while he was home.

She admired him all the more for the life he'd chosen to lead in Bangor when he had all this at home. Her heart yearned for him to come back to Bangor. It was the only hope for a future for the two of them.

She smiled at him, wishing she could erase the worried look in his eyes. "It's all right. An hour or two won't kill me." She lifted one corner of her mouth, but the joke fell flat.

"I suppose I'd better get back home," she said finally, though she didn't want to leave his side. "I've hardly seen my family."

"Of course. I have to finish preparing my sermon for tomorrow anyway."

They walked back up the hill to the terrace.

"Goodness, where were you two? It's not polite to disappear at your own party." Mrs. Brentwood eyed her accusingly.

"I'm sorry," she whispered.

Warren spoke more firmly, "We were hardly gone more than a few minutes. I just wanted to show Espy the gardens and dock."

"Very well."

"I need to leave," she said. "Thank you for inviting me to your tea."

"Leave? You just arrived."

"Espy doesn't have too much time before she must return to Bangor. She'd like to be with her family."

His mother's lips pursed. "Oh, well, of course, if you have to. It was a pleasure to make your acquaintance."

"Likewise."

The ride back was quiet. Espy stole a few glances at Warren every now and then, and as if sensing them, he turned to her and smiled, but said very little. She wondered if he were as perturbed by how little she had fit into his world.

• • •

On Sunday morning, the congregation settled down with rustlings as Warren made his way to the pulpit, his hands trembling, his knees unsteady.

The hymns had been sung, the announcements made, the offering collected, the Scriptures read. He reached the heavy wooden pulpit, gripping each side as if holding to a raft in the stormy waters. The congregation that stared back at him did appear as a vast sea. A sea of faces, their gazes expectant or impassive.

The dream he'd had so long ago came back vividly in that instant. He glanced down at himself—even to the robe and surplice he was wearing. He relived the feeling of utter helplessness. *Dear God, I have no pearls of wisdom to give them. What possessed me to think I had?*

The words formed in his mind: *But I have.*

His heart began to thud. *Lean on Me and not on your own understanding.*

His heart swelled as an awareness of the Lord's presence began to fill him, an awareness such as he'd never experienced. His eyes scanned the congregation once again, this time without terror but with wonder. He found Espy, sandwiched between Angela and Alvaro. He smiled and she responded shyly.

A sense of power filled him, but this was not his own.

He looked down at his Bible. "Please open to the book of

327

Romans, chapter one, verse three." He read, no longer feeling shaky. "Concerning his Son Jesus Christ our Lord, which was made of the seed of David according to the flesh; and declared to be the Son of God with power, according to the spirit of holiness, by the resurrection from the dead."

He looked back at the congregation, letting the words sink in. He began to preach, feeling a power flowing through him, a power that originated from the Scriptures in front of him. He preached the glory of Jesus Christ, and what it meant for their lives in the present.

The eyes of his listeners showed him they were listening. There were no rustlings or coughs. When he closed, there were a few seconds of silence, then Pastor Curtis came up to him. "Thank you, Warren." The firm clasp of the man's hand on his shoulder and the brightness in his eyes told Warren he was pleased. Warren bowed his head and moved back to his seat. The pastor spoke a few words of commendation, receiving assenting murmurs from the congregation. And then they sang a final hymn, said a prayer, and the people began rising and moving. Pastor Curtis came up to him, where Warren still sat in a daze.

"Come along, let's greet the congregation. I'm sure everyone is waiting to say something to you. You were stupendous, young man. I knew you were gifted, but you have surpassed even my expectations. That seminary has certainly taught you a lot in a short time."

As he spoke, they walked down the steps from the altar and headed toward the entrance of the church.

Warren was stopped and greeted by several people, people he'd known all his life. But now they were looking at him differently, with a deference he'd never seen before. He wanted to say he didn't deserve it; it had been God's Spirit in him.

He remembered his prayer in his room back in Bangor. God had answered his prayer, he realized in new wonder, but he'd chosen this moment to pour out His Spirit. He thought about Peter.

It wasn't until he'd stepped out into the water from the boat that the Lord had shown him he could walk upon it.

How he wanted to tell Espy. His eyes had been scanning the congregation. He let out a breath of relief when he saw her standing in a corner.

"Excuse me a moment, Pastor Curtis. I need to say something to Espy."

"Very well, my boy. Hurry back, these folks want to talk to you, not me."

"Excuse me . . . pardon me, ma'am." As quickly as he could without shoving people, he wended his way to Espy's corner.

When he reached her, he couldn't hold back a big grin. "I'm glad you didn't leave."

She responded with a wide smile of her own. "Warren, you were wonderful!"

"Did you really think so?" Besides Pastor Curtis, hers was the only one whose opinion he valued, he realized in that moment. He knew that he'd reached people that morning, and that it hadn't been due to himself. But he did yearn for Espy's approval.

The warmth in her eyes and tone filled him with such delight he couldn't help reaching for her hands.

"Yes, I did." Gently, she pulled her hands out of his clasp.

Feeling a sense of disappointment, he let them go, but said immediately, "Will you wait for me?" He made an apologetic motion with his hand toward the front entry, "I'm not sure how long I'll be."

She seemed to hesitate. He breathed a sigh of relief when she said, "All right."

"I'll be as quick as I can." Then he realized how difficult it must be for her to be in this church. "I have a better idea. Come with me." He reached out a hand but she drew back, a horrified look on her face.

"Why not?"

Her eyes grew rounder. "How can you ask that? They'll think you're with me. It will ruin all you've done."

He chuckled, realizing that God's anointing was still with him, because he felt none of the fear he would have at one time of being seen with Espy. He took her arm and drew her along with him even though he could feel her resistance. "Since I didn't do anything, it makes no matter."

"What do you mean?"

He glanced down at her. "I mean, it wasn't anything I did, but the Holy Spirit."

He took Espy's hand.

They reached the entrance to the church and Warren stood beside Pastor Curtis, Espy on his other side, her hand tucked firmly in his arm.

"Hello there, Espy. I didn't know you were back. When did you arrive?" Pastor Curtis showed only surprise, not suspicion.

The next minutes were taken with greeting people. Warren noticed how people's glances slid to Espy with few greetings her way. He only realized after having been distracted by speaking to several church members that Espy's hand was no longer on his arm. He looked quickly to his side and was relieved to see she was still there, standing quietly. She gave him a tight smile.

"Hello, Espy." A middle-aged woman smiled warmly at her before nodding and smiling at Warren.

"Hello, Mrs. Thompson." Espy returned the woman's smile. At least this woman seemed genuinely glad to see Espy. Warren had no time to listen more as a gentleman came up to him and clapped him on the shoulder, addressing the pastor. "You'd better watch it, you might be out of a job."

Pastor Curtis only chuckled in return. "That's the whole purpose. I have to train up my successor."

Finally, when everyone left, Warren turned to Espy. "That wasn't so bad, was it?"

She only gave another strained smile, and he wished there was something he could say to make things better. But he realized it would take time for the church people's image of Espy to be erased. They needed to see the godly lady she'd become.

"Are you back for good, Espy?" Pastor Curtis asked her.

"Just for today. I'm taking the stage back at one." She glanced at her watch. "Goodness, I must hurry home."

Warren's face fell. "Must you take the early stage? I was hoping to take you home to Sunday dinner."

The pastor, as if sensing an awkward silence, patted Espy on the arm. "It's good to see you, my dear. I hope you won't be such a stranger anymore. I'd love to hear about your life in Bangor. You're looking very well."

His glance encompassing them both, he said, "Seeing your time is short, I won't take up any more of it." He turned to Warren. "We can talk about your sermon sometime this week." With a nod to them both, he headed toward the sanctuary.

Warren took Espy by the elbow and led her out into the bright sunshine. The street was quiet now, most people having headed home to their Sunday dinners.

Espy broke away from him at the street and began heading in the opposite direction.

"Whoa, where are you heading off to?"

"Home. I told Angela I'd help with dinner."

"I'll take you then. But I hope you'll reconsider taking the later stage. You can come to our family dinner. I'll take you to the stage afterward."

She said nothing and he had to quicken his pace to keep up with her. "Hey, slow down. Where's the fire?" When she kept walking, he touched her arm. "Listen, Espy, I know it was hard for you to return here, and I do so appreciate that you came all this way to hear me preach."

He swallowed. "I looked out at all that sea of faces which

looked so forbidding, and yours was the only friendly one. You were my lifeline."

"I'm glad. But that was before the Lord filled you," she said in a voice filled with awe.

They smiled at each other in understanding, and for a moment, everything between them was as right as if they were in Bangor.

Warren took a deep breath. "Anyway, I still appreciate your being there. I know it was hard meeting my parents yesterday. They weren't very friendly to you. It'll take them a little time to get used to . . . to our friendship, but I assure you they'll soon accept you."

"Will they?"

"If they have a chance to know you. That's why I'd like you to come to dinner today. I know they're stuffy and dinner may seem like a formal affair, but it'll be better than yesterday, I promise."

She stopped, facing him. "I really don't think it's a good idea."

"You have nothing to be ashamed of, Espy. You're not the person you were. You just have to give people a chance to see the new you."

Her smile twisted. "After yesterday? I don't think your parents would welcome me back there twice."

"You were just too nervous." His mouth hardened. "Besides, it's the only way for Mother to understand that you're my friend, and that she must accept you as such." He leaned toward her. "Please come, Espy."

"Very well." The words seemed dragged out of her.

26

When Espy left Warren at her door, her heart was breaking. As she looked at him through the crack in the window curtain, his long stride taking him back up the street, she knew she must leave.

She couldn't subject him—or herself—to another excruciating few hours at his parents' house. They came from different worlds. Their time in Bangor had served to blur those lines, but now the Lord had brought him back home. She would not be a stumbling block to him.

"Espy, is that you?" Angela's voice called out from the kitchen. "Dinner's on the table."

"I'll be right there." With a sigh, she pulled away from the window. There was a lot to do before the stage left the livery stable.

Warren took the buggy back to Espy's house at a quarter to one, determined that things would go better this time with his family. He'd had a brief talk with his parents, making it clear how much their acceptance of Espy meant to him.

At least there would be no guests.

He pulled up at Espy's gate, hitched the horse to a post, and hurried to the front door.

After a few knocks no one came. Beginning to feel alarm, he knocked harder, wondering if they were all in the back part of the house.

Finally, he saw a shadow through the curtained window. The door opened, revealing Espy's mother. "Hello, Mrs. Estrada. It's nice to see you."

The woman pushed a loose strand of hair away from her face. "Lookin' for Espy?"

"Yes, ma'am. Is she ready?"

"More'n ready, I'd say. She's already gone."

"Gone?" He reined in his panic. "Gone where?"

"To the station. She walked with Angela and Alvaro." She looked past him. "Were you planning to take her? Would've been helpful to have the buggy, though she didn't have a lot to carry."

"Do you mean the livery stable?" At Mrs. Estrada's nod, he stepped back. "Thank you. Sorry to disturb you."

He hurried to his buggy and whipped the mare into a canter as soon as he left the row of houses. *Lord, get me there on time. Please don't let Espy leave.*

Fighting down mounting panic, he threaded his way through the more congested traffic near the hotel and livery stable. He finally found a spot to tether his horse and buggy and wiped the sweat from his brow with a handkerchief, relieved to see the stage still parked at the curb.

"Excuse me, please," he repeated as he made his way through the people in his way. Finally, he saw the back of Espy's straw bonnet. Breathing a prayer of thanks, he reached her just as Alvaro handed up her bag to the driver to put on the roof.

"Espy."

She whirled around, fear in her eyes. "Warren!"

Breathing heavily, he stared at her. "You were just going to leave?"

She swallowed. "I'm sorry, Warren. It's . . . it's best this way."

He nodded to Angela on her other side. Alvaro came back to his sisters. "Warren, where'd you come from?"

As if sensing the tension in the air, his welcoming smile died, and he let the hand he held out drop to his side. Angela touched Alvaro on the arm. "Why don't we go and wait over there?"

"Sure."

After they left, Warren struggled to marshal his arguments. "What's best this way?"

She moistened her lips. "I don't belong with your family, Warren."

"But you belong with me." Her umber eyes widened. Feeling more and more conviction with each word, he gripped her arms. "Marry me, Espy. I love you."

Tears filled her eyes even as she began to shake her head. "N-no . . . you don't mean that."

His lips tipped up at the corners. "What do you mean I don't mean it? You know how long I've been in love with you but was too scared to admit it?"

She pressed her lips together, her head shaking more vigorously. "You were right not to admit it. You belong here. God has brought you home and given you a ministry. I would just sully it."

"I don't care about that. God has washed your slate clean, just as He has mine. Together, we can brave anything. Please, Espy, give us a chance . . . unless you don't feel the same about me." He cleared his throat, feeling ashamed. "I haven't always treated you right, and I'm sorry for that."

Her hand touched him. "Oh, Warren."

"Please marry me."

She stared at him a long moment. Slowly she began to shake her head. "I can't marry you, Warren. It wouldn't be right, I'm sorry," she whispered brokenly, breaking away from him.

He tried to hold on to her but she pulled away.

"All aboard," the coachman's stentorian tone rose above the babble of voices around them.

Espy picked up her skirts, almost running to the coach. Out of breath, tears blurring her eyes, she was the first to climb aboard. Ignoring Warren's cry of "Espy!" she settled into the farthest corner. Soon, other passengers were filling the space, until once again she was packed tightly with the other passengers like herring in a tin.

Warren's face appeared over those crowded at the entrance, his gaze entreating her. She mouthed the words "I'm sorry" before looking away.

• • •

The door slammed shut. The coach jostled as male passengers climbed onto the roof and the driver onto his seat. With a loud "Whoa!" and a crack of the whip, the coach began to move. Only then did Espy lean forward to look out. Angela and Alvaro smiled and waved. Warren came to her side of the coach just as it moved beyond her line of vision, and she had to crane her neck for a last glimpse of him.

Ignoring the chit-chat of the passengers around her, she bit into her lip, watching the last houses of Holliston move past her.

He *loved* her. Even as her heart sang to hear at last the words she'd dreamed of hearing for so many years of her life, she had to give him up. He'd been through enough with his parents to endure any more.

Closing her eyes, she prayed for strength to stick to her refusal. Time and the reality of everyday life would confirm it to him.

Feeling the tears begin to well in her eyes again, she fished out her handkerchief and closed her eyes, dabbing at the corners discreetly.

No one ever died of a broken heart, she told herself, repeating her mother's oft-told words.

Dear Lord, heal my heart, because I don't know if I can bear this pain otherwise.

• • •

Warren stood at the edge of the street until the last cloud of dust died down from the coach's wheels. He'd surprised himself with his proposal, not having planned it, but he knew it was right. He and Espy belonged together.

He still felt in a state of shock at Espy's refusal. Was it because she didn't want to leave her life in Bangor, or because she couldn't endure returning to the scene of her shame in Holliston?

"I'm sorry, Warren." Angela's soft voice intruded on his thoughts. "I didn't realize she hadn't told you she was leaving."

He glanced toward Espy's sister and brother with a sad smile. "That's all right. I should have known. I guess it wasn't easy for her to come back."

Angela's lips tightened. "I'll say it wasn't. This town treated her shamefully. If I could get away, I would, too."

The three of them walked away from the livery stable. Warren offered them a ride home but they declined.

Relieved, wanting to be alone, Warren climbed aboard his buggy and reined in the impulse to just follow the stage all the way to Bangor.

He'd have to return home and tell his parents Espy wasn't coming. They'd be relieved.

His shoulders slumped, wondering how he was going to endure the coming days. He'd committed to working with his father, so he couldn't go to Bangor until the fall. He'd write to Espy, of course, but he knew words on paper would not be enough to sway her.

• • •

Warren could only attribute it to God's grace to enable him to get up each morning and go to work. He spent his free time in God's Word or talking with Pastor Curtis.

He wrote to Espy every day, determined to wear her down, if nothing else. She didn't reply, though every day he searched the pile of mail with eagerness and had to endure the stab of disappointment when there was no letter from her.

The pain went from a sharp, stabbing hurt that made every action an effort of will to a dull ache that never quite left even when he managed to immerse himself in his daily activities.

He corresponded with John, who rejoiced in what the Lord had done in Warren's life and encouraged him in his decision to stay the summer.

Warren confided to him that he had proposed to Espy. John wrote back that he and his wife could tell Espy was hurting but she had kept silent about the cause. They promised to pray for God's answer.

We rejoice in your desire to join your life to Espy's. We can think of no finer wife and helpmate. She has grown tremendously in the Lord since she first came to us from Holliston. However, only God knows who is the best person to accompany us through life's journey. Marion and I promise to pray diligently about this, and I encourage you to do the same. If Espy is the one for you, the Lord will make a way.

The words were heartening when he read them, but they offered little comfort in the long hours of each day when Warren was forced to carry out his duties with all diligence. He pored over the Scriptures on faithfulness: *A faithful man shall abound with blessings. . . . Well done, thou good and faithful servant: thou hast been faithful over a few things. . . . I thank Christ Jesus our Lord,*

338

who hath enabled me, for that he counted me faithful, putting me into the ministry.

He desired with all his heart to be faithful to the Lord, even if it meant working at his father's firm.

A month had passed. He'd gone through the July Fourth celebrations. Once again, they'd put on a lobster feast to raise money for the needy, with Christina doing most of the organizing and Angela and her friends doing most of the work cooking. Warren had enjoyed the event once again, getting the most satisfaction from working side by side with the other members of the club cooking and serving the food to the community.

But it hadn't been the same without Espy.

Now, the rest of the summer seemed to drag on, with nothing to look forward to but autumn and his return to Bangor. His season of spiritual dryness had passed, and he was eager to study Scripture again under godly men.

He was looking through the window down toward the mill yard when there was a knock on the door. He turned, startled to see Pastor Curtis standing there.

"Hello! Come on in. What brings you here?"

The pastor didn't seem his usual, jovial self; his brows knit in consternation. He entered, motioning to the open door. "Mind if I close this?"

Warren blinked, not used to having the door closed unless he was dealing with figures. "Not at all."

The reverend said no more until he'd taken a seat. Warren chose the chair beside him. "What is it? Is something wrong?"

The reverend placed his hands on his knees and peered at Warren until Warren began to feel something had happened concerning him, but he couldn't think what. Had someone had a complaint about him in church?

"I've discovered something quite startling about Espy Estrada."

Every fiber of Warren's being went on alert at the sound of her name. "Has something happened to her?" His voice came out shaky.

"Nothing like that. It's a good thing—in an awful kind of way." He shook his head, as if still puzzling things out.

Warren's pulse became more erratic as he waited. "Please tell me."

"Another young woman has come to me, accusing Mr. Stockton of making inappropriate advances to her."

The blood began to pound between Warren's ears so he could hardly make out what the minister was saying.

"She, too, used to work for the Stocktons. Annie Green. She left when the professor kept finding her alone and making insinuating suggestions. Mrs. Stockton never discovered anything, and she didn't dare say anything, afraid no one would believe her."

Pastor Curtis shook his head. "But it bothered her mightily when Espy was accused, especially when her scandal was made so public. When she saw Espy at church and began hearing all the gossip resurrected, she said she had to tell someone. She doesn't think it's right that Espy still lives under that cloud."

Warren stood, unable to sit any longer. He rubbed the back of his neck, trying to take things in. "You're saying Espy was innocent of any wrongdoing? But what of how Mrs. Stockton found them?"

"Espy told me it was the professor who kissed her, and before she could do anything, Mrs. Stockton saw them. She wouldn't believe anything Espy said at that point and demanded she leave the house."

Warren stared at the minister. "Espy told you this? Why didn't she say anything to me? Why did she let me believe she was guilty of what everyone was saying about her?" He felt hurt and betrayed.

"Would you have believed her?"

The blunt question stopped him short. "Perhaps not then, but when I found her in Bangor and she seemed so changed. I thought

340

we became friends. Why didn't she trust me enough to tell me what really happened?"

The pastor shook his head. "You'll have to ask her, but perhaps she wanted you to believe in her without her having to defend herself."

Warren felt a shaft of guilt shoot straight to his soul. He thought back over his conduct with Espy. He'd always judged her according to his high standard, even when he'd fallen far short of it himself.

As if sensing his distress, Pastor Curtis stood and came over to him, clasping his shoulder. "You care for her, don't you?"

Warren nodded.

"I thought as much. That's why I thought you should know. I believe Annie. I'm going to speak to the Stocktons. I think it's high time Espy's name was cleared."

"Let me know how it goes." Warren flexed his fingers, coming to a decision. "I'm going to Bangor—after I speak to my parents."

As if understanding the look of determination in Warren's eyes and tone, Pastor Curtis nodded. "Sounds like a good plan to me." He winked and stepped away. "You have my blessing," he added with a chuckle.

Espy got off the streetcar and trudged the final blocks home. She felt wearier than most evenings. Mr. Hill had been particularly demanding, making her retype the letters he'd dictated when he decided to change one sentence and add another sentence.

The days were long and stuffy on the fourth floor of Peabody Manufactory. Lunchtime only reminded her of the times with Warren.

She reached her street and began the final trek. Suddenly she noticed a tall male figure at the entrance to the gate of House of Hope. Her steps slowed, not daring to believe his familiar form.

But noticing her, the man straightened and began walking toward her.

"Warren," she whispered. He hadn't told her he was coming to Bangor, and it was nowhere near the autumn yet. She hadn't written to him, though she'd devoured every letter of his. But she had not wanted to encourage him in any way, no matter how much the silence cost her.

Now, seeing him, she feared something had happened to someone in her family and he'd come to break it to her in person.

She hastened her steps, almost breaking into a run.

"Warren," she said, hardly able to speak.

He was smiling. He held out both his hands, and without thinking, she reached out her own. "Hello, Espy. It's so good to see you."

The next second, he swung her around, his arms tight about her. She clasped him around the neck, breathing in the scent of him, that faint woodsy smell, feeling the lightweight wool of his sack coat against her cheek. Then she remembered, and she began to pull away. He tightened his hold on her. "No, you're not."

She looked up at him. "Not what?"

"Getting away from me."

"Warren, you mustn't."

"Mustn't what?"

Her cheeks grew warm and she looked down, to lips, the edge of his white teeth visible. "You know . . . this—"

"Why, when you are to be my wife?"

Her gaze flew back to his eyes. They were laughing into hers. *I mustn't let him ruin himself. Mustn't encourage him.* "You can't say such things."

"Says who?"

She twisted a hand helplessly. "Everyone. Your parents. Christina. It would ruin your reputation, your ministry."

"I told you I don't care." He chuckled, leaning down and touch-

342

ing his lips lightly to hers. She drew in her breath. "I've been wanting to do that again since the first time."

"You have?" The words popped out of her mouth.

"Mm-hm. But I didn't dare. I felt so bad that I hadn't stuck by your side last summer when everyone was accusing you, even when I believed those stories." His eyes searched hers. "Espy, why didn't you tell me the truth?"

She found it impossible to swallow. Tears filled her eyes. "How do you know?"

"Another young woman has told Pastor Curtis that Mr. Stockton made advances to her, and because of it, she left their employ. She felt terrible when you were accused but didn't dare say anything because Mrs. Stockton never found out in her case. Now, seeing you again, and hearing the murmurs of gossip, she felt convicted to tell the truth about Mr. Stockton."

The horror of it all came back to her in a wave and she shuddered, lowering her face against Warren's shoulder. "Hey, there," he said softly, "it's all right. I didn't mean to upset you with this news."

"What has happened . . . to the Stocktons, I mean?" Her voice came out muffled.

"Pastor Curtis has handled it all. He spoke to the Stocktons first. He gave Mr. Stockton the opportunity to clear your reputation. When he refused, Pastor Curtis made an announcement at church, in effect saying that recent evidence has come forth to prove that you did nothing inappropriate in the Stockton household. He asked for the Stocktons' corroboration right there in church, and Mrs. Stockton stood up and said it had all been a misunderstanding."

Espy couldn't imagine it. She'd lived under this cloud for so long, though it had ceased to be a part of her new life in Bangor where no one knew. But having gone back to Holliston had shown her how alive it still was.

"You can come back now and hold your head up. No one is

going to misjudge you again, Espy. Now," he said, tipping up her face with a fingertip under her chin, "will you allow me to propose to you once again?"

"But your parents—they still won't approve." She floundered around for reasons.

"I've made it clear to them that you are my first and only choice for a wife, and they have accepted that." He looked down. "Espy, please forgive me for assuming you were guilty, and having the temerity to suggest that you were good enough for me now because you had repented from your past and lived a new life."

"Oh, Warren, don't you see how much more I loved you because you were willing to marry me, believing I was guilty?"

He looked at her with wonder. Then a smile began in his eyes and traveled down to his mouth, curling it up at the edges. "So, you do love me?"

She blushed, looking down at his necktie. "Did I say that?"

He squeezed her waist. "You can't lie to me, you know."

Her own lips tugged at the corners. "No, I can't, can I?"

"So, is it a 'yes' this time?"

She looked seriously into his eyes once again. "Are you sure?"

"I'm sure that you are God's choice for me. I don't know what the future holds—where we'll live, what ministry the Lord has for me, whether in Holliston or here in Bangor—but I can't imagine doing it without you at my side."

Then he bent down and touched her lips once more with his, except this time they stayed there, lingering.

An abrupt whistle and raucous laughter caused them to jump apart. He grinned ruefully, letting go of Espy slowly. "I guess this is not the place for such behavior."

He took her hand into the crook of his arm and led her to the gate. "So, what shall it be, yes or no?"

She tipped her head then took a deep breath before speaking, feeling she was jumping into a great unknown. "Yes."

"That's my Espy." He motioned her to precede him. "Shall we tell the Talbots?"

She took his hand. "Yes, let's . . . dearest Brenty."

He pretended to frown. "Will I have to get used to hearing that infantile nickname for the rest of our married lives?"

She laughed up at him. "Only when I am feeling most affectionate."

Joining her in laughter, Warren walked hand in hand with her to share their good news.

FICTION FROM MOODY PUBLISHERS

River North Fiction is here to provide quality fiction
that will refresh and encourage you in your daily walk
with God. We want to help readers know, love, and
serve JESUS through the power of story.

Connect with us at www.rivernorthfiction.com

- ✔ Blog
- ✔ Newsletter
- ✔ Free Giveaways

- ✔ Behind the scenes look at writing fiction and publishing
- ✔ Book Club

MOODY
PUBLISHERS
www.MoodyPublishers.com